Twice A Quinceañera

Twice A Quinceañera

YAMILE SAIED MÉNDEZ

KENSINGTON
PUBLISHING CORP.

www.kensingtonbooks.com

KENSINGTON BOOKS are published by
Kensington Publishing Corp.
119 West 40th Street
New York, NY 10018

ISBN: 978-1-4967-3706-9 (ebook)

ISBN: 978-1-4967-3705-2

First Kensington Trade Paperback Printing: August 2022

10 9 8 7 6 5 4 3 2 1

Printed in the United States of America

This one is for Linda Camacho

Chapter 1

Nadia

One month before the wedding day

If only there were a way to one-click a magic remote control to rewind, speed up, or pause time! If only there were a way to get a second chance, to do things right once and for all.

It wasn't the first time Nadia Palacio wished for this. But now, sitting in her car as she tried to gather the strength to face her family, the desire was stronger than ever. The difference was that this time, it wasn't because she regretted what she'd done. Quite the opposite.

Finally, she'd stood up for herself like she stood up for other people. She just wasn't ready to deal with the consequences. Not yet.

What she needed was a pause button that would give her space to breathe. To think. But even if her world had come crashing down, Planet Earth still kept spinning like a music box ballerina.

Instead of a waltz, the sounds playing in Nadia's mind were like Thor having a demolition party with his hammer in her life.

Since last night, she'd done a lot of breaking.

She'd broken up with Brandon, her fiancé of five years. Her

boyfriend since high school. She'd demolished his lies, his endless gaslighting.

But she hadn't come out unscathed. She'd walked out of the fight with a heart smashed to smithereens and her confidence the size of the dust motes dancing in the sunbeams that slashed through the windshield of her car.

And now, no matter how Nadia broke the news to her family, her Wonder Woman alter ego would go down the toilet. Part of her wanted to barge inside the house to get it over with. It's not like she was a teenager who'd stormed out of the house, screaming an empty threat never to return, only to do so three months later with her tail between her legs to own up to her errors.

But that's how she felt, sitting in the driveway of her parents' home.

From the moment her family had arrived in the United States from Argentina when she was twelve, Nadia had been happy in the split-level cream-colored house. She still made her run for it at the first chance she got, with a full-ride scholarship under her arm and the expectations of the whole family on her shoulders. When she returned a few years later, it was with two shiny diplomas and a set of fancy letters at the end of her name: Nadia Palacio, JD.

The first professional in the family. Not just her parents, Ernesto and Virginia, and her sister, Isabella. No. She was first in the whole Palacio clan, an irrational number of people scattered all over the world, most of whom were getting ready right at this moment to make the trek to Orem, Utah, to celebrate Nadia's wedding with her trophy fiancé, Brandon.

Except that there wasn't going to be a wedding anymore. Brandon was vacating their apartment—her apartment—as she tried to gather the courage to come clean to her family.

Nadia placed her forehead on the steering wheel of her sensible slate Subaru Outback. "Ay. Dios mío, help me," she whispered. She wasn't particularly religious. But she needed divine intervention now more than ever.

She waited for a heavenly voice to tell her what to do, how to do it, or at least, comfort her and assure her that everything would be all right. But the only sounds were the birds fluttering among the trees and Tinkerbell the Yorkie barking at them. Maybe the gods were sending her a saving message, but Nadia didn't speak bird nor dog. She was on her own.

She dried the sweat off the palms of her hands on her magic black slacks. They were magic because they had the power to erase her curves from the eyes of the jerks at the law firm. It had taken four years, but after holding off indecent advances and demeaning comments, she had her first solo case in a family feud over some property. There was something soothing in using the law to help other families fix their problems when she couldn't even face her parents.

As if she had summoned the devils from the office, her phone chirped and vibrated in her pocket, startling her. She glanced at the screen and read:

Remember to stop by the office for the Hawkins file. It's Friday/funday, but I can meet you there if you need me.

She winced, picturing the leering smile of Laramie Hunt, the main partner, her boss.

She was going to ignore the text, but if she was boring, like Brandon had said, she was also petty.

I already stopped by early this morning.

Her stomach churned when she saw the three dots that meant he'd been glued to the phone to reply. Finally, she read:

Good girl! Text me if you need any advice. I'm alone this weekend. Say hi to Brandon for me!

"You creepy mother-effer!" she said, imagining how Brandon would laugh at her if he knew she couldn't swear properly, even when she was by herself.

Instead of replying, she took a screenshot. She saved all these conversations, just in case.

"Tía!" Olivia, her niece and goddaughter, called her from the front door, waving her in. She was sixteen and idolized Nadia, who adored her back. "Abuela's asking why you haven't come in yet!"

"I'm coming!"

She swallowed her nerves, her guilt, and remorse for what she'd done. She fought the urge to turn the engine back on and drive all the way to the end of the world. Not Argentina, where her family was from and most of the Palacio clan lived, though. No. She couldn't face them. She'd go to Alaska, and from there, to Siberia. Maybe she could take up fishing or some other strenuous work that would leave her too exhausted to think of how close she'd been to the goal she'd been chasing since junior year in high school and she'd just flushed down the toilet. Literally. Along with the engagement ring, which for five years she'd pretended to love but had dug into her finger, scratching and wounding her skin and her self-esteem.

"Dale, Tía!" Olivia called again. She'd been trying to use more Spanish, bless her heart. The combination of the Palacios' Argentinian accent with her father's Puerto Rican had left her with a mix only the family could understand. With college already in sight, and eager to follow in Nadia's footsteps, she insisted on only speaking Spanish in the house.

Nadia opened the door and headed out under the burning July sun. Her high-heeled, black Jimmy Choos, one of her only indulgences, scraped on the salt-eaten cement of the driveway, and when she balanced on her right foot to inspect the damage, she saw the ruined leather of the peeled heel. But before she let out the frustration that had been building inside her, her mom said, "We can't be late to the fitting, mi amor! What were you doing in the car for so long?"

Nadia's armpits prickled with sweat.

She should've made a run for it. Now it was too late.

She fixed a fake smile and met her mom's eyes, knowing she was about to break her heart. "Mami . . . we need to talk."

Her mom clutched at her heart, her face transformed in an

expression of joy. "You're pregnant?" Nadia almost took her shoes off and ran away for real.

"You must have done something," her dad said, breaking the ominous silence that had fallen in the kitchen after Nadia's announcement. "You two seemed so happy and in love last weekend at dinner."

The silence that followed was oppressive. Even Tinkerbell had stopped barking at the multi-colored lights the suncatcher cast on the tiled floor or the birds outside the window. Olivia texted furiously behind the kitchen counter. Most likely updating her mom—Isabella, Nadia's sister—about the new family drama.

Nadia should've started with her good news from work. The daughter of two workaholics, she should've known news of a possible promotion would have softened the blow. But after her mom's jumping to conclusions, and her dad's bellowing "¡Otro nieto! ¡Qué alegría! Gracias! Dios mío!" all the way from the second floor, she'd had to act fast. Things were already out of control.

"Yes, that's it. You must have done something. Brandon's like a son to us," her mom said, as if she'd arrived at the only logical explanation. Nadia curled her toes in her shoes as her mom continued, "Tell me exactly what you said. I'm sure it's a misunderstanding. I'll call Lisa—"

Nadia slammed her hand on the table, and when her mom flinched, she immediately regretted it.

"Mami, you're not calling Brandon's mother!" Her voice quivered as she tried to modulate to a tone that was firm but not disrespectful. "*I* didn't do anything. We're through. There won't be a wedding."

"But the family's on their way!" her mom, Virginia, added, wringing her hands.

Nadia had a vision of her family in Argentina, England, Spain, Canada, and even Australia, packing their bags to make it to *the wedding of the decade*, as they had dubbed it. Some of them had been saving for this event for years. Others had just wanted to see with their own eyes if the Palacios' exile in the United States had been worth the distance and sacrifice.

Her wedding had been her parents' chance to show off to the rest of the family how happy their daughters were. Isabella's wedding had been small, held during a year the visa requirements for the US were excessive, banning most of the family from traveling. Now things were better, but Nadia had ruined everything.

This was such a mess.

"Mami, don't worry," Nadia said. "I don't know how, but we're going to figure it out."

Her mom raked her fingers through her dyed-black hair and sighed. "I guess I better call the dress shop and tell them . . . They might not return the money for the dress *or* the bridesmaids' dresses. You know that, right?"

Nadia's stomach clenched. She had been so stunned with the breakup the night before that she hadn't considered the ramifications. She had paid for most of the wedding expenses, but her parents had helped with a lot, too.

"You'll get your money back," she said, patting her mom's hand. It was cold like marble, as though Nadia and her mother were discussing the death of a family member, and not her marital status remaining the same. "I have savings . . . and—"

"It's not about the money," her dad said.

Nadia's shoulders relaxed. Now maybe her dad would gather her in his arms, and she'd cry while he patted her shoulder and told her that everything would be okay. They'd get out of this problem together. She'd always wished he'd protect her and comfort her, and yet, he never had.

"It's just that I can't believe you let this drag on for so long," he said. "I saw this coming years ago, but when I warned you, you and your mother told me I was being unsupportive."

Olivia's breath intake helped Nadia remember not to lash out.

"What do you mean?" she asked, trying to brace herself for the onslaught.

"I didn't want to say it, but . . . *I told you so*," he said, showing the palms of his hands as if he held the truth there. "Remember when you were sixteen and came back crying to the house for the first time?"

Nadia nodded.

"Bueno, I told you that little fight was just a glimpse of something major from the future. But . . . I was the bad guy for saying he'd leave you one day and then it would be too late to get a do-over."

"What do you mean, *too late*?" Nadia lashed out.

"Well, you're not getting any younger, am I right?"

"Papá—"

"I know, I know," he interrupted her. "But just when I was warming up to him, he calls the wedding off?"

Nadia hated that he was right, at least partly. There had been signs from the time she and Brandon went out on their first date. She'd had to pay because he'd "forgotten" his wallet at home. The truth was, he didn't have a job, and his mom had banned him from using the family's emergency credit card like his own personal trust fund. Through the many years together, they'd broken up more times than she could count. This time, it was different. But yes, what terrible timing. Now that her dad had started to love Brandon like a son . . .

But her dad was also wrong. She wasn't old by any means. She wouldn't turn thirty until next month, anyway, but in her family, anyone unmarried by the age of thirty was an anomaly.

Anxiety, her old friend, started constricting her chest. This was a cue for Nadia to get a breather. She might not have a remote to pause time, but she needed to be alone if she was to avoid a fight.

"I'll be right back."

"Where are you going?" Virginia asked desperately.

"To the bathroom, Ma. Is that okay?"

She turned away to climb the stairs before she could see her mother's expression grow even grimmer. But the worst was how worried Olivia looked, standing behind the kitchen counter, clutching her hands like she was praying.

Nadia wanted to reassure her, but she had nothing to give. She turned away.

The eyes of dozens of versions of her sister and herself judged her from the portraits on the wall on either side of the stairs. School pictures, dance recitals, the awkward years of braces, the fleeting months through the high school cheer team. In all of them, she had the same overeager expression of having reached a goal, only to go chasing after a higher one. Never stopping to celebrate a single victory, because there was always something else to achieve; something better to chase.

She'd been exhausted for years, striving toward the marriage goal line, and now that it had disappeared—no, that she had erased it—she didn't know what she was running to. There were only ten steps up the stairs, and she was already out of breath.

In the kitchen, her parents whispered furiously. The phone rang. Tinkerbell started barking again.

Finally, she reached the bathroom at the end of the hallway and closed the door behind her.

"You're so screwed," she said to her reflection in the mirror.

Gosh. She looked terrible. She had broken out on her chin and nose, and she cursed the out-of-whack hormones that were making her life miserable. She needed a lash fill after all the crying last night, and her hair clamored for a deep conditioning.

She had broken up with Brandon, not the other way around. She hadn't been brave enough to tell her parents this tiny fact, though. If they sided with him, she'd never get over it. It was better if they never knew what had really happened.

She had a flash of coming home last night, exhausted after

an intense week at work, and from stopping at the gym so she could look perfect on the wedding day. Brandon on the computer with—

Her chest seized, and she started hyperventilating.

She splashed cold water on her face, but instead of feeling better, she felt her stomach lurch. Stars exploded in her eyes. This was more than anxiety. Maybe she was having a delayed-onset panic attack, and she didn't know how to deal with it anymore.

She closed the frilly decorated toilet seat and sat with her head between her legs, breathing deeply but not too deeply. The last thing she needed was to pass out and create a bigger drama. She tried to relax her shoulders, but her muscles were so knotted up that she didn't know how to let go of the tension.

Brandon was right. She was too stressed, too boring, too predictable.

She'd only tried to do everything her parents, her boyfriend, her bosses, society, and the whole effing world expected of her.

When had she started ignoring what she really wanted and started pursuing what others *told* her she wanted?

Once again, she had the flash of a memory. She was in the bathroom at school, crying, and Honey Thomas was telling her, "He's everything a girl should want, Nadia. The fact that he wants you back when he could have anyone else has to make up for the rest. There's no perfect man . . ."

They'd been fifteen years old, and she'd already felt like a failure, because Brandon kept treating her like a rag. But for the first time in her life, instead of blaming her past self for the stupid choices she'd made through the years, she felt a surge of compassion for the girl she'd been, that little Nadia.

She pressed the balls of her fists on her eyes, and once the stars stopped blinking and her eyes adjusted to her surroundings, she noticed the magazine rack in the corner of the room next to the bathtub. It hadn't been there last time she'd been home. Olivia must have put it there to browse when she soaked in long, candlelit baths.

How her mom had changed!

She used to rage against the magazines Nadia and Isabella bought with their babysitting money. She said they were trashy, full of stupid advice and—whisper—*porn*. But now, she seemed to have no problem that her granddaughter enjoyed them. Not that Nadia was jealous of Olivia. She adored her niece, but still, it was hard not to have hard feelings.

Someone knocked on the bathroom door, and she got startled.

"Nadi, are you okay?" Isabella asked. What was she doing here so fast?

Olivia must have asked her to come, and although she hadn't thought of going to her sister for comfort or support, now she was grateful that her niece had called her. No one else had asked her how she was.

"I'm okay," she said, her voice all nasal and teary. "I'll be out in a second."

She braced herself for Isabella bullying her into opening the door. But her sister just said, "Okay."

The sound of retreating steps told Nadia that her sister had gone back to the kitchen.

What had come over her? When they were younger, Isabella wouldn't have relented until Nadia opened the door and told her everything. Then she'd enumerate each and every thing that Nadia had done wrong. But now, she'd left her alone.

Still, Nadia needed a minute until she could go back to the family.

She grabbed the first magazine off the rack, the one with a beautiful, sexy Latina on the cover. Maybe that's what Brandon had expected her to turn into all these years, and he'd gotten tired of waiting. She had wanted to be that sexy Latina, too, but she'd never been that kind of girl.

That had been Isabella, who'd married a Puerto Rican boy

before she graduated college. Their parents' disappointment only lasted until Olivia, and then Noah, came along. Thank God for her niece and nephew.

She thumbed through the glossy pages of the magazine. She had never aspired to being part of the glamorous Latine jet set in the United States. But she had believed that after pursuing her law degree and achieving it—with honors—she was finally reaching her American dream. The one that was promised to her.

Lies. All lies. Degree or no degree, her life had been an endless run on a hamster wheel.

Where had that magic of celebrating herself stopped? When she decided to quit her volleyball team to cheer for the boys' team? When she'd learned to ignore the voice in her heart telling her to run far from Brandon Lewis, even if he was the gift of God to womankind?

She wasn't sure.

She threw the magazine on the countertop. The pages flapped like the beating of paper butterflies, until it landed on the floor with a smack. It was open on the center spread, all crooked and wrinkled. She regretted her outburst the moment she saw the water she'd splashed from the counter seeping through the paper. She didn't want to ruin her niece's magazine. What right did she have?

But as she was about to put it back on the rack and go down to face her family again, the glittery pink headline of an article grabbed her attention:

Double Quinceañera: A New Trend That's Here to Stay

Under the caption was the picture of a Latina woman in a showstopping gold dress that hugged her body almost obscenely. She had her head thrown back in a burst of laughter, her luxurious dark brown locks fanning on her shoulders. A glass of bubbly in her hand, and a court of friends laughing with her, celebrating.

That picture was everything Nadia had been chasing her whole life yet hadn't known. A celebration for her achievements. A night with her friends and family, and maybe love, but not necessarily.

She read on,

I never had a quinceañera when I was fifteen, and while I understood why my parents would rather save that money for college, I still envied my friends' elaborate parties for their coming-of-age. Now that I'm financially solvent, I wanted to have a cake and eat it, too, with pink decorations and balloons, and a flute of champagne to toast to the amazing things I accomplished and those I'm choosing to manifest for my life in the future.
— *Silvia in San Antonio, TX*

Nadia gasped for air. She had been holding her breath without realizing it as she read and reread the article.

Double quinceañera?

She hugged the magazine against her chest. Who cared that she was wrinkling the pages even worse? She'd buy another one for Olivia. But the words of that woman, Silvia? She could've written that article herself.

A double quinceañera to celebrate her thirties. What a revolutionary idea!

What if . . .

But no. She brushed the thought away. She couldn't just throw herself a party for her birthday, now, could she?

But why not?

Her birthday was just a day after her botched wedding date. She'd chosen especially so she could say she had achieved marriage before her thirties.

Nadia went through the particulars of switching gears from a wedding to birthday party.

She'd spent years planning the wedding of her dreams, as far as her circumstances allowed it.

She'd have to get a different dress, but the food was paid for. Now, the venue . . .

Her lawyer brain turned on as she went over the contract. Or what she could remember. She didn't remember the specific jargon, but she was sure the language had focused on the payment. As long as the place was paid for—and it was. The balance had been met for months now—she could host a rave, if she wanted to.

If the owner agreed to let her take over the contract that Brandon had signed, even though he hadn't contributed a cent to it.

She imagined the shock on Brandon's face when he heard what she was planning.

No. Not what she was planning. What she was *doing*.

It was set, and once she settled on something, she didn't turn back.

"Predictable? Me?" she asked aloud, as if she were picturing Brandon in front of her.

Resolute, she opened the bathroom door and headed downstairs.

There would still be a Palacio family party to show off her accomplishments, even if she didn't have the trophy fiancé anymore.

"Double quinces, here I come."

Chapter 2

Marcos

Marcos pressed the IGNORE button on the dashboard of his Subaru Outback. Two seconds later, his phone started ringing again. The car was too old to show the caller ID, and it wasn't like he'd take any random calls. He should've put his phone in the cup holder like normal people did, but after his parents' accident three years ago, he always made sure to leave it far from reach to avoid any distractions. He was supposed to be on call 24/7, but he was already on his way to the venue. Could this person not let him enjoy his last minutes in silence?

When he'd agreed to help with the family business, he never expected that he'd be nothing more than a glorified operator, directing calls here and there. His parents had always made it look so easy and relaxing, the business of making people's fairy-tale dreams come true. How had they done it for so long?

Well, by *they*, he really meant his mom.

He immediately regretted thinking about her, the late Monica Hawkins. He still had a voice mail in his phone that he hadn't had the courage to listen to. Her last voice mail to him. Three years after her death, the heartache was still so great that when the phone rang again, he pressed the ACCEPT button. Anything was better than dealing with his grief and its twin daughters, guilt and shame.

"Where are you? I've been calling you forever, and it kept going to voice mail," Sarah, his sister, barked.

A little kid cried in the background. His baby nephew, Elijah. If Marcos had been stuck in a car with his high-strung sister on a road trip, he'd be crying like that, too.

But his sister had too much on her skinny shoulders to also deal with his immaturity, so instead of replying with a cutting remark, he said, "Hi, Sarah. Yes, I'm okay. Thanks for asking."

She scoffed on the other side of the line, but when she spoke again, her tone had softened. "We're on our way out, and I want to make sure everything's okay. How was Dad this morning?"

Marcos raked his fingers through his long, curly hair, all sticky with sweat after two hours burning down his anxiety at the gym. He sighed at the memory of his dad just sitting next to the window while Santiago, the home-care nurse, came in to give him his bath and do his therapy with him.

Although most days, his father didn't remember who Marcos was or why he was angry at him, he'd still sent him a scathing look that made Marcos relive every single mistake he'd committed in his life. Not like he didn't deserve it. But still.

A part of him told him he should've stayed back in LA, but he brushed the thought away quickly. Wasn't that what had brought so much sorrow to his family to begin with? If he'd come home at least once before the accident, then the last memory of his mother wouldn't be that wounded expression that made him want to burrow to the center of the earth to swim in molten lava and disappear.

"Dad's fine," he said, slowing down so a Honda could merge into the lane of southbound I-15. LA freeways were wild, but traffic in the Salt Lake Valley was worse than he remembered, especially navigating in this relic of a car, the same one Marcos had driven in college. If that back seat could talk.

"Santiago was there, and I took the chance to go to the gym."

His sister clicked her tongue, and after a moment of silence, as if she were debating whether or not to say anything, she added, "I don't get your obsession with going to the gym when there's one set up at the house . . ."

He rolled his eyes and started bouncing his left leg. Of course, she didn't get it; otherwise, why would she think the old Bowflex contraption from the early 2000s was acceptable? The treadmill didn't go above a four. If he didn't run every morning, he couldn't quiet the restlessness. He needed a release of some kind, and after breaking up with Bree, he hadn't been with anyone else. Not that he could confide this in his sister, so he said, "I have everything under control. Go on your trip and have fun with your family. I promise Dad will be okay, and the weddings will all go smoothly as—"

"I have you on the speaker," she cut him off, probably sensing that a gaudy retort was coming. Had his voice given him away? He was almost thirty, but with Sarah, his mind always reverted to that of a boy of thirteen.

"Hi, Marcos," said Nick Barrios, his sister's husband.

He bit his lip to suppress a chuckle. He should've known that his virginal-minded brother-in-law was listening in to every word he said, waiting for the chance to pounce and bring him back to the fold of the church. He was a Mormon bishop, the leader of a congregation of about three hundred people in their neighborhood, which gave Marcos a childish and irrational urge to make him as uncomfortable as possible at every chance he got.

"Heyyy, Nicky Jam!" he said.

Nick laughed, like every time Marcos said this silly joke. Nick and Nicky Jam were at the opposite ends of the Puerto Rican spectrum. Nick was tall but slight, clean-cut and polished. He parted his brown hair to the side and had trouble keeping his glasses from slipping down his freckly nose. Nicky Jam was a legendary reggaeton artist, and he looked it, all tatted up, pierced, and ripped.

Laughing, Marcos glanced to the car beside him and caught the woman's smile. He winked at her, more out of habit than anything, and returned his attention to the road ahead. His exit was coming soon, and with all the construction, he wasn't sure where he should switch lanes. "Like I was saying, Sarita," he said. "I got everything under control."

The silence that followed wasn't the vote of confidence he'd been going for, and he rubbed his chin as if his sister had slapped him.

"I know you have the best intentions, Mark," she said. The childhood nickname made him shrug like a scolded little boy. But he'd asked for it when he'd called her Sarita to bug her. "But this month will be crucial, especially with the lawyers looking at every detail to make sure Dad can handle the business. His brothers will snatch the property away from us."

His dad's brothers were both outstanding Mormons like Nick, but unlike his brother-in-law, who was one of the most decent human beings he knew, the uncles were scum. Their religion hadn't stopped them from stripping their brother of his inheritance once Gramma and Grandpa Hawkins were gone. Religious men like his uncles made Marcos break into hives. Maybe that's why he kept trying to make sure Nick wasn't like them?

The only thing his father had received in a trust was a once-dilapidated farm that, under Marcos's mom's help, had flourished into a profitable wedding venue.

Early-onset Alzheimer's had incapacitated his dad, Stuart Hawkins, and Uncle Monty and Uncle George had swooped in, claiming that Stuart couldn't hold on to the ancestral property in his condition. The reason behind it was that the farm, where his parents had hosted thousands of weddings over the years, was prime real estate, and they wanted to develop it into a golf course or some nonsense like that.

Family . . .

His exit was coming up. He cut in front of a black Tesla, and when the guy honked at him, Marcos blew him a kiss. The look on the other guy's face made him laugh.

"Don't laugh, Marcos," Sarah said, totally misunderstanding him, as usual. "The farm means a lot to us. Do it for Mami. It's the least you could do after—"

"Sarah," Nick said softly, and Marcos felt a rush of gratitude for his brother-in-law.

His sister knew how to punch where it hurt the most. Marcos had returned like the prodigal son, but no one would roast him a calf. He'd have to work for it.

"Sorry," said Sarah, and the baby started crying again in the back seat. "Thanks for covering for me. Like I said, it's all set up for the twelve receptions, from Thursday to Saturday."

Marcos had heard this a million times, but she couldn't help herself, could she? She had to repeat it every time.

"—Kenzie can do almost everything, but you have to help, okay?"

"I know," he said, feeling like a chastised child.

"Listen, before I let you go. I was going over the venue's voice mails last night, and this woman, Nadia Palacio, called. She called me again this morning, but her message was all cut off. Can you make sure everything's okay? I mean, these bridezillas are something else!"

"Don't worry," he said, feeling back on his turf. He could deal with disgruntled customers better alone than with his worried sister. "I'll take care of it."

He could practically see Sarah's shoulders dropping with relief.

"Now go and have fun . . ." The desire to say it was so great that he let the words rush forth. "And, kids, remember to use birth control if you don't want to come back with a little bun in the oven. Three babies in three years would be too much, even for Mormons."

Nick laughed nervously, and Carly, Marcos's three-year-old niece, said, "I want a little bun, Mamá! I'm hungwy!"

Marcos burst out laughing, and his sister hissed, "I'm going to kill you, Marcos. You just wait until I get back home!"

Still laughing at the memory of his niece's tiny voice and the image of his sister trying to explain his last words, Marcos drove the final blocks to the farm, where the venue was. Like every time he cruised down the tree-shaded roads of tiny Mountainville, he breathed in a combination of resentment and contentment. He was home, whether he liked it or not.

When he was in high school, he couldn't wait to get out of here, this oppressive place that set irrational expectations no regular human could achieve. His parents wanted him to be perfect, just as everyone else around him seemed perfect. Marcos knew his friends well enough to see through their appearances, though. He could never hide who he was, what he felt, what his values were.

He'd moved—run away—to California. But in all the years, there hadn't been a day that he hadn't missed the sight of the majestic mountains, still snowcapped in late July, and the breathtaking beauty of the bright blue sky. That is, when the sky didn't turn hazy with all the summer fires in the mountains. Still, the smoke made for wonderful sunsets.

How many times had he gone outside to take out the trash (his chore from the time he was four all the way to his teenage years), only to stare at the sky, mesmerized, and find his mom in the front yard, doing the same thing?

If only his mom were still around. Other than his Mediterranean looks, he hadn't inherited a lot from her besides her love for beautiful things.

She'd tried to coax him back without success every year, trying to lure him with the promise of hikes and camping trips in the canyon, but Marcos and his father were like two stubborn mules. They fought too much.

They were the same, for all they liked to point out what they hated about each other.

Had liked.

His dad didn't talk to him anymore.

He turned the last corner, and like always, the sight of the old barn surrounded by the willow trees—which had been here since before the Mormon pioneers occupied the land—made him smile. In spite of all the memories. Mostly sad memories, but those, he couldn't blame on anyone but himself.

It was only fitting that to atone for the sins of his past, he should be back here, the place he'd detested as a teen. It was also the least he could do for his mom's memory, his dad's acceptance, and his sister's love.

He hadn't understood how his mom didn't get tired of dealing with the drama of a bride who was nervous about a wilting bouquet, or a new pimple on her chin that nobody really cared about. Or of the mother of the bride trying to live her fantasies through her daughter, no matter the cost. Or the groom with the typical deer-in-the-headlights look when he realized he'd made the biggest mistake of his life, but it was too late to bail, and there was no alcohol to lend him courage. But, hey, they were on the verge of scoring once and for all, and they might as well go through with the charade of happiness.

"You're becoming old and cynical, Hawkins," he said to himself, proving that yes, he was doing just that. Becoming old and cynical.

He parked in the spot that had been his father's. The only other car was a Nissan. Kenzie, the assistant—his assistant for this month—was already here.

He had yet to arrive earlier than her, but he didn't want to risk spending any more time alone with Kenzie than was necessary.

"Good morning," he said as he walked into the office, hitching his gym bag higher up his shoulder.

She turned and gave him a radiant smile. If he were a weaker man—like, the man he'd been last year—that smile would put him in serious danger. Not that he'd made a vow of chastity, but he didn't want to swim the murky waters of revisiting an old high school squeeze.

"Hey! Looking good," she said, waving adorably. She wore a high-necked white blouse that hugged all the right places, but he'd trained himself to just look at the face, just in case.

He smiled shyly, once again raking his fingers through his tangled hair. "What's new?"

She leaned back on her desk, where there were framed studio portraits of her three kids. No traces of the ex-husband in any of the family pictures, but it wasn't necessary. The kids resembled Ryder like three drops of water—blond, blue-eyed, rosy-cheeked. He and Marcos had run track together in college. Marcos had never dreamed that the eyes that used to laser his back in every race would get cloned in such cute kids. Not that Marcos envied Ryder or wanted kids anytime soon—or ever—but the bastard didn't deserve so much when he'd been such a douche.

"Ah, same old same old," she said with a modest shrug, tossing her long, dyed-blond hair over her shoulder. She'd been a brunette until tenth grade. "The kids were with Ryder this weekend, and I was just home all alone last night, bored to death! I kept hoping you'd call for dinner or something." She fanned her long lashes like a seductive butterfly.

She was relentless. He had to give her that.

"Oh," he said, "I meant, at work. Anything new at work?"

Her wounded look made him feel like trash. But he couldn't afford to leave any openings in his anti-relationship shield. She'd take any. Proof of that was how she'd taken his innocent question about a new local restaurant as a possibility for them to go out and try it. Never in a million years.

Her face turned to stone as she said, "Just that woman, Palacio, who called this morning to cancel the wedding."

"Cancel the wedding? What?" Almost noon on a Friday was

definitely too early to start dealing with this crap. "Isn't the wedding like at the end of this month?"

She shrugged, her lips pursed. "She left a rambling message this morning. Do you want to listen to it?"

He shook his head. What if the woman wanted a refund? He tried to remember the exact wording of the booking contract, but he couldn't recall the details in small print.

"What did she want?"

Kenzie shrugged. "She says she's stopping by to talk with you."

"Why me?" he asked, more to himself than anything.

"You're the boss," she said, shrugging that shoulder again. "I'm on my way out to lunch now. I'd stay to handle her, but Sarah told me you'd have everything under control." She stared at him like she was challenging him to ask for her help, to say he needed her to deal with this situation.

But he didn't want to owe her anything. Kenzie would take any chance to pretend that kiss in high school had meant anything at all.

He looked at the clock. Eleven-thirty. He could still take a shower before the woman showed up. Somehow, he had to channel the bride-charmer energy that the women of his family possessed, and he couldn't do it stinking of sweat.

"It's okay," he said, heading to the upper floor, where there was a shower. "I'll handle it."

He felt her eyes on him, and he decided that he'd shower in the gym from now on.

Chapter 3

Nadia

"A double quinceañera?" Her mom looked at Nadia as if she'd lost her mind. She turned toward her husband. "Ernesto, talk some sense into your daughter, please!"

Nadia had expected them to help her pull off this last-minute party she hadn't even cared about half an hour ago. Judging by her mom's reactions, it was time to change tactics.

"Papi, it will be all on me. I promise you won't have to do anything."

She said *do*, but she meant *pay*. She knew her parents' objections to the breakup or this follow-up party didn't really have to do with money. Not totally, at least.

He put a hand up. "Except deal with the family, hija. They already speak about you enough."

The family. The family lived thousands of miles away. She hadn't seen half of them in years, since they'd all visited Argentina ten years ago when Noah was still in diapers. She hadn't even met the other half in her whole life. How could the opinion of literal strangers matter at all in what she—a professional, independent woman—did or thought?

She felt the anger rising inside her. Anger that wasn't really directed at her parents, or even the family. She was angry at Brandon, for wasting the best years of her life. She'd spent her twenties acting like they'd been an old married couple, when he . . . when he had a very different idea of what an old married couple was supposed to be like. But when she'd flushed her ring down the toilet, she'd promised herself that she wouldn't give Brandon any more of her precious time. Her biological clock was ticking, and not that she wanted to find a replacement for him, but she wanted to live, be free, celebrate herself once and for all.

But celebrations meant different things for her parents, who had given her straight-A report cards and her honor degrees a cursory glance and a "That's your job, after all." She'd been lucky they took her out when she'd been her law school's salutatorian. That's why she'd been waiting for this wedding to be the celebration of all her accomplishments. The cherry on top of the complicated mille-feuille cake that was her life.

Now, here she was.

She sat on the chair, mainly because her feet were hurting and she didn't need blisters on top of everything else, and also because she was tired. Exhausted in every sense.

Isabella placed a hand on hers, startling Nadia. She looked at her sister, expecting the same disappointed and terrified look as in their parents' eyes, but instead, she found understanding and support veiled behind a small smile. The rare sight was enough to infuse Nadia with the courage she lacked to put her foot down.

Figuratively. She was too old to throw a tantrum, and her heels had already suffered enough for a morning.

"The venue is paid for. With *my* money," she added. Her mom gazed down at the table, but Nadia still saw her rolling her eyes. "I can't get a refund with only a month's notice. The plane tickets won't be refunded, either," she said, enumerating with her fingers for emphasis. A true Virgo sun, she'd transfer all of this to a list as soon as she got the appropriate stationery for it, but for now, all this info would live in her head. "We can still see the family and show them our *grand* life. We can still have a celebration. For my birthday. God knows, I've gone many birthdays without even a cake!"

She was on the verge of tears. Why was she so emotional? And then, with horror, she realized she'd forgotten to take her birth control pill this morning. She was so sensitive to even the slightest medication, but never before had she been so careless.

Not that there was any risk whatsoever that she'd get pregnant. She didn't even have to count the days since she and Brandon had had sex to make sure she was safe. They had truly lived like an old married couple, including the sex. Or lack of.

How had she been so clueless? She couldn't even remember the last time they'd done it, let alone shared a moment of spontaneous passion that left her reeling. What had she thought? That the wedding would fix their inexistent chemistry? That all of a sudden, he'd turn into the attentive, cool life companion he'd never been? She'd only had one boyfriend like that, back in college. Not a boyfriend, exactly; that boy had been a . . . fling. She had never even known his real name, but everyone had called him Rocket. He'd been the star of the track team, and the one person she'd slept with other than Brandon.

She'd never confess it to anyone, not even to her own journal, but lately with Brandon, in their rare, most intimate moments, she'd close her eyes and think of Rocket, his muscular tanned arms and legs, his long curly hair . . . The way he'd smiled later, caressing her back, as they talked about their dreams of the future, and what the purpose of life even was. She knew then, ten years ago, that they weren't meant for each other. Their goals were so different. But damn! She'd never forgotten him or his kisses, or the way his fingers and tongue . . .

The memory doused her in heat.

She fanned herself, and her dad, unaware of her thoughts,

thank God, handed her a cup with water. "No need for theatrics, Nadia Noemí. I know it must be hard that Brandon broke off the engagement, but you've never been a drama queen, and you won't start now, when you're una mujer hecha y derecha."

He meant well, she knew he did, and still, she had to clench her teeth not to unleash all her fury. Once again, she reminded herself she wasn't angry at him.

But at least her parents had calmed down a little, and although she hadn't said much, or nothing, really, Isabella seemed to be on her side. Olivia was nowhere to be seen. Sent back home to avoid watching her aunt spiral, no doubt.

Great. Now she was a bad example for her goddaughter.

"But you're just going to throw a party for yourself, hija?" her mom asked, dismayed. "A wedding without a groom?"

Isabella brightened at that, but her lips were pressed, as if her thoughts weren't appropriate enough to share.

"No, a quinceañera for an adult, Mamá. A treintañera, they call it," Nadia said, smoothing the tablecloth with her French-manicured hand. Ah! If only life's wrinkles were as easy to fix. "We'll get to dance a waltz, Papi. We'll have cake. We celebrate my life, which is only a representation of your hard work. Don't you see?"

Despite the extra zest she put into the last statement, her parents didn't seem convinced. Maybe they sensed she wasn't being totally honest. It was going to be a celebration of *her* hard work, but she hadn't known how to put it politely and respectfully.

"And the venue is okay with that? What about the dress?" Her mom always went straight to the point.

Nadia shrugged. "I'm meeting with the venue owner at noon. But what can he really say? No? Everything's been paid for already. I can do whatever the hell I want with my money." The stunned silence alerted her to her slip of the tongue. H-E-L-L was considered a swear word at home. "Sorry, it's been too much, but considering, I think I'm handling it well? Give me some credit, please."

It was the closest she'd come to begging them for their support.

She looked at her family around the table and added, "Do you want to come along to talk to him? I'm okay either way . . ."

She left the invitation bouncing, but neither her parents nor her sister took the bait.

"You need to sort this out by yourself, nena," her dad said. "Dealing with the family will be a lot. We won't leave you stranded like your novio did, but think. This is hard for us, too. We lost a son."

He might as well have stabbed her in the heart.

Her dad had never acted like he minded having two daughters, no one to pass on the Palacio last name to. But evidently, Nadia hadn't understood what it meant for him to have a son.

But knowing the amazing relationship her dad had with Jason, Isabella's husband, she should've known.

Nadia bit her lip and looked at her sister.

Isabella sighed. "I'll help you with anything you need, but today I have Noah's baseball tournament. Jason's at work until late, and I'm in charge of the team's refreshments, and I don't have anything ready yet."

Nadia wanted to remind her she didn't need to cook anything from scratch for a bunch of teenagers who poisoned themselves with McDonald's and Taco Bell behind their parents' backs. But she knew she'd never break through Isabella's obsession with babying her son. Like a martyr, Isabella would even endure being eaten alive by mosquitos at a baseball game for Noah.

She hated baseball as much as she loved her son. As much as once upon a time she'd loved her husband, Jason. A baseball-obsessed Puerto Rican. Maybe all relationships soured with the passing of time. Maybe, all the movies and stories lied about what love really was. But then, the everyday little moments were erased from the movies and stories.

But instead of waiting for her happily ever after, Nadia would create her own. One without a man beside her to tell her what to do, to put her down, to treat her like an employee or, worse, one of his bros. Like Jason did with Isabella, but who was Nadia to mix up her sister in her messes? Isabella knew better than anyone the balance in her sentimental life was in the red, worse than Nadia's even. Gosh.

At least Nadia didn't have children to think about.

Nadia shrugged. "I'll go see him on my own. I've been dealing with his daughter, but she's out of town. Still, I met him last year, when we first signed the contract, and he was nice enough, remember?" Her parents' expressions softened as she took charge of this, and she saw a chance to insist on the most important matter for her. She looked at them and asked, "But please, will you at least come to the celebration?"

Her mom crossed her arms and pursed her lips. She looked at her husband to be her spokesperson, as usual.

He cleared his throat and said, "Of course, we'll be there with the whole family." Nadia reached out her hand to take his. He pressed it softly and added, warning in his voice, "I hope this party is what you really want, exposing this failed engagement in front of everyone. I hope you don't end up regretting this indulgence."

Other than her fling with Rocket, she'd never strayed off the narrow path her parents and society had marked for her. She'd never questioned it. But if celebrating her life once and for all was an indulgence, she was more than ready to take the first step into uncharted territory.

Nadia was lost. She'd never been to the venue on her own. She had always been with her parents, and her dad had driven, or with Brandon, and every time, they'd been arguing, so she hadn't paid attention to the route.

Her phone insisted on sending her to the other side of the neighborhood, and unless she wanted to ruin her beloved Jimmys by traipsing over a hay field and an orchard—which she didn't, thank you very much—she needed to find the tiny road that would lead her to the rustic yet romantic barn to celebrate the greatest day in a person's life.

"Please," she prayed to no one in particular. No one in her family had wanted to come, but she hoped any angel on duty had a little free time to answer her plea. "Where is this place?"

Was this a sign that she shouldn't go through with this ridiculous idea? Maybe she should've called one of her friends for advice, but lately, she'd been so distant from her friends, she'd been embarrassed to call and let them know she'd kicked Brandon out and the wedding had been called off.

Most of them would pretend to be shocked, but then, behind her back, they'd gossip that they'd seen this coming all along. All except for Stevie and Madi, the two friends who really mattered. But Stevie was in Texas for summer sales. And most weekend mornings, Madi was unreachable, leading a yoga retreat in any studio along the Wasatch Front that would hire her.

Still, sooner rather than later, Nadia had to update her friends on the change of her marital status. She'd have to wait until she was in the right mental space, though.

Madi and Stevie were her ride or die, but with the rest, she'd have to be careful. Most of them were friends with Brandon.

In the magazine article that had planted this idea in her mind, there were photos of accomplished women celebrating with friends and family, showing off their bachelorette-hood with pride. Or those who had families of their own had included their kids in celebrating their mother and wife like a queen.

She wanted that. She wanted to feel cherished and adored. And if she had to provide the setting, food, and music for her family and friends to do just that, then so be it. She'd already paid for it, after all.

A bell chimed, and Nadia grabbed her phone to check the messages. Maybe Brandon was dragging himself back to ask for forgiveness, which she wouldn't extend, but she wanted the satisfaction of saying no. But when she looked at the screen, there were no notifications. She glanced at her smart watch, and nothing. Finally, she noticed the dashboard and saw the bright orange light indicating she was out of gas.

"Motherfuh—" she muttered.

She didn't know if she should turn back to the main road and ask for directions and get gas in the meantime, or just keep going. Whenever this happened to Brandon, and the idea of being stranded had sent Nadia into a panic, he'd brush her off and continue just to spite her. They'd usually arrived at the gas station running on fumes and the electric charge of one of their showstopping arguments.

She slapped her forehead. Why, oh, why had she put up with him for so long?

She decided to keep going, even though she'd been down this road at least three times, and the young moms with their strollers and Diet Cokes eyed her suspiciously from the park.

And then she saw the peeling wooden sign that indicated EN-CHANTING ORCHARDS and pointed toward a long road lined with trees—she didn't know what kind—and a riot of wildflowers. It was still unbelievable that in the Utah desert, there was an oasis like this. Slowly, she coasted along the lane, and at the sight of the pond with swans, the old barn, and the most majestic mountain in the Wasatch Front in the back, she gasped. This was paradise.

She'd made a million mistakes in her relationship with Brandon, but she'd chosen the perfect place to celebrate their union. Now she'd reclaim it as the location to celebrate her independence.

"Thank you," she replied to whichever supernatural being had answered her prayer.

She parked between a minivan and a black Subaru that looked uncannily like hers, only with California plates.

On an impulse, she reapplied her lipstick. She didn't want to look like a heartbroken woman. She wanted to appear strong and confident, to convince the venue owner that the double quince would be so much better for his business than a regular wedding. Selena's red always made her feel pretty and powerful, so she reapplied it carefully.

She felt her neck prickle, like someone was looking at her. She peered out and looked to the second floor of the barn, but there wasn't anyone at the window. A swan couple, one black and the other white, glided on the water. One of them trumpeted, and the other replied.

Swans mated for life; she'd read that somewhere. Even birds knew how to choose their partners. She felt a pang in her stomach again but tried to ignore it.

Her hands prickled with nerves. Before she got cold feet, she got out of the car. Her shoe made a crunching sound when she stepped on the gravel, and she bit down a string of swear words. She'd never been the sweary kind of person, but this was a special circumstance, and if anyone deserved to send everything to hell, it was her.

She didn't want to ruin her shoes, but the alternative—going barefoot—was unacceptable. She slammed the car door, startling the swans.

"Sorry!" she said to them, but they didn't even look back at her and continued gliding on the pond with grace and arrogance.

The breeze from the nearby canyon felt heavenly on her face. She'd been baking in her work pants and gauze blouse, but this was the good thing about Utah summers: They were dry, and when in the shade, under a breeze, the heat was bearable. Not like in Rosario. She remembered feeling both revived and suffocated by the humidity there.

She tried to put all her weight on her shoes' tiptoes so she wouldn't ruin the heels even more in the gravel, and when she reached the flagstone path, she sighed in relief. There were two signs. One pointing toward the office, and the other, more like a mini billboard, announcing SHANNY AND LUKE, SITTING IN A TREE.

Yesterday, when the wedding was still on, she'd come home to propose to Brandon what the sign could read for them. They'd gotten into the habit of sharing cutesy, cheesy phrases at night. It had been the only romantic-like thing they'd still done, and she had looked forward to sharing what she'd come up with. Something that now she couldn't even remember. In the shock, she'd erased it from her mind. She'd only known he'd love it. But now, it was all for nothing.

She tried to plaster a smile on her face.

Fake it till you make it had been her mantra all her life; that is, until yesterday. But if she hadn't changed her schedule without telling him, she might still be in wedding-planning la-la land. No. It was better to be alone than to be miserable and lonely.

Nadia opened the office door and came across a very pretty woman about her age. The stereotypical Utah Valley girl. With creamy skin and long luxuriant blond hair, a lash-extensioned, manicured, Botoxed, tanned beauty that all the guys of her generation had snatched up as a wife. How many times had Nadia been told by one of Brandon's friends or another that Latinas were just for fun? Was that why Brandon had stuck with her? Hoping the fun would resurface?

She shook her head to dispel her thoughts. She mirrored the woman's smile and asked, "Excuse me, do you work here?"

The woman nodded. "Yes, I'm Kenzie Van Leck, and you are?"

Nadia didn't know if she should try to offer a handshake or not, but sensing an invisible barrier that Kenzie seemed to project, Nadia crossed her arms. "I'm Nadia Palacio. I'm here about the Palacio-Lewis wedding?"

Something flashed in Kenzie's eyes. "Oh," she said, in a tone Nadia didn't know how to read.

"The venue's owner . . . is he here?" She looked around like a dork, as if the old man were hiding and, at the sound of her voice, would jump from behind a box and exclaim, "Surprise!"

Kenzie pursed her lips and glanced upstairs. "Marcos was in the shower. He's almost done getting dressed." She pressed her lips as if she didn't want to grin at the thought of Marcos in the shower.

Marcos? Not that a regular Utah guy who looked descended from a Scandinavian god couldn't be named Marcos. She'd met plenty of Marias who didn't have a drop of Latinidad in them, but still . . . she half-hoped they were talking about the same person.

Nadia's mom always said, "Para gusto los colores," meaning that to each her own, but Nadia had never been the kind of girl who went for older men. The way Kenzie talked about this Marcos guy suggested there was a connection of some kind between them.

The old guy Nadia had met with last year could certainly have been considered attractive by some women, with his sharp blue eyes and easy smile, and a head of luxurious curly blond hair. But he had to be pushing his early sixties or even more.

She tried to suppress an all-body shiver and said, "Okay . . . should I wait for him here while he finishes?" She tried not to imagine the old guy in the shower, attractive or not.

Kenzie nodded and pointed at a lush turquoise chair in the lobby. Nadia sat down and looked around her at the portraits of previous couples, all smiley and accomplished.

How many of those are still happily together? she wondered. And then she chided herself for being so cynical.

She saw the portraits of the three kids on Kenzie's desk. They looked just like her, with no trace of the old man in them. Maybe they were from a previous marriage of hers? That would explain her giddiness still, after three kids.

Usually, people that lit up like a Christmas tree at the thought of someone were still in the early dating stage, or the honeymoon one, when sex was finally allowed and expected to produce children in their ultra-conservative Utah Valley community.

Finally, the sound of footsteps on the stairs announced the arrival of el tal Marcos.

Nadia rose to her feet and turned to face the staircase. This wasn't the venue owner she'd been expecting. Something in the way he moved seemed oddly familiar and sparked the beginning of a memory in Nadia's mind. But if this was the venue owner, he was too young and good-looking for a sugar . . .

". . . daddy!" she exclaimed softly before she could stop her words.

The man stopped in his tracks, and the white flash of a grin crossed his super-tanned face.

Nadia turned her gaze at Kenzie, who was watching the newcomer with the same expression Nadia had seen on those Catholic saints experiencing religious ecstasy. This girl clearly wanted a piece of that—

"Ah," the man said. "Miss Palacio?"

Enveloped in the scent of a cologne she would've recognized anywhere, he walked up to her, stretched out his hand, and shook hers. When they locked eyes, Nadia got pulled back in time, to the weeks in college when she hadn't been stuck with Brandon—they'd been on a break.

The magical weeks she'd been in love with the boy from the track team she'd met at the Hispanic Student Association. He usually waited for her to get out of the library just to chat, and then the rest of the summer . . . that summer she'd thrown caution to the wind and let herself go, really having fun for the first time in her twenty years.

The man seemed to be going through the same time-turning shock. His light brown eyes widened, and a cloud of regret passed across his face.

They both spoke at the same time.

"Nani?" he asked, and Nadia said, "Rocket?"

Chapter 4

Marcos

Marcos Hawkins had done many stupid things in his life. He was the first in line to acknowledge his reckless past and cast a stone. He was helping his sister in the family business to atone for his misdeeds, after all. But one of the biggest mistakes of his life had been not learning the full name of the one girl he'd met in college who had made him lose his mind and, for an instant at least, imagine what it would be like to settle down like his parents had begged him to.

They'd met at a Hispanic Student Association party at the U, the University of Utah. When he asked his roommate, Hernán Rivera, who the long-haired girl with the attitude was, Hernán had warned him to stay out of her way. "She's Brandon Lewis's, bro. You don't want to get in trouble."

Of all the things Hernán could say, he had to go with the one that most sounded like a challenge. Marcos was even more interested in the girl than ever. Brandon Lewis was the star point guard of the basketball team that had made the sweet sixteen round during last March Madness, but Marcos wasn't intimidated in the least by the long shadow his rival cast. So long, it reached all the way to a meeting of Hispanic students, in which he'd never step in.

But still, Marcos was lured by the confidence in the girl. Her dark eyes were bright and inquisitive, and maybe because he couldn't keep his gaze off her, she finally noticed him standing by the stage. He wished the track team had a little more leverage, or any at all. He'd decided to throw for three from half-court, even if he had no business shooting to begin with. He was an optimist, though.

He summoned all his charm and smiled. To his delight, she smiled back. And shockingly, she was the one who made the first move. Before he knew it, she was walking in his direction.

Marcos wasn't a newb when it came to the ladies, and he enjoyed the game of the chase, both being the chaser and even more, the chased. The thrill of the hunt was, in fact, the only thing he really liked about relationships. But when she flashed that smile at him, tossing her brown curly hair over her shoulder, his previous Casanova airs left him in a puff.

"Hey, welcome to our meeting. I'm Nani. How are you?" She leaned in and kissed him on the cheek, and in a reflex movement, he kissed her back. When she leaned closer to him, he pulled her in a brief embrace that made him hyperaware of her every curve.

He didn't believe in love at first sight. But he believed she'd bewitched him with that kiss. If not, then how to explain that years later, he still remembered the scent of her lemon shampoo and the softness of her fingertips on his forearm?

For the first time in his life, he'd been speechless, and Hernán had chimed in, unfortunately. "This is Rocket, and you're Brandon Lewis's girl, right?"

The look of disdain that came over her made Marcos smirk with admiration—and his heart swell with . . . hope.

"I'm no one's girl," she said, chin lifted, shoulders squared.

"Call me Nani. I'm the assistant to the president of the Hispanic Student Association, and I want to make sure I know every single student that's part of it." She looked at Marcos, who was mesmerized by the certainty in her voice and the latent power in her.

Having attended Lone Peak High School, arguably the most competitive school in Utah Valley, he had met plenty of overachieving girls who, if given the chance to mature a little, could've changed the world. Some of them didn't make it past that first summer after high school before sporting a rock on their fingers. Most had dropped out halfway through freshman year when their Mormon missionary returned and popped the question on the way home from the airport. But here was a girl who would go far if she really kept her independence. If she always remembered she didn't belong to anyone.

"Hi, Rocket," she said, laughing. "Tell me about yourself."

They were the same age, barely twenty-one, but she was so much more mature and composed than he was. He wanted to impress her, so he brushed aside his penchant for sarcasm and arrogance and told her about his dream to travel the world as a photographer, but felt the pressure to choose a practical career like business management to help his parents out.

"I understand," she said. "I've always known I wanted to be a lawyer, but sometimes, I fantasize that I went for dance. Or singing. Something artistic, you know? But my parents . . . I'm first generation, and I can't let them down."

Hernán, bored by the conversation already, left without a word and headed toward the clique of girls that were dancing amongst themselves while most of the guys watched them like wolves. This was the reason Hernán had dragged Marcos into the meeting, the promise of Latina girls they could hook up with. At least for fun. Hernán needed someone with papers if he wanted to stay in the country, after all, and in that case, love would have to take a step back.

But Marcos didn't want to be anywhere else that wasn't next to Nani. She was a flame, bright and warm, and he craved her like a man who hadn't seen the sun for years.

Years later, in the darkness before dawn, on his loneliest nights, he realized he should've taken her by the hand and made a run for it right then. Before he chickened out like a fool, leaving the field open for Brandon to swoop back into her life and reclaim her, erasing the candor and warmth that made Nani who she was.

But he'd been intimidated by her, and so much in awe. Nani, on the other hand, seemed to bask in being the object of admiration. Although she'd declared she wanted to meet everyone else in the meeting, she spent the rest of the time with Marcos, and in the few instances that she had to leave his side, they looked for each other with a hunger neither one could explain.

They continued the conversation in the parking lot, where they kissed for the first time.

Marcos didn't remember who'd made the first move. He hadn't felt butterflies in his stomach or seen the proverbial fireworks even during his first real kiss in eighth grade. But with Nani . . .

Time had stopped and bent on itself and expanded until he couldn't imagine not kissing her soft lips, tangling his fingers in her long hair, breathing the scent of her dark skin. He'd never dated a Latina girl before, and the first taste left him hungry for more.

The next morning, they met for a run in the park, and after the run, they'd gone back to his apartment, and made love in a way that put romantic movies to shame. It had been so much more than sex. They had connected spiritually, but if he said that aloud, Hernán and the rest of the guys would've laughed at him.

They spent the whole summer together, dividing their time between school and each other. She attended summer term because she was an overachiever and wanted to graduate early, and he did because he'd flunked freshman year and had to make up his credits.

To keep up with the joke from the first night they met, they called each other by their nicknames: Nani and Rocket, and he felt free to be a new person just for her and honored that for him she was just Nani.

But when fall semester was just around the corner, and his friends' names adorned the sign in his parents' wedding venue, he caught Nani's eye and saw that look.

The look asking for more.

She'd never demanded anything, not even to know his last name or his past, but he realized that she longed for it. She deserved more, too.

She longed in silence for more than he could ever give her.

In her, there was the promise of everything a man could want, but he didn't feel like a man yet, not at barely twenty-one. She was going far. She could one day be president of the country, head of the United Nations, a world leader. She was already a woman who knew exactly what she wanted.

And he was just a boy with nothing to his name.

A niggling voice in his mind told him he'd never be able to keep up with her. That if anything, he'd pull her back. So, he did what he did best. He ran.

He made a big deal out of a small argument. He dropped out of school, left the team, proved his father right, broke his mother's heart, and changed his phone number.

But worse than that, he turned his back on the one girl who'd made him want to be the best version of himself. He was too scared by the whole prospect and too lazy to even try, so he left to tour the world, as if looking for a treasure when he knew too well he'd left the true jewel back home.

By the time he owned up to his mistake, it was too late. Hernán told him that she was back with the basketball player.

Marcos made himself forget about her. He was resolved not to even learn her full name. Still, in his dreams, he smelled her hair and felt her fingers tracing his spine.

And now here he was, standing in front of her, like the tongue-tied boy he'd been almost ten years ago.

"Nani," he repeated, emotion rising inside him like a geyser.

She nodded but didn't return his smile. Her eyes were still sharp, but there was a dullness around her, as if the knocks of life had tarnished her brilliance. Irrationally, he wanted to kiss every inch of her to make her shine with pleasure, like he'd always known how to do in his narrow college bed. But he had no right to even think about that. He'd forfeited it when he'd run without an explanation.

He stood rooted in place and put his tightened fists in his pants pockets.

"Marcos," Kenzie said, slinking toward him and draping a hand over his waist. "If you want, I can help Miss Palazzo."

"Palacio," Nani corrected, and he could feel Kenzie flinch beside him.

He stepped away from his assistant and her territorial and inappropriate gesture, and said, "Go to lunch, Kenzie. I'll handle it."

Kenzie's face flushed a red color he'd only read descriptions of but had never seen in real life. "Well, I just wanted to help."

"It's okay if she stays," Nani said, crossing her arms protectively, as if she were already too wounded to deal with more. And for her sake, he shrugged. "Sure, Kenzie. I didn't mean to imply . . ."

What? That he wanted to be alone with Nani, as he'd been fantasizing for years? That Kenzie bugged him to death, but he didn't have the guts to put her in her place, both because he didn't want to humiliate her and because, perhaps, he did like the attention, as wrong as it sounded.

"Come in—I mean, take a seat." He motioned to the plump chairs his mother had just reupholstered before the accident.

The two women sat opposite each other and instead of choosing sides, he leaned against Kenzie's desk, crossing his arms, too.

"Tell me what brings you here." He didn't know what to ask. He was so completely out of his element.

Nani was getting married. Why else would she be here?

His insides quivered when he noticed how she took a deep breath and squared her shoulders. "I was hoping to meet Sarah to explain the situation. Sarah and I have been working on my wedding coming up. It's scheduled a month from today, but something came up."

A lead ball fell in his stomach, although Marcos tried to keep his face impassive. She was here for her wedding. Scheduled a month from today.

What had he expected?

That she'd wait for him all her life when he had run like a coward? She hadn't been the kind of woman to keep waiting for morsels, and he doubted she'd have changed so drastically in the years that had passed.

"Actually," Kenzie said, taking charge, "Sarah's out of town with her family, and Stuart, well, he's not available at the moment or for the foreseeable future. Marcos is in charge now."

The remaining twinkle in Nani's eye went out.

Marcos couldn't stand to see her so desolate. "Three years ago, my parents had a terrible car crash, in which unfortunately, my mother passed away. My father suffered a brain injury, and added to early-onset Alzheimer's . . . he's trudging along, but . . . lately, he's been unable to work. I stepped in for a month, since my sister had a personal commitment." He'd never said all of this aloud, and even to his ears, his voice sounded mechanical and expressionless. But his heart shattered every time he thought of his parents, making the long drive to California to surprise him, since Marcos wouldn't come home. They'd never made it.

Nani composed her features and lowered her gaze. "I'm so

terribly sorry to hear of your loss. I hope your father recovers soon."

He hoped that at least his father would know him and accept his apology. Even if he was three years too late.

Nani squirmed in her seat, and she looked up at him with such sorrow in her eyes, a knot formed in his throat. "I'm sorry for any inconvenience this may cause, but my reception is all paid for in advance, and actually . . . I needed to let you know there won't be a wedding, after all."

A fire flared inside Marcos's chest, but he tried to quench it when he saw the pain in her face, although she tried to sound collected. "I'm sorry to hear."

"What happened?" Kenzie asked, pursing her lips in a pout.

Nani took a deep breath and, tapping the palms of her hands on her lap, said, "That's personal, but the thing is, there won't be a wedding to celebrate."

Marcos noticed there were fresh scratches on her ring finger, but no ring.

"We offer no refunds," Kenzie said before Marcos could lie and say that he was sorry her wedding was canceled.

In spite of the nonchalant facade, Nani was obviously distressed. How could he feel such elation when the situation brought her so much heartache? But the truth was that for the first time since the terrible news of his parents' accident, he felt alive about something.

Nani wasn't getting married after all, but the wedding business was in the red. Even if he wanted to, Marcos couldn't offer a refund. He'd promised Sarah everything would go smoothly. Once again, Marcos Hawkins, overpromising. But this time, he literally couldn't afford not to deliver on his promises.

"I understand," Nani said. "And the truth is, my whole extended family from Argentina and other parts of the world already made arrangements to attend. Believe me, I'm aware that a wedding can't be canceled as easily as the engagement was called off."

Despite her words, and judging by the waves of sorrow he felt from her, Marcos doubted the break in the engagement had been easy at all. Nani's hands were clasped on her lap, but her fingers were shaking. She bit her lower lip, and the red was so sexy. He had the irrational urge to gather her in his arms and protect her and love her, but that train had left the station a long, long time ago.

"What do you propose then?" Kenzie asked curtly.

Marcos sent her a pointed look, and in a more subdued tone, she added, "I mean, how can we help you?"

Nani swallowed and smiled. She opened her mouth, but no sounds came out. He'd never seen her struggle for words; she was the most eloquent person he'd ever met. Finally, she opened her Louis Vuitton purse and took a rolled-up magazine from it. She thumbed through the pages nervously, and then placed the magazine on the small coffee table that separated her from Kenzie.

Marcos and Kenzie leaned in. The headline of the article read:

Double Quinceañera: A New Trend That's Here to Stay

There were pictures of celebrations with pink balloons, fluffy dresses, and a lot of smiley, happy faces.

Tenderness bloomed in his heart. Is this what Nani really wanted? Is this what hid behind her Wonder Woman mask?

Kenzie's cheeks were bright red again, and she said, "I don't understand what this has to with us. We're in the wedding business, not in the birthday party one."

Nani nodded. "I get that. But a quinceañera isn't just a birthday party. It's a coming-of-age of a young girl being presented to society."

"You're not a young girl," Kenzie said.

Did she realize how bitchy her voice sounded?

"I'm aware of that, thank you."

The room turned chilly.

Nani continued, "In fact, I'm a very accomplished woman on the verge of turning thirty years old."

Kenzie's face registered her shock. "Thirty? You don't look that old . . ."

"You're thirty, too," Marcos said.

"I'm a mother," Kenzie replied, as if birthing three babies had granted her an ageless status that put her above every other woman, including Nani.

"I'll be thirty the day after my original wedding date. I decided that instead of canceling everything—and since I already paid the venue, including food, cake, and entertainment—I'd use the resources to celebrate my treintañera, my double quinces."

Kenzie pursed her lips, tapping a finger to her chin. Making calculations, no doubt.

"I think it's a wonderful idea," Marcos said, and Kenzie sent him a hurt look like he had betrayed her.

"We have a reputation to maintain," she said. "We specialize in weddings, and this party feels like . . ." She made a gesture with her hands as if trying to pull the right words out of thin air. "Like the anti-wedding, you know what I mean?" she exclaimed. "Miss Palacio, there are other places that can host your birthday party. I know that in Salt Lake or Provo, there are halls that do these kind of Hispanic celebrations. Maybe one of them can accommodate you, since there's nothing in your contract that says you can switch the nature of the event?"

The silence was deafening, and Marcos saw the change that came over Nani. Once again, he was a lovestruck twenty-year-old boy in awe of such power coming from this woman.

"I'm well aware of all the places that specialize in quinceañeras, or like you said, *Hispanic events*. And as you also said, there's nothing in the wedding contract that explicitly prohibits me from changing the nature of my party. I paid for the space. What happens at my party is my decision."

Kenzie looked trapped, and Marcos felt bad for her, but why was she so adamant in denying Nani her request?

"Listen, Kenzie," he said. "You know our situation. We can't offer Miss Palacio a refund, and like she pointed out, we can't tell her she can't have her party here. She already paid in full. Besides, maybe this will be an opportunity for the business to branch out?"

"Branch out into what?" Kenzie shot back. "Mark, think of your mom's legacy."

Marcos set his jaw. He hated that Kenzie had invoked his mother and her legacy, as if she had ever known his mom like he did. But then the thought came to his mind that Kenzie had worked very closely with his mom for more than five years. Maybe Kenzie had known Monica Hawkins more than he had, after all.

Nani gathered her magazine and said, "Marcos, I'll leave you and your wife to discuss the details—"

"Wife?" He and Kenzie exclaimed in unison, although their expressions couldn't have been more different. Kenzie had blushed a delicate shade of pink, a smile lighting up her face, but he felt like Nani had punched him.

"Oh," said Nani, noticing Marcos's horror. "You're not . . . together?"

"No," Marcos said before Kenzie could say something that would ruin his image in front of Nani even more.

There was a silence that made him wish for a time machine.

He needed to break the ice. "But going back to what you were saying about my mom's legacy, you know she had a quinceañera in Uruguay, right?" he said.

Kenzie shook her head. "I had no idea. I don't understand what this *quincy* thing is supposed to celebrate. Like, a sweet sixteen?"

Nani sighed as she rose to her feet. "It's so much more than that. I don't expect your business to change the model and start catering to the *Hispanic* community." Marcos heard the emphasis on *Hispanic*. "But, I mean, it can be a turning point for Enchanting Orchards. In any case, I'm glad we're clear that our contract doesn't forbid me from hosting my party here."

She looked at Marcos, and his stomach flip-flopped. "I'll forward you a few changes, like the saying in the sign for example, and the decorations. I understand that I might have to pay more. Luckily, I'm an accomplished, independent woman, and that won't be a problem."

And with that, she turned around and walked out.

Chapter 5

Nadia

Nadia wanted to run out of the place, but more than anything, she wanted to retain her dignity. She couldn't do one without wrecking the other, so she took slow, deliberate steps to the exit.

Outside, the sun shone mercilessly. A breeze blew, and she opened her arms so it could dry the nervous sweat that trickled down her arms.

Great.

The botched wedding, canceled engagement, and the confrontation with the one man who could destroy her whole life had done what she'd been avoiding for years. What she believed she'd conquered: nervous sweating, the kind that burned her skin and bleached her clothes.

When she and Brandon were super young and had a fight and then made up, he'd teased her about her nervous sweat that ruined her clothes. She'd been studying for the bar, and he was upset that she didn't have the energy for sex at two in the morning. She'd given in, of course, anything to avoid another fight that would jeopardize her relationship with him, and he'd joked her toxic sweat was proof that she had acid for blood, which explained her temper and drive.

She'd laughed, but his caustic words had eroded the little self-esteem she'd been clinging to during those difficult months. When she passed the bar the day after, she hadn't even had the strength to celebrate.

But now, she knew better. She was proud of herself for standing up to that woman, Kenzie, and her jabs about Hispanic culture and celebrations.

Nadia jammed the key and unlocked her car. The remote had run out of batteries months ago, and the screw was too old and rusted for her to replace it.

Maybe she should pour a couple of drops of her armpit sweat on it, she thought self-deprecatingly, but instead of laughter, all she got was a pounding headache.

She sat in the sweltering car and turned the key.

The car rumbled, sputtered, and died.

"Ay, not now."

Not when she wanted to make a dignified departure. Hadn't her parting words been that she was a successful, affluent woman?

She winced.

Those were the kind of words Brandon would say when he didn't get his way.

Don't you know who I am? he'd bellow or say through clenched teeth.

She always hated when he tried to throw his weight around, all because he'd been voted One of Utah Valley's Most Promising Teens years ago.

She'd been salutatorian in law school, but her parents had said it was second place. She almost never thought about it anymore, except for when her self-esteem was at the bottom of the barrel. Like now.

She tried to turn the car on one more time, but the car was dead.

Don't force it, said a voice in her mind. *The ignition can burn!*

"Why, why now?" she asked, fighting the urge to bang her head on the steering wheel. She'd seen the warning sign, but didn't want to stop to get gas, thinking she could do it next time. She never tried to push that little mile, and the one time she did, she face-planted.

How was life fair?

Her car had said, *No more ignoring me!* And here she was now. Stranded.

What a metaphor for her life!

Not seeing the signs until it was too late.

It had been the same with Brandon.

Her stomach grumbled, as if asking her not to forget it had been cramping for weeks now.

How long until her body finally broke down, too?

Whom was she kidding, trying to portray a steely persona, when inside, she felt like a melted marshmallow?

She was sure that chick, Kenzie, and the guy of her dreams, Rocket, were laughing at her, heading back to a shower or whatever the hell they did in between clients.

She stopped that thought before it had time to grow legs.

First of all, she wouldn't even think of that guy as *her* Rocket. His name was Marcos. She could never make this mistake aloud.

To call him Rocket in public would be a humiliation she would never recover from.

Second, but really, most importantly, she had to call someone for help.

The first person to come to mind was Isabella. Her sister had been sympathetic to the tragedy. Running out of gas was their shared nightmare. She'd understand and come to Nadia's rescue.

She dialed her sister's number.

It went to voice mail, but when Nadia was about to leave a message, she saw her sister's number flash on the screen. She was so relieved, she could have cried.

She tried to speak, but she couldn't say a word. She took a shuddering breath.

"Are you okay?" Isabella asked in that motherly voice of hers.

Nadia wished she could nestle in her sister's arms and ask her to fix her mess. Not only about the car. No. It was everything. Her whole life was spinning out of control.

Before she burst into tears, she remembered she was still in a parking lot. For all she knew, Kenzie was watching her from the window. Besides, Nadia wanted to show her sister she had things under control. That she wasn't falling apart. Because for all their camaraderie, chances were high that Isabella would go to their mother with the gossip, and they'd call Brandon's mom, and then he'd get involved, and . . .

No.

She had to get it together.

"Bella," she said, and she was so proud her voice didn't even waver. In the background, someone yelled, and she remembered her sister was at Noah's baseball game. Still, she had called her, so now she had to ask, "You're going to think I'm the worst. Again. But for the first time in my life, I ran out of gas. Where are you, and can you give me a hand?"

Isabella sighed, and Nadia felt the heat creeping up to the roots of her hair and beads of sweat explode on her forehead.

But Isabella wasn't judging her. That much was obvious when she said, "I can't. I'm in Salt Lake. Where are you?"

"Mountainville," Nadia said.

A shared sigh echoed on both sides of the call.

"Believe me," Isabella added, "I want nothing else than to get out of this horrible heat, but you might do better calling road assistance. Or what about Madi?"

"She's in a yoga workshop."

"And Stevie?"

"In Texas," she said.

There was a small silence, and Isabella asked in a tiny voice, "And Papi?"

Nadia didn't want to call her dad for this.

"It's okay," she said. "I'll call road assistance." Before she hung up, she added, "Hey, Isa—" She hesitated. She didn't want to be rejected twice in a phone call, but she decided to risk it and be vulnerable. Brené Brown would be proud. "Do you wanna come over later tonight? I need a heart-to-heart." She said this in the fake English accent they used when they were tiny and had played at having tea with the queen.

Ah, those glorious days of pretending in which she'd learned all her most harmful coping mechanisms!

"Good job, Papito!" Isabella screamed, her voice squeaky and thunderous at once through the speaker. Nadia pulled the phone back from her ear, but the damage was already done. Her eardrum wouldn't recover for days.

"Ouch," Nadia said, switching her phone to the other side and rubbing the injured ear with her finger.

"Sorry, Noah just made a home run. Bases loaded." The enthusiasm was genuine, and Nadia didn't want to be a jerk.

"Yay," she said, swinging an imaginary matraca. And then she laughed.

"I'll come tonight. Okay?" Isabella said.

Okay. She had this. She could make things work if her sister was by her side.

What a welcome change this was.

"Okay, I need to get out of this parking lot. You won't ever guess who I saw," she said.

"I can't wait for—dale, Papito!" Isabella yelled again, and this time, Nadia wasn't able to pull the phone back in time.

Her other eardrum was also completely paralyzed and damaged.

They said goodbye, and Nadia dialed Stevie's number. She might be in Texas, but she would know what to do. Stevie, who always sold more alarms or pest-control contracts than any other guy on her team; who'd go canyoneering for weeks at a time and then go skydiving, paragliding, skiing, and running like it was nothing. She'd know what to do. She had friends all over the world, and she might know someone who could help Nadia.

A few seconds later, she got a generic text: "Sorry. I can't talk right now."

And then the three dots.

Nadia bit her lip as she waited.

And when she glanced back at the phone, she read, "T doors. Tlk Ltr?"

Muttering aloud, Nadia translated, "At doors. Talk later?"

Stevie's *A* key had been busted since they'd gone to Lake Powell last summer, and she had insisted her phone was waterproof. She was more of a workaholic than Nadia and hadn't had time to replace her phone yet.

Nadia chuckled as she gave the message a thumbs-up. For all she knew, Stevie Choi was replying to her message as she climbed one of the world's highest seven peaks. She was the polar opposite of their other friend—magical, ethereal Madison Ramirez.

Nadia tried not to, but she had to confess she envied Madi, a yoga master, a perfect girl, a perfect everything. Her life was perfect. She was warm and spunky like a ray of sunshine. Maybe things went her way because she'd been a saint in a previous life . . .

Then what kind of person had Nadia been in other lives to deserve so much misery?

The universe answered with another stomach rumble.

"What do I do now?"

She'd never called road assistance. Never had the need to. She could change a tire. She could refill wiper fluid and jump-start a dead battery.

She could not create gasoline out of shame and fumes, or even her toxic sweat, though.

She tried to turn the engine on one more time. There was no use.

With a sigh, she got out of the car and rummaged in the trunk, the secret space of mess that she allowed herself as she took it everywhere she went. Finally, she found the tiny gas container under a pile of papers.

She searched on her phone for the closest gas station. She'd passed it on the way. She should've stopped, but she hadn't wanted to be late to the meeting with Mr. Hawkins.

And then she'd waited for him to get out of the shower.

She wanted to scream.

Why was she so bad at seeing the signs?

The gas station was only one mile away, but she was wearing her nice Jimmys. The driveway was cobblestones and gravel. By the time she was on the main sidewalk, the leather heels would be shredded.

Could she maybe call an Uber there and back?

"Do you need help?"

"Rocket," she exclaimed, whipping around. She hadn't heard his approach at all.

Crap.

She bit her lip, face burning in embarrassment, but when she looked up at him, she made sure she had a confident smile on her face.

"Hey . . ." she almost said *Rocket* again.

She couldn't remember his real name.

Damn it!

He smiled genuinely, and those freakishly bright brown eyes of his made her stomach somersault and flip-flop like a fish at the end of a line. Something trickled down . . . there, and she prayed it wasn't her period. She had to use the bathroom. Her body was a freaking ticking bomb.

"Do you need help . . . Nani?" he said, obviously not recalling her name, either.

A tenderness came over her and almost made her ovaries explode.

"Nadia," she said, and she sounded so curt, but hello. She

had to place some rigid boundaries now, didn't she? "My name is Nadia Palacio."

"Hi, Nadia Palacio," he said, offering a hand to shake. The way he enunciated each syllable of her name would have made her swoon if she hadn't been a jilted bride. No. Not jilted. She'd been the one to break up the engagement. She had the upper hand. Didn't she?

"I'm Marcos Hawkins," he said, and actually walked toward her and shook her hand. "Nice to meet you again, Nadia. This introduction is like . . . ten years overdue." He had a dimple when he smiled. His arms were sinewy and the hair on them golden brown.

She realized her armpit stains must be massive, and she clamped her arms next to her torso.

"My car is out of gas," she said, showing him the canister. "You don't happen to have some gas at hand, do you?"

She looked around as if hoping to see a gas dispenser. Weren't wedding planners, or whatever he was in the industry, supposed to be prepared for any emergency?

But no dispensers popped out of the pockets of his tight jeans. Instead, he held a key that looked identical to the one for her car. They were, after all, the same make and model and color. Talk about coincidences.

"I'll drive you to the gas station," he said.

"Oh, no," she replied, panicking at the prospect of spending time alone with him in a car. She knew what things he was capable of in a small space.

Or what he'd been capable of, she reminded herself. It had been ten years, but her body remembered, judging by the tingling, for crying out loud.

She showed him her phone. "I'm calling an Uber. I was about to . . . hit this button when you showed up."

He clicked his tongue and got inside his car. "Come on, Nani," he said. "You're going to ruin your pretty shoes. Besides, by the time an Uber makes it here, we will be back, and you'll be well on your way."

She bit her lip again. She was all flustered that he'd called her Nani, like it was nothing. It had shaken her to the center of her solar plexus to hear her nickname on his lips again. Those luscious lips he'd licked. She noticed they were cracked. His lips had always been cracked back then, too.

He noticed her noticing and said, "The dryness. I'm not used to it yet. I've been cracking and peeling like a lizard for days."

She rummaged in her purse, took out a tube of lip balm, and passed it to him.

"It's sealed," she said, just in case. "Still unused."

He laughed. "I know what *sealed* means, nena. And thank you."

"A favor for a favor," she said, with a shrug meant to brush off the smile of gratitude.

He took off the wrapper and wiped his mouth before he applied a thick coat of balm. The cherry scent of the ChapStick, mixed with the pineapple from the car's air freshener, took her back to her teenage years.

"Thank you," he said. "My lips are kissable again."

Before Nadia protested or changed her mind, he turned on the engine. In that moment, Kenzie came out of the office and headed toward the white minivan. The look she sent in their general direction made Nadia grateful she wore a bracelet charm against the evil eye.

Marcos, unfazed, rolled down the window and said, "See you later, Kenzie!"

"See you later!" she said in a bright voice, but when she looked at Nadia, who had climbed onto the passenger seat, Kenzie's eyes promised war.

Nadia scoffed. She didn't have time for this kind of conflict. She didn't care what was going on between Marcos and Kenzie.

Panic hit her again.

What was Nadia doing in Rock—Marcos's—car?

What was she thinking?

What was Brandon doing right now? Did he miss her? Did he even care?

Marcos drove off.

Nadia held the gas canister on her lap. She tapped her fingernail on the plastic, like she was asking all the questions bubbling in her mind in Morse code.

"No," Marcos said, turning at a corner. "There's nothing between us."

"Us?" she asked, distracted, off guard at his confession.

"Us?" he said, confused. "Kenzie and me." And then his face sobered. "But yes, you and me, too. There's nothing between us, either, so relax."

It was the truth. There had been nothing between them for a long time. But still, the words hurt. It was like being rejected all over again. Like when she'd realized Brandon didn't love her.

Brandon, who'd tried to gaslight her. But Rocket had left without an explanation.

He'd been her everything.

Brandon, that is. Brandon had been her everything, and Rocket . . . he'd been a fling, a . . . distraction. She knew better now. She wouldn't let herself be seduced by his long hair, strong arms, and luscious lips. Not even now that they were moisturized.

She cleared her throat to try to reset herself. She didn't want to appear unmoored in front of this man.

"What do you mean we were nothing?" she asked in spite of herself. Her temper was bubbling. "We even talked about moving in together, and one morning, you were just gone."

The memory of the pain when she realized he'd left her hurt even more now than it had ten years ago.

He kept his eyes on the road and shrugged. "It was for the best."

"What do you mean?" she asked, seething.

"You went back to the basketball player. You were about to marry him, right? So I think that's proof enough that we were nothing more than—"

He paused as if allowing her time to either contradict him or add a few words, but she wasn't going to make things easy for him. Favor or no favor.

"Nothing more than a good memory," he said, with the ghost of a smile. She saw so much pass through his eyes. Por Dios! His voice was so velvety soft that Nadia's eyes prickled at feeling just how sweet and tender the memories must be for him, too, to still talk about them with such tenderness.

"Those were good times," he added.

After a couple of seconds, she added, "Yes, they were."

Damn.

She couldn't believe she'd said that aloud. She must be drunk with grief and exhaustion. But the best was his reaction.

His face should have been in a museum. It should have been on billboards nationwide, warning women against thieves of hearts and reason. If she didn't know better, if she hadn't vowed to show the world she was an independent woman who could survive without a man by her side, if a part of her still didn't have a tiny hope that Brandon would come back to her and beg her to reconsider, to still have the wedding, then she would have fallen for Rocket's smile and sent all her resolutions, false hopes, and expectations to hell.

Finally, they arrived at the gas station.

"Here we are," he said, opening the car door.

The pulsing of sexual tension was unbearable, but thankfully, a gust of fresh air dispelled it like feathers in the wind. She hadn't felt that kind of tension for a while, but her whole body vibrated with it. *Resonated with it*, Madi's voice corrected in her mind.

The breeze came to her rescue once more to cool her down.

She got out of the car and stood in front of the pump.

"Are you okay?" he asked with such concern in his voice, she didn't know how to react.

"Of course I'm okay," she replied, flustered, looking around in circles, proving that she was, in fact, not okay. She hated that he knew her more than her longtime fiancé ever did.

"Do you know how to do it?" his voice was still compassionate.

She'd have preferred mockery or flirting. Compassion was too close to pity. And pity was something she couldn't accept.

"Yes. I know how to fill out a tank, silly."

"Careful with the flow. The canister's only a two-liter, and this is a fast pump," he said.

She took a deep breath and hardened her features.

"I know what I'm doing. Thanks."

"Okay," he said, nodding once. "Do you want anything from the store?"

She wanted a Diet Cherry Vanilla Dr Pepper, but she didn't want to owe him any more favors. She shook her head, and after a second or two of hesitation, he headed inside the gas station.

"Come on," she chided herself. "Get a move on, Palacio!"

She was ever obedient, even to her bossy alter ego. Her heels clacked against the concrete as she went around his car and carefully placed the container on the ground like the sign at the pump instructed.

She bent over and jumped right back up when someone wolf-whistled. She whipped around to see three teenagers in an old-fashioned jeep filled to the brim with camping gear. This gas station was right at the mouth of American Fork Canyon, and people from all over the world flocked there to enjoy hiking the breathtaking landscape, including world-famous caves she hadn't been to since a field trip in eighth grade.

"Hey! You little brats!" she called, and the boys pretended they hadn't done anything.

Cheeks burning, she squatted as she carefully pressed on the dispenser but almost nothing came out. A few drops of gasoline leaked down the sides of the red plastic container, her neck prickling at the furtive looks the boys sent her and her famous J.Lo butt, as her family called it. She moved her feet out of the way so she wouldn't ruin her shoes even more. Why hadn't she let Rocket do this for her?

Rocket. She had to stop using this nickname in her mind. It did nothing but bring back memories hot enough that she might be putting her whole town in danger here at the gas station with her flaming thoughts.

She peered over at the store, and he was waiting in line with a couple of drinks and something else she couldn't see. Once again, she craved a cold, caffeinated soda. Brandon always made fun of her irrational love for Dr Pepper. She'd told him how, as an eleven-year-old, she'd loved the sweet taste of a drink no one back home in Argentina had known.

Thinking of Brandon made her sweat again—now with rage.

She was so mad at him all over again that she was irrationally afraid she'd combust, and then create an explosion and ruin the whole world and burn it down. All the world except for Brandon, of course, who never stayed around to see the mess he'd made.

Why was this pump not working?

"Okay, chill," she said to herself, and got her finger out of the pump trigger to try another hose. A few drops of gasoline went over her fingers, and instinctively, she wiped them on her pants.

Now she'd stink forever. What had she been thinking?

She tried to see if the machine had charged her for anything even though it was obviously broken. With a flash of horror, she realized the pump wasn't working because she hadn't paid. In fact, she didn't even have her purse with her. It was still in *her* car.

"Fu—" she exclaimed, just as Rocket was heading back her way.

She wanted to stomp and throw a tantrum like a two-year-old. The teenagers were still behind her, though.

"Everything okay? Ready to go?" Marcos asked.

She turned around, her cheeks flaming like flares.

When he saw her expression, his eyes got all concerned. He had a plastic bag bulging with stuff.

She closed her eyes for a second. Her ears were buzzing. Or maybe it was the teenage boys, whispering like harpies behind her—what were they saying?

"What's wrong?" he asked, his voice rising, his gaze flickering behind her to the boys.

"Hmmm, I left my purse in my car," Nadia said, and she had a flashback to being eighteen and telling Brandon she'd forgotten to take her pill that morning. The shame still ate at her.

The silence fell and bounced like a rubber ball. Her chest pounded.

"Okay," Marcos said matter-of-factly as he pulled his wallet out of his pocket. "I got it. It's just a few bucks. It's not like that summer when gasoline was almost five dollars a gallon, remember?"

She remembered no such thing, but she appreciated the gesture. Not only that he was paying for it, but he even filled the canister. Also, he wasn't being a jerk about the whole situation.

If Madi had heard her thoughts, she'd have said, *Your bar for not-jerk behavior is very low, love.*

Nadia would've agreed with her.

"I'll Venmo you," she said, and bit her lip, exhaling the stress that left her in ripples. "Once my phone is . . . charged."

"No problem, Naaa . . . dia," he said again.

He looked beyond her, and his embarrassment at almost having called her Nani vanished like it had never been there. Later,

Nadia would remember this moment and wonder how a person's expressions could change in the blink of an eye. First, his eyes lit up, and lines fanned out from the corners. The light spread to his mouth that was now a smile, and then, he started chuckling. Soon, it was a belly laugh.

He put the bulging bag on the ground and clutched at his stomach.

"What is it?" she asked, and couldn't help smiling, too, because his laughter was *that* infectious.

The boys behind her started laughing, too. She had a nagging suspicion Rocket was laughing at her. Enraged all of a sudden, she turned around, and the tallest of them, a freckly Asian boy, nodded. "Some are born lucky. I hope to get some of that luck in my future," the boy called out, his hands around his mouth like a megaphone.

"Amen!" the other two echoed, saluting Rocket.

"What?" she asked, rounding on him. "Do you know them?"

He wiped his face, and his voice was so strained, it seemed he was trying hard to stop laughing. "Kai helps at the venue sometimes. Why?"

"What were they saying?" she asked. Her voice sounded tiny and teary. What she really wanted to say was, *Don't tell me they were making fun of me. I know I'm a mess. I know it, and I don't need anyone else to tell me this.*

Rocket seemed to hear the request lurking behind her question. He smiled kindly at her.

What was it about this guy, whose smile could disarm her like this? She had been happy with him during their fling. Until he'd run and left her. Left her to go back to Brandon. This instant connection she felt with him was irrational, like everything she'd done since yesterday. She couldn't figure it out, and like every time she wasn't in control, her frustration and fluster turned into anger.

Her anger wasn't really directed at Marcos and the boys, but they were there, laughing and smiling like she was a bimbo and didn't understand anything. Brandon had laughed at her like that a lot.

Marcos wasn't Brandon, although it was hard not to be angry at all the men in the world right now.

It wasn't directly his fault that she'd gone back to Brandon after he'd left, but his action of running away had unleashed a series of motions that ended with her stranded with no gas, being made fun of by teenage boys.

"Let's go," she said, seeing how he wasn't going to tell her what was so funny, the boys had become his favorite people in the world.

She got back in the car, the canister of gas between her feet, and she wondered if it was safe to carry it like this. She wasn't going to ask him, though. All her life, people had commented on how smart she was. But she was only smart in a bookish way. How had that helped her in real life?

She was mad at Brandon, but honestly? She could only blame herself for everything that had happened in her life.

Rocket filled his tank, and then the teenage boys drove away, toward the mountains. He finished paying for the gas, and when he got back in the car, gave her the receipt.

"Here you go," he said.

"Thanks," she said without glancing at it.

He rummaged in his plastic bag and grabbed a bright yellow can. "Here," he said. "Have you tried this?"

"What is it?" she asked. She wasn't a soda person other than Diet Dr Pepper. But the words YERBA MATE in bold texturized letters on the front of the can intrigued her.

Yerba mate was an herbal tea that a lot of people in South America drank instead of coffee or along with coffee, like her dad, who liked to mix a tiny teaspoon of instant coffee in his morning mate to give it a boost.

Argentines went everywhere with it. She'd seen photos of Messi, the soccer player, heading to games with his mate in tow. But Uruguayans were even more fanatical about it than Argentines. She wasn't sure if it was an insulting term, but her dad had told her that Uruguayans were green bellies, panzaverdes, since they went nowhere without their mate, not even the movies or church.

When she had met Rocket and she'd found out he was part Uruguayan, she'd offered him a mate. The traditional one, made with ground toasted leaves and hot water in a gourd, and drunk with a bombilla, a straw with a filter at the end.

He'd shaken his head. "I'm not a mate person," he'd said, as if he were saying *I'm not an air breather* or another barbaric thing like that. She had insisted. She'd seen him drink coffee, although he'd told her he did it to bug his Mormon family. Mormons' health code prohibited them from drinking coffee.

This can he was handing her made mate look like an exciting energy drink.

A yerba mate–flavored energy drink?

"I've never tried it," she said. "And I don't like energy drinks, so probably I won't like this."

"You turned into a purist?" He rolled his eyes. "Try it!"

She laughed. "Oooh, a purist," she mimicked.

He shrugged a shoulder. "I'm a former D-One athlete, lady. I went to college and know my words, for your information."

She popped the can open, and the gas fizzed. "I see. Oh, it's not carbonated?"

"Not this kind," he said.

She tried to read the nutritional facts, but the print was too small.

She took a sip of the drink, expecting to hate it, but her tongue exploded in a symphony of flavors.

"How much caffeine does this have?" she asked.

"A lot," he said, laughing again. "But no carbs."

No carbs?

"It's sugar free," he said. "Although, why do you bother checking that?"

"I'd rather not count my calories. I like to eat them in the shape of bread, thank you very much."

"With butter," he added, licking his lips, and the gesture, so innocent and indecent at the same time, made something pulsate in Nadia that she wouldn't admit, even under torture.

"I have to limit my intake of carbs," she said. "Diabetes runs in the family, but you? You're so lucky. You still look like when you were in college."

He shrugged and opened his mouth as if he were about to say something. She expected him to be totally predictable and tell her she looked the same, too, although they'd both know it was a lie. But he didn't.

"Here we are," he said when they reached the parking lot. Kenzie's car wasn't back.

She got out and poured the gas in her tank. Hopefully, she could make it to the gas station by her apartment. She couldn't risk forgetting to fill up and being stranded on her way to work on Monday. Silently, she vowed to never let the needle go below the halfway mark ever again.

"Do you think it will start now?" she asked.

He nodded like he knew all the secrets of the universe. And because she felt like a wet, abandoned duckling, she believed him.

She turned the key, and her car came alive after the first try. The engine rumbled; the wheel vibrated under her hands. She was so relieved she could have cried.

She remembered Marcos was standing right next to her, still watching her like he was worried about letting her go on her own.

"About the party," she said. "I paid for dance lessons, and a couple of . . . activities. I'll get back to you on Monday with some details? And questions? My whole family is coming. It'll be . . ."

"Wild," he said, and that smile was still there.

"You can say that again." He nodded knowingly, and she

added, "Anyway, nice to see you." She stopped herself from saying *Rocket* at the last second.

"Nice to see you, Nani," he said, with zero qualms.

She drove away, and before she took the turn at the end of the driveway, she looked in the rearview mirror. He was still watching her.

Chapter 6

Marcos

Marcos saw her drive away, praying to the god he didn't believe in that he looked cool and composed. Inside, his blood churned and boiled like the ocean waves he'd seen once in Nazaré, Portugal. He'd been there to photograph a wedding, which was held at the same time as a surfing competition. Now that he thought about it, it made sense that his friend Declan, a merman if there ever was one, a person addicted to the ocean, had chosen that spot to tie the knot with his soul mate, Cody.

He remembered the awe at watching a tiny-looking human ride those otherworldly walls of water and raw nature power. And then the awe turned into envy. Marcos could surf, but not well enough to try to tame one of those monster waves.

Now, his heart fluttering, his legs shaking, he had the urge to run far, far away. Get on an airplane back to Portugal. Plant his feet on one of those flimsy surfboards. Anything but be here, feeling the tug-of-war his mind and heart were playing.

"Ugh!" he groaned, mussing his hair, as if he could rip the

fantasies his mind was conjuring at a rate of one hundred per second, all of them starring the girl of his dreams and him.

Nani.

Thinking of her, seeing her in the flesh, and having her close enough to touch was his definition of torture.

Because no matter what his feelings had been this last hour since he'd seen her, or whatever fantasies his mind created, there was no way he had a chance with her again.

Not when she'd just broken her engagement and was finally on the path to reclaim her life. Not when he was here to atone for the sins of the past two decades of his life.

But then, his body and heart were sabotaging his best intentions.

When he was little, his mom had warned him that all the consequences of his reckless decisions would one day catch up to him. She'd been right, of course.

His day of reckoning was here, when he least expected it.

His Mormon queen of a sister, Molly Mormon, aka Sarah, would tell him there was no such thing as punishment, but the consequences to his acts. And it's not even like he was mad at God. He doubted there was such a god as the one his mother and sister had believed in. But in case there was one, he wasn't even mad at that kind of guy. He pictured this deity a little like his father, except older and sterner, and with a long beard that reached his belly. Which was nothing like his father, as Stuart Hawkins wasn't even old enough to have a full head of white hair.

If he were being honest, Marcos wasn't even mad at the young boy he'd been, who had put him in this predicament with Nani. If he hadn't run away that day in college, his life wouldn't have turned out any better, because that young Marcos Hawkins had been a jerk. He hadn't improved much, but at least he knew what kind of guy he was.

The young Marcos Hawkins would have destroyed the

beauty and power that was Nadia Palacio. Hadn't his father once told him he broke everything he touched? And if he had destroyed Nani, then the world wouldn't know the luminous woman Nani had turned into. Not that she wasn't luminous before. She'd been blazing. Now she was a force.

To play along with the clichés his mind was firing at him, he agreed that at the time, he'd only been a moth.

Marcos the Mothman.

He laughed, increasingly more aware that the swans were looking at him with concern from their pond.

No, back then, he hadn't even been a moth. Instead of running toward the light, at least for selfish motives, he'd run in the opposite direction. His excuse was that with that decision, he had wreaked the least of damages. What a liar he was.

A liar and a coward.

His head hurt as he thought of what could have been. Visualizing the paths his actions would make and the ripples of unintended consequences, he'd taken the one that seemed the least harmful.

The truth was, he'd taken the one that led to the worst outcome. Stuck in the family business, out of his element, his family's last hope to get at least a scrap of redemption.

He finished drinking his mate and threw the can in the garbage container outside the venue. The catering and decorators had started their job for the wedding tonight. This wedding was for an unusual client: a middle-aged couple getting remarried after ten years apart.

He'd never met them in person. Sarah had taken care of all the particulars. But he was curious about the circumstances, so he wanted to see what kind of thought process drove a man to remarry a person he'd loathed enough to get divorced from.

Marcos waved at Marty, the caterer, and as he was walking into the office, which was blessedly Kenzie-free, his phone rang.

He didn't recognize the number, and there wasn't a name. His first impulse of sending it to voice mail almost won, but he resisted. If the call went to voice mail, then he'd have to listen to it and see the record of his mom's last voice mail that he hadn't been brave enough to open yet.

His mom's literal last words.

He hadn't told anyone about it, not even Sarah. Every time he saw that unheard message, he'd feel like a fraud and a murderer and liar. To complete the nightmare, he'd have to call the person, most likely another bridezilla.

No. There was no point in procrastinating.

He brushed his hair out of his forehead and clicked ACCEPT.

"Marcos Hawkins speaking," he said in the breezy voice he'd learned as a call center employee when he was sixteen, his first job.

"Hello, Mark?"

The other voice didn't belong to a bridezilla.

The man sounded so much like his father, Stuart, back when he was well, that unexpected and unwelcome tears prickled Marcos's eyes. His breath solidified in his lungs, and he gasped, as if he were at the last mile of an ultramarathon in the Salt Flats of Northern Utah. Another trip in which he hadn't stopped by to visit his mother.

It took him a second to understand what the man was saying. And when the voice and the words registered, he realized it wasn't his father. Of course, it wasn't. It was Uncle Monty.

"Mark, do you hear me?" Uncle Monty insisted.

Marcos hated that his uncle used this nickname; it was only for family, the close kind, not extended. The last thing he remembered his uncle Monty saying to his mother was that these Hawkins kids were all hers, not part of the family that had walked the prairie with the Mormon pioneers.

"I'm here," he said, to ground himself before his anxiety took over. Why did he revert to being a little child when people from the past saw him? All his flaws came crashing back down. Here, he couldn't pretend to be the cool Marcos Hawkins. He was Mark the troublemaker.

"As I was saying, I'd like to come and talk to you later today. I have a business meeting and then a church activity that I need to take care of. But the church is nearby my folks' place, and I wanted to stop by and talk to you, if that's okay."

Marcos saw nothing okay with this proposition, but if anything, his mother had taught him to respect his elders. And his uncle qualified as one—a crooked one, but one nonetheless.

"I'll be here," he said. "We have a reception at seven, which means that if you're going to stop by, I can't meet you after six, because that's when most of the families show up for last-minute preparations."

His uncle clicked his tongue, but his voice was pleasant when he replied. "I'll be there at five. How's that? That way, you can take care of business."

"Sounds good," he said, and his voice sounded so tiny, he was embarrassed. If his friends from Cali heard him like this, they wouldn't believe he was the same person. But he was. Marcos Enzo Hawkins contained multitudes.

There was a pause, and Marcos's stomach growled. He regretted not getting a sandwich at the gas station, but he'd been embarrassed for Nani to see that when it came to food, he still hadn't changed at all.

"See you later then," he said.

"Yes, see you later. And oh, before you go, it's nice to talk to someone civilized instead of your sister. I don't know what happened with our sweet little Sarah, but she's been impossible to deal with. She was sure you wouldn't even consider talking to me. But I'm happy you're more approachable. I'm sure we can reach an agreement. George will be happy to hear. Bye now."

He hung up, and Marcos felt like a fool. His uncle had played him right where he wanted him.

Sarah was going to kill him.

After he'd eaten, and his mind cleared a little from the fog of his blast from the past and the conversation with his uncle and the shame that ensued from that, Marcos felt a little more like himself. He'd put on a black suit and, magically, this new person took over his actions and thoughts.

It was time to act like the legit venue owner everyone but him thought he was. Maybe if he pretended long enough, he'd start believing this wasn't the worst idea his sister had had yet.

The gravel crunched with the weight of a vehicle, and he looked out the window.

An elegant but old-fashioned emerald-green Jaguar drove up the driveway.

A man in a navy suit and a sprig of flowers in his lapel stepped out of the car. He looked around with a satisfied expression on his face.

He was tall and had a ruddy face and a receding hairline, but he seemed to have accepted the relentless hair loss in a dignified way. He didn't seem to be trying to hide the fact that his best hair days were gone. He was fit, the sleeves of his suit jacket tight, but he also had a small beer belly. He was grinning so widely, his face would be hurting later. Marcos knew this from his experience of walking red carpets when he'd accompanied Bree, but then, he'd been faking his happiness. This man radiated joy.

Kenzie greeted him at the entrance of the venue.

"Mr. Locke!" Her chirpy voice reached the office window from downstairs. It didn't sound like she was faking her gladness, either. Marcos guessed that in a way, seeing a couple remarrying and finding love again after a divorce was healing for her. She could flirt all she wanted with him—and others—but he'd seen the way her eyes got all velvety and soft when she talked about her good-for-nothing ex-husband, Ryder.

She was good at her job, but it was time for him to show up. Marcos took a deep breath, buttoned up his jacket, and headed downstairs. He'd tied his hair back in a neat ponytail, but out of habit, he still brushed a ghost strand of hair behind his ear.

When he reached the entrance, the man and Kenzie were chatting like old friends. But still, the man didn't flirt with Kenzie at all. And in spite of her friendliness and exuberant enthusiasm, she, too, was all proper, keeping a respectful distance from him.

Marcos was impressed.

The man saw him approach and smiled back at him. Marcos was grateful he'd listened to Kenzie's advice and tied back his hair and put on his suit to receive the guests instead of wearing running clothes, like always. His mom and dad used to mingle with the guests, anticipating emergencies and mishaps, as inconspicuously as possible. Earlier, Marcos had taken the pin with the name Enchanted Orchards from his father's desk and placed it on his own tie. It had been his mom's idea; in case a person needed help, they'd know who to ask and not spend time looking around like a needle in a haystack.

Kenzie seemed impressed, too, at his appearance. She nodded and winked so briefly, Marcos wondered if it had really happened.

"Good evening, I'm Marcos, a pleasure to meet you," Marcos said, trying to find his composure after the overwhelming sense of validation for getting Kenzie's approval. Some habits were hard to break. He wanted to sound professional and competent. He stretched out his hand for the man to shake.

"Good evening, Marcos," the man said. "I'm Gary Locke."

"It's a pleasure to meet you, Mr. Locke. Congratulations on your wedding day!" he said with sincerity.

The man got all bashful, the tips of ears flashing hot red in spite of his shrug, as if to hide his feelings. The change from confident giant to blushing groom was so instantaneous and unexpected that Marcos smiled, and his cold, cold conscience marveled at the vulnerability of this man. Another tiny corner of his mind wondered if it was all for show. He'd met his share of con artists; he'd been on the way to becoming one if he hadn't met Nani back in the day and fixed his ways, but he hated being a cynic.

Kenzie had a call, apparently, because she placed her hand over the earpiece that she always wore to arrange all details. She looked up at Marcos, and he braced himself for an emergency.

But Kenzie just smiled briefly and said to Marcos, "I'm heading to help Marty with the canapés delivery. I'll be around if you need me. Excuse me."

He nodded briefly, sending a prayer to whatever saint was on call for her efficiency and professionalism. She'd tried to get him to wear an earpiece, but he'd said no. Now he regretted it. If he was going to do a good job, looking the part wouldn't be enough.

"She's very good at her job. Same as Sarah," Mr. Locke said when she walked away, but unlike other men, he didn't stare at her curvy figure. "Thank you and your staff for helping me throw my bride the wedding of her dreams. I couldn't have planned this without you."

"It's our pleasure," Marcos said, and to his surprise, he wasn't even lying or pretending. "Like you said, Kenzie and Sarah are devoted to our clients."

Making people happy had been his family's obsession for years. But the hard work had taken a toll on Sarah and her family. After their father's health deteriorated, she had taken over the business, and she had given it her all. But the truth was, she had her hands full with her kids. When she came back, she'd hopefully see that Marcos had kept his promise of keeping the business on its feet.

"They sure are." Mr. Locke laughed as if he'd just remembered something. "Sarah told me they're not used to dealing directly with the grooms. It's mostly brides, especially their mothers. There are a couple of overzealous grandmas here and there, or a bride's father, when his wife makes him, but seldom the groom."

Marcos nodded. In an industry devoted to celebrating love and family, men were blatantly absent.

He cleared his throat and asked the million-dollar question, "What makes you the exception to the rule, then? Is it because it's the second time around?"

He regretted the questions instantly. It wasn't his place to pry.

But Mr. Locke nodded, seemingly not offended at all. "Julia, my bride, has been the backbone of our family since we were babies, in our early twenties."

Marcos racked his brain for a polite way to ask how they'd gotten here, a second chance. And why. But he didn't need to worry, as Mr. Locke shared of his own free will.

"For our first wedding, we were poor freshmen. She was a first-generation college student from Wyoming, and my family was okay financially, but not loaded. I'm the middle child of ten. I have six sisters and three brothers."

Marcos whistled, his mind like a calculator going through numbers of what a fortune his parents must have paid for all those weddings.

"Exactly," Gary said. "But you know what? When they realized Jules's family was stressing about the cost, they paid for everything. Even the dress and the flowers and everything that's usually the bride's family's responsibility."

"Things are changing," Marcos said, his fingers fidgeting with his *unprofessional* (as Kenzie had called it) thread bracelet tied around his wrist. "Now, it's more balanced out. Families split the costs, or sometimes even the groom's family takes over, like yours did," he said, thinking of the Coronels' wedding next week. The boy's family was from Mexico, and they were footing the bill to make sure he and his bride got the celebration they deserved. None of the peanuts-and-mints nonsense.

The Coronels weren't well-off, but they were still throwing a three-day bash ending up in the celebration. They'd chosen this venue because it was outside city limits and could party until five in the morning, unlike the others that only allowed until ten to respect city limits. The mother of the groom had explained to him that since they had family coming from all over the world, they couldn't do a one-hour line shaking hands and a hot chocolate bar. But the poor bride's mother had been horrified. The groom's family had said they'd take care of the reception.

In fact, Marcos remembered Nadia's file had said her wedding would be until the wee hours of the morning, too. He wondered if she'd keep the extra time for her double quinces. He smiled, thinking of what a revolutionary idea it was to throw herself a treintañera.

Mr. Locke must have thought Marcos's smile was because of his words about his soon-to-be wife again. He continued, "Jules was so grateful my family paid for everything, but this debt—a perceived debt, but one nonetheless—took a toll on our marriage. I mean, our humble reception was all my parents could help with, and I won't make it the culprit in our failed first marriage. But it certainly contributed to it. I cheated on her."

Marcos was stunned. This wasn't the confession he had expected.

Mr. Locke patted him on the shoulder and said, "Not with a person. No. I was never unfaithful with another person. But I paid more attention to my businesses and career than our relationship. She took care of the kids and the house. I never realized how unhappy she was until she turned forty-five, and our last child moved out. She said she was depressed and didn't have a reason for living anymore. I never saw it coming."

The story, sadly, was common enough.

Mr. Locke kept talking. It was like now that the words had started flowing, he couldn't stop them. "The fighting started. I was offended. I took her words so personally, you see? Hadn't I given her everything so she could stay home with the kids? Everything but my attention. She did the most important work, but I pretended I was doing her a favor for not having her work out of the home. The last vestiges of our relationship collapsed. The kids, two boys and a girl, all married in their early twenties, too, took her side. We got divorced, and I was angry for a long time. We saw each other again when our first grandchild was born. Now, he's five, and we have three more on the way. But Duncan was the bridge."

Mr. Locke's eyes became luminous, and Marcos looked away from him. The brilliance in them embarrassed him a little, and he didn't know why.

"After Duncan was born, Julia and I started meeting for breakfast once a week, and then we'd head over to watch our grandkid. She seemed to like that I changed diapers and played with the baby, something I'd never done with our own children. I felt this was a second chance God was sending me. I worked hard to have her fall in love with me all over again. I'd always loved her. And she did, too, because she's loyal and generous, but the truth was, because of the man I had been, she hadn't liked me for a long time. When I had the idea to propose for the second time, my children were all on board. They helped me do the whole production for the Instagram photo, you know? But I wanted to throw the party of the year to celebrate our love and her forgiveness. To celebrate, you see? Not as something to get over with quickly. You never know if life will give you a second chance. I got it, and I'm damned grateful, pardon my French."

A warm feeling came over Marcos.

"That's a . . . wonderful story." Marcos swept his gaze over the decorated venue and was proud Enchanted Orchards had played such a big part in the love story. "It all looks perfect."

Mr. Locke smiled. "She'll love it. Thank you."

"Thank you," Marcos said, feeling like this stranger had given him a key. He didn't know what the key would open yet; there were so many locked little boxes in his heart and his mind that he chose not to look into anymore, because it all hurt so much. But he put the imaginary key in the imaginary pocket of his imaginary pants for a day when he'd need the advice.

Mr. Locke turned to rearrange some name labels on the table. "The kids fight if they're next to each other. I just remembered I changed the seat configuration at the last minute."

Marcos patted him on the shoulder. "I'll be around, making sure it all happens just as you had dreamed for your bride."

His heart burned with determination, and for the first time since he'd arrived back home, he understood why his parents had done this all their lives. Helping people start their lives together with a bang that would sustain them through the hard times.

Mr. Locke left to talk with the DJ, and Marcos saw a car arrive in the parking lot and park in the place reserved for the horse-drawn carriage.

He suspected he knew who it was, but just in case, headed over to ask his uncle to move the car before he got too comfortable.

"Uncle Monty," he said, as his uncle was getting out of the car. He was suited up, too, but not in the celebratory outfit or work outfit kind of way. Uncle Monty's suit had a churchy aura.

His uncle turned his piercing blue eyes in his direction, the Hawkins signature eyes that the three brothers had inherited from the Scandinavian ancestors up in the old family tree. But there was nothing of the kindness Marcos had seen in his dad's eyes, encouraging him to do his best all his life, even when there was no reason for hope.

"There you are, Mark," Uncle Monty said. "I worried you'd forget, so I took a little longer to arrive and help you save face. I remember how many times your parents waited for you to show up to work, and you never did."

"Those were other times." Marcos clenched his fists and put them in his pocket so he wouldn't punch that sanctimonious smirk off his uncle's face. "I need to get back soon though, so . . ."

"It will only be a few minutes," he said.

Marcos shook his head. "Come around and park in the back. Our guests are arriving already. I expected you an hour ago."

His uncle sighed like a petulant child, but he got back in the car and moved it around the parking lot, revving the engine and sending dirt and gravel in its wake.

"Oooh," Marcos said to himself in the voice his sister would use. "He's angry . . ."

He missed Sarah suddenly, and regretted that he hadn't been a better brother. He walked over to the parking place where his uncle had left his Audi, so he wouldn't get too comfortable and waste his time.

"Hi, Uncle. Nice to see you," he said, trying to channel his good host energy, put a mask on. The good energy from his talk with Mr. Locke was fizzling out from seeing his uncle, and he resented this intrusion.

But his uncle seemed oblivious.

"I see you're upset. But you have to understand, the church meeting went a little longer than I expected. But it's all the Lord's business. Take it up with him, if you're offended."

Marcos wondered what Lord his uncle was talking about. He doubted Jesus would be okay with his church treated as a business, but he kept his comments to himself. There was no sense in arguing about the church. Not now or ever.

"I have to head back to the reception soon. But, like I said, nice to see you."

His uncle nodded and sighed again, but he didn't say it was nice to see Marcos, too. He extended a hand that held a manila folder. "Here," he said. "These are the property documents that appoint my brother Stuart as the guardian of the ranch. But since he's not the guardian anymore, we're putting it up for sale."

Marcos tried to swallow the knot in his throat, but the knot was lodged. He felt like throwing up.

"You know this is my parents' work and glory, to use one of your favorite phrases from the scriptures you love to read and quote," Marcos said.

His uncle clenched his jaw.

"Why are you doing this?" Marcos asked. "Why do you want to destroy their legacy?"

"I don't want to destroy anything," his uncle said. "But it's not fair that you kids pretend you can run the business, when it's obvious you can't."

"How is it obvious?" Marcos asked, aghast. "We're booked until next year. We're in the top ten wedding venues in Utah County, the world's wedding reception capital. How are we floundering?"

His uncle shook his head. "Really, Mark? You want to do this job the rest of your life, and be chained to it like your parents were? We all know you'll run at the first sign of trouble. And if you're looking good now, it's only because you're riding on your parents' hard work from before the accident, and all your sister has done ever since. She's . . . unpleasant, but she's hardworking. I'll give her that. You, on the other hand—who are you trying to deceive? We all know you can't do this job. You're a good athlete, but let's be honest, business was never your strong suit."

This was his uncle's first mistake. If anything motivated Marcos, it was being told he couldn't do something. It was like he'd been dared, and he'd never turned down a dare.

He would save the wedding venue and keep it in his father's and mother's name forever, whatever the cost. But what about his freedom? The desire to run hit him like an anvil.

He'd deal with it later.

"We're not giving up without a fight," Marcos said. "My lawyer will be getting back to you on Monday." He felt a lot more confident in his words at the look of contempt on his uncle's face. He didn't even have a lawyer.

"You're making a grave error. You and your sister are making the biggest mistake of your lives. Have you thought that you're never going to get a better offer than mine? You're going to regret this."

Uncle Monty sounded like the jerk he'd always been. A gaslighter. An emotional abuser like most of the Hawkinses, except for his dad. Where had Stuart come from? A pumpkin?

Marcos shrugged.

How many times had he been given ultimatums? Too many to count. And by people he loved and admired. From someone like Uncle Monty, it was easy to laugh at the desperate words. He decided to take a leaf out of his mother's repertoire of saying "Tomalo de quien venga," and if his uncle thought he was doing something wrong, then he must be doing something right.

He saw Drew, the horse handler, approaching, wearing a perfectly fitted tuxedo, but he looked stiff, uncomfortable. Which was natural, after all; a rodeo champion, Drew was used to jeans and flannels, but he, too, made concessions for the job that he loved. Marcos would do the same, even if he didn't love the job yet. But he was going to try.

"Thanks for the vote of confidence, but now, excuse me. I have to go." He tipped an imaginary hat to his uncle and left.

He wondered how in the world he'd keep his uncles out of the venue. But for all that was sacred, he'd make it work. He swore on his mother's grave.

Chapter 7

Nadia

Nadia needed a girls' night. Margaritas or rosé. Some tender loving care to soothe her wounded heart and destroyed ego. Something that would help her get back to her senses. What in the world had she done?

She climbed up the stairs to her condo, dreading the moment when she'd open the door and have to face her new reality. The higher she stepped, the deeper her heart plunged into a dark ocean made up of flashbacks from the night before. Every time she thought she'd risen above the crest of a new wave of grief, another one would come crashing into her, leaving her gasping for air.

But it wasn't like she could just crumble around her downstairs neighbors' stroller and plastic baby cars. Nadia Noemí Palacio couldn't lose it in public. She kept trudging home, the choking memories relentlessly flashing like unblockable pop-up ads.

Last night at this time, she'd been so happy on the phone with Madi. They had finally connected in spite of their different work schedules. Every time Nadia was off work, Madi was just starting hers. After all, her clients were mostly busy women like Nadia, who tried to reconnect with their bodies and souls after they'd given all to their jobs. Nadia had yet to take her up on her invitation to return to the studio for a healing sound bath. The first and last time she'd attended one of these sleeping yoga classes, the gong's vibration, meant to unstick feelings in her body, must have worked its magic, because Nadia had the first panic attack since she'd been in college.

The experience had left her raw, frayed at the edges. Madi, in her loving patience, tried to give her the space she needed to make the choice to attend a class again.

Nadia had been telling her about the flowers and last-minute details for her wedding. For years, Nadia, Madi, and Stevie had planned their dream weddings, even when they didn't have boyfriends, and even when Stevie said she'd never get married. *Especially* during those times. One would have thought every detail would be checked a month from the actual wedding. But there were so many unexpected things that popped up.

Brandon's betrayal was something Nadia had never antici-pated.

Maybe ten years ago, when they were still practically kids. But not now.

Madi had cut her with a comment about her boyfriend and one of the yoga instructors in charge of the retreat, making Nadia laugh all the way from her belly. Little had she known that would be the last honest-to-goodness moment of laughter she'd have in a while.

"I tell you! Sometimes he's so embarrassing! We were all chaturanganning, and Jacob starts snoring! The yogini super-vising me was about to blow a gasket—"

Nadia had opened the door, and she'd been surprised to hear voices coming from hers and Brandon's room. At first, she thought it was the TV, because although one of the voices was definitely Brandon, it had that quality of coming from a device. She'd placed the groceries on the counter. A weird vibe in the

air made the hairs on the back of her neck and her arms stand
on end.

Madi, oblivious that there was a problem, kept chattering
like a chipmunk on the other side of the line.

Something inside Nadia told her she needed to find out what
was happening right now, or she'd regret it forever.

Obeying her instinct for once in her life, she headed to the
room on tiptoes. Her heart beat in her throat. She'd hung up the
phone without saying goodbye to Madi, who must have thought
the call had spontaneously dropped, because the service in this
apartment in the newly developed part of town was dreadful.
Nadia hated the carpets in them on principle. At home with her
parents, there were no carpets, except the rugs that were washed
every other day. But this time, she was grateful for them. They
muffled her steps.

"Now, look at me from this angle," Brandon's voice had
asked.

A girl laughed.

Nadia was frozen in place. Who was he talking to? She had
the urge to turn around and run away, pretend she hadn't been
here at all. Pretend her life wasn't about to change forever. Be
destroyed. But Nadia was never one to run away, not even if the
monsters in her nightmares ate her up alive.

Without being able to help herself anymore, she opened the
door.

Brandon had been in bed. Alone. His hands in . . . la masa,
as her mother said. But on the TV, which she had detested from
the beginning but he had insisted on, was the video of a Latina
girl. She looked so young, playing coy in what looked like a
hotel room. The angle of the video moved to a close-up of her
naked breasts and then lower to . . .

Nadia didn't even want to think about it.

The girl laughed, and there was a glimpse of her face. Nadia
had gasped. Not because she knew her at all. But because the
girl looked uncannily like a younger version of herself. If one

thing was true about Brandon, it was that he had a type. That type was a younger Nadia.

For all she'd tried to diet and exercise, through the years, her body had changed, and she would never get to be that reedy kind of girl anymore. The worst, or the best, was that she really liked the way she looked now. She'd grown into her woman's body that he'd criticized over and over, claiming he just missed the good old days—of what? Her having an eating disorder? Grad school, the bar exam, a career, and life in general were stressful enough without good food and a healthy body.

She held her breath, knowing what she must do but already overwhelmed by what this meant, not only for her, but for so many people.

Nadia must have stood frozen, looking at the screen for a while, because she jumped when someone touched her shoulder.

Brandon.

"Don't touch me!" she'd bellowed and jumped out of the way. "Don't touch me with those filthy hands!"

He'd looked like the proverbial deer in the headlights. He looked older, too, a distorted version of who he'd been in college. What? Did he think time only passed for her?

She had loved him still, changing bodies and all. Wasn't that what love was all about?

She had loved him. Now, he was disgusting to her. Because unlike him, she knew she was growing towards the prime of her life. Brandon, on the other hand, had peaked in college and kept trying to be that guy. Pathetic.

She'd said nothing of the kind in that moment. She'd been too horror-struck. Too numb. The words had come hours later that night, when she kept reliving the moment over and over, trapped in a loop.

He'd tried to explain. Of course, he tried to turn things upside down, the gaslighting jerk. "This video is from years ago," he'd said.

"When?"

"Before we were engaged. We were on a break."

"When I was studying for the bar and you kept traveling to El Paso for work?" Her voice was hoarse; she was upset that she'd been so clueless.

But really, had she been clueless? There had been so many signs! The trips. The interest in trying new things for sex when she'd been too exhausted for even the basics, and she'd wished they could just snuggle. His scathing comments about her looks.

He'd done everything for her to discover the truth, because he was too much of a coward to confess, but she had been a coward, too. She didn't have the emotional bandwidth to face the facts. And now? Now they had come to collect with interest. A month away from the wedding.

He'd shrugged like it was nothing, like he wasn't destroying her. "I said we were on a break. I wasn't cheating. I haven't seen this girl in years!"

"But you're jerking off to a video of her right now!" she'd yelled, and she was aware that the neighbors were listening, paying attention to every word she said.

"If it makes you feel any better, I do it to pictures of you, too, when you're on a trip or working. I don't do it to videos of you, because I don't have any. You're stuck up that way."

She'd slapped him, and it had felt so, so good.

"Do you think I should feel grateful? You disgust me. Get out right now."

He hadn't even looked back. He'd left with a spring in his step, like he had been waiting for the right moment, and it had finally arrived.

He was physically gone, but he'd been emotionally checked out for years.

If Nadia was going to move on, like she'd promised herself, she had to stop feeding the ghosts of her past.

Brandon's cheating wasn't her fault. She wasn't perfect, but she didn't deserve this kind of treatment. No one did.

The apartment still smelled of Brandon's cologne. And her

eyes filled with tears when she saw the engagement ring she'd chosen herself—and paid half of, because it was beyond his budget—sitting on the kitchen counter on top of a paper towel. He must have fished it out of the toilet. The ice cream she'd brought last night had melted and dripped on the carpet.

She couldn't help it. She started laughing. And once her emotions were unleashed, she couldn't stop. She laughed when she thought that at least she had trained him well. How many times had she bitched at him to put a paper towel or coaster so there wouldn't be a ring-shaped water stain? Too many to count.

But then, soon, the laughter turned into tears when that mean voice in her head told her that, yes, she'd trained him well, for someone else.

The hurt and the sorrow were so great, her legs buckled, and she collapsed on the shaggy living-room rug and cried and cried until she thought she was hearing things.

But no. It wasn't her imagination. Someone was softly knocking on the door.

Her sobs stopped, as though sounds from the most dramatic telenovela had muted. She imagined what she must look like, hungry, heartbroken, abandoned on the floor. Pathetic. She almost laughed, but stopped herself just in time. She was on the verge of hysteria.

Were the neighbors finally coming en masse to ask her to move out of their decent and overpriced condo that she was ruining with her antics?

"Nadia," someone said. "I could take the door down, but I'd rather not. Nadia, open up, babe. Are you alive?"

It was Stevie.

What was she doing here? She was supposed to be selling alarm systems in Texas.

"Of course she's alive," Madi added, her voice like chimes in the wind, even if she sounded outraged. "Nadia, can we come in?"

"Open up right this second," said Isabella, her sister, no Fs given, sounding very much like the mom she was, coming to put things in order.

"She might need some space," Madi said behind the door.

"¡Qué espacio ni ocho cuartos! I'm not going to allow you to wallow in self-pity, Nadia Noemí! Open this instant or—"

"Or what?" Nadia yanked the door open, interrupting her sister midsentence.

At the sight of her, Isabella's and Stevie's eyes widened at the same time, in the most astounding show of synchronized shock that would win them Olympic medals, if there were such a thing.

Why did her mind always go to competitions?

"Hey," she said, wiping her nose with her sleeve. "What are you doing here?"

Stevie managed an office of twenty salesmen, mostly men. Her team always won the first spot in the company-wide competitions in September. She never missed a day of work.

"I'm flying back Sunday night," Stevie said, kissing her on the cheek. "Madi is trying to get back, but she can't leave the workshop without a sub." She waved her phone in her hand. On the screen was the ethereally beautiful Madi, her eyes teary with worry.

"Hey, love," she said. "I have to hang up now, but now that I've seen you're alive, I have to go. I'll be there tomorrow, okay? Then we'll find him and kick his ass."

Coming from sweet, warrior-of-light Madi, the words stunned Nadia into silence. But she moved out of the way so her friend and her sister could walk into the apartment.

"When you texted that you were coming home, I was in Spanish Fork," Isabella said, her voice like sandpaper scraping a sunburned face. "At another baseball championship game. Do you know how hellish the freeway is with the construction going on? And your poor friend here is exhausted. Show a little more gratitude."

Nadia sighed and saw her neighbor across the hallway going into her apartment. She was a white woman who was easily in her fifties but looked ageless, beautiful, and graceful with her white gauze robe and long blond hair. She had a small Yorkie called Prince that looked just like Tinkerbell. But Nadia didn't know her neighbor's name.

"Good afternoon," Nadia said.

The neighbor nodded in greeting and turned as if to walk into her apartment, Prince peeking over her shoulder like a baby. But right before she was about to close her door, she turned around, a blazing look on her face. She smiled at Nadia and said, "It was about time you kicked his ass out. It's hard at first, but you got this. Brava."

Her raspy smoker's voice reverberated on the stucco walls and all the way to Nadia's heart.

Before Nadia, Isabella, or Stevie could react, the woman was gone.

The three of them exchanged a shocked look that left Nadia super happy that she, too, had synchronized with them. She clamped a hand over her mouth to hide her burst of laughter.

But then, the mean voice in her head said, *See? Everyone knew but yourself. Pathetic.*

Why did an imaginary voice have more power than what real people said? Nadia didn't know.

"Come inside before the whole condo makes a petition to kick me out," she said.

She moved aside, and Stevie and Isabella barged in like the Ghostbusters, ready to annihilate a particularly vicious band of demons.

"Have you taken all his trash out already?" Stevie asked, her strong, unwavering voice contrasting with the exhaustion rimming her big brown eyes.

"Yes," Isabella said, literally rolling up her sleeves. "We'll obliterate him from your existence."

"He must have taken everything but that," Nadia said, pointing at the ring sitting on the counter.

Their bravado left in a sigh.

"Oh," Isabella said, walking toward it. "May I?"

She'd always loved that ring. The one on her left hand was tiny. Jason had offered to trade up for a bigger rock, a real one, now that he could afford it. But Isabella stubbornly refused, citing that the tiny, cheap little thing was a testament to their young true love, and she couldn't part with it for a bigger one now that times were better. The liar.

"Don't!" Nadia exclaimed just as Isabella's loving hands were slowing down to cradle the precious. Isabella's face whipped so fast in her direction, Gollum would've been proud and jealous of her reflexes.

"I threw it down the toilet. Bran—he . . . must have retrieved it before he left to . . . I don't know what his purpose was when he decided to fish in the toilet for it, and I don't know if he disinfected it and sanitized it or put poison on it. Don't touch it, though."

"Poison?" Isabella scoffed. "He's not that smart or resourceful."

"He did put a paper towel underneath it," Stevie observed in her practical, no-nonsense voice.

"He did do that. You trained him well," Isabella observed.

Nadia shrugged. "Too bad my only accomplishment so far is teaching him how to place a paper towel on a counter. Too bad he never learned not to cheat, or how to love me. Or all those things that are kind of important when you're about to get married."

Her eyes filled with tears as she hung her head so her sister and her best friend wouldn't see them and reach the same conclusion that kept blaring in her head: *pathetic.*

"Ay, Mamá," Stevie said, walking toward her with arms wide open. "Come here, mi amor."

Nadia had been needing a hug since last night. This is exactly why she'd run home to her parents. How couldn't they understand she just needed a hug?

She snuggled into Stevie's arms. Her friend must have just washed her long, brown hair, because it was still wet and smelled of lavender and a whiff of disinfectant. Maybe it was the pest-control chemicals she'd been selling since April. Stevie's dad was from Korea, and her mom was a Latina, Utah born and raised. She had Peruvian ancestry, but she didn't speak a lot of Spanish. Stevie had grown up speaking both Korean and English, but when she met Nadia and Madi in seventh grade, she'd picked up Spanish scarily fast. She knew how to use all the endearments and the swear words, the most important words in any language.

Isabella watched them with longing but didn't join the bear hug. For all the rep that Latin families had of being exuberant and loving, her family was terribly cold and emotionally unavailable sometimes.

"Tell us everything," Stevie said, taking her by the hand and leading her to the sofa.

But Nadia shook her head and said, "I know I stink like a goat. I've been stress-sweating since this morning, and no deodorant is cutting it anymore. Give me a few minutes, and I'll be back and tell you everything. Why don't we get food?"

Automatically, she turned toward her sister for this request.

"It's on its way," Isabella said, and although her arms were crossed, her voice was soft. "I couldn't cook it myself, but I already ordered it before I got in the car. It should be here before you know it."

Feeding people, especially her family, was Isabella's superpower.

The Palacios had a hard time being all touchy-feely, but they showed their love in other ways.

Nadia headed to the shower, kind of afraid of seeing what she'd find. A torn notebook page with a scribbled note? A lipstick graffiti on her mirror with the mark of Brandon's lips? A trail of rose petals leading to their bed and him waiting naked under the covers?

He'd done all those things in other instances, after other fights in which she'd sworn never to take him back. She always had.

But this time, the counter in the bathroom was clean. There was nothing on the mirror. And the bed was carefully made, as if he wanted to leave no doubt that this time he wouldn't be waiting under the covers. She was a little relieved, but above all else, disappointed in herself, that in spite of it all, she'd still been hoping.

There was no hoping her way out of this breakup. This time, the gap between them was real. Irreparable. Insurmountable.

At least the apartment and everything in it was hers. She'd bought it herself.

Why hadn't she seen the signs and saved herself the misery? No. It wasn't her fault that he was a cheater. But it *was* her fault she'd let things get to this point. Brandon was a coward. He'd been throwing hints that he didn't want to be married and start a family, and she had ignored them.

Even the neighbor woman, who'd never exchanged more than a few words with her, had known.

Nadia opened the faucet and let the water run down the drain with her tears and regrets and the shame.

By the time she was out of tears, she had everything planned out.

She turned off the water and walked out of the shower, welcoming the sharp cold of the tile on the soles of her feet, shooting up her legs. She hoped it wasn't her sciatica acting up. She put on a set of lacy underwear just for herself. There was no one to impress, lure, tempt, or entertain. She did it just for herself. To feel pretty under the circumstances. And then she put on her fluffiest robe, pulling from the corner of her crowded closet. His matching one was still there. He'd never worn it, because she had insisted on saving them for the wedding. Saving robes for the wedding, when he couldn't even stay loyal?

How sad that she'd thought a Mr. Lewis embroidered over his heart would be incentive enough for him to go through with the plan.

She combed her curly hair and let it fall down her back instead of tying it up in a sock bun like she always did on Saturday nights, preparing for Sunday brunch. To hell with brunch!

This whole weekend, she intended to stay in bed all day to lick her wounds, and then go back to work on Monday with all the force she could muster to conquer the world.

Wasn't that how Nadia always fixed her problems? Allowing herself a little time to grieve or lick her wounds, and then she went out and kicked everyone's butt.

But she was tired.

She was grateful Stevie and Isabella were here with her. She'd heard the doorbell and the murmur of voices. The scents of delicious Mexican food made her mouth water. But she kind of wished they would leave her to deal with things on her own. She didn't know how to tell them everything that had happened with Brandon. She was so embarrassed.

She took a deep breath and opened the bedroom door.

The cool air was the best face toner in existence. And then she saw the lit candles, heard the spa music coming from the spy speaker on the counter, and saw the food carefully plated on the small living-room table, fluffy pillows around it and a fruity cocktail in wide-mouthed stemless wine glasses.

"Is that—?" she asked, pointing at the drink.

"Fun and flouncy, yes," Isabella answered, without a glance, as she finished up in the kitchen.

Brandon had always made fun of the wine spritzer made with rosé, soda, and frozen fruit. He'd called it ratchet. But Nadia loved it, and she was emotional because her sister remembered.

"We have cookies in the oven," Isabella said. "Those are mine. I found a baggie of dough in your freezer, and thought, why not?"

There were no better cookies than her sister's. Nadia felt a wave of gratitude and emotion flow from the pit of her stomach and crest in her chest. Her eyes filled with tears again.

Her friend and her sister looked at her with bated anxiety.

"Thank you. Everything is perfect," she said.

Stevie sat on one of the heart cushions and patted the next one. "Come, sit and eat before it gets cold."

Nadia obeyed and deeply inhaled the scent of her favorite food: tacos al pastor and enchiladas from Cancún Querido, her favorite restaurant in the whole wide world.

The place was a hole in a wall that she'd found in middle school because she had a friend from Mexico whose mom made the most celestial corn tortillas ever for the restaurant. The family had been deported the following year, and Nadia had been devastated. She'd kept going for the tortillas, because she missed how nurturing they were to her soul, even if they weren't as good as her friend's mom's. And she'd gotten her desire to become a lawyer to help people like her friend. Sujei Muñoz had been her name.

She took the first bite of the salsa verde chicken enchilada on her plate, and a bone-melting feeling of safety swept over her. She loved the combination of flavors and how they exploded on her tongue. How she appreciated the time it had taken some hands to make this divine food.

Stevie and Madi loved Cancún Querido, too, and Isabella ordered takeout from it more often than she'd ever acknowledge.

Nadia and her friends, and even her sister, didn't have a lot in common, but love for food was one of them. Madison Ramirez, Madi, was Puerto Rican on her mom's side, and she was Argentinian on her father's and stepfather's, too. They had a joke that Madi's mom had a thing for South Americans. That's how she and Nadia had become friends at the beginning. They'd both connected with Stevie over a bowl of Korean barbecue, and the rest was history.

But Nadia's parents were both from Argentina and didn't understand their daughter's devotion to spicy foods. To her, Mexican cuisine was a work of art, and she ate it with a kind of reverence Brandon had always made fun of.

They ate in silence, with the binaural beats in the background.

When her stomach was full, she took a sip of rosé, which she mainly loved because it was secretly her favorite color, and said, "Thank you. This is just what we needed."

Isabella and Stevie exchanged a look that Nadia interpreted as *Time to dish.*

She braced herself for their questions, grabbing a pillow and hugging it tightly, as if she'd drown if she let go.

But instead of asking about Brandon, Stevie said, "Now. What is this wonderful idea of having a double quince?"

Nadia's cheeks burned. Double quinces sounded so ridiculous, she felt she was going to die of embarrassment. "Why? So you can make fun of me?" she asked, in the sharpest, bitchiest voice she could muster.

Isabella rolled her eyes. She was about to say something when Stevie placed a hand on her arm to stop her.

To her credit, Stevie didn't speak right away, either. Instead, she sipped from her rosé and said, "No. So your sister, and Madi and I—who love you like a soul sister, by the way—can help you make it the best quinceañera, single, double, triple, or any other multiplier, the world has ever seen."

A knot grew in Nadia's throat. But she wasn't about to cry. She shook her head, confused. "So, you're not here to hear what happened with Brandon, or to change my mind?"

"Of course not!" Isabella exclaimed. "We're Team Nadia one hundred percent. Now, tell us all about it, because I don't really know how it works."

Loose-limbed after the shower, the food and wine, *and* the support of her girls, Nadia shimmied on the cushion as if she were making a nest.

"You both know perfectly well what a quinceañera is. You

had one, Isabella, and you"—she pointed at Stevie—"have to remember Madi's. It was the event of the year."

That party had catapulted Madi into high-school royalty. But thankfully, she hadn't left Stevie and Nadia aside for her new friends. Some people still talked about the dance that had gone on until the cops showed up, but then they, too, had stayed to eat and dance way past the city curfew.

Isabella and Stevie exchanged a cryptic look that kind of pissed Nadia off.

"What?" She took another sip, as if she needed the encouragement to confront them.

Stevie shrugged one shoulder. "Nothing . . . it's just that—and understand, I'm with you one hundred percent—but what's the motivation behind this?"

"What she means is, was your wedding acting like a quinceañera, like, was it standing for your life celebration instead of marking the beginning of your life with Brandon?" Isabella said. "You needed him then, but now that he's not part of the picture anymore, I mean . . . I don't even know what I mean."

Isabella had never held her alcohol well. For all that she mocked Nadia's preference for rosé, she got all cloudy-minded after the first couple of sips.

"I didn't go into planning my wedding as a surrogate for my quinceañera, if that is what you're alluding to. No."

"Okay," Stevie said. "At least that's clear."

Nadia's mind was a whirlwind. "I mean, it's true that I've had the perfect wedding planned since we were freshmen in high school."

The three of them would get together every once in a while to work on their future receptions, with PowerPoint presentations and all. It had been meant as a joke, but the truth was that Nadia had used those mock plans as a foundation for her real wedding. And although she wouldn't admit it, not even to her sister and one of the friends who knew her the most, she was a little embarrassed. But honestly, hadn't they been raised to aspire to that? To be wives and mothers, all while putting their careers aside? She had a flashback to the "Why I Want a Wife" essay she'd read for her gender studies class, and how she had vowed never to be that kind of woman.

"I didn't want to have a wedding to make up for not having a quinceañera, Isa," she said, tired.

"Then why?"

Nadia shrugged. "Why does anyone have a wedding? To have a husband? Like I've been drilled to do all my life?" she asked, lasering her sister with a murderous look. "You had both. You tell me. Or were you too young when you got married that you didn't even think about why you were doing it?"

Isabella got that wounded puppy look on her face. Nadia wished she could take her words back.

"Ouch, Nadi," Stevie said, "you're being extra mean with the person who's by your side no matter what: your own sister."

Madi might have been teaching yoga, but she had left her spokesperson behind: Stevie, who idolized Madi and took her spiritual advice to heart. Stevie had an older brother, Felix, whom both Madi and Nadia had had a crush on in middle school. But she had no sisters, and her cousins all lived in California.

Madi was an only child. She had a weird reverence for blood sister ties. Once, Madi had told them spiritual sister ties were strong, but she envied anyone who had a blood sibling and would've given anything to get one.

Her friends weren't the envious kind of people, but suddenly, Nadia realized she had what—who—they'd most needed all their lives: an older sister to pave the way.

Nadia sighed and prodded her sister with her foot, knowing Isabella was terribly ticklish in the legs.

Isabella squealed, jerking away from Nadia, spilling wine on her shirt.

"Sorry, Isà. I didn't mean to."

Everyone knew Nadia meant she was apologizing for way more than the wine.

Stevie nodded, satisfied. "I'm glad you're not getting married to Brandon. He's obviously not your soul mate."

"Obviously, Stephanie Marie Choi," Nadia said, satisfied with the look on Stevie's face at hearing her full name. "Otherwise, he wouldn't have cheated on me with every vagina carrier that crossed his path. But you know what? I get it. He doesn't love me, and what's worse . . . or better, or whatever?"

"What?" Isabella and Stevie asked, leaning forward as if to hear better.

"I actually don't love him either, you know? I haven't for a long, long time."

The air seemed to be sucked out of the room with this bomb of a revelation.

Nadia hadn't known it until she said it. She wasn't drunk—yet—and she wasn't emotional. This was the first time she'd allowed herself to tell the truth.

"Why didn't you say it before?" Isabella asked, sounding a little annoyed that it had taken Nadia so long to own up to the truth.

"I guess I was afraid of being alone. After fighting for him and getting him, I didn't want to give him up. I guess he was my Ashley."

They nodded, as if this explained everything. They'd all had a strange fascination with *Gone with the Wind* ever since their eighth-grade teacher had shown it at school in the civil rights unit. Madi and Nadia had loathed the way slavery had been portrayed, and they hate-watched it with Stevie and Isabella.

Isabella, being the oldest, a college freshman to boot, had helped them write a petition to the district enumerating all the things that were wrong with the movie, so they wouldn't have to subject future students to that kind of white-supremacy propaganda. The district had agreed with them, for once, in a record development and turn of events that had made the local paper and inspired a counterprotest that, thankfully, got nowhere.

That surge of power from having been heard, and the memory of Nadia's friend Sujei's family being deported, had fueled the girls' desire to go to law school. But then, Isabella got married at nineteen. Madi discovered that she was less interested in human laws than in what the stars had to say, and she became a yoga master. She got a degree in business only so she could one day own a studio. Her dream was to own a state-of-the-art facility with a salt cave, which is why she was willing to travel across the Wasatch to earn the money she needed.

Stevie had a rougher detour. She had a baby at sixteen. She kept the baby, but Tristan died of SIDS at five months. He would be Olivia's age by now. His death broke her and almost ended her. With the love of Nadia and Madi, little by little, she went back to her pre-baby plans, getting her GED and all. With the need to get as much money as possible in a short amount of time, she went into summer sales. After all, Happy Valley was supposed to be the direct-to-door industry capital of the world. It was only meant to be for a summer, to get enough money for tuition. She'd outsold every other salesman in the industry. But that September, instead of enrolling in college, she went to Europe on her own, backpacking from town to town, picking up languages and experiences along the way and leaving a trail of broken hearts. When her money ran out, her job was waiting for her in April.

After then, it was hard to give up the freedom that summer sales provided. Her mom had told her the baby had ruined her life, and for the last few years of adventure after adventure, Stevie had made sure to prove her wrong over and over again. When Stevie was in town, she volunteered at a Planned Parenthood clinic in downtown Salt Lake, accompanying girls and women so they didn't have to go through procedures alone. But other than march at the Capitol every time women's rights were under attack, she had nothing else to do with the law. Her dream now was becoming her own boss. In what industry, she didn't know.

One by one, all the girls had found their own paths in life.

The only one to keep on going with the original plan was Nadia. Not because she was in love with the law, but because she needed things to make sense. Also, because she felt she had no other choice. After all their sacrifice to come to this country and stay in it, her parents deserved the pride of having a child who was a professional. After Isabella got a new last name and two kids instead of the JD, it was up to Nadia to give them that prize.

Even if the prize turned out to be an Ashley sort of dead end. *Ashley* was their code name for that one goal that they thought was a holy grail and turned out to be the pits.

Although they had hated everything about the movie (well, maybe not the costumes. They all had wanted a Scarlett O'Hara green dress), they referenced it every time they were together.

"When I got Brandon, and secured him, I realized there was no love. There is cariño, you know? I think I'll always have a special place in my heart for him. I love his family—"

"You mean the kids," Stevie said.

Nadia shrugged. "Yes, although his sisters detest me. But if I'm being honest? I'm a little . . . relieved," she said with a sigh. "I just don't want to be stuck with a wedding venue and flowers and food and entertaining the family that's about to start trickling in, and nothing to show for all my life."

"You're a freaking lawyer," Isabella said. "You always find a loophole to any contract."

She sounded so sure of Nadia. Maybe because having a degree had been Isabella's dream all her life, and she couldn't imagine a more perfect accomplishment. The truth was that Nadia loved her job, but like Brandon, reality hadn't met her expectations. Once she'd secured the position at the firm, the glow of it had dimmed, and now she was stuck doing so much work for such little credit. Her soul just wasn't in it. If she'd been able to practice a different kind of law, then it wouldn't have been so bad. She'd wanted to go into immigration or refugees' rights and defense, but her parents had insisted there was no money to be made there, and if she was going to put so much life and money into something, she should get the most out of it, too. Her job sucked, but it paid very well.

"Now that I have the venue and the flowers, and the DJ and band, and the food, I decided for once to celebrate the quinces I never had," she said.

"And where did you get the idea from?" Isabella asked.

Nadia took out the magazine from her purse. "From here," she said, and opened the spread to the middle.

Isabella and Stevie read in silence. She studied their faces with a small smile. When Isabella turned her gaze to the image of the woman laughing with her friends, she smiled and her eyes filled with tears, which made Nadia feel like crying, too.

Maybe she was a little tipsy already.

"That's what I want," Nadia said. "My family celebrating *with* me."

"And *for* you," Isabella said. "People seeing you as the center, once and for all."

Nadia nodded. "I mean, your quinceañera wasn't extravagant, but it was beautiful." She'd been nine years old, and she remembered the gnawing envy she felt for her sister, seeing her like a princess in her blush-pink dress. The whole family hadn't been there, because the flights were so expensive, and Argentina was navigating one of its endless economic crises. Only Abuelo Leonardo and Abuela Catalina had made it. They had also come back to Utah for Isabella's wedding four years later. Nadia had been fourteen then and dreaming of her own quinceañera. But that year, her dad had an accident at work, painting a building. Their parents couldn't afford a bash.

They had said they'd make it up to her, but by the time her sweet sixteen came around, her school was going to Washington, DC, to the student model UN that her class had won at BYU. She'd chosen the trip. And then it was impossible to celebrate again. She'd had a birthday cake and candles here and there. But her dream of having a quinceañera had never come true. She'd never brought it up again, because she didn't want to hurt her parents with irrational requests. They'd given her pretty much everything they could.

"Now I can pay for it on my own," she said.

"Madi says her quinceañera was one of the highlights of her life," said Stevie. "It was one of the highlights of mine."

Stevie had her first kiss there, with a boy from the soccer team she'd liked since sixth grade, but who moved to New York that year.

"I mean, Madi says it was a little embarrassing to walk in to all the kids from school looking at her. The neighbors said it was like a wedding without a groom. And in a way, it was. Because she made vows to herself that day," Stevie said, her eyes shiny, as if the disco ball from Madi's quinces were still casting light all around them. "And her family made those vows, too, you know? It was like a show of support and this rush of energy and love. Sometimes when I'm sad or depressed, or discouraged, I think back on that day, and my heart swells with that love and joy for how happy she was."

Nadia nodded. That party had shattered every record. Someone—they never knew who, because all the neighbors had been invited—called the police for disturbing sounds. When they arrived, one of Madi's uncles, who had been expecting this to happen, had shown them the special permit they'd gotten from the city to play music until midnight. The person must have eaten their heart out when they saw a picture of Madi, with most of the police department, the firemen, and the EMTs who hadn't wanted to miss out on the action, on the newspaper's front page.

"I can't imagine what that night did for her," Nadia said in a dreamy voice. Then she turned to her sister. "What did it mean for you, Isa?"

Isabella sighed.

"My quinceañera was a magical night. More so than my wedding, to be honest," Isabella said, her gaze cast down as if she were ashamed of looking them in the eyes. "I mean, I'm eternally grateful for *my* husband." She lifted her chin defiantly. "If I had to do it all over again, I'd marry him at nineteen in a heartbeat over and over again. I love the life we have together, and our children, Olivia and Noah. Still, that night of my quinces? I felt like a princess. A celebration for being me."

"Exactly," Nadia said. "I want that. Why is it so revolutionary that I don't have to wait for anyone else to do it for me? That I took charge and celebrated with the people I love and that love me back."

They nodded.

"Which makes me think," Stevie said, "why didn't Olivia have her quinces last year?"

Isabella rolled her eyes. "Jason and I wanted to do it for her, but she refused. She says it's embarrassing."

"Why don't we celebrate hers and mine together?" Nadia asked. Because like always, she thought of her family first.

"No," Isabella said. "Thank you, hermana, from the bottom of my heart. But if I were to take over your party, we'd end up fighting. I'd want to go through the process of choosing things like the cake and music, and decorations and guest lists, with my daughter. It's part of the experience. And she doesn't want to. So there."

True. That's what Nadia had loved about her wedding planning. How close she'd become with her sister and mom.

"Now, as far as planning. What are we doing?" Stevie asked.

Nadia scratched her head. She should have put on more conditioner. The air was so dry, her scalp was itching horribly.

"Let me get my binder," she said.

Her legs were numb from sitting cross-legged on the floor, but she wobbled on her feet and got her planning binder. It was like a physical version of Pinterest. She did have a board, or rather several, of course, but she needed tangible things, so she'd kept all her dreams in a binder.

Brandon had hardly looked at it.

She opened it up to the beginning. She'd started collecting ideas when she and Brandon had moved in together when she was twenty-three. Almost seven years ago.

"Should I chuck it?" she asked, more wondering aloud than anything.

Stevie placed a hand over hers and patted it. "Aw, mi amor. No. At least, not all of it. Just a few things."

They sat at the round kitchen table as they turned the pages.

"The highlight video has to be redone," Isabella said.

Stevie ripped out the video script page that documented Nadia and Brandon's chronology. All the years they'd been together, on and off, since they were sixteen. A lifetime.

In spite of what she'd said about not really loving Brandon, Nadia felt a pang like a stab. It still hurt to see her dreams discarded so easily. So casually. She stood still, holding her breath, as Stevie placed it facedown on the table, delicately, like a surgeon excising a tumor.

"Seating charts," Isabella said, all businesslike. "Not like his whole family had RSVPed to come. But even with the few who deigned to, like his parents and sister, taking them out of the list frees up the space."

The seating charts had been hell and a half to arrange. Brandon's mom wanted to have a spot everywhere. Trying to accommodate her whims had been for nothing.

So much wasted life! And all for people who didn't really appreciate her.

Was he going through their memories and throwing them away so casually, too?

Isabella placed a blank seating chart in front of her. She had a daring look on her face. "So? We keep the main table and the guests all around, fanning out in order of importance? Or how do you wanna do it?"

Nadia's chest seized again. Her smart watch vibrated.

Elevated heart rate, it flashed once, like a warning wink.

This emotional roller coaster couldn't be good for her.

"Who am I going to invite?" Nadia's voice was panicky. "Maybe this is the wrong idea. Maybe I should just . . . donate the money to the venue. They can't refund me. It's in the contract."

Maybe she should do that. Donate the money, run away to a place where no one knew her and she knew no one, and start all over again. What a failure she was!

Brandon, her heart called, and she hated it, this dependence she had on him, like a bad addiction. She hated him. And she hated herself for having been such a fool, and for continuing to be one.

"You can do that if you really want. Donate the money, I mean," Stevie said, draping her arm on Nadia's shoulder. She probably recognized the signs of Nadia's impending anxiety attack. "But I'm proud that you took charge this way, babe."

Nadia shook her head, but she didn't even try to shake away Stevie's comfort. Her skin throbbed with the need for a warm hug. "I didn't think things through. I'm going to make it worse. Everyone is going to laugh at me. This is going to be a mess. The one time I do something spontaneous. I hate this," she said.

Now it was Isabella who spoke, in her soft, motherly lullaby. "I know this feels overwhelming now, but it'll pass. It always does. And when that moment comes, and we're all celebrating the amazing, blazing bitch that you are, won't you be happy you didn't cower at the first obstacle?"

The clutch in Nadia's chest eased a little. Maybe . . . maybe her sister was right, after all.

Wasn't she always?

"But the family . . ." she still said. "What will they say when they arrive, and there's no wedding?"

The new invitation cards wouldn't arrive in Argentina and the rest of the world on time.

"We can place the new invite in their hands once they're here. What are they going to say? That they're not attending? And miss the party of the decade? Imagine Abuela Cata's face when she sees you in a killer dress and celebrating your degree and career."

Nadia shrugged, trying to erase the image of her grandmother shaking her head at her, disappointed, telling all her friends once she was back in Rosario. The complete opposite reaction her sister wanted to encourage.

"Everyone's going to hate me," she said.

"They won't. Everyone on this new list will want to be there," Stevie said, with a conviction Nadia envied. "I promise you that every single person in that party will be a Nadia stan." She made a Rosie the Riveter gesture that made Nadia laugh.

And then, Nadia exhaled and turned the page to the centerpieces.

"We replace the pictures," Isabella said, matter-of-fact. "We have to get you a photo shoot, and then we replace them in the frames. No biggie."

Nadia must have made a face, because Isabella added, "Unless you want something different?"

"It's just that another photo shoot . . . I hadn't thought of that." Nadia's skin prickled with ghost hives at the memory of her bridal photo shoot. The photographer, a friend of Brandon's, had been an absolute jerk.

Isabella shrugged. "You'll want pictures, Pitufina."

When they were little, Isabella had loved that Nadia sounded like Smurfette when she cried, naming her Pitufina for moments like this, in which the emotions got the best of her.

"Dress," Stevie continued, ripping the pages of the dress design, the dress on which Nadia had spent a fortune and several months of hunger and deprivation so she could fit into it. She'd had the dress for five years. She'd never expected the engagement to last this long and then fizzle like an old dog's fart. The alterations had also cost her a fortune. All for nothing.

"Cake," Isabella went on, ripping off the page for the groom's cake that Nadia had designed. A stack of all his favorite sports teams: BYU (although he'd played for the U), the Patriots, the Yankees, and Oklahoma City.

Each page that came out of the binder was a layer of the weight in her heart coming out. It hurt, but it was necessary.

In the end, there were only a couple of pages left.

"*Now* we make a list," Isabella said.

Nadia's heart fluttered. She loved lists. Finally, something she could take control of. Stevie and Isabella dictated the most important tasks, and she wrote down the bullet points in her best calligraphy:

"Invitations."

"Dress."

"Cake."

"Flower arrangements."

"Music."

"Video."

"Party favors."

"Send-off? We're staying to celebrate all night, but there has to be a showstopper moment, you know?" Stevie said, and then she voiced what was going on in Nadia's mind.

"Father-daughter dance," Isabella said at the end, looking into Nadia's eyes.

Nadia nodded, her eyes misting.

This was the one thing she wanted to give her parents.

"Honeymoon?" she asked.

She didn't want to go by herself. Especially not to Disneyland.

"No trip. For now."

"Okay," said Isabella. "On Monday, we call around and rearrange everything else."

It was a little more complicated than she'd anticipated.

Planning a wedding had taken years of her life. She hadn't considered what would happen if it didn't go through. Now she knew better. And replacing a broken party for a made-up one wouldn't do.

It all had to be done from scratch.

Would this be a sign for the rest of her life?

Chapter 8

Marcos

The happy couple—the Lockes—and their guests were gone, leaving behind a trail of cast magic in the shape of confetti and burnt-out sparklers for Marcos to sweep up before the cleaning crew arrived the next morning.

All the laughter and joy burrowed inside Marcos like those annoying wood worms that ate through the old storage shed. He knew by experience that before hope demolished his defenses, he had to cut it.

Hope for what, after all? The future? Was it really hope that motivated people, or did people just want something so much that they decided to ignore any and all warning signs?

For all Marcos knew, Gary Locke and his wife would decide this second chance was another mistake. That they'd rather be alone than spend years, their golden years, with someone they didn't really love.

Marcos picked up a broken glass and threw it in the garbage bin.

If he had a second chance at life, would he be too jaded to

give himself the opportunity to try again? Would he decide that once you know something is bad for you the first time, you run in the opposite way? Or something good. Some*one* good.

Someone like Nani.

He could never think of her as Nadia.

After she'd left him standing in the parking lot like a fool, he'd known he was in trouble. The wedding was at its peak, Kenzie fluttering along the tables with Marty making sure everything was going according to plan, when he'd gone into the office.

The music floated to him through the window, and the song that he and Nani had danced naked to when they were still so young, when they'd felt arrogantly invincible, started playing—"Bailar Pegados." Incomprehensibly, a DJ in New York had created a new remix of this ballad from the '90s that had the cheesiest lyrics ever. It quickly spread like fire, and now it played on every radio station, even the English-speaking ones.

It was worse than with "Despacito" a few years ago.

In the office, with no one to watch him but the ghosts of his past, he let himself be swept away by the music's magic in rewinding time.

He was back in that student apartment. The scent of lemon shampoo from her wet curly hair enveloped him. He could still feel the softness of her skin on his fingertips. Now, her dark brown eyes were soft and beautiful, but with a hardness that hadn't been there ten years ago.

He wanted to find Brandon and punch him.

In a perfect world, Nani would have had the happiness she deserved and still celebrated her double quinceañera. Even if she'd still been with Brandon. Why had she suffered so long with that tool by her side, that piece of ballast that dragged her down for years?

But then, what a relief.

Finally, she was free of the fiancé, and it had nothing to do with Marcos.

This was his chance . . .

"My chance for what?" he said aloud. He could've slapped himself.

He shook his head at the intrusive thought. Where had it come from?

A chance for what? He already had a plan. He'd revive the family business and prove to everyone he wasn't a good-for-nothing who always left things for others to fix and finish. Even when the urge to run was so strong, his legs couldn't stop twitching.

Why had life sent him this temptation?

He wished he didn't want to know the whys behind the wedding cancellation. He felt like he didn't have the right to ask. And inwardly, he'd thanked Kenzie's brashness, although Nani had deflected the question like a pro. She was a lawyer, after all.

And even if calling off the engagement had been her idea, he knew Nani must have been hurting.

Weddings got canceled all the time. It happened more often than people thought. His parents had always made sure to treat each cancellation on a case-by-case basis. If one of the members of the couple had a health emergency, things could be moved around. Once, a groom had tragically died the day before the wedding. Marcos's parents had attended the funeral and donated the flowers as part of their condolences to the grieving wife-to-be, now not even a widow. Sometimes it wasn't possible to refund the money. Not because they didn't want to. But because their cash flow wasn't the best, and the employees and vendors still had to be paid for their preparations and work.

The wedding venue kept his parents happy and busy, but they had no false expectations of ever becoming rich in this industry, because they considered the human aspect of everything.

For them, this was all about the people.

Not for the first time, Marcos realized he was in over his head. All his life, he always thought of himself first.

In fact, it had always been Marcos first, second, third, and last.

Now, he had to consider how his decisions affected so many people.

Like this double quinces business. Now that the high of seeing Nani was fizzling out, and he was crashing back to reality, he wondered if agreeing to go along with her plan was smart at all.

Quinceañeras for Enchanted Orchard, in the heart of one of the whitest counties in the state?

In a flash, a memory came to him. He remembered his mother telling him about her plan to start hosting quinceañeras. To turn that into part of the business to serve her community. Some people like Kenzie had thought it would destroy her business. But she loved quinceañeras. Secretly, so did Marcos.

When he was ten and attended his cousin's party in Colonia, Uruguay, he'd been so jealous of her, wishing there were a similar thing for boys.

"Every day is a celebration for boys. This world caters to them. To *you*. Girls don't get to have this kind of party or recognition many times in life," his mom had said while they sipped bitter mate with Abuelo Walter and Abuela María Laura Rocha.

After they came back to the States, there had been a few setbacks to her plan to do quinces, and weddings were more profitable, but his mom had always wanted to expand. Maybe this was a sign from her.

He looked at Nadia's file.

Nadia Noemí Palacio. The party was slated for September 20. Slightly after the peak of wedding season. The busiest months in Utah Valley were April, June, and August, with a minor uptick in December, after the semester break.

His mother had always warned him not to be married in December. The cold and the threat of snowstorms made it hard for guests to arrive and limited the celebrations. But he'd always thought that the pictures looked breathtaking, like something from a fairy tale, even if his toes and fingers nearly froze during photo sessions.

He loved looking at people from behind the lens. Although he wasn't a professional photographer—meaning, he didn't have a degree for it—his shots had won awards and kept him on the go. Like he liked to be.

And now, he was a prisoner to his parents' legacy, and in a way, he felt horrible for resenting this.

If he quit, he'd be the hijo de puta—no offense to his mother, may she rest in peace—that everyone believed him to be. He couldn't take this last thing away from his father.

The image of his uncle Monty swam in his mind.

Talk about hijo de puta . . .

But really? The money from their share of the land would be wonderful. After the money ran out, then what?

Marcos knew enough about cutting corners and seeking the path of least resistance to know that if he took Uncle Monty's offer, he'd regret it. Not now. Not in a few years. But one day, he would.

Besides, if he closed the wedding venue, what about the people who'd already paid deposits? He couldn't return the money now, because the books were in the red. But if they sold? Still, he'd be breaking so many brides'—and their moms'—hearts.

He couldn't do it.

Nani's face replaced Uncle Monty's, and after her, all the other people whose dream weddings he'd been helping to make come true.

It would have been so easy to return her money and not see her ever again, but his heart jumped with an electric jolt at the thought of seeing her.

A text chimed.

I know you're finishing a wedding. Sorry for interrupting. Is it okay to talk on Monday at lunch about changing some arrangements? Or should I talk to Kenzie? If so, what's her

number? The office mailbox is full. Thanks. Oh, this is Nadia
Palacio, by the way.

His heart sped up as he thought about her, sending him this
text, with last name and all. As if there were other Nadias in
his life.

He had the urge to reply that she could talk to Kenzie. That
way, he wouldn't have to deal with Nadia directly.

But this was a second chance at something that had been
beautiful once and he had ruined. He had no hope of ever getting together with her again. He didn't deserve anyone like
Nadia, much less Nadia herself. But she was magnetic, and he
couldn't ignore the temptation.

And just as regular old Marcos usually ran away from com-
promise, he always ran straight to disaster, too. If this time,
the wrecked heart was his, he was too curious about Nadia to
consider the consequences.

He replied:

Monday at the end of the day works better for me.

He wanted to add something more but didn't know what.

The first time, he'd come into her life during a break from
Brandon. He still didn't want to be under that loser's shadow.
But more than anything, he wanted to be with her. And help her
give the middle finger to the rest of the world.

Besides, the company needed the money from this event and
any other publicity that she might bring.

Wanna meet here?

After a few seconds, her answer flashed in his screen.

Yes.

Marcos loved physical work. He loved helping the cleanup
crew. Putting everything where it belonged. Ready to leave the
place immaculate for the next day. All his life, his father had
told him to study hard so he wouldn't have to do this hard manual work. Marcos had grown up fearing it, but the truth was
that now, he enjoyed the quiet and the feeling of having some

control in life at all. There was something therapeutic in putting things where they belonged after a big celebration.

His friends in California had laughed when he told them he was coming back to Utah to work in the wedding business.

Bree had been skeptical, so much so that they decided to call it quits. Things between them had never been rocky. Theirs had been a calm arrangement. An apparent one-night stand between two grown-ups who were lonely but enjoyed each other's company. Not because there was love or a strong connection, but because they were both decent people who were tired of being alone and had a lot of baggage to actually search their fairy-tale happily ever after.

Bree worked as a handler for celebrities. A Latina whose family had moved from Mexico to Idaho three generations ago, she'd come to LA with the dream of becoming the next Hollywood superstar. But when the only auditions her agent got her were for cleaning ladies or other background characters, because she was racially ambiguous—whatever that meant—she'd quit.

"My ancestors didn't go through every imaginable trial for me to end up tending tables after a no-line role."

He knew what she meant.

They had met tending tables together, until a friend got her the job as a handler. At least she got to walk the red carpet. Not as she had envisioned it when she was a teenager, but still. She and Marcos got along well. They cooked together and lived like an old married couple without all the emotional baggage.

So when he announced he was going back to Utah to take over the family wedding business, she'd shaken her head and said, "I love you. Not like a soul mate, but as a human, and I wish you the best. But I won't uproot my life for this."

He understood her one hundred percent and didn't resent her at all.

Still, he missed their chats and walks. She had been a good person in his life; perhaps, the best friend he'd ever had.

Bree had been the transition that he needed to ease back to his old life without falling into old patterns of running away.

"You're running toward," she'd told him. "I'm proud."

"Toward what?" he'd asked.

She'd shrugged and kissed his forehead. "The new Marcos. Fixing things with the family who loves you. You're like the prodigal child, but instead of wanting to take, you want to give. That's good."

He'd hugged her for a long time, and then he'd said, "Take care, Bree. Don't give up on your dreams."

She'd only smiled, and he'd known she wouldn't give up.

He had no experience running a business, but he could fake it till he made it. Now, after the first wedding, he felt his confidence start to grow.

After the guests were gone, Kenzie's mom had brought her kids to pick her up. They were adorable, but boy, was that something he couldn't get into. Not when his life was in shambles. Kenzie needed some time on her own to figure out who she was. They both needed time on their own to figure out how to function without depending on others.

Not alone. Because that was miserable, too. He knew from experience.

Besides, he needed no degree to understand that Enchanted Orchard was in danger of not making it after this fall's events.

With a heavy heart, he left the office, making sure all the lights were off.

As he drove up to Salt Lake County, he did something unexpected: He planned.

There were two events on Saturday. Two small weddings. On Sunday, he'd rest, and then he'd tackle the week like one of those waves from Portugal.

On Monday, he'd interview the new helpers and talk to Nadia about what modifications would be happening in her event.

The house was quiet when he arrived. The nighttime nurse's

car was there. He felt a light relief that he didn't have to spend time alone with his father.

He opened the door, and his heart clenched at the absence of his dog Bandit running to greet him. Bandit had been gone for two years, but Marcos hadn't had the heart to take the leash from the hook.

He stopped in the kitchen and got a Diet Dr Pepper. That had been his mom's only addiction.

Unable to put off the inevitable anymore, he headed into his father's room.

Heidi sat in the chair and read to him. The nurse was a white woman in her fifties. Tall and big-boned, she had a pinkish and youthful face, but her short hair was snow-white. He stood by the door, listening to her pleasant, kindergarten-teacher's voice, as she read from *The Little Prince*, which once upon a time had been his dad's favorite book.

The Isabel Allende novel that his mom had bought for the road trip to California three years ago sat unread on the night-stand, waiting for her return.

He leaned on the doorjamb, and Heidi's eyes flickered in his direction without breaking the narrative. They were bright blue and lively, like the forget-me-nots that carpeted Albion Basin in July.

His dad must have felt the shift in the vibe or something, because he opened his eyes and looked at him so intensely, Marcos's heart started pounding in his chest.

"Alexander," he said in a clear voice, which added to the cruelty that was early Alzheimer's. Then he added, in his perfect Spanish that only held the faintest trace of a gringo accent, "¿Cómo estás, hijo?"

Marcos's heart did all kinds of convoluted twists. He wanted to run to the end of the galaxy. Anywhere but here. Alexander had been a cousin from Uruguay whom Marcos didn't remember. He'd spent a year in Utah when he was in high school, and because of visa protocols, he'd never been able to come back to visit. Apparently, he and his cousin looked a lot alike, although his dad always liked to point out how Marcos was a lazy bum compared to the hardworking Alexander.

But his dad looked at him with so much love and tenderness that he stood rooted in place until he recovered his bearings.

After his heart rate slowed down a little, he took a deep breath that made his neck crack. He couldn't help but smile back at his father's quizzical look.

"Hola, Papá," he said.

He hardly ever spoke Spanish with his parents. Being the youngest in the Hawkins household, he hadn't had as much exposure to Spanish as Sarah, who was completely bilingual. Not Marcos. He understood everything, but sometimes his tongue couldn't form the words that were in his heart. As a young teenager, he'd been so frustrated by this that he'd given up even trying.

But his father now believed he was Alexander, his friend and oldest nephew on his wife's side. Now it was Marcos's time to pay for the neglect and the silence. But the interest that had accrued was too high and too painful.

Still, he complied.

"Have you heard from Marquitos?" his dad asked, and his voice was so tender and loving. "Your aunt wants to talk to him, but he doesn't call back. That boy . . ." His father didn't end the sentence, but Marcos still filled in the blanks: *That boy is a bad son. He breaks our hearts. We're so worried about him.* And on and on.

Not that his parents had ever said all these things aloud, but still, Marcos didn't need to hear them spoken when they blared in his mind nonstop.

"I'll tell him to call," he said in Spanish, sounding like the worst gringo of all.

His father nodded and closed his eyes.

Heidi smiled at Marcos and nodded too, as if saying he'd done a good job.

Why didn't he try to be more like his cousin when it actually mattered?

Now it hurt like a bitch.

It hurt that his father didn't know him. That his father's memory was stuck in the days before the accident. In the brief moments when he recognized Marcos, there was the accusation in his eyes that Marcos couldn't stand.

"Is everything okay, Heidi?" he asked. "Do you need me to bring you something? It's almost midnight."

She shook her head and stretched her neck. "I'll read for a few more minutes, and then give him his medicine, and turn off the lights. Santiago will be here at eight, and then tomorrow evening, Carmen will take over. Any concerns?"

He had so many concerns.

But what was the point of voicing anything? What happened if the business went belly-up? Who would pay for all the nurses and all the things his father needed?

Marcos had no judgment against people who needed to send their loved ones to home care, but he'd never forgive himself if *he* did. If he took his father from the house, then he might as well sign his father's death sentence, and he couldn't have that on his conscience, too.

Heidi went back to reading, and Marcos headed to bed.

He flicked through his social media. Too bored with the political arguments and soccer rivalries and the things that in the past had been important to him, he quickly put his phone away.

And then he got the temptation to search for Nadia. How many times had he looked her up without any results? He hadn't even known her real and full name, so he'd wasted hours looking for a ghost. And now, as soon as he typed her info into the search bar, countless posts popped up. Articles in the newspapers about her talent and accomplishments. She'd been the first Latina salutatorian at BYU.

In all the pictures, she was either alone or with friends. There was no trace of the fiancé anywhere. She'd apparently erased him from her posts, as if he'd never existed. Had Brandon at least been the one taking the photos?

Their lives overlapped so much. Marcos was surprised to see that he and Nadia had so many friends in common, including Jason Hernández, her brother-in-law. Jason had gone to school with his cousin Alexander and played with him on the high school varsity baseball team.

Marcos had an ache in his chest looking at her pictures through the years. So many people in common. Their mothers had even been online friends.

A picture from her college years on her timeline left him breathless. It was the photo of their friend group that Hernán, his best friend, had posted without tagging him. Marcos remembered that day as if it had been yesterday.

It was toward the end of the summer, and after an afternoon at the lake boating in someone's father's boat, they'd gone back to the dorms and stayed up watching *The Lord of the Rings* while Nadia explained to him all the mythology since *The Silmarillion*. He hadn't cared about the movies. He just loved her voice and how much she knew and cared about.

Back then, Marcos and Nadia hadn't really known a lot about each other, but they had meant everything to each other. In the photo, she was by his side, naked shoulder to naked shoulder, smiling from ear to ear, their faces red from the sun.

His heart swelled as he thought of that boy he'd been. So confused and unmoored. And of all the pictures to repost, she'd reposted this one.

He saved it to his camera roll and went to sleep.

Saturday was a blur spent on weddings and the hospital.

After unclogging a stubborn toilet in the bridal changing room, Marcos was running back to the kitchen when he got a phone call from Hernán, his college buddy.

He wasn't going to answer. Kenzie had been blaring in his earpiece that the freezer wasn't working for some reason, and he'd almost chucked the equipment into the toilet he'd just fixed. The only thing that stopped him from doing so was knowing he'd be the one to fish it out. Putting his hand in that bowl once had been enough. But he had a hunch about the call, and when he briefly glanced at the screen, it was Hernán's name on the caller ID. His college buddy was now the father of three little girls under seven years old, soon to be four. His wife, Rachel, had been in the hospital since the day before.

Marcos took off the earpiece and turned it off. The freezer could wait for a few minutes. "Hola, peluca," he said, leaning against the hallway wall and cupping his hand around the phone. From the party, the voice of Shania Twain was twanging "You're Still the One" while two hundred people joined the chorus. "What's the news?"

"She's here! All eight pounds of Nina Rivera!" Hernán's pride and joy oozed out of the phone speaker. "I just sent you a picture. Isn't she lovely?"

Marcos glanced at the screen. It was all megapixels of pink rolls and a headful of dark curls. A tiny pink bow rested on her forehead. People said all newborns look alike, but this little girl, tightly wrapped into a baby burrito, was definitely a one-of-a-kind beauty. Marcos's face softened. How could she be so pretty when she was a mini clone of her father? They were like two drops of water, although now, Hernán was bald, his legendary headful of hair having been shed along the way from college to fatherhood.

"Ay, ¡qué linda!" Marcos said. "Congratulations, dude. For being such an ugly son of a bitch, you sure make cute babies with Rachel."

"Me and Rachel need to ask you something important."

Marcos stiffened. Kenzie—arms crossed, foot tapping—was staring at him with a murderous expression on her face.

"I'll come over to the hospital after this wedding, okay? You can tell me in person," Marcos said, and after a quick goodbye, he hung up. Then he turned to Kenzie and said, "Before you ask, my friend's wife is in the hospital."

The annoyed expression gave way to regret. At the mention of *hospital* her mind must have gone off into a terrible scenario, not the birth of a baby. "Oh, I'm so sorry," she said in a soft voice. "Just check the freezer when you have a chance, okay?"

And before he could clarify the misunderstanding, she went out to help with the bride and groom's going-away carriage.

Later that night, he stopped by the hospital with some flowers that had been left from the last reception. He could barely stand on his feet anymore, but he didn't have to fake a smile for Rachel, who looked so happy but tired as she nursed her new baby.

Taking advantage that Marcos had sat in the ugly nursing recliner, Hernán took the baby from Rachel and placed her in his arms, taking him by surprise.

"Aw, you look good like that, Marcos!" Rachel said.

Hernán sent her a curious look, and she added, "Don't give me that look! You know in my book, you're the handsomest papi in the world. Just noting that Marcos looks good with a baby in his arms. I have a couple of friends I could set you up with—"

"Hold up!" Marcos exclaimed, and when baby Nina blinked, startled by his voice, he added in a whisper, "Is that what you wanted to tell me? You didn't have to ambush me like that!"

Hernán and Rachel laughed, and after a conspiratorial look, she said, "Actually, we were wondering if you'd be her godfather."

Marcos hadn't expected this. In his childhood religion, babies weren't baptized, so he wasn't sure what a godfather was supposed to do. His friend must have seen the thoughts warring in Marcos's mind, because he said, "Dale! That way, we can officially be compadres."

"But what does it mean? What do I have to do as a godfather?"

He loved being an uncle to Carly and Elijah, and an honorary one to Hernán and Rachel's girls. But a godfather?

"Basically, a godfather is a stand-in father, just in case," Hernán said.

His words only muddled the waters. Marcos was now borderline panicky.

First the venue, and now a baby?

"In case of what?"

Rachel gently elbowed her husband and said, "A girl can't have too many father figures in her life, don't you think? Good men who will protect her and support her and take care of her if the parents aren't around."

"Don't worry, Hawkins," Hernán said with a smirk. "I'm not about to die and leave you a little one anytime soon. Just say yes and count it as your good deed for the day."

"For a lifetime, you mean!" Marcos had reservations, but he still smiled, as his friends cheered and called him compadre.

He was still smiling the next day on his Sunday-morning run. He got back home in time to say goodbye to Heidi and hello to Santiago, who congratulated him on becoming a godfather and showed him pictures of his own two godchildren from Mexico. Twin boys who were his best friend's kids.

Marcos's good mood soured when Sarah called to make sure things were okay.

"Everything's under control."

She clicked her tongue, annoyed. "Listen, nene, Kenzie's worried about that woman changing her wedding reception to a quinceañera. You know we can't refund her a single cent. The numbers—"

"Are in the red. I know. Listen, she'll pay extra for the new decorations and stuff. She was already paying extra for going past midnight. And I have an idea—what if we do quinceañeras after her party?"

"I don't know . . ." she said. "That's something Mami and I always talked about, but it never worked for some reason."

"Maybe this time it will," he insisted.

He could hear the gears in her brain working super hard as they both tried to come up with ideas of how to keep the property and afford their father's treatment. Three home-care nurses weren't exactly cheap. He didn't even want to calculate the price of medications.

"Oh, I didn't tell you the other day, but Uncle Monty came to see me," he said. "He had all these documents . . . I need to talk to that Laramie guy, the lawyer."

"Ugh," she said with disgust. "I can't stand that guy."

"Me either," he said, "and he knows it. He told me he's too busy with another case, so he's assigning us to another lawyer in his firm."

"Piece of sh—"

"Mami, can I have more ice cream?" his niece Carly asked, and he could imagine the embarrassment Sarah felt that she'd almost been caught swearing.

Marcos laughed.

"Stop it," she hissed into the phone receiver. "One day you'll see how hard it is to be a parent, Marcos, and then I'll be the one laughing."

"No, you'll be the one helping me out, right?"

Not that he had the intention of ever becoming a dad. But he was a godfather now. That had to give him some respect in her eyes. His heart started beating hard as he gathered courage to tell his sister the news. He felt like a teenage boy confessing that his girlfriend was pregnant.

"Guess what?" he said. "Hernán and Rachel had a baby girl yesterday. Her name's Nina."

"Aw, what a cute name! Tell them congratulations for me, please." Her voice had softened.

"And . . . they asked me to be her godfather, and I said yes."

There was a silence so deep that he wondered if the call had dropped. "Are you still there?"

She cleared her throat and said, "Yes, I'm just surprised."

Marcos felt heat rise from his stomach to his face all the way to the tips of his ears.

"What do you mean? You don't think I'll be a good godfather?"

She laughed, but there was no humor in her voice. "I think you'll be great. I guess I'm just jealous I didn't think to ask you to be my kids' godfather."

Now he was the one stunned into silence. "But you all don't baptize babies."

"I could have still asked you to be the honorary padrino, right? My poor children will just have to do with being your niece and nephew . . ."

"I'll always be their stand-in father figure. I mean, Nicky is the best father a kid could want. But I'll cheer them on and support them and—"

"Okay, okay, I get it. And thank you. I know you will, little brother."

They stayed silent for a few seconds, in which Marcos tried to process his emotions.

Then a baby cried on the other side of the line, and Sarah said, "I have to go. Congrats on becoming a grown-up, finally," she said. "And good luck with that woman, Palacio."

He felt himself blush to the roots of his hair. Sarah, who must have had a secret sensor of his moods and emotions, noticed the effect that the mere mention of Nadia had on him.

"Marcos? Is there anything else you aren't telling me?"

"Nothing, Sarita," he mumbled.

"Don't you dare, okay? We agree to do her party, but her rebounding on you isn't part of the deal, okay?"

"What? What gives you that idea? I . . ."

"The clock doesn't tick only for women, little brother. A damsel in distress, your defenses lowered after becoming a godfather . . . Just keep her at a distance. She's a very beautiful woman, and you, little brother, have a reputation that precedes you."

"You're so unfair," he muttered. "I'm perfectly able to keep things professional. I mean, look how Kenzie and I—"

"I know, I know," she said. "Just . . . be careful, is all."

"I will. I promise."

Not entirely convinced or relieved, Sarah hung up, but her words still circled his head like little white birds in cartoons.

Sarah, the rational sibling, was right, of course.

Marcos had been by Nadia's side the last time Brandon had broken her heart, or the last time he knew about. The bastard had cheated on her and finally messed things up so badly that she broke up with him weeks before the wedding. Although she'd hate him if he said so aloud, Nadia was a damsel in distress. And although he'd never been a gentleman or cavalier at all, Marcos would be lying if he denied he was dying to rescue her from her problems. At least by helping her throw this party.

But what if Marcos gave way to his feelings, the irrational desire to have a second chance with her, to see if this time around, things turned out differently? What if he offered her his heart on a platter, and she went back to Brandon after all?

Marcos didn't want to be a rebound, like his sister had said—or a shoulder to cry on—anymore.

When he met Hernán in the afternoon at the park, he told his friend about his blast from the past.

"Maybe it's a sign for you to settle down, Marcos," Hernán said, as they pushed two of his girls, Lucy and Lily, on the swings.

Luna, the oldest, was playing tag with other kids in the grass surrounding the playground. They were all little replicas of their mother, blond, freckly, and blue-eyed. Little Nina had inherited all the Latin genes from her Chilean dad, it seemed.

"I don't need a lady to settle down," Marcos said, and noticing the look Hernán sent him, he added, "Or another person. I'm too busy with my dad and the business. And now, add the goddaughter that you and Rach gave me into the mix, thank you very much. There's no room for anything else."

"It's always all about timing with you, eh?" Hernán said. "Bad timing, I mean."

"The one time in college was the perfect timing," Marcos added.

"And you messed it up by running away," Hernán said, and he couldn't argue with that.

Later, they took the girls to In-N-Out, and then they headed to their homes. Marcos wouldn't have acknowledged this even under torture, but he kind of envied his friend. He'd lost his hair, and freedom, but he was adored by his girls. While Marcos headed home to a night of loneliness and silence.

In spite of Marcos's promise to his sister and his words to Hernán, he was excited, because the next day, he'd be meeting Nani.

And if he had a chance, he wouldn't run from her anymore. He'd chase *her* for once.

Chapter 9

Nadia

"The reason I didn't go home yesterday, Mami, isn't that I don't love you or I don't trust you. But I didn't want to see Lisa and have to comfort her while she cried because her son cheated on me for years," Nadia said, trying to connect the call to the Bluetooth. There was a patrol car behind her, and she didn't want to get a ticket for talking on the phone so early on a Monday morning.

Her mom sighed.

Tinkerbell yapped in the background, and not for the first time, Nadia wished she could've trained her fur-sister better. She hadn't even had a coffee yet, and her head was about to explode. If this was a sign of things to come, then she didn't want the rest of the week to arrive.

"All I said is that she wants to talk. Also, she was wondering when you're returning the veil to her. It was her grandma's," her mom said.

The blasted veil. But Nadia deserved all the drama and tears she'd had to shed because of the stupid veil. All this drama for not being brave enough to put her foot down when Lisa had suggested she wear her grandma's veil that had been passed down as a family heirloom.

Not that Brandon's sister had even worn it, but Nadia had been stupid enough to give in.

How could she have been so clueless? She had no idea. She wanted to tear her hair out, which wasn't the best course of action, seeing as how she had a photo shoot for her new invites to think about.

The news of her broken-off engagement hadn't spread at all, surprisingly. She'd enjoyed the quiet weekend, without her mom pestering for details she didn't know yet, her ex-future mother-in-law crying, and the barking dog.

But now, she had to face the fire, and she needed a damn coffee at least.

She put the blinkers on, pulled over, and when the cruiser passed her, she let out the breath she'd been holding. But in doing so, she got a crick on her neck.

"Ay," she moaned.

"This is too stressful. Isn't it?" her mom asked, sounding teary. "Why did you bring this upon yourself? You know you can ask Brandon to give you another chance, right?"

Nadia muted herself for a second so her mom wouldn't hear her scream, "Like hell I will!" When she mildly recovered, she unmuted and replied, "Okay, Mami. You're right. I'm sorry this is too stressful for you. It's my fault."

She imagined her mom stiffening at the sarcasm dripping from her voice.

She couldn't hold her frustration anymore and added, "But what did you want me to do? Continue with the wedding to a man who doesn't love me?" She hadn't told her mom the details of the breakup, or the extent of the damage to her self-esteem, but she knew any mention of any kind of disrespect for the Palacios would be enough to convince her mom that this had been the only sensible course of action.

Her tactic worked, because when her mom spoke again, her

voice was slightly offended on Nadia's behalf. "Of course not! I didn't want you to go into a marriage that's going to make you unhappy. But things won't be easy. Abuela arrives tomorrow. She just called to remind me, as if we could ever forget."

Nadia sighed again, but this time, she didn't mute herself.

A heavy silence fell on both sides of the call.

Nadia's mind and heart were in turmoil.

Even after Isabella and Stevie's pep talks Saturday night, the whole double quinces party seemed a little ridiculous. But she held on to it because of Madi, who on Sunday night had arrived at Nadia's apartment exhausted but loving as always, to cheer her up.

It was also true that Madi's visit had almost backfired, but in the end, it had given Nadia the boost she needed to trust her first impulse to celebrate her life.

Madi had proposed to read the tarot cards to Nadia to see what her next move would be.

Nadia had hesitated. The cards were never nice to her.

"There's nothing to fear, love. The cards don't lie, but they can help elucidate a dilemma," she said, as she lit a circle of candles around the lambskin rug she had placed in the living room.

"Elucidate?"

"You know, illuminate your path," Madi said, leading Nadia to a meditation pouf.

"Okay then," she said, and picked the traditional set, the Rider–Waite, because after years of friendship with Madi, Nadia was familiar with the meaning of these cards. Madi wouldn't be able to make up an interpretation to make her feel better.

"Ready?" Madi asked, her amber eyes shiny as if she had a light inside her. Her hair, highlighted by the sun and now the candles, fell in perfect waves that framed her heart-shaped face.

Nadia nodded, closed her eyes, took a big breath, and picked a card.

"Ay," Madi whispered, the dismay in her voice making Nadia shiver with dread.

She peeked at her friend through half-open eyes, wanting to make sure Madi didn't switch the card, but afraid to look at the image on it.

"Is it that bad?"

Madi gulped. Her eyes were wide with horror, and her mouth pressed in a line as she nodded. "It is the past, though, so of course, it's not . . . nice, love."

Nadia glanced at the card. A man lay on the ground, ten swords stabbed into his back.

"A little obvious, no?" Nadia said, trying to smile but unable to do so.

"Draw another one," Madi commanded.

Nadia did so.

The three of swords. Now it was a heart stabbed by three swords.

Tears prickled in Nadia's eyes. She'd gotten many three of swords over the years. This wasn't new, but it still hurt.

Madi's eyes were teary, too. But she recovered first. She shook her head, sending her goddess hair flying off her shoulders, and said, "We know the past sucks. Now let's pick one for the present, and then another for the future."

That's when Nadia started downing the rosé, so the rest of the night was a blur. This morning in the car, while her mom cried silently on the other side of the phone, she only remembered the card for the present. It had been the ten of wands, a person carrying a bundle of sticks on their back, the weight so heavy, it made the person's legs buckle.

She could feel that weight in her soul.

Then for the future, she'd gotten the Tower. The card depicted lightning hitting a mountaintop tower and setting it on fire, and two people jumping from the windows.

"I give up!" Nadia had said, too sad to even cry. "Let's call it a night, Mads. My life is going to suck, right?"

"But the Tower isn't all bad, love!" Somehow, Madi was smiling.

"Destruction. Upheaval. What else? Oh, yes, chaos. That's what it means."

Madi had taken Nadia's hands to calm her, which worked. "Look at the light. It means divine intervention. Also? After the chaos comes reconstruction. The Tower means a radical change that can lead to your best life. I mean, take another one to elucidate some more."

Nadia had humored her, because she wanted to go to sleep.

The next card had left them both speechless. It was the ten of cups.

"Oh, my goddess!" Madi had exclaimed in her ethereal voice.

Nadia had just stared at the card as an odd calm fell over her. There was a couple holding each other while facing a beautiful house and a green garden. Two children played joyfully next to them. A river flowed over green pastures, and in the blue, blue sky, a rainbow held ten golden cups arranged along its arc.

"The having-it-all card," Madi had said in reverence. "Hold on to this feeling in your heart, Nadita. I know it will come true."

Nadia had placed the card under her pillow, and then she'd packed it in her purse, not like a compass, but like a talisman against all those things that would come before she got the promises in the ten of cups.

But what if Nadia cut her losses? What if she disappeared from the earth and didn't show her face ever again? What if she ran?

But as soon as the thought had come into her brain, it left. She wasn't a runner or a quitter or a coward.

And she had done nothing wrong. The one who had to disappear was Brandon, which he might as well have already done. She hadn't heard or seen even a trace of him since Thursday.

If anything, she was trying to rectify the wrong of taking his disrespect for so many years.

"Everything will go okay with Abuela," Nadia finally said. She must have sounded resolute, because her mom didn't even argue. In fact, she sighed in relief. Nadia continued, "Just please don't say anything to her yet. I know how hard it is, but I want to be the one giving her the news. She never loved Brandon."

Her mom's relief reached her through the phone. "Ay, hija! I won't say a thing."

After a few more mutterings about not proving Abuela right, her mom hung up.

Abuela Catalina and Abuelo Leonardo were the only ones from the whole extended family who visited often.

Abuelo didn't care one way or another for Brandon. He was the typical grandfather. But her grandma was a different story. She was sharp and intuitive, and ever since Nadia was seventeen, she'd been warning her about Brandon. For Abuela not to love someone, the person had to be a piece of work. And now Nadia saw that her grandma hadn't been wrong in her years and years of observation. It was still a kick to her ego, because other than Brandon, she'd always done everything she was supposed to.

Proving Abuela right would be a pill too big to swallow. She hoped she didn't choke and die when she came clean to her.

Abuela had grown to love Isabella's husband, and Nadia had hoped it would be the same with Brandon after the actual wedding, as if a simple piece of paper could really change anything.

To make matters worse, now Nadia had to face her boss. He'd been a bitch about time off for her wedding. "You've been together for years, living in sin. What is that performative piece of celebration going to do?" he'd said, pretending to joke, when she'd asked for time off before the wedding, too. She'd been saving her vacation time for years. He had no choice but to give it to her. Still, she wanted to do the best at work, so she could finally get that raise she'd deserved for so long.

When she finally arrived at the office, Shanice came up to her quietly and said, "Are you okay?"

Shanice, a small Black woman who'd immigrated from Haiti in her teens, was the most experienced paralegal in the office.

The firm would collapse without her expertise, but Laramie and the partners treated her like a glorified secretary. In her late forties, she was the heart and soul of the firm. She'd been on Nadia's side from day one, warning her and advising her at every opportunity.

In turn, over the years, Nadia had convinced her time after time to stick with her until she got made partner. Secretly, she hoped one day she'd open her own firm, and Shanice would follow her. But could she afford her?

Nadia told herself Shanice was one of the reasons she didn't walk out of this toxic environment.

"I heard a few things over the grapevine about your wedding. Is it true?"

Nadia was technically one of her bosses, but in reality, they were good friends now.

So she didn't take it as if the woman was trying to fish for gossip. That wasn't Shanice. If she'd broken her impeccable code of conduct, then the rumors had to be loud like firecrackers.

Nadia nodded briefly. "I couldn't take it anymore, so I kicked him out. Everything in the apartment is mine. Even the car. Even his phone, so I disconnected his line. He can call me a bitch all he wants, but the truth is, he never even paid me back for his part of the phone bill. He's such a tool that he doesn't even know how to transfer his number out of my account without his mom's help."

Shanice shook her head, but her eyes were blazing when she placed a hand on Nadia's shoulder. "You did the right thing. Now to be strong, so the leeches here don't try to get any kind of advantage out of this situation."

Nadia swallowed the knot in her throat. Shanice was right. If there was any advantage he could have over this development in Nadia's situation, Laramie would find it and exploit it.

She had to snap out of her private life matters and protect her career, which was the only thing keeping her sane at the moment.

"Have you had a chance to look at the Hawkins papers?" Shanice asked in a businesslike, cold manner.

Hawkins . . .

The name circled in Nadia's head for a second that stretched into eternity. And when she made a connection, her hands shook so hard, she spilled coffee on herself.

"Hawkins?" she exclaimed.

She'd known this, but she hadn't known Rocket's real name was Marcos Hawkins. The firm's clients. Her client.

The one case that could make or break her career.

"Yes, Hawkins," Shanice said, lasering her with her gaze. "Did you not read them?" she muttered through clenched teeth. The walls had ears in this office. "Laramie wants to be done with this case by the end of the month," Shanice said, helping Nadia blot the coffee out of her pants.

The papers. They were still in her car. She hadn't even thought about work, with everything else happening in her life. So unprofessional. She'd never been this way before. Not even when they had the scare with her mom, thinking she had breast cancer because the mammogram had shown a mass.

Then, Nadia had still shown up at work and done her best, and when Shanice found her in the bathroom, crying with relief when she got the phone call that all was in the clear, she was so pissed that Nadia hadn't taken the day off.

"The partners take a day off after they come back from golfing to recover from their vacation, and you don't even give yourself time to breathe or to eat. You're vanishing into nothing!"

Ever since then, Shanice had made it one of her life's missions to make sure Nadia ate well. Nadia loved the feeling of being smothered with love and pampered, because at her parents' home, she was pushed so hard to be the very best that she could be that the demands at work didn't seem like a bad deal at all.

"I'll give you another set of copies. You only need to get the owner to sign the papers. The client is putting a lot of money in this development, and Laramie thinks he found a way to make the actual owner fall. Mr. Hawkins has to sign himself, though."

Nadia cursed the bad timing and her lack of awareness. When she was planning the wedding, she'd never really realized that the venue owners' last name was Hawkins, which of course now she knew was Marcos's, as well. But what were the odds that her first job was to work with the family of the man whose venue was hosting her big bash?

She spent the morning fielding phone calls. The ones that Shanice redirected were regular firm clients who paid fortunes to have their wealth administered by others. So much money, and they really didn't know what to do with it.

The calls that came through her personal cell that she reserved only for business were people she helped for close to nothing. She had a passion in finding loopholes in complicated immigration cases. Maybe it was her South American resourcefulness, but no matter what, Nadia always got the job done. Perhaps her methods weren't traditional or proper enough for other attorneys, but she always found a way to help families stay together. And because she had a stupid sense of justice that led her by the nose, she always tried to make sure that everything she did benefitted as many people as possible.

Laramie and friends—or Laramie and crones, as she called them behind their backs—had employed her after witnessing one of her mock trials in law school. Laramie had been there with his cowboy hat and boots. Nadia generally had a good obsession for the whole cowboy archetype, although no man she had ever dated had anything to do with nature or farms or the country in general. Perhaps it had to do with her vague memories of the family ancestral home on the outskirts of Rosario in Argentina and the seemingly endless afternoons riding horses by the Paraná River with Abuelito Luis, who had passed away when Nadia was ten. Whatever her attraction to cowboys had been got demolished with Laramie's affectations. She'd heard Shanice say the man had never even ridden a horse or cleaned a stall, but he liked to play the part.

Whatever the case, he'd been impressed by the simple way in which Nadia had solved the team's problem. A simple but fail-safe way. And they'd employed her. She'd been delighted to get a position in a company in Utah so Brandon didn't have to move away from his job and start his search again. Their children, when they came, could live close to cousins and grandparents.

But then she realized the firm used her like a secret weapon, and she grew bored of saving others millions that she never saw trickling down to her back account, in spite of what her economics professors had said in college.

What she hated the most was that Laramie always passed on her marvelous findings and solutions as his own, never giving Nadia any credit. When she'd finally gathered the nerve to point it out in a meeting with Mr. Miller, the main partner, the man had been astounded, and had rebuked Laramie, who'd acted offended and aloof until he proposed a way for her to become partner.

She'd been on the verge of striking out on her own, setting up shop and helping people the way she wanted to do. And now, the familiar urge knocked on the doors of her heart once again.

She had found a way for the Ravello family to remain together despite the impossibility of it all. The parents had been in limbo for years, waiting for a way to legalize their situation, and when they had thought everything was bleak, Nadia had found the way out. The way to the light.

"Now, we have this meeting with the judge in the morning. Be there on time. Remember, no feelings. They just care about the facts. We'll ask for a second chance," Nadia told them.

Mr. Ravello had thanked her profusely. Right then, Shanice brought her lunch and said, "Now, go over the documents and tell me what you think."

Nadia peeled the wax paper of her Cuban sandwich and kicked her shoes off under the table, since it was her break.

She read the papers. No, she inhaled them. The case seemed very straightforward. The property in question, a farm, was part of a family trust. It had been assigned to the oldest son, a Stuart Hawkins.

The trust specified that the property had to remain under the care of a direct blood family relative. It had been with Stuart for years, and the farm had succeeded, and even though he'd tried to buy off the two other brothers, they had never budged. Nadia understood they had been biding their time. Now that Stuart was incapacitated, they saw their chance to swoop in and tempt his children.

Marcos had seemed incredibly well-equipped to run the venue and everything it entailed. But Nadia saw how hard it would be for him to feel trapped to his parents' dreams when the easiest route would be to sell their part to his uncles.

The payout was considerable, which meant that the brothers would get at least ten times as much from the developer that wanted to incorporate the farm and convert the idyllic views into a neighborhood of mansions only a few very privileged people could afford.

Ethically, she couldn't be in charge of this deal.

At all.

She felt a moral obligation to warn Marcos, but if she did, then she'd never get that promotion to partner she'd been chasing for so long.

But before money, she always considered the moral standing of anything she did.

She had to find a way to warn Marcos without violating her client/lawyer confidentiality. Stuart Hawkins was very much alive, and it would take a vampire and vulture to get him to sign these papers. It wouldn't be her.

Shanice popped in after lunch like an alarm. She had her lips pressed and said, "So?"

Nadia shrugged. "I'll have to talk to Laramie. I can't go through with this."

"You know he won't be happy. His cut from this deal will be massive. He's already looking at airplanes and houseboats in Lake Powell."

Nadia exhaled. "But if I don't, then I will never forgive myself."

Shanice nodded. "I'll leave you to it."

Nadia used the bathroom and made sure she had nothing in her teeth that might diminish her credibility. She walked to her boss's office, and he was there, waiting, sitting at the window, looking at the majestic mountains, where one of the typical late-summer fires was burning.

"Oh, Nadia," he said, overemphasizing the *D* in her name and making it sound like a *TH*. "So tell me, when can I expect the final arrangements for the Hawkins deal to be finished? I asked you this weekend, and I was disappointed you weren't available."

She clenched her teeth and squared her shoulders. "Actually, I'm here to let you know I can't work on this case anymore."

He furrowed his brow. Laramie didn't like changes to his calculatingly laid plans. "What do you mean? You're the one who said that if Old Man Stuart can sign, then it will be legally binding. Our client wants this finished before the end of the month so construction can start before the end of the year."

"There's a conflict of interest," she said, trying to swallow the knot in her throat. "I have a personal relationship with Marcos, Stuart's son, and I—"

"But you were just engaged to someone who had nothing to do with the Hawkins spawn. Now that your wedding is off, you don't have a connection to this venue anymore."

She noticed the use of the past tense in the verb. How did he know? He was like a shark, smelling for a bleeding wound.

She nodded. "It's got nothing to do with my wedding being

called off. Marcos Hawkins and I were good friends a few years ago, and morally, I need to warn him of what his uncles are trying to do."

Laramie's face dropped the mask of persuasion. "Listen, chica, I'm not going to lose this commission just because you got cold feet before your wedding."

"That has nothing to do with this. It's morally wrong to urge your client to attain a signature under duress," she said.

"But not illegal," he said. "In the law, there are wrinkles where legality doesn't reach, and I happen to like working in those spaces—in the wrinkles. How do you think I made my fortune?"

Her face was flaming. She was tired of him and his attitude. "Then consider this my resignation," she said. "I can't be part of this anymore."

"Aha! You're willing to lose your equity in the company for a business that has nowhere to go?"

She thought of all the families who'd started by celebrating at Enchanted Orchard. She remembered the pride on Marcos's face when he was working at the venue. Even Kenzie and Sarah flashed before her eyes. Nadia hadn't been unemployed since she was fifteen.

But she couldn't continue with this anymore.

"No. I won't do it anymore. Find yourself another trick pony."

There. Lightning had struck the Tower. Now it was time to jump out the window.

Her head held high, Nadia gathered her belongings and left the building. With the bad references the firm was bound to give her, she wouldn't find a job anywhere else. At least not as a lawyer, but damn, did she feel free and powerful!

At home, unemployed and lonely, Nadia went over the list of things she needed for her party.

1. Dress
2. Pictures
3. Decorations
4. Cake
5. DJ
6. Dancing lessons
7. Guests

Nadia wasn't a procrastinator, but the magnitude of the tasks ahead made her feel like a real-life version of the ten of wands. She was lightheaded and winded.

She couldn't do it all alone. Too bad this morning Stevie had flown back to Amarillo, Texas. She'd be back for the party, and she'd support over the phone, but it wasn't the same.

Madi was teaching every evening, and Isabella hadn't answered her calls yet.

Nadia had the impulse to call her mom to ask to borrow Tinkerbell as a support animal, at least. But Abuela and Abuelo's flight landed the next morning, and soon after, the rest of the family would arrive. Her apartment would fill to the brim with too many people for her to also add a dog into the mix.

She took a long swig of orange juice straight from the bottle, now that for the first time in her life she didn't have to worry about sharing anything with anyone. She'd never lived on her own, and she really loved the freedom to walk around in underwear if she wanted to and drink from the bottle.

But when her phone buzzed and startled her, she spilled juice all over herself.

Nadia blotted her blouse with a paper towel and answered the phone.

It was her sister.

"Hey, Nadita," Isabella said, sounding a little out of breath. "Just a heads-up that Kate just called me. That's why I didn't answer your call."

Nadia's hair bristled. Kate was Brandon's sister. "Is it about the veil? Because if it is, tell her I'm going to use it as toilet paper, so don't even bother—"

"Actually," Isabella interrupted, "she only wanted to let you know she went ahead and canceled the honeymoon."

The fight left Nadia in a huff.

The one item Brandon had taken care of, because his dad had been a pilot all his life and they had airline and hotel credits, had been the honeymoon. For Brandon and the Lewis family, erasing any traces of the failed honeymoon was as easy snapping their fingers.

"She paid the one-hundred-dollar cancellation fee and sounded like she had mortgaged her Botoxed lips for it, the bee-otch," Isabella said.

Nadia plopped on the couch. "She didn't ask you to pay it back, did she?" Fire was about to come out of her ears, nose, eyes, and mouth if her sister said yes.

But Isabella replied, "Forget about her. Now, I imagine you called me about the dress, right? How about we go shopping tomorrow evening? I found a couple of places that are open until nine."

"Tomorrow the family arrives," Nadia said.

"Exactly," replied Isabella. "We'll need an exit plan for a couple of hours, at least."

Nadia loved the way her sister thought.

"I can't go tonight, because I promised Olivia I'd take her driving. She's had her permit for months, but she's never been behind the wheel, pobrecita."

"And Jason?"

"At Noah's game." Isabella's voice had turned icy, and Nadia was about to ask what was wrong, when her sister asked, "What else is on the list?"

"The list?"

"Yes, nena. The list. I know you have one in front of you right now."

It wasn't technically in front of Nadia, seeing how she was

sprawled on the couch, but still, she got up and walked to the counter, where she'd left the piece of paper.

"I'm meeting the venue owner about decorations tonight," she said, and the promise of seeing Rocket made her heart sputter.

"Photos?"

"I'm calling right after I hang up with you," she replied.

"Okay, it sounds like a plan. Good luck. Chau chau."

Nadia had wanted to tell her about her job, about how she had quit, but she knew her time with her sister was over for the night.

Isabella was always on the run, and even a phone call with her left Nadia feeling like she'd run a race, too. She wanted to go to bed, but she was seeing Marcos tonight, and there were so many things to do.

Before she lost momentum, she dialed the photographer's number.

"Ryanne speaking," a voice said on the other side of the line.

"Oh, hey, Ryanne, this is Nadia Palacio, hmmm . . . remember Brandon Lewis?"

Later, when Nadia thought back on the conversation, she couldn't really pinpoint when things started going downhill. Had it been when Ryanne couldn't remember her although she had clear memories of Brandon? Was it when she said she needed an appointment the following week?

In any case, if quitting her job had made her feel like she was jumping off a tower on fire, listening to Ryanne was like burning alive.

"What do you mean you won't be able to take photos and video of my treintañera?" she asked, trying to pull on her pants with her shoe stuck in the narrow leg.

She wanted to get into her screen and strangle this girl.

"Well . . ." Ryanne said. "Brandon did promise me the wedding of the decade. I already had contacts in *Utah Valley* magazine. But now . . . I don't want to be involved in this sham of a party. I mean, this is an anti-wedding, and I don't want to give my clients the wrong impression." She popped her gum and yelled to someone, "See you later, Suzie!" shattering Nadia's eardrum. And then she added on the phone, "Sorry about that. That was one of my videographers. The thing is, I was also giving Brandon a big discount. And he's my friend. I don't want to betray his trust, you know? He was very loyal to me when I was getting started."

Nadia tried to swallow some choice words that were crowding in her mouth. Brandon seemed to be very loyal and a good friend to everyone except for her. And this girl. Who did she think she was?

"I can match his price and even pay full price," Nadia said. "This will be an incredible party. I, too, have contacts in the magazine. You might get good exposure."

"I don't eat exposures, sweetheart," Ryanne said, and the sound of her whiny voice grated on Nadia's ears.

"I know. And I said I'd still pay even more than what Brandon was paying you."

"The thing is, he never even paid a deposit, but I have quite an extensive waiting list. Someone else might jump at the chance. I'm just not the girl for the job," she said.

Nadia, who had been pacing all over her apartment as she tried to persuade Ryanne, plopped on her bed.

She was right. This girl Ryanne, whatever relationship she had with Brandon, wasn't the right person to photograph her double quinces.

Nadia didn't want it stained with his memory, or name, or whatever baggage he'd been carrying that Nadia hadn't known about.

"Okay, I guess. Thanks for leaving me hanging," Nadia said, and hung up, knowing that the woman would be seething at not having had the last word in the argument.

It was a small victory that couldn't fill the crater of humiliation Nadia felt in her heart.

"Great," she said. "Now to get another photographer."

She didn't even know where to start. She and Brandon had

bought boxes of disposable automatic cameras to place on each table so later on they could see the wedding through their guests' eyes. The idea had seemed adorable.

But now, it seemed that those candids would be the only pictures she ever had of her double quinceañera. They would look nothing like the photos in the magazine.

She couldn't have that!

She was jobless, without even unemployment benefits, since she'd been the one to quit (without a two weeks' notice, to boot), but by all that was holy, was she going to get the best photos money could buy.

She opened her laptop and went over the list of photographers. She started calling from the top, but when they heard the party was just a few weeks away, they hung up on this crazy woman right away or, on one occasion, tried to take advantage of the situation and quoted her three times the regular fee, then even more when he found out the party would be extending until later on in the night.

She could delegate this task to Stevie, who was an excellent negotiator and the most likely to get a good deal, but she felt bad passing on her problems to her friend, who was in the middle of her selling season.

Nadia hadn't wanted to be a bridezilla, and she wasn't going to become a birthdayzilla, either, and confirm everyone's worst suspicions.

Her phone chimed with a calendar reminder. It was time to meet Marcos at the venue. She didn't have time to get ready if she was to arrive on time.

She could ask him to meet over the phone or FaceTime. But she knew she needed to take a look at the place to have a better idea of what needed to be done. She wouldn't have a groom to fill in the space with his fake smiles. The whole weight of making the party a success would fall on her. Ten of wands, all over again.

Especially when she remembered she had to warn him about his predatory uncles and their true plans for the venue.

Thoughtlessly, she pulled her hair up in a ponytail and headed down to her car. If only she could run away from the mess she'd gotten herself into! All eyes on her. She could've played the "poor jilted woman" card. But no. She had to go and put on the strong woman facade.

If anyone saw into her eyes long enough, though, would they see how much of a three of swords she was?

She didn't intend to give anyone the time to even glimpse into the lonely little girl, crying because she was tired of running toward the trophy that others got just for showing up.

Why was everything so much harder for her than for all the other people she had ever met? Even for Isabella, who was perfect in every way.

What was Brandon doing right now?

She pulled into Enchanted Orchard's parking lot, but she hesitated before getting out of the car. She made a note of where his car was parked. This time, she wouldn't make any embarrassing mistakes, like trying to get into his instead of hers.

Today, there would be no running out of gas. Her tank was full. No going to the gas station together for snacks that her hips absolutely didn't need.

Everything was under control. *She* was under control.

She looked around her as her lungs expanded with the first full breath she'd taken all day.

This was a special place.

The sky wouldn't be dark for a couple of hours, but the venue was softly illuminated by fairy lights that crisscrossed atop a gazebo, next to the pond where the swans glided.

She couldn't stand it if it was all demolished to build houses or a golf course.

The willow trees swayed by the pond like they were dancing and telling her *hello, you crazy witch. Ready to keep on dumping money on this stupid party? What if you had instead donated this money to a group that could use it or paid your loans or sent your parents on vacation?*

But was it really so wrong to do this with her own money? She hadn't had a birthday party since she was ten years old. There was always something or another. Why was it so hard for the world to understand that it was okay to celebrate her life?

She believed in the motto of not leaving a trace behind. But that phrase worked in national forests or the canyon. Not in life.

The people—the women—history remembered were the trailblazers who left just that, a trail. And she intended to do just that.

The little flame inside her heart grew to wildfire proportions when she realized Marcos was walking in her direction. He looked as if he had been waiting for her to have the nerve to get out of the car.

He wore jeans and a T-shirt, nothing special, but he looked like a romance hero, dark and tall and a little rakish. He waited for her to make her way to him and raked his hand through his hair like he had in college when he was wrecked by nerves before a meet.

Her stomach somersaulted.

She didn't want to be feeling this tingling sensation at the mere sight of him. But what was it? Muscle memory? Parts of her body remembering what his fingers and lips felt like?

When she was in seventh grade, her class had gone to the Hare Krishna temple in Spanish Fork, forty minutes south of Orem, where her parents lived. The class had run with llamas and learned mantras they chanted with the strongest man Nadia had ever seen in her life. And then he had talked about a mural on one of the walls of the temple, portraying the course of a person's life. From birth until death.

"Cells completely renew themselves after seven years," he explained. "After that time, your body finally turns into a completely different body, although something deep inside your essence still remembers everything, of course."

Contrary to popular belief, she didn't remember a lot of things from school without having to study all night. But she had remembered this statement for the rest of her life. And as the years with Brandon went by, she'd thought that the cells in her body didn't remember who she had been in Argentina, or who she had been with Rocket, the mysterious boy she'd spent a glorious summer with. When she turned twenty-eight, she had mourned that the last cell of her lips maybe had shed and didn't remember the softness of Rocket's lips on it. Hadn't this been a sign of how unhappy she had been with Brandon?

The fling with Rocket had been so decadent and pure that she had never told Stevie or Madi about it. Her sister would've been horrified she'd slept with another man so soon after breaking up with Brandon, so she hadn't told Isabella, either. It was her only secret, as was the agony of knowing that even though he was finally just an arm's length away, he could never be hers. She wasn't even completely her own yet. But she was trying. She was broken in ways she didn't know how to fix. She only knew that if she couldn't fix herself on her terms, no one else would come and do it.

"Thanks for meeting me today," she said, and like a dork, extended her hand for him to shake.

Marcos took it and . . . kissed it.

Time stopped in an instant, and for a second, they remained like that.

Now my hand will forever remember the touch of his lips, she said in her mind. *Even if every skin cell burns and falls, when I die and my flesh decomposes, I will feel the electricity of his lips on my hand.*

She knew she was being dramatic, but since Thursday, her life had been nothing but a series of dramatic events.

He looked uncertain and then gave her a small smile. "I'm

sorry," he said, shrugging. "Yesterday I was with my friend and his little girls all afternoon, and I had to pretend to be a footman and servant for two hours. I guess I saw a princess, and the action just seemed natural, Nani."

Something quivered inside her when he called her Nani, and she felt something like a pull from her belly toward him, as if he were magnetic and she had no control of her actions.

But she wasn't that kind of woman. To fall for stupid gestures or silly words.

She just laughed, dismissively.

"I haven't been called a princess in a while, Hawkins," she said, because there was no way the name Rocket would escape her lips. If it did, it would take the last trace of self-respect she possessed, and she had forbidden herself to fall so low. Not even a tower crane would lift her again.

It was so tempting to fall for his gestures, but what if she gave in and he ran again?

She shook her head at how stupid she was in her choice for men. There had been two. One she had to kick out, and the other had run from her life when things were perfect. No. She could never lower her guard with Marcos. She'd never put herself in that situation again.

"I appreciate your meeting with me, but Kenzie had several questions about the cost. I think she was overwhelmed." She tried to laugh, but then thought she sounded slightly unhinged, and so she stopped herself. "I had thought working with brides required a steel mask and temperament. Maybe I'm too much?"

She had tried to joke, but her voice had cracked at the end of the sentence.

"No," Marcos said, and he took her hand. "It's really not you. She's going through some personal things, and the company is, too. She's just really stressed, and when you called, you caught her at a bad time. I'm sorry. Really, I hope you don't take it personally."

Nadia swallowed the knot in her throat. Of course, she knew

better than taking things personally. She prided herself in having a thick skin. But the events of the last few days had left her raw, like when she'd been a junior in high school and crashed with her bike and got road rash in places she didn't even know existed because they had never seen the light of the sun—in front of the whole boys' basketball team.

But why was she always the one giving others a break? When was someone going to think about *her* feelings and treasure them? She was tired of being strong. She just didn't know how not to show this fake face anymore. She didn't know how to drop the charade. She felt like that old Leonardo DiCaprio movie, *The Man in the Iron Mask.* She was the woman in the steel mask. And with the heat of the volcano that roared inside her, a volcano that was too much for some people, the mask had melted and become so natural, now people confused it with her own personality, and the truth was that she was tired.

The only person who knew her without it was a boy who hadn't even known her true name. Years ago. She knew she had changed. He had almost not recognized her, but in a way, that same vulnerable girl who wanted to be spontaneous was still there.

She shrugged, and her voice was all thorns when she said, "I don't care. But anyway, thanks for meeting with me. I was hoping that the decorations could be swapped for something less wedding-ish and more . . . neutral, you know? Kenzie did say there were things in your hall's storage that could work."

"Come on, then," he said, and led her to a cabin that looked abandoned and gave her chills.

Chapter 10

Marcos

He offered an extended hand, and she took it. That vulnerability and trust. It disarmed him. Because if she really knew Marcos, the one who could never commit to anything, then she'd be running the opposite way, screaming.

The sunset was streaking the sky in colors that took his breath away. The fires burning in California, Idaho, Colorado, and right here in the Wasatch Front, leaving devastation and heartbreak all around, had made this sunset possible. He knew a metaphor was there, but he couldn't really think with Nani by his side, in her running leggings, like that time they'd gone on a run and ended up in her dorm bed.

"That's a beautiful sunset," Nadia said, following his gaze. Then she continued walking ahead, gingerly stepping on the cobbled path. At the end stood the small cabin that the first Hawkins in the valley had built for his young wife. They'd raised five children there, but no one had lived in that house for generations. The family now used it as a storage shed.

In high school, Marcos had sometimes hidden there when his

anxiety was too intense, and he couldn't stand being close to anyone. His parents had known, of course, as they had known everything, even though he never shared much with them. They'd always been there for him. But he hadn't been there when they needed him.

Maybe if he hadn't run the last time, then his illness and loneliness wouldn't have made such catastrophic damage to his father?

But what good came of *what if*s and *should have*s?

The swans glided on the pond, and as a sign of respect, Marcos nodded at them.

"What are their names?" she asked. "Is there a story behind them?" Her voice was soft now, after the barbed comments about Kenzie, but had a huskiness to it that tugged at the center of his solar plexus. He didn't know why she had this effect on him.

"Their names are Helen and Paris," he said, and noticing the smirk on her face, he smiled.

"My mom had this thing for Greek mythology," he explained. "She had never been a reader when she lived in Uruguay, but she loved the movie *Troy* and then started looking up everything she could about mythology. She was obsessed with the story of Paris and Helen, and always lamented that they didn't have a happy ending. Some of the retellings of what happened to them are terrible."

He felt her shiver, and he wanted to encircle an arm around her shoulders, but that wouldn't have been professional. So he controlled himself.

"When she got serious into the wedding business, she adopted two swans that were at this bird rescue in Salt Lake. One of them had been wounded during a hunt, or something like that."

"A hunt? Like in hunting swans? Who does that? Are we in the sixteenth century?"

He nodded, feeling his mouth curve into a smile. "That's exactly what she said, too. She was so sad, so she brought them to the farm. I was fifteen or so, and she nursed the wounded one—the white one, which is Paris—back to health. Helen, the black one, wouldn't leave his side. Eventually, with the years, she brought more swans to fill the pond. And like birds do, they started having babies. I'm sure there was some inbreeding involved, but whatever. This pair is everyone's favorite."

Her rubber sandal slipped on one of the flagstones, and without thinking, he held her by the elbow. She didn't shake him off, and somehow, his fingers traced all the way down to hold her hand. He told himself it was to keep her safe, in case she slipped again. But the truth was, her hand and his fit perfectly together.

"I saw a picture of the swans, the cabin, and the big barn in the *Utah Valley* magazine. Then I followed on social media. I would scroll over the timeline and imagine my reception here," she said. Her eyes got shiny when she said this, but she lowered them too quickly for him to notice if it was from the pollution or because the memories hurt too much.

"I hear that all the time," he said. "Word of mouth, my mom's reputation for being the wedding fairy godmother, and the beautiful swans are responsible for most of the business we get. Sarah and Kenzie have done a wonderful job with marketing."

They arrived at the abandoned cottage, and he let go of her hand to unlock the door.

"You haven't been back in here in a while?" she asked when the door wouldn't give.

"I was actually here last week, trying to find blue and silver foil. But the door is broken. It was me, after sneaking out so many nights when I was a teenager. We should actually remodel this whole thing, but . . . it has character."

And memories.

"Do you still live here?"

"Nah," he said with a shrug. "I should. I mean, that would

mean an expense I wouldn't have to worry about, but . . ." His glance flickered away from her sharp eyes. The sky was quickly turning dark purple, and far from the city lights, the first stars were glittering like crystals. The temperature had dropped quickly once the sun had sunk behind the mountains. "It's best for my dad to be closer to town." He held the handle firmly and pushed with his shoulder until the door gave way.

The scent of his mom's perfume still lingered all this time later and hit him like an embrace. He tried not to lean into it, because if he did, he didn't know what could happen.

Nadia walked ahead of him.

Before she stumbled into the things that filled the cottage like a museum of good memories, he followed her to the middle of the room. After he pulled a string from the ceiling fan, the light came on. He picked up the old milk crate his sister had left below the fan and placed it by the door.

Nadia blinked as her eyes adjusted to the harsh light. She gazed around, and his heart pounded painfully at the sight of the family pictures. Everything around him made him hurt. His mom's paintings. She painted Enchanted Orchard from every point of view, trying to catch the perfect way the light hit it at different times of the day. But her favorite subjects to paint were people, especially couples and families. Her embroidery of sayings and intertwined initials. There were even the remains of wind chimes on the farm table that she never finished assembling.

Nadia stood in front of the last Hawkins family portrait perched on top of the fireplace. It had been taken right before Marcos left for college. He had given his parents hell that day. He didn't want to take family pictures, but his mom, who had none from her family in Uruguay, had convinced him to stand for one shot. Just one. He agreed on the condition that he took it with his own old-fashioned film camera. His parents, surprisingly, had agreed.

The paid photographer woman had stood graciously to the

side as young Marcos had set up his manual SLR camera on a tripod that he had to lean against the wooden fence so it wouldn't topple. They'd all been laughing by the time he had figured out the timer. He still remembered the kiss of the sun on his skin and the way the overgrown grass had prickled his naked ankles as he made his way to his family for the shot.

"This is a great portrait," she said.

The words left his lips before he could stop them. "I took it." He was proud of this shot and grateful his parents had been so patient with him, even if they hadn't understood him completely.

There was a brief silence, and then Nadia asked, "You're a photographer?"

"Sometimes," he said.

"Did you also take all these other pictures?" Nadia asked, turning back toward the portrait and crossing her arms, although the cottage still held the warmth of the day.

Marcos chuckled. "No, that was my mom."

"I would have loved to meet her."

Marcos knew that his mom would've loved to meet Nani, too, and that she would've enjoyed tremendously helping her with her double quinces. Which is why they were here, right? They were trying to find decorations and not explore his past.

"Should we . . . go look for some treasure?" he asked, motioning toward the stairs with his head.

Nadia nodded. She had a curious expression on her face that he didn't know how to read. He didn't want to read it. He was low-key scared of her questions and sharp mind that seemed to be connecting the dots of the picture of his life.

As if to shoo these fears away, like he used to erase imaginary monsters when he was a kid, he clicked on the lights as they climbed to the second floor. Until they reached a sort of loft, where there were rows upon rows of shelves with bins carefully labeled in pretty calligraphy.

"This is better than a bridal store," she whispered, awe in her voice.

She walked along the shelves, her hand softly brushing the bins, as if she were hoping they'd tell her secrets. Her shoulders were high and tense, and he had an irrational urge to place a hand on them to take some of the weight she carried. Instead, he peered out the round window of painted glass.

For a moment, the only sounds were her footsteps muffled by the worn-out beige carpet. This was both Marcos's favorite and most dreaded moment of the day: the time when day became night. Bree had called it his sundown blues, the few minutes when he struggled with the feelings of flying off like a runaway kite into a vortex.

"What do you think of this for my party?" Nadia asked.

Her bright voice brought him back with a pull. Her turned toward her, still half in a daze of memories and regrets.

Somewhere, she'd found a feathered top hat and placed it on her head.

He laughed, not able to imagine who would've worn that at a wedding, but then he thought it must have been left over from a cotillion dance.

"That looks elegant," he said. "You'll have to wear a tux for it to match."

She pursed her lips and narrowed her eyes as if assessing the suggestion. "Maybe if the tux is bright pink?"

"Bright pink?" he said, hyperaware of the flirty tone of his voice. Maybe it was habit? Whatever the cause for this switch in mood, he grabbed the excuse with both hands like a desperate man. "I took you for a black and neutrals kind of girl."

"Black and neutrals is for work, Hawkins," she said, taking off the hat and walking off to put it away.

He didn't want her to lose the smile on her face. So he said, "You're looking for pink? You should've said so earlier."

He walked toward her, held her hand, and led her to a shelf a couple of rows over, where a wooden sign read EVERYTHING PINK in his mom's curly handwriting.

"Now we're talking!" she exclaimed.

He felt like he'd hit the jackpot. Finally. There was that smile he hadn't seen in ten years, which still took his breath away. The girl she'd tried so hard to bury when she was around him, his Nani.

His Nani, unceremoniously trying to grab a heavy bin she couldn't reach.

"Let me take that for you," he said.

She moved out of the way, and he lifted the big box that wasn't really that heavy and placed it on a small table by the windowless wall. He imagined his mom doing this over and over with brides through so many years. But surprisingly, this time, the grief wasn't choking or crippling. It was like this bittersweet glow in his heart. Light with just a cast of shadows to show off its beauty.

"Ready?" he asked, hoping that inside, she'd find what she'd been looking for.

She opened the box and gasped. An explosion of pink, light gold ribbons, and iridescent glitter popped out.

"Look at that!" he exclaimed.

She bit her lip, and when she looked at him, her eyes were sparkly with joy.

"This is perfect," she said, taking out one of the vases with a string of pearls and lace. Everything in this box was so unlike the Nadia everyone saw. So much like the Nani he had loved.

"Feathers, pearls, lace . . . you were born in the wrong century!" he said. "Lucky for you, it is the Roaring Twenties again."

"Thank you," she said, and then the cloud of a doubt showed on her face. "You're sure it's a fair trade for my decorations? Will I have to pay extra?"

The decorations that she had exchanged had been beautiful, but kind of generic. Carefully braided twine and dry flowers around delicate glass orbs with pictures of what looked like the happy couple Nadia and Brandon had been. Pretended to be. Who would have thought that on the other side of those smiles was so much hurt and betrayal?

Marcos was sure Kenzie would have no problem placing those decorations elsewhere.

He waved a hand in front of him as if shooing a fly. "Don't even think about that. All this pink stuff has been here for who knows how long?"

"I know . . ." she said, doubt in her voice. "It looks pretty ancient, but I know that with Isabella and my mom's help, we can spruce it up."

"They all approve of this then?" he asked.

She shrugged. "My mom really hasn't said anything about the party yet. She's still hung up on the breakup. She's heart-broken. She loves Brandon." She paused, and then she added, "Sometimes I think she loves him more than I ever did, in a non-creepy way—oh my gosh, don't look like that!" She tried to laugh, but sounded so sad, like she meant that her mom loved Brandon more than she did Nadia. "She always wanted two sons. You know? She loves sports, and growing up in Argentina, she didn't really have a chance to play at all. But she just had Isabella and me. Now she has Noah, my nephew, and my brother-in-law, Jason. She's going to miss Brandon, that's all."

"And your dad?" Marcos asked, his heart about beating out of his mouth with wanting to go to Nadia's family and ask them what was wrong with them.

But then she said, "My dad never liked him. Which doesn't really mean he's one hundred percent in on the treintañera train, either."

"Will they come around, you think?" he asked, leaning against the wall.

"They have to. At least outwardly." A mischievous look flashed in her face now.

"Why?"

"My grandparents are arriving tomorrow, and after them, it's the whole family."

He felt a pang of jealousy. His grandparents in Uruguay were long gone. After his mother's death, his contact with the extended family had kind of died. Even with his cousin Alexander.

"You're all very close?"

"At least for show, we are," she said. "Which is good enough for me. After the party, I know I'll get to see way more of my abuelos and aunts and cousins. I'm actually thrilled about that, because I would've been on our honeymoon. Now I get to stay and enjoy the family."

"You mean, you'd rather be with all of them than in a fancy place, with your new husband, spending all your time together having the adult kind of fun you have been dreaming about all your life?"

That was a nod to their past.

And by the downcast look that came upon her, he knew he shouldn't have brought this up.

One night, after a particularly affectionate moment that made him smile every time he thought about it (and there had been many times he'd gone back to that happy and catastrophic moment in the years since), he'd said his parents planned and organized and hosted weddings, and one thing had led to the other, and he'd asked her about her dream honeymoon. By the way her eyes had widened, he knew the question had awakened possibilities in her mind that he hadn't intended. She must have thought he was asking for future reference. He'd just been curious. He'd been twenty-one, and a wedding was as far from his mind as a trip to Mars.

But it hadn't been the same for her.

She'd wanted to be like most of her friends and get married young. And she had told him that for a honeymoon, she'd love to go to a special place neither one had ever been to and make new memories that would last for all eternity.

After that night, there had been a weird wedge between them. The wedge turned into a gap, and then a chasm he wasn't ready, or able, to jump or bridge, and eventually, he'd run in the opposite direction.

"Where were you heading?" he asked, like always, looking away from the feelings he wasn't ready to face now—or ever.

She shrugged. "Disneyland. Can you believe it?"

"Disneyland?" He scoffed. "Doesn't his family own a travel agency, and his dad was a pilot? You could've gone anywhere in the world!"

She shrugged. "We'd never been there together, he said, so it qualified. By the time we settled for it, I was so tired of fighting."

"And where would *you* have gone?"

Her eyes sparkled again, as if a part of her that had been asleep up until he'd asked arose from the ashes. "You're going to laugh . . ."

He placed a hand over his heart. "Never. I promise."

She bit her lip, her eyes flickering over his face as if to catch him the moment he broke the promise so easily given.

"I always wanted to go to—" She mumbled something he didn't catch.

"Where?"

She took a deep breath and looked him square in the face. He braced himself for her confession.

"Argentina," she said. "I always wanted to go there."

He narrowed his eyes. "But you were born there. Didn't you move here when you were like ten?"

"Twelve, actually," she said, turning away from him, her ponytail slapping him like a whip. "Other than Rosario, I've never been anywhere else in my own country. I want to go to the Iguazú Falls, to Patagonia, to the Andes . . . I don't know," she said, a little out of breath, as if the mere thought of getting to know the place of her birth left her gasping for more. Then she turned toward him, and the soft look on her face stirred a feeling inside him he'd never experienced before.

He felt so . . . seen.

He, too, wanted to go to Uruguay, to see if maybe he'd find the pieces of him and his family he felt were missing.

That good-for-nothing Brandon.

If Marcos had been in his position, he'd have taken her to the end of the galaxy, if that had been her wish.

"But did he know where you wanted to go?" he asked.

She pressed her lips and nodded quickly. "I thought he'd surprise me with a trip to Santorini, in Greece, you know? I could've gone with Madi and Stevie, my friends, but I would've been delighted if he even thought of that. I had no problem paying half, even. When he first said he'd booked us a room in Disneyland, I thought it was a joke. I even thought he'd take us to Argentina, after all. I made sure my passport was ready to go. And then . . . oh well."

"At least he didn't ruin your experience of Santorini or Argentina forever."

"That's a silver lining I hadn't considered. Thank you for that." She winked at him, and he had to swallow the thick knot in his throat.

He didn't know what to say.

Suddenly, he realized how hot it was up here in the storage. Sweat beaded on her hairline, making tiny curls come to life. His hands prickled, and a desire to breach the two-step distance between them took hold of him.

She was still biting her lip, her chest rising and falling fast.

What would she do if he stepped toward her and smoothed that little curl on her temple with a brush of his thumb? He knew he wouldn't stop there, and he really couldn't afford to throw a wrench into his already complicated life. Or hers.

She didn't deserve it.

As if to argue with his thoughts, she took a step in his direction, her lips parted, her eyes like they were daring him to take her around the world right now. But what if he made a move, and she rejected him? For all he knew, he was the only one of the two whose body wanted to pick things up from where they left them ten years ago.

"Should we take those to your car?" he said, breaking the spell.

She exhaled, her shoulders dropping, but not like she was disappointed. More like she was relieved.

"Sure," she said.

They headed down. As in a team, she switched the lights off behind them and then locked the door at the top of the stairs that led to the hallway.

He carried the box of decorations to her car.

"Thank you," she said. "I'm sure we'll have plenty for the tables and more."

"If you and your friends or your sister want to take another look, just stop by anytime. I know Kenzie guards this like a dragon's treasure, but I'll let her know it's okay if you stop by."

"Gracias," she said, with a little complicit smile. And then her look changed, as if she needed to tell him something and didn't know how.

The roar in his ears when she said a simple thank-you couldn't drown the voices telling him that he'd been a fool.

"You look like you want to ask me something," he said.

The fairy lights danced around them now that the sky was inky black.

She chuckled and ducked her head. "Am I that obvious?"

His heart was hammering so hard in his chest that he couldn't catch his breath.

"Tell me," he whispered, lifting her chin with his index finger.

She took a deep breath and, rolling her eyes, finally said, "It's just that . . . I need pictures, you see? And the photographer canceled on me when she found out the wedding was called off. Do you know of a photographer that can take a job with such little notice?"

Did he ever.

There was a high-pitched roar in his ears as she kept talking. How many times had he wanted to photograph her and never had the courage to do so those months they'd been together? He'd regretted it over and over, and now this.

She must have mistaken the swirling feelings competing in his heart for reluctance, because she waved a hand between them. "Actually, never mind. You must be so busy with the business, but if you have a contact, I'd really appreciate it. I called everyone in the area, but I couldn't find a single photographer, can you believe it?"

He couldn't. Couldn't believe his luck.

"I can take them," he said.

She must have not expected this offer; that much was clear from the way her eyes widened in alarm. Or was it surprise?

"I mean," he hurried to add, "I, sometimes, shoot at destination weddings and such. I haven't done it in a while, but some of my pieces have been in popular wedding publications. I've never done a quinceañera, much less a treintañera, but if you want . . ."

"I'll pay you," she said.

Payment was the last thing in his mind. But this was important for her. He wanted Nadia to have the best images to remember the night she reclaimed herself.

"I'll go over the calendar and send you a few tentative dates?" he asked.

"I'd love that. Thanks," she said. "Thinking every detail for the party would be crossed, I scheduled family activities down to the minute, and now . . ."

For a second, she stood in front of him in silence. Her arms crossed tightly around her body.

His heart and his body were screaming for him to kiss her, once and for all. But he wouldn't make a mess of her life again. She sounded too stressed already.

"I better go," she said, getting into her car. "My family arrives tomorrow, and . . . anyway. Good night."

"Good night and good luck." He held the door of the car open for a second, but then he moved out of the way and closed it before he did something stupid. And she drove away.

Chapter 11

Nadia

In Nadia's defense, she didn't sleep a wink all night. Besides, the Salt Lake City airport had been remodeled, and she didn't recognize anything around her as she drove in circles, missing the freeway exit time and again. The renovations had been finished for a few years, but Nadia had been nowhere close to flying anywhere that whole time. She'd been busy with school and then work to take even a weekend off to go to Vegas or even St. George.

Lost in the maze of the highways, confused by the voices of three devices giving her GPS directions, and flustered under her mother's watchful eye, Nadia once again took the wrong exit or entry or whatever.

In the passenger seat, her mom remained silent, clutching her giant floral purse. But when the devices all said in unison, "Recalculating," she let out a sigh that contained almost thirty years of frustration.

"There's your sister," her mom said, pointing at the white van heading in the right direction.

Isabella and her family, along with Nadia's dad, had left

twenty minutes behind them. But of course, her perfect older sister never got lost.

"We'll be okay, Mami," Nadia said, trying to sound soothing. "You'll see. I'll drop you off on the curb, and then I'll get a parking spot."

Her mom sighed again. "I hope I find your father on time. I don't want the family to arrive and see us arriving in different cars."

Nadia wanted to kick herself. Why hadn't she insisted her mom drive in the minivan with her sister? Instead, she had her mother in the passenger seat, and her dad, holding Tinkerbell the Yorkie, was in the back seat of Isabella's van, acting like a petulant child.

They'd decided Nadia's car was too casual and non-elegant to receive the older members of the family. There were weeks to go before the party, and like she'd told Marcos the night before, they were scheduled down to the minute with activities. There were so many details she still needed to figure out.

She went over them in her mind one more time:

Dress.

Cake.

Music.

Photos.

This morning, she'd been tempted to text Marcos that she'd found someone else to take the photos. But the idea of calling more people, who would either say no or ask for her (still not even dreamed of) first child as payment, exhausted her. At least she could cross one item off her list, even if Rocket would be the one on the other side of the camera.

Her hand prickled with equal parts excitement and embarrassment for the previous nights, and she dried them on her jeans. She could've done with a nap, but a nap wasn't in the schedule, at least until after the party.

In an attempt to get some breathing room, Nadia had suggested her family spread out their activities over the whole month they'd be in Utah. Since she wouldn't be leaving on a honeymoon now, she could spend time with the family after the party. She hadn't mentioned the little detail that she didn't have a job anymore. But her mom had insisted they keep the itinerary. The arrangements for pedicures and family outings to restaurants and excursions had been done with months of anticipation to ensure availability and good prices. Her mom didn't have the bandwidth to go over the process again, even if secretly, everyone wanted to just chill.

No wonder every time the family gathered, it was the most stressful time of their lives. Each time they were together, it was as if they had to make up for the months and years they hadn't seen each other.

But knowing her mom, and how she was on the verge of an emotional explosion, Nadia kept her mouth shut instead of complaining. Her mom's stress was pulsating in toxic, quiet waves. She always got so nervous when the family arrived. It had been the same ever since Nadia was little.

The house had been scrubbed from ceiling to basement. Even the crawlspaces had been scoured, because what if Bisabuela Hortensia wanted to inspect?

Never mind that Bisa was in her nineties and unlikely to be climbing anything or crouching anywhere, but Nadia didn't want to be the reason her mom had a disgusto. It was enough that the wedding had been canceled.

Just thinking about the way they'd break the news was giving her hives. She'd slathered lotion on her skin, but there was an angry patch of eczema on her hand that wouldn't be soothed with anything.

Maybe she should've hydrated more. Internally.

It was one in the afternoon, and Nadia hadn't even been able to drink a sip of water.

If only she had the excuse of her job to keep her away from the airport! But if her parents got wind of her resignation, and the fact that she didn't have a job lined up, then they'd freak. One drama was enough to last her a lifetime.

Not for the first time, she regretted her life choices and wondered why she hadn't decided to become a cloistered nun. But then her mom would've complained that she preferred God to the family. The family came second to nothing, not even deity or divinity.

A giant plane flew overhead, and her mom said, "Ay! I hope that's not them."

"Mami," she said, trying to sound pleasant. "They haven't even landed yet." She took the right turn this time. "The app will tell us when they do, and where to wait for their suitcases and everything else."

Her mom's phone rang—the ringtone was a Bad Bunny song, and if her mom would stop and listen to the lyrics for a second, she'd have the whole family bleach their ears and brains. But since Noah and Olivia liked it . . .

"See? It's your father," her mom said, exasperated, and then she replied more politely, "¿Bueno?"

Her dad's voice blared in the speaker. "It's a circus in here. Where are you, gorda?"

Her mom hated that her dad called her gorda. He said it was an endearment, but her mom always took it literally and would stop eating for days, only to succumb to her hunger and binge on carbs.

"Your daughter took the wrong turn, Ernestito. We got lost, but she's dropping me off right now."

Her dad was the one that sighed now. "We should've driven our car."

Tinkerbell barked in the background.

He hated not being in control, but he got too nervous driving into the airport, and ever since Isabella had gotten her license, the sisters had been the ones in charge of heading to the airport for family pickup.

"I hope Jason remembers he has to pick up your cousins in the evening," her mom said.

Because the parents had insisted the whole family come to the airport to receive los abuelos, they were doing multiple runs to Salt Lake from American Fork. Apparently, they thought the cousins wouldn't know about Uber or taxis. But to their parents, sending the family in a taxi was the same kind of sin and crime as leaving them stranded in the desert. It would be an unforgivable offense.

Of course, they couldn't wait in Salt Lake all those hours, which they had done in the past, but now not only Isabella's kids had protested. Nadia had also reminded them that los abuelitos weren't as young as they used to be, and with new airport security, they couldn't just wait forever.

Nadia parked by the curb and said, "Tell Papi to meet you by luggage claim. Isabella will be there. Look for Olivia. She has the signs. I'll go park and be right back."

Huffing and puffing to show her discontent, her mom got out of the car, and Nadia headed to the parking lot.

She should've canceled everything.

She felt so bad that she had put her family in this situation. Maybe she should've told her abuelas about the wedding cancellation to better manage expectations. But she'd been so distraught, she hadn't wanted to ruffle her mom's feathers. Her parents were in their fifties, not elderly or ancient by any means. Sometimes they got frustrated that she treated them like old folks and fussed around them, and other times, they complained that she didn't really take care of them.

She just went along, following her sister's example. It was better to err on the side of caution.

It took her forever to find a parking spot, and she had to leave her car on the top floor of the parking garage. She left it next to a van that looked like her sister's. She headed back to the terminal. Her phone had no signal, so she had no idea if her family was texting her or if the airplane bringing the family had arrived.

She was glad that for once, she'd forgone fashion and worn comfortable sneakers that allowed her to run if she needed to.

The airport was crowded to the max. She had never seen it this way!

Suddenly, she remembered it was a Wednesday. The day that a lot of Mormon missionaries left for their assignments, and when a lot of them came back to the place where the church was based. She had never been a Latter-day Saint, but a lot of her friends growing up had been. It was like the Catholic Church in Latin America. Like in every religion, there was a little of everything, good and bad. There were the hardcore members, who lived and breathed for the church. There were the casual ones, who only attended special occasions. And then the ones who hadn't stepped into a church for years.

Brandon was part of this last group. His parents and sisters were very active in the church and lamented the fact that Nadia wasn't even a member. She had tried to see what it was all about and even had discussions with the sister missionaries, but her mom had put el grito en el cielo.

No daughter of hers would leave the family faith, not if she was just trying to fit in, and now, looking back, Nadia was glad she hadn't actually done it. She had already changed herself enough for the sake of "love." And because she loved herself, she better find her family in this chaos. If los abuelitos and the rest had to wait in the middle of this crowd and got lost because of her, then she would never forgive herself. She knew her mother never would.

Running without a plan wouldn't help anyone, so Nadia made herself stop and look for the international arrivals monitor.

She found the one that showed the flight coming from Orlando had landed but didn't mention when. She panicked.

Purposefully, she made her way through the balloons and

banners and crying babies. By the third Starbucks sign, she saw Olivia, her niece. She was like a replica of her mom, Isabella. They were identical, even to the little dimple next to the corner of their mouths

"Olivia!" she called, and three other girls looked in her direction.

Even in that, her sister had chosen well. At least Olivia wouldn't suffer because of her name, like Nadia had growing up.

She headed toward her niece, as all the while, a voice in the back of her head told her to make a run for it. To book herself a trip to the Maldives and come back in a few months, when all her savings had run out.

But although the idea was so attractive, so many things held her back. And they weren't all bad.

She wasn't like Brandon, who must be on a beach somewhere. Free from everything. But then Nadia imagined her friend Madi reminding him about karma, that in a few years, Brandon would be all alone. It was one thing to be thirty and independent. It would be quite another when he was pointed at as the creepy uncle who thought he was cool and funny, but no one could stand.

"Tía!" She heard Olivia's call above the cacophony around her until a small hand clutched hers.

"Finally!" Olivia said.

"This is a disaster!" Nadia exclaimed, laughing. "How are we going to find everyone?"

"Abuela and Abuelo are right by the luggage carousel. Except for Mami. She was planted next to the escalator, or as close as she can get with all these missionary homecomings."

"I wish I'd booked their tickets for another day or time."

They looked around until they saw Nadia's mom and dad, their expressions stunned. "What is happening today? This is bedlam!" her mom said, while her dad tried to pacify Tinkerbell.

They huddled next to the Starbucks, and then Nadia said, "I'm going to go check for Isabella."

She left before her mom called her back. She sent Olivia a smile of apology. Nadia's mom adored her granddaughter. As strict as she had been with the girls, she'd been permissive and adoring to her Olivia. But Nadia didn't want to listen to the barking Yorkie or her parents bickering over how many people were at the airport or the fear that someone would recognize them and ask about the wedding.

"No sign of them yet?" Nadia asked.

"There they are!" said Isabella pointing ahead.

Nadia turned to see her family coming down the escalator.

Emotion overtook her.

She felt like when she'd been twelve years old, welcoming her grandparents to Utah for the first visit to her family's new home. She saw that Isabella was full of emotion, too. Her eyes were brimming with tears at the sight of Abuela Catalina.

Abuela was tiny but had a big personality. A little like Tinkerbell, whose barks Nadia could hear through the multitude and the clamor of voices.

Abuelo Leonardo stood before her like a bodyguard. Tall and handsome with his gray beret, although it was hot outside. They looked like movie stars, in their best clothes and bifocals that got dark with the bright sunlight coming through the airport windows.

"Abuela!" Isabella yelled.

Their grandma saw them and waved furiously.

Her family was here!

But . . . her grandma looked so much smaller than she remembered. And although her hair was darker than ink, and her lips carefully delineated and painted in red, Abuela Cata looked fragile, like a small doll that was crumpling under the harsh brightness of the sun. Bisabuela Hortensia clutched to her arm, looking ahead as if she knew exactly where she was going.

Nadia ran the distance to the escalator, and they all fell into each other's arms, hugging tightly. Nadia let out the sob that had been kind of choking her.

"You're here!" she said.

Abuelo tried to shield them from the crowd coming down the escalator, but then he said, "Let's move out of the way, chicas."

They headed to the foot of an artificial palm tree, and Nadia turned to hug the rest of the family that had been following the abuelos.

Tío Román and Tía Aimée and their teenage kids were so grown, Nadia hadn't recognized them. Tía and Mom talked on FaceTime or Messages every Sunday, and she had seen the kids in the background or the pictures her aunt shared online. But she was shocked at how much older they looked in person. Thiago and Mercedes were eighteen and seventeen. Last time she'd seen them, ten years ago, they'd been all big brown eyes and easy smiles. Nadia hoped they'd all get along.

She was glad to see them hugging Olivia and kissing her on the cheek. Best friends already. But when Thiago tried to kiss Noah, Nadia's nephew put up his hands and walked back, saying, "Whoa, whoa. Chill, bro. A handshake is okay."

Isabella and Olivia blushed to the roots of their hair, but Thiago and Mercedes didn't seem offended.

"This is incredible," Tía Aimée said, looking around with eager eyes.

Until she saw Nadia's mom, her sister, and she ran. The two sisters hugged each other, crying and laughing, oblivious to the people around them.

Nadia loved this for her mom. To finally have her family together. She just wished she didn't have to give them the bad news of her broken engagement. Not all of them would react the same way.

"Let's get out of here," Isabella said, leading them all to the luggage carousels.

Jason was already there. He had turned his NY hat backward and rolled up his sleeves for the task ahead. His gold chains glinted under his T-shirt and contrasted against his copper skin, tanned after spending all summer at a baseball pitch or another.

"Welcome, everyone," he said. "We're missing one piece, but I think the rest is here!"

He pointed to several carts stacked with at least twenty suitcases bursting at the seams.

"How did you know what to get?" Bisa asked, astounded.

Jason shrugged modestly, but then he pointed at Isabella with a motion of his chin and said, "It was all her, Bisa. She asked everyone to send her a picture of their luggage and asked them to tie blue and yellow ribbons to the handles, so they were all easy to find."

"¿Qué dijo?" Bisa asked in a whisper that carried through the clamor inside the airport.

Nadia's mom leaned over to translate for her. Jason had spoken in Spanish, but Bisa had a hard time understanding his Puerto Rican accent.

Tía Aimée sent Isabella a congratulatory look. "Well done, Isa. Well done."

Isabella beamed at her husband, and still glowing, led the family to the parking lot.

Nadia was driving her mom, Abuela, Abuelo, and Bisa. Tía and her family were going with Isabella, along with the luggage. Nadia's dad was traveling back with Jason and Noah.

A few minutes into the drive, when Nadia's heart rate was finally settling down after all the chaos at the airport, Abuela pointed at the mountains. In the province of Santa Fe where they lived, it was all llanura, endless plains. Although Abuela had seen mountains before, the surprise of seeing them there, just like that, never wore off.

"No snow yet?" she asked.

Nadia shuddered, even just thinking of the cold months ahead. "No! It's too early in the season, although in September, you never know. It can be scorching hot one day, and the next, we can get a surprise flurry storm in the mountains."

A surge of warm pride flooded her when she realized how well the Spanish rolled off her tongue, although she hardly spoke it anymore.

"And where's the novio of yours?" Abuelo Leonardo asked, going straight to the point.

"In English, it's fiancé, Leo," Abuela said. "Remember, Jason explained novio is just an enamorado?"

"It can also be the groom," he argued back. Then he turned to Nadia and insisted, "So where is your novio, Nadita?"

She knew the moment of truth was coming. She'd planned different ways to phrase the explanation, and still, the words choked in her throat and heat rose to her face. She glanced in the rearview mirror at her mom.

Virginia's face was red like a beet, as well, and a little suspicion grew inside Nadia's heart. "You told Abuela?" she said in English, knowing she was breaking all etiquette, but she couldn't think in Spanish.

Her mom stuck out her chin and shimmied her shoulders. "Unlike other people, I don't keep secrets from my mother." The words, more than the fact that she was speaking in slow but still-perfect English, stopped Nadia from even gasping in surprise. "Maybe that's why you don't underst—"

"Now, now, girls," Abuela Catalina said in a soothing voice in Spanish. She had placed a hand over Nadia's shoulder and another on her daughter's shin. Four generations of women from the same family in the same car. "Don't argue. I might not speak English, but I feel the tension. Don't you, Mamá?" she said, turning toward Bisa. But Bisa was still mesmerized by the mountains in the distance. She was turning one hundred years old in October, but she had the sharp gaze of someone half her age, as if she couldn't get enough of this world she'd lived in for one hundred years but still didn't really know much about.

"We're not fighting," Nadia and Virginia said at once, both sounding appalled and embarrassed.

"No need to lie, either," Abuela Catalina said. "Now, Nadi, yes, your mami told me about the fight with Brando."

"Brandon," Bisa cut in without tearing her eyes from the car window. "His name is Brandon, Catalina! Ten years hearing about this gringo! The least you could do is get his name right, don't you think, hija?"

The silence that followed was among Nadia's most surreal times of her life. She didn't want to make eye contact with her mom, because she felt a bubble of laughter rise inside her. As with tears, she knew the moment she started laughing, she would lose it. And she was driving.

Four generations of women from the same family find sad end when one of them, the driver, gets unhinged due to years of emotional suppression.

No.

That wasn't the kind of headline she wanted to add to her collection of media appearances. If anything, she'd have preferred it had something to do with:

Local woman finally takes control of her life and kicks out her fiancé for being a cheater.

Or better yet:

Local woman finds the spine that she had lost in early puberty.

She needed to chomp on some gum. She needed a drink to douse the fire that was consuming her.

In her mind, she went over the contents of her glove compartment, but she knew there wasn't even a whiff of mint from a piece of gum, not even a chewed-up one. She'd given it up last year after a severe case of gastritis.

She glanced down her door and saw the top of a can peeking out. The soda mate thing that Rocket—Marcos—the hot Uruguayan boy of her dreams—had given her at the gas station. She had not intended to confess she was drinking this Americanized version of mate, but if she didn't give her body something liquid, she would die. In a swift movement particular to those spending too much time in the car commuting for work, she uncapped the can and took a long swig. It was warmish, because outside, the day was about one hundred degrees. And maybe it was the carbonation, or the caffeine, but after she took a swallow, she was seeing constellations.

"What are you drinking, mamita?" Abuela Catalina asked.

Her mom shot her a look that was a plea for equal parts silence and curiosity.

Nadia took another swig and passed the can to her grandmother. "Mate. It's like a soda."

The exclamations that followed drowned any talk of Brandon. Abuela Catalina and Nadia's mom, Virginia, argued about the crime it was to put mate inside a soda can.

"With cinnamon?" Virginia asked, grabbing the can out of Nadia's hand and inspecting the label.

"And passion fruit?" Abuela added, grabbing the can from her daughter. Then she switched to Spanish and said, "Look, Mami," shoving the can in front of Bisa's face. "What do you think of this capital offense? I knew when these kids stopped visiting in Argentina that all the family customs were falling by the wayside."

Nadia kept her eyes fixed on the freeway ahead, trying not to smile about having caused mayhem over a simple drink.

"How can you share with people if everyone has their own little can? It defeats the purpose of mate," Abuela said.

She had a point. Maybe that's why Nadia had been so reticent when Rocket had introduced her to it; something in her DNA had recoiled from this sacrilege. Unable to resist her curiosity anymore, Nadia looked at the back seat through the rearview mirror.

Bisabuela Hortencia had turned her body to look at Nadia for the first time, and she had the most complicit little smile on her face.

"Well?" Abuela Catalina insisted.

"Give me that here, Mami," Virginia said from the passenger seat.

But before Abuela could do as Nadia's mom requested, Bisa grabbed the can from her hand, looked at it, and said, "Sexy can."

The words sucked up the air in the car.

She then took a long swig, tipping her head back. To the other women's anticipation, these women who'd been born of her, she smacked her lips and took another sip.

"So?" asked Nadia. "What's the verdict?"

"I like it," Bisa said.

Nadia laughed, and soon, her mom and Abuela Catalina followed. And before they arrived to Nadia's childhood home, both Abuela Catalina and her mom had tried the mate soda, too, and declared that it wasn't that bad after all.

"Sexy can," Nadia repeated under her breath as she helped her dad bring the luggage out of the van's trunk.

"What are you whispering to yourself?" Isabella asked, briefly pausing to act like a general directing the masses. "Are you practicing how to tell the family?"

Nadia was surprised and did a double take. "You mean you drove with Tío Román and Tía Aimée and didn't say a thing? Not even one of the kids spilt the news? Not even Papá?"

Isabella shook her head. "We talked about everything but. They didn't mention anything, and of course, I didn't either."

Nadia wasn't so sure. Silence didn't mean a thing. She knew from experience that the fact that no one talked about a problem didn't mean they weren't all aware of what was happening.

"Well, Mami told Abuela Cata," Nadia said with a shrug.

"Of course," Isabella said. "I'll never forget how she told Abuela I was pregnant before I could even tell Jason."

Yep. That was her mom, all right.

"Do you think I should do it now, before Mami shares her version of things?" she asked Isabella.

Her sister sighed as she considered. She scratched her chin

where she was breaking out and said, "You should definitely tell los abuelitos and Tío Román's family. The tension of keeping this secret is bordering on toxic."

"And go over the whole spiel tonight again, when the rest arrive?" Nadia could hardly breathe from the anxiety of going through the seven rings of hell of coming clean to the family.

Isabella placed a hand on her shoulder. "I'll support you no matter what. But you'll see, after saying it once, saying it again won't be that hard."

"Easy for you to say," Nadia said, pulling up the handle of one of the carry-on pieces.

"Tonight, when we pick up Tío Ricardo and his family, and Dolores, Jason and I will ease them into the change of plans."

A huge weight fell of Nadia's shoulder. She'd never felt so grateful to her sister as in this moment. "Thank you, Isa. I owe you big-time."

Tío Ricardo and his husband, Tío Francisco, and their twin girls didn't worry Nadia. They were easygoing and understanding. But she'd been nervous telling her cousin Dolores, who now went by Lola, a book editor in Barcelona. Nadia had always looked up to her. Honestly? She was low-key starstruck by her own cousin, who'd edited an award-winning novel. Lola's brothers, Agustín and Pedro—a basketball player in a B team and a model, respectively—wouldn't make it until right before the wedding, er, party. By then, hopefully, their sister would have broken the news, and they could decide if they still wanted to come or not.

"I can pick up Gianna and Marcella tomorrow and tell them in the car," Nadia said.

Isabella pouted. "Aw, I wanted to pick them up!"

"We can both go?" Nadia whispered with the last bit of air remaining in her lungs.

Gianna was everyone's favorite family member, after Bisa, that is. She had moved with her mom to Australia when she was ten. Her dad, Tío Lorenzo, had died the year before, and after that, she hadn't had a lot of contact with the family. Nadia's mom had sent her a wedding invitation just out of courtesy, and everyone had been surprised when she'd replied that yes, she and her plus one, her girlfriend, Marcella, would be attending. She then proceeded to make a family WhatsApp group. Every morning, Nadia woke up to three hundred notifications, mostly memes and laughing emojis.

The thought that all these people had put their lives on pause for her, and she still hadn't come clean to them, paralyzed Nadia.

For an irrational instant, she considered driving to Brandon's parents' house and asking to see him. Maybe they could still fix this? Maybe they could just get married and then call for an annulment?

"I can't tell them," she said, her mind reeling. "There has to be another way to fix this."

She needed to talk to Brandon. She'd pay him anything, the last of her savings, so he'd go along with her plan. She took her phone out of her pocket and stared at it.

"Hey, don't even think about it," Isabella said in such a sweet voice, grabbing the phone from her hand.

"Think about what?" Nadia said, and when she looked up at her sister, she felt a pang in her chest. There were tiny wrinkles fanning from her eyes that Nadia had never noticed before. But her eyes were so soft and understanding.

"You're thinking about calling Brandon, aren't you?"

Nadia swallowed the swear words that had crowded her mouth. "How do y—"

"I know you as if you were my daughter," she said. "Actually, I think I know *you* better than I know my own daughter. Who knows what is going on in Olivia's head? But you? I see your thoughts as if they were my own. It's his loss. You did nothing wrong."

Nadia grabbed Bisa's quilted duffel bag and almost dropped it.

"What's in here?" she asked, carefully lowering it to the ground.

"You know Bisa," Isabella said with a chuckle. "Most likely, it's cans of Campbell's soup in case she doesn't like the ones they sell here."

Nadia picked up the bag again with her left hand. Without the ring to bite into her finger, she realized she could use her left hand more than she had in the past without torturing herself.

"Wouldn't it be easier if—" She took a big breath to confess that she had been the one to break up the engagement. With good reason, but still.

"If you forgave him? If you begged him to come back?" Isabella asked, and she took the bag from Nadia's hand. "No, love. Keep going like this, because you're doing great. I'll tell everyone now, if that's what you want."

"Chicas," Abuela Catalina called them from the door. "We're eating lunch. Come on in!"

Nadia and Isabella stood side by side for a second. And then Isabella said, "Let's go face the lions, sis."

And they walked into the house to the whole family sitting down, as if they had been waiting for them.

"So?" Abuela Catalina said in Spanish, sitting at the head of the table like the matriarch that she was. "When are you going to tell the rest of the family all the truth, Nadita?"

Nadia made an effort not to roll her eyes.

She hated that nickname. She knew her grandma loved her, but that nickname was the beginning of one of Nadia's worst mental spirals ever.

Nadita sounded like little nada, a little nothing. And that's how she felt many times, comparing her achievements to her sister's, and her cousins', and honestly, everyone else's in the world.

Her parents sat side by side at the kitchen island, their hands clasped.

"What truth?" Noah, her thirteen-year-old nephew, blurted out, and then he said, "Ouch, Olivia, what did you elbow me for? It was a simple question."

Olivia muttered something, and Noah repeated, "Ouch."

"Olivia"—Isabella's voice cut through the thick tension in the kitchen—"go up to your room right now. Leave your brother alone once and for all."

"My room?" she asked, and the sound of her voice reminded Nadia so much of Isabella's at that age that she felt like time had moved back. "This is Yaya's house—"

"Whatever," Isabella's voice boomed.

"Isa," Nadia said softly.

Her sister was only taking out her frustration and stress on her daughter. But it wasn't a good look on her, or Olivia, or anyone else.

Isabella, of course, didn't take it well. "Please, Nadia, don't interfere. You have no idea what's it's like to be a moth—" She interrupted herself just in time, but the damage was already done.

Nadia's eyes prickled, but she wasn't going to cry in front of everyone.

"I said go to the spare room upstairs until you can behave, Olivia," Isabella said, and this time, even her husband's face was tomato red.

Olivia looked at her father for help, but he knew better than anyone not to contradict Isabella in front of the family.

Noah felt bad, judging by the dismayed look on his face, but even he, too, was helpless when Isabella got like this.

Olivia went upstairs as quietly as possible, and Nadia felt even worse that her niece had been humiliated because of her. So many things were going wrong because of her. If she'd put up with Brandon and not exploded at him, then they could all be celebrating now instead of arguing.

"Listen," she said.

"I don't understand anything," Bisa muttered, but she was

looking at the window, and Nadia didn't know if her great-grandma was talking about the situation or something else.

And then Abuela Catalina said, "I'll translate, Mami."

Nadia's mom sent her a look like it was her fault that when she was emotional, she could only think in English.

Nadia wanted to get it over with.

"I'm sorry. I'm going to speak in English," she said, gazing at everyone who was staring at her.

"The kids can practice their English. It's better this way," Tía Aimée said to Tío Román, as if he had protested. Thiago was asleep on the sofa in the adjacent family room, and Mercedes had a look of resignation that Nadia recognized only too well. She made a mental note to make it up to her younger cousin.

"I can't think in Spanish when I'm nervous, and before I lose my nerve, let me explain," she said.

"Are you pregnant?" Tía Aimée asked, and then she added, "Why did you kick me, Meche? It was just a question."

Nadia wanted to run out of this crazy house, but she'd only have to come back and try it again later. So it was now or never.

"There isn't going to be a wedding after all."

The words echoed and bounced against the walls of the house and against the walls of Nadia's heart and mind. Realization sank in, and everything that went along with breaking up with Brandon. More than a decade of her life, gone in flames. Gone in a cloud of fart! Leaving a bad smell and taste, and a whole lot of wringing hands and knotted stomachs, and debt.

She was grieving like someone had died. Because someone really *had* died when she'd made her decision: the person she'd been for such a long time. She wasn't really sure who she wanted to be from now on.

Maybe she didn't have to figure it out in front of the family, who were tired after a grueling trip. Maybe not even before the celebration of her birthday. But she wanted to be who she was without Brandon by her side.

Would this be too hard for her family to understand?

"—should've stayed in Miami, I tell you, Leo," Abuela Catalina was telling Abuelo. Nadia was dissociating, so she really couldn't process what she was really feeling right this second.

"Is he dead?" Tío Román asked. "Because the only way a man wouldn't want to marry someone as beautiful and accomplished as you is because he's either dead, like literally, or in his soul."

No one translated this, and Nadia didn't really need an interpretation to feel like she was being enveloped in a blanket of love. She came back to her body and realized she was shaking.

"Gracias, Tío Román," she said, and she was so proud she wasn't crying. "He's not dead. Actually, I don't really know if he's dead or not, because I have not seen him or even heard from him for more than a week."

"But you lived together," Abuela Catalina said, twisting the knife in Virginia's heart.

"We used to," Nadia said. "But there's no wedding."

A murmur like the rising waters of the river filled the kitchen.

But then Nadia's dad, Ernesto, stood up and said, "We wanted Nadia to tell you all. I know this is a big surprise, because like her, we've been waiting for this day for many years. But the reason we didn't say before you got here is because everything about your trips had been set and paid for. It would've been more expensive to change flights and hotels or cancel altogether. We wanted to see you, though, and Nadia's thirtieth birthday is coming up. It's actually the day after the wedding would've been. She can't get a refund on the venue or anything, but we're celebrating her thirtieth like a double quinceañera."

"A double quinces?" Mercedes asked in English. But her eyes were lit up with anticipation, which, when added to the sight of her dad speaking up for her, helped Nadia feel better about her life choices.

Ernesto took out a magazine from the kitchen drawer. He flipped the pages, and when he found the center spread, he showed it to his brother, who then passed it to Mercedes. The rest of the family gathered around her to look at the article and pictures. Nadia and Isabella made eye contact. Her parents must have bought another copy of the magazine. If that wasn't love, then what was it?

Noah was looking all over the family's faces as though he hadn't understood a word, even in English. "You mean this is why Uncle Brandon didn't come to my game on Saturday? He'd promised! You mean, like, Uncle Brandon—"

"He's not your uncle anymore," Olivia said from the top of the stairs.

And in the most incomprehensible development of all, Noah burst into tears and walked out of the house.

Jason looked at Isabella, who in turn looked at Nadia, and said, "See the unintended consequences?" And she ran behind her son.

Chapter 12

Marcos

With the Locke wedding behind him, now it was time for Marcos to dive completely into the Coronels' festivities coming up. Still, his mind was on Nadia and how she was doing. Her family was arriving from all over the world this week. How had they taken the news of her canceled wedding? He'd texted her a couple of dates that worked for a photo shoot for the updated invitations, but she had said her evenings (his preferred times to catch the golden hour) were filled to the brim with family commitments.

He stared at her contact on his phone, his finger hovering over the text box. But what right did he have to check up on her? It's not like they were friends. Besides, he didn't want to breach any professional boundaries. Once her party was over, he'd never see her again.

The thought was like an infected sliver in the tip of a finger.

He'd never had a problem moving on from a relationship, and it wasn't like his thing with Nadia was even new, but he'd never had any closure. Knowing he had no one to blame for this but himself didn't help him feel any better.

Just as he was about to send her a message anyway, he got a text from Hernán. Another update on baby Nina. When Marcos asked him how the baby was doing, he replied by sending a flood of pictures of not only the baby, but also of Lucy, Lily, and Luna.

Who would have thought that Hernán Rivera would become such a besotted father?

Marcos liked every single picture.

Rachel's mom is in town and the girls are with my sister. I got a couple of hours to myself. Wanna hang out?

It was like college all over again, like time hadn't gone by at all. Marcos glanced at his watch. He couldn't leave now. At least not for a while.

Someone has to work . . .

A second later, Hernán tapped back with a laughing emoji. He'd always had an infectious laugh, and Marcos could almost hear it in his mind. He chuckled as another text came through.

Call me when you're free, working man. But not now because Nina just fell asleep. She's the lightest sleeper.

Marcos was tempted to call, just to spite him. But he decided not to at the end. He still had mild PTSD from when he'd done this to his sister Sarah when Carly had just been born. Unlike what people said about him, Marcos learned *some* of the lessons life threw at him.

But he needed a soundboard. This time, he didn't even think before he called Bree, his ex-girlfriend. He needed the perspective of someone who hadn't known him as an irresponsible teenager to remind Marcos that he'd changed.

She answered after the first ring. "Hey, stranger. What's up?"

He regretted calling her the moment she answered. Bree was working hard at rebuilding her own life. It was unfair to ask her for help with his. But right as she answered the phone, he got a call from Kenzie. He felt like he was in the middle of a tug-of-war he didn't know how to get out of. He pressed IGNORE on his assistant's call.

Music sounded in the background from Bree's side.

"Hey, B," he said. "If this is a bad time, I can call you later."

"Regretting that you called me already?" she asked, laughing, and he laughed, too. Bree knew him too well.

Before he could make up an excuse, she said, "Actually, I'm at a job." He smiled in response to the smile her voice painted in his mind. "I had an audition for a hair product commercial."

"You did? I'm proud of you, Bree!" He was genuinely happy for her, and more when she replied, "Not only that, but I got the part. We've been filming all day. We're just wrapping up." She said something else, obviously to a person on her side of the world, and Marcos smiled, imagining her fulfilling her dreams.

Good for her.

"I'm happy for you, Bree. I really am," he said, and he didn't even have to fake it.

"I have no one to thank for this but you, because after you left, I mean, after we parted, I analyzed my life choices and realized I want to be an actress, damn it! I'm not going to stop until I get there. At least I'll do it with awesome hair along the way."

"I had nothing to do with this," he said. "It was all you for going after your dream."

There was a brief silence.

Before it tottered on the precipice of awkward, he asked, "So, what's new? Has it been all work and no fun?"

"Actually . . ."

He shouldn't have asked anything. But he couldn't leave her hanging like this.

"Actually what?"

She laughed nervously. "I've been seeing this person. This guy," she said. "I met him a few weeks ago, and he's really nice."

Marcos had been thinking about closure. This was the perfect ending to his chapter with Bree. He had to let her go now that she was finally flying.

"Really? I'm so glad for you, B. I really am."

She exhaled, like this had been the hardest confession of her life.

He was happy for her. But Marcos was only human, and he still felt a pang of . . . what? Lost chances? Regret?

No. Not regret.

It was envy.

He and Bree had been like roommates with benefits. There had been no magic between them. Not like with Nadia, then or now. It was impossible to deny that the last time he'd seen her, something inside him was pushing him to pick up where they'd left off. But there was like an invisible barrier that Nadia projected and he didn't dare cross. No matter how fast he ran or how strong his legs were, he could never turn back time and fix the past.

"And you?" she asked. "Did the girl who works at the venue finally catch you?"

He shouldn't have told her about Kenzie's quest to snatch him. Which is why he didn't tell her he was going to be a godfather or about Nadia. She'd roast him.

"Don't even joke about that."

"I mean, she's gorgeous, and she wants you," Bree said. "What's stopping you?"

The sound of crushed gravel lured Marcos to the window. A gray minivan approached, followed by another car.

Competent and dependable, Kenzie was welcoming the Coronel family as they came for last-minute arrangements and the dance lesson to help the groom, Anthony. He'd wanted to be ready for the first dance with his bride and her father-daughter dance.

Kenzie was lovely, but for all the flirting, she didn't really want Marcos. She wanted Ryder back. She was trying to use Marcos to win back her ex-husband, but this was a game Marcos wasn't about to play.

What was stopping him?

He wanted to be loved for who he was, not replace someone else. Which was really what was stopping him from giving in to what he felt for Nadia.

He didn't want to be a rebound with her again. He wanted her to want him for him. Not to fill the missing piece in her heart and make do with him.

"I'm a busy man," he said. "That's what's stopping me. That, and my uncles breathing down my neck for the property."

"And why don't you sell then? What's stopping you from that?"

Marcos considered, and then he realized what she was doing. "Did you learn this question at therapy?"

She laughed. The sound was like sunshine made soundwaves, and it made him smile. "Yes, I learned it last week before I decided to start auditioning again. What's stopping you? I keep asking myself, and now I pass on this technique to you."

Blessed Bree. He wished he could hug her. He missed her. He missed the warmth of her arms. But they were both better off doing what they needed to do. "Thank you, B. I'll Venmo you my part of the cost of therapy."

She laughed, and he could picture her throwing her head back. That was something he'd always been proud of, his ability to make her laugh. And that he'd never broken her heart.

Someone called her, and she said, "Break's over. I have to go. I'll call you soon."

They said goodbye, and he realized he hadn't even asked the name of Bree's new love, and that actually, he didn't need to know to be happy for her.

Marcos went back to his present. He had a wedding business to manage.

Who would've thought? Marcos had been known for so many things in his life.

Marcos, the menace. Marcos, the player. Marcos, the heartbreaker.

Marcos, the runner.

Marcos, the avoider.

Now he was Marcos, the wedding planner. The irony of it all! Marcos, the nonbeliever in commitment, the nonbeliever in true love. Here he was, making other people's fairy-tale fantasies come true.

It was time for him to go down and make sure the dance lessons were going according to plan. Most likely, Kenzie had called to ask questions about how to turn on the sound system, which had given them a hard time this past weekend.

But then, music started blaring from the speakers as he was halfway downstairs. Since no one but smiley portraits were watching him, he let himself shimmy with the rhythm of the song. Talking with Bree had left him in a good mood.

Until he walked into the vaulted-ceiling main room of the barn and came face-to-face with Nadia.

"Hey!" they said in unison, but they both went silent when, without thinking, Marcos leaned in to kiss her on the cheek.

So much for being professional.

"I . . . well, one of the things in my calendar was dance lessons here. I didn't notice until an hour ago. Sorry, I didn't know you'd be here, too."

Nadia was wearing a cream-colored, loose dress, and her curly hair fell all the way to her hips. Her skin had a golden glow, and when he'd kissed her, she'd shuddered a little. She looked like a goddess, and he'd have worshiped at the feet of her altar if only she gave a sign.

"Hola," a diminutive older lady, who had Nadia's piercing eyes, said behind her.

"Hola, señora," Marcos said respectfully, glad for the chance to sound like a grown-ass man and not like a tongue-tied teenager.

From the other end of the room, Kenzie waved him over and called, "Marcos, we have a problem. Come over!"

Nadia winced at the bossy tone in Kenzie's voice. She crossed her arms, and the warm surprise of seeing Marcos vanished from her face.

The little old lady stared at Marcos curiously. Then she leaned into Nadia and whispered in Spanish, "You didn't introduce us, Nadi. If this is your novio, why is that girl—"

"No, Bisa," Nadia said, stepping between Marcos and the old lady. "This isn't my novio. I don't have a novio, remember?" She glanced at Marcos over her shoulder, and after a couple of seconds, she blinked hard, as if she were waking up from a dream. More like a nightmare. "You know what, Bisa? Let's go—"

"No, don't go," Marcos said softly, reaching out his hand. "Give me one minute, and I'll be right back." Then he turned toward the old lady and said, "Señora, permítame un instante. Ya mismo vuelvo."

The old lady nodded at him, her eyes widening. "Ay, además de super guapo es tan amable, Nadia, no me habías dicho—"

He gave Nadia the opportunity to save face and did not listen in on the rest of her sentence. It was obvious she thought he was Nadia's fiancé. He one hundred percent, absolutely, irrevocably was this woman's eternal fan and defender. It was hard not to be, with someone who'd just said he not only was handsome, but also polite.

But by the time he reached his assistant, she was all flustered, talking with the Coronel family and wildly gesticulating with her hands. Her cheeks were bright red, and she had a sheen of sweat on her upper lip.

"Hello, ladies, so great to see you," he said to the Coronel bride, her mother, and the groom's mother and grandmother.

So many women.

The groom, dressed in distressed black jeans and a vintage Nirvana shirt, sat at the window seat, scrolling on his phone. Marcos had the urge to smack the kid on the back of his head. He couldn't be older than twenty. What was he thinking, getting married? If Marcos had been the bride's father, he'd have a stern conversation with the wannabe-husband. How was he going to support his daughter?

But before he got carried away with anger for a daughter he didn't even have, he turned to Kenzie and said, "What's going on?"

She signaled for him to step over a few feet away.

"Excuse us," he said to the Coronel women and followed Kenzie to a spot next to the entrance.

"What's wrong?" he asked.

"I've been trying to call you, and you sent me to voice mail." She put a hand on her hip and tapped the tip of her kitten-heeled shoe on the floor.

"I was on an important call," he replied, as his face reddened.

She blew a strand of hair out of her face. "The dance instructor didn't show."

It took Marcos a few seconds to process this info. He went over the independent contractors and vendors in his mind. He couldn't think of or even picture who the dance instructor would be.

"Remind me who he is again?"

Ever since he'd taken over the wedding venue, he'd felt like he'd been on a constant state of being quizzed, and he kept flunking every test.

Kenzie gave him that tiny smile of disbelief and vaguely contained violence that had made her the most ruthless and successful cheerleader in their high school. "That Spanish guy, Carlos Sauvignon. Remember him now?"

Marcos had never actually seen the man in person, but he'd always thought his name was pretentious and maybe even fake. He was, in fact, a Spanish guy, like from Spain, who taught ballroom at BYU and who'd been on the list of independent contractors. Most families were okay with the groom and bride, or the bride and her father, just going through the motions of a dance. But others who took the celebrations more seriously, or just didn't want to embarrass themselves, chose to hire a dance instructor.

"Marcos," Kenzie said, bringing him back to the problem at hand.

"Did you call him?" he asked, as the Coronels conferred in a corner and Nadia and her elderly lady friend stood at the other end of the venue. He couldn't keep his eyes away from her, but he glanced back at Kenzie for her reply.

She just stared at him, tapping her shoe.

Silly of him to ask. Of course she had.

"He ghosted us?"

She nodded. "My calls go straight to voice mail." Her voice dripped venom.

She didn't add anything, but he could just as well hear her thoughts.

This kind of thing had never happened with Sarah in charge.

And then she said the rest: "We have a reputation of being impeccable in all our commitments, Mark. We can't afford to refund anyone."

Silence rang in his ears.

If it had only been the Coronel family, he would've put his ego aside and taught them the dances himself. His mom had been adamant he learned how to look good at a party.

But he couldn't do it with Nadia here. He was too self-conscious for that.

And then, an idea lit up in his mind like a lightbulb in a cartoon.

Without hesitation, he took his phone from his pocket and texted the Batman emoji, dropping a pin with the location of the wedding venue.

Hernán would know he needed help and call him back.

"Who are you texting?" Kenzie asked. "Didn't you hear what I just said?"

Three dots appeared on the screen. Hernán was typing a message.

what's the emergency?

Marcos put a finger up for Kenzie to be patient for two seconds. With a huff, she turned on her heels and headed back to distract the Coronels. The switch in her expression, from frustrated to radiant as she turned toward the clients, impressed him.

Marcos typed:

I need a dance instructor at the venue right now. Can you help? I'll pay you of course.

His compadre lived only a few blocks away. He had a couple of hours to spend, and he happened to be an expert dancer and teacher. Back in the day, he loved teaching his Latin moves, but that had been forever ago.

Hernán's reply was a thumbs-up, an emoji of a man running, and another of wind that, actually, looked more like a fart. Hopefully, though, it meant his friend was on his way.

Marcos had to buy Hernán some time.

"Hey, Kenz, do you know how to connect my phone to the speakers, like Bluetooth or something?"

She looked at him as if he'd asked if he knew how to tie a double knot.

"Did you get ahold of Carlos?"

He handed her the phone. "No, but we're going to be okay. We're going to improvise."

Kenzie's hand jerked so hard that she dropped the phone. Marcos caught it in the air.

"I know improvising is like a swear word for you, Kenz, but please, humor me. I'm trying to do the right thing here. I'm not Sarah, but I care about the venue and our clients. Please play along."

By now, he'd been holding her hand. Her nails were cutting into his skin. For a couple of seconds, she watched him intently, as if trying to catch him in a lie while hoping she didn't.

"If this doesn't work, we'll have to refund the money. And you know—"

"I know," he said.

He turned toward the Coronel family.

"Hey, Anthony," he called to the groom. "Get over here. Your bride is waiting for you."

Right on cue, the bride in question, Abby, blushed to the tips of her ears.

Anthony sent her a cheesy smile.

"Please, excuse our dance teacher's tardiness. His wife just barely had a baby this week, and he's in baby la-la land," Marcos said, trying to sound both apologetic and amused.

The explanation worked like magic. The mention of *baby la-la land* was even more powerful than the word *bride*.

The mothers of the groom and the bride grinned at each other.

"How charming," Señora Coronel said. She was a little older than Abby's mom, who couldn't be over forty.

"While we wait, please remind me what dances we're practicing," Marcos said.

Together, the mothers filled him in on the kind of dance they wanted Anthony to learn. Abby had been in the high school dance company, and she could dance pretty much anything. Marcos looked at Anthony through narrowed eyes, and the boy shrugged. "I have two left feet, apparently," the boy said. "Sorry about that."

"No, you don't," Abby said, rushing to his side and kissing him while the moms pretended not to see.

Anthony winked at Marcos with an infuriatingly smug expression on his face.

Kids these days . . .

Marcos left the happy couple throwing compliments at each other and the moms chatting excitedly with Kenzie. Finally, he was free to head where his mind and heart had been the whole time.

"Nadia," he said, and to call her attention, he placed a hand over the small of her back. "I'm sorry for the delay."

At the touch of his fingers, he felt her shudder. When she

turned her face up to his, her eyes were blazing as she moved out of his reach. He shouldn't have touched her without consent. First the kiss, and now this. He had no right to take these kinds of liberties with her, or with anyone else, for that matter.

"I'm sorry," he said at once.

She lowered her lashes and said, "It's okay."

Although she didn't say the words aloud, he heard them all the same: *Don't do it again.*

He silently vowed not to.

"Hija, ¿no me vas a presentar con tu novio?" the older lady asked, and then, obviously thinking he didn't speak Spanish, she switched to English. "So great to meet you after so many years, Brandon, is it?"

Nadia paled so suddenly, he thought she was going to faint. Marcos hadn't been wrong before. The older lady thought he was the groom?

He looked at Nadia quizzically. Hadn't she told her family?

She guessed the questions in his mind, because she put a hand up, as if to stop his thoughts reaching the wrong conclusion, and said, "Marcos, this is my great-grandma, Hortensia. I call her Bisa. Bisa, this is Marcos."

"Pero, ¿cómo?" Bisa's face was all vulnerable and confused. "Is Marcos his middle name? You should've told me earlier, mi amor! You're even more handsome than in the photos, querido. You look like the tennis player, no, Nadita? Rafa Nadal?"

"Bisa, por favor," Nadia said, raising her hands as if in a prayer that her great-grandma wouldn't embarrass her anymore.

Then his mind made the connections. Great-grandma; that vulnerable look on her face; Nadia's dismay.

Although this woman didn't look like a crone from the movies, she must be stepping over her century and clearly had some signs of impairment he recognized from his dad, who was much younger, but already suffered the effects of early-onset Alzheimer's.

He crossed his hands to stop himself from touching Nadia. All he wanted was to hug her and whisper in her ear that he understood. That he didn't mind that her great-grandma thought he was the fiancé. The world had to be so confusing for her. He didn't mind playing along.

But how to say all that, with so many people around them watching the woman's worried conversation from afar, without hurting Nadia's feelings, too?

The fact that she'd still shown up for a dance lesson made her appear like a giant in his mind.

"Here I am," a voice said from the entrance. "Sorry I'm late."

Hernán was wearing a pair of joggers and a white T-shirt with the faces of his wife and daughters. In any other person, Marcos would've thought he was really trying too hard. It was kind of ridiculous. But the truth was that Hernán really was in love with all five of them, his pride and joy.

Immediately, all the older ladies, including Bisa, flocked to him.

Hernán was already dancing as he walked, as if he'd done this a million times. In a swift move, he grabbed Marcos's phone from Kenzie's hand, flicked through the screen, and after a couple of taps, the music started playing. Ed Sheeran's "Perfect."

Nadia groaned, and when Marcos turned around to see if it had really been her, she was pretending to look out the window. Her shoulders were shaking, and he wondered if she was laughing or crying.

The rest of the people were completely bewitched by the song, singing and swaying along the floor. Hernán adjusted Anthony's hands on Abby's waist, and paired up the mothers, so they could practice the waltz, too.

"To loosen up," Hernán said, and the two women nodded with a smile.

Hernán was magic this way.

In a matter of minutes, the mood of the room turned from tense into celebratory and exhilarated.

When the music switched to the radio mix of "Bailar Pegados," the Coronel grandma said, "This is way better, kids!" as she grabbed her daughter-in-law's hand to dance.

Marcos fought the urge to glance at Nadia to see if she remembered this song.

"You can't stand there," Hernán said, shimmying his shoulders at the beat of the song as he walked toward Kenzie.

Trying not to make eye contact with Hernán in case he paired him with his assistant, Marcos turned toward where Nadia and her great-grandma were standing.

Bisa smiled like a young girl, but Nadia still faced the window. She was furiously tapping at her phone.

Kenzie laughed, and then Marcos saw that Hernán was teaching her how to twirl and get back into step, as the bride's mother tried to copy the footwork from behind them.

No hay mal que por bien no venga, Marcos's mom used to say, and once again, he saw proof of her words.

He'd never seen a group of people more at ease with an instructor. Maybe the T-shirt was like a neon sign that said Hernán was a safe guy to be around. Maybe it was the infectious abandonment with which he moved, totally unselfconscious of his dad bod, as he joked about his belly.

Whatever the case, Marcos was grateful his friend had taken control of the situation. Until he saw him heading toward Nadia, and his heart jumped to his throat.

But instead of taking Nadia's hand to join the party, Hernán stood before Bisa and said, "¿Bailamos?"

Bisa's face lit up, as she carefully followed Hernán to the middle of the room, where everyone made a circle around them as they danced.

Cross-armed, Nadia watched the scene unfolding in front of them with a slight smile on her face. Marcos walked toward her but kept an acceptable distance that would prevent his itching hands to even accidentally even bump into her.

"Is that the same guy from college? What's his name? Germán?" she asked.

"Hernán," Marcos said.

She laughed softly. "Remember what a player he was? He must have kissed everyone in my dorm sophomore year."

"Everyone?" he asked, raising an eyebrow.

She turned toward him and looked him straight in the eyes. "I was kissing someone else in sophomore year."

He tucked that rogue strand behind his ear, and he bit his lip to prevent himself from saying something stupid.

"I'm talking about you," she said.

And then she was the one looking flustered, as if she didn't know where the words had come from.

He saw her pinching her arm through the long sleeve of her dress.

Then, her gaze on Hernán and her grandma demonstrating the waltz, she sighed and added, "Sorry about Bisa. She's very healthy physically, and she's very sharp, but all of a sudden she has these episodes, and she forgets something we were just talking about."

He understood the pain in her words, but let her talk.

"She's been planning on the wedding forever. She knows that Brandon and I broke up, but she keeps forgetting. She thinks . . ." Her voice trailed off, as if she couldn't say the words. Then she took a big gulp of air, like she was about to jump from an airplane without a parachute. "She thinks that you're my fiancé, you see?" The words rushed, drowned by the music, and he felt such a tenderness for her that his eyes became misty. Dang it. He didn't want to get emotional, but he knew what she was going through. And it wasn't easy.

"At least she got stuck in something happy," he said, taking a step toward her. Hernán had switched the music to a Franco De Vita ballad, and the young couple was slow dancing, looking into each other's eyes, away from the world.

Now it was Marcos taking a big gulp to confess something. "My dad got early-onset dementia in his late forties. He did okay for a long time, but when he and my mom had the accident and she died, it's like he died, too. He got stuck in a limbo, like this loop," he said, and she was looking intensely at him, like she knew exactly what he meant. "A loop in the past when things between us weren't the best. When he woke up and heard the news that she was gone, he just got mad. He's angry at me, as if I had killed her, you know? The only time he talks to me is when he thinks I'm my cousin Alexander."

She had a look of sympathy, and this time, she was the one who reached and placed a hand on his arm, placating, soothing, understanding.

Bisa had sat down in one of the plump chairs that lined the walls of the ballroom, and she alternated between clapping and taking sips from a can of soda mate. Nadia laughed softly, and she wiped her eye surreptitiously, but Marcos noticed.

Wanting to change the subject, she said, "I booked the dance lesson months ago, and then I forgot about it. When I got the notification in my phone today, I asked Bisa to come with me."

"She likes to dance?" he guessed, watching Nadia's great-grandma tapping her foot on the floor.

"And she'd bored at the house," Nadia said. "Everyone is so busy getting reacquainted, and gossiping about me, that I had to get out of there for a bit. Bisa got in the car before I could finish asking her if she wanted to come along."

As if Bisa had felt their gaze on her, she said, "You two, tor-tolitos, practice your dance! Don't be shy!"

Nadia groaned and tried to cover her face with her hand. But Marcos saw the look on Bisa's face again, that heartbreaking moment when she realized she'd said something wrong, like a scolded toddler.

"I'm okay dancing if you are," he said softly. "We can go along for her sake."

She took a sharp breath, and when she looked at him, he was disarmed to see her eyes were full of tears. He didn't know if it was seeing the young couple lost in their world, their moms now dancing together, or the image of Bisa, living an alternate reality, or all those things combined, but he felt the grief coursing through her and this new chapter in her life. She was trying so hard to do the right thing at all times. She looked exhausted.

"What dance were you and Brandon planning?" he asked.

She laughed now, and when she blinked, the tears were gone. "We weren't planning on anything, actually. He didn't want to dance. I signed us up anyway, in case he changed his mind and didn't want to look ridiculous. That threat always worked with him."

"And what are you dancing at your party?"

She shrugged. "I don't know. I guess I'll still have a father-daughter dance with my dad. He said he'd meet us here, but I don't know what's taking him so long. Maybe he just forgot."

He hated to see her so heartbroken.

Apparently unable to remain seated, Bisa was up on her feet again, dancing a salsa with the Coronel grandma.

"Come on, Nadia and novio! Don't be shy," she called again.

Bisa was having the time of her life, but the pain in Nadia's face seemed so deep, it rattled him. He knew that pain of slowly losing someone you love who really doesn't remember you anymore, even though you're right there next to them.

Hernán sent him a not-too-subtle hint with his head. By the way Nadia stiffened next to him, she had guessed what his friend meant by the signal. He should've pretended not to understand. He should've made up an excuse to go check on something up in his office.

But instead, for the first time in weeks of trying to behave, Marcos went along with his impulse.

Heart hammering in his chest, he stepped in front of her and offered his hand. He wouldn't touch her without her consent again. "May I have this dance?"

She scoffed, as if she thought this was a joke, but he was dead serious.

He looked at her as softly as he could, hoping she could see he meant it.

"Are you for real?"

From the corner of his eye, he was aware of Kenzie looking at him with a strange expression.

"You paid for dance lessons. Let's dance."

Her eyes lit up when she bit her lip and smiled. Finally, she nodded, took his proffered hand, and headed to the dance floor.

Chapter 13

Nadia

A couple of weeks ago, if anyone had shown Nadia a video of her dancing with her college fling turned impossible crush, she would've thought she was having a fever dream.

But here she was.

In Rocket's arms, dancing to the song she'd picked for the cheesiest, most ridiculous first dance—"She's Worth It" by a British boy band Olivia loved, Megaheart.

How had Hernán known?

And then she remembered she'd put it down in one of the forms she had filled out months and months in advance. She had picked this song, fantasizing that her groom realized she was the girl from the lyrics.

Her groom, the love of her life. Brandon, of course. Not Marcos from her craziest fantasies.

This practice dance was all she'd get with him.

Now, instead of lamenting the twists and turns that life had taken her for, she grounded herself in the moment. That is, as much as she could while gliding across the floor under the eyes of an unlikely audience.

She tried to keep a modest distance from Marcos, touching as little skin as possible, but then Hernán blurted out, "Are you like brother and sister dancing? You're giving these two a terrible example!"

Marcos replied by pulling Nadia closer to him. Her breath hitched when her breasts pressed against his chest. She looked up and wished she hadn't. His mouth was so close to hers that if she stood on tiptoes and swung to the side, like the rhythm of the song dictated, the crucial distance would be breached. She could almost taste the mint of the chewing gum he must have popped in his mouth before he came downstairs.

Marcos seemed to guess her thoughts, because his mouth quirked in an almost-smile. His eyes were blazing coal as he led her all over the floor, expertly, like all he did in his life was dance waltzes with jilted brides.

She closed her eyes to savor the sensations going over her body like electric currents when he started singing softly. He knew all the words.

She turned her face away, the room and the others blurs of color and movement.

"Why this song?" he asked, dipping his head to brush her ears with his lips.

"How do you know *I* picked it?"

"Come on," he said. "I saw the forms, and it was your handwriting, Palacio. Besides, Kenzie said the one time he was here, he looked like he'd rather go to war. He's a jerk, and we all know it. I thought we were all clear on that."

A shot of resentment jumped in Nadia's heart. Why was Kenzie revealing all these things behind her back? But then, Nadia realized the anger wasn't only directed at Marcos's assistant, who must have been eating her heart out seeing Marcos and Nadia dancing. No. The one and only owner of her anger was Brandon.

And herself.

"You're right. I picked the song even though Brandon didn't like it."

"So why did you stick to it?"

The chorus was rising, making the emotions swell in her heart.

"Because I like to pretend the lyrics are about me," she whispered.

Marcos didn't say anything for a little while, but when she felt the muscles of his back move smoothly under her hand, Nadia's thoughts took wings. Only a thin piece of fabric separated her skin from his, and she fantasized about what it would feel like to trace her way down his spine. Would he still be ticklish, like he'd been when they were young?

But then he broke the silence. "The lyrics are beautiful. I saw a documentary about this band. The songwriter's sister wrote a poem, and he made it into a song. Everyone thinks it's about the love of his life, but in an interview, he confessed she wrote it to her past and future selves. He said loving yourself like a soul mate is the most radical thing you can do." Marcos's voice faded away with the melody.

She didn't know what to say. She's never thought of herself as the love of her life. Of course, it wasn't necessary to be a religious person to know that the great commandment in the Bible and other sacred books was to love one's neighbors as oneself, as with God.

But she hadn't thought of that in a long time, so worried had she been about Brandon loving her like she wanted to be loved, that she'd forgotten that the only person who could love her unconditionally was herself.

"I don't know if I can do it."

"You're doing it," he said in her ear, her heart beating hard against his as they glided on the floor. "What's stopping you from loving yourself with abandon?"

The song was coming to an end, and then it abruptly switched to a reggaeton in Spanish that had been blaring on the radio all summer. Nadia laughed when she saw the Coronel grandma giggling like a little girl while she tried to twerk.

With an expert hand, Marcos twirled Nadia and dipped her. Unsmiling, she looked straight into his eyes, and when his flitted to her lips, she lowered her lashes, scared of the intentions he wasn't fast enough to hide.

Her whole body craved for him to kiss her. But of course, he didn't. Like the other night in the storage room, he seemed to project a wall between them. Nadia didn't blame him. She was a mess, and he seemed to have his life under control. Who was she to come and complicate it?

The whole room broke into applause, and when Marcos brought her back up and she opened her eyes, it took a few minutes to get her bearings back.

She wasn't alone dancing with a charming prince in the clouds.

She was in the ballroom of the venue, surrounded by the Coronel family, and to the side, she noticed more people had arrived: her dad, uncles, and a gaggle of her cousins, including Lola and Gianna, whose mouth was wide open in shock. The men all looked like they'd been rolling around in the mud, judging by the sprigs of grass on her dad's salt-and-pepper hair and the mud in her uncles' shoes. What had they been doing?

Bisa saw them, too, and waved them over. She and the Coronel grandma seemed to have become best friends as they stood arm-in-arm. "Come here, Ernesto, and dance with your daughter, now that she practiced with her fiancé."

"Fiancé?" everyone in the room repeated with shock.

Without missing a beat, Marcos stepped up to the challenge, and stretching out his hand, said, "Don't take too long dancing with your dad, love. I'll miss you."

Chapter 14

Marcos

He had no idea where the words had come from, or why he'd gone along with Bisa.

Nadia's grandma might not remember this moment in a couple of hours, but he would. The rest of the people around would, too, even if they'd all pretended to go along with the ruse.

He hated his past self for having run from Nani.

He hated his future without her.

He was a coward and a fool.

But Marcos wasn't a liar.

If anything, he was an honest, cowardly fool in love, and wherever they had come from, his words were true. She was his love, and when all this was over, he would miss her.

It had been a long time since he'd felt this, the sensation of both falling into an adventure and rising in a high no chemical could mimic. For the last several years, as soon as his heart tugged him toward someone he was mildly interested in, he'd turned around and ran. But now, with Nadia, it was as if the years apart had been a blink.

Sometimes, like when she'd been ignored at a good audition or had a bad day tending tables, Bree liked to imagine alternate realities. She had liked to pretend that in another dimension, instead of tending tables or applying for roles with no lines, she was a superstar greater than J.Lo or Salma.

Maybe in another reality, Marcos hadn't run, and he'd gotten to dance like this with Nani every night, calling her his love, and missing her every second he didn't spend with her.

But he was stuck in this reality, one in which he was just the owner of the venue of her failed wedding plans.

How could he feel like this after all this time? Marcos hardly knew her. He hadn't even known her fully ten years ago. But the heart doesn't understand the logical brain. And right now, his illogical, flimsy heart was telling him that he'd love this woman until the day he died and beyond. He couldn't have her, because he didn't deserve her. He wouldn't be an obstacle in this journey she was on.

The journey to loving and celebrating herself.

He'd do anything to help her pull this party off, though. If that meant going along with her great-grandma, who thought he was Nani's fiancé, then so be it.

"I'm sorry," Nani said, looking embarrassed, as if she'd been the one blurting out the deepest secrets of her heart. "She forgets things. She mixes things. She thinks—"

He touched her elbow with his fingertips and felt her shudder. "It's okay. I know what it's like. Don't stress about it."

"But don't you mind? It's so annoying that she thinks . . ." She bit her lip, as if she couldn't even say the words that her great-grandma thought he was Brandon, and his heart hurt for her.

He minded. He would've given anything to say he was hers forever and always, but he'd lost that right ten years ago, and he knew life doesn't give you second chances. At least, not to him.

"We all know the truth. I mean, if she's like my dad, correcting him only helps for a few minutes, and then he goes back to thinking I'm my cousin. Seeing the truth in his eyes hurts every time. Why make her go through that? I don't mind."

She held his hand and pressed it in a gesture of gratitude.

"Really, though," he said. "Go dance with your dad."

Nadia's dad's eyes were narrowed as he walked toward them. It wasn't until he almost reached them that Marcos noticed he was limping. Badly.

Nadia noticed, too.

"Oh, no, Papi," she said, taking the two steps that separated them. "What happened?"

One of the other men helped Nani walk her father to a nearby chair. "He thinks he's still a pibe in his twenties and tried to dribble past this big Russian guy from the other team, and he fell like a boulder on his own hip."

Nani sighed as she closed her eyes.

Marcos wanted to help, and he didn't know how.

"The worst is that next week we have a rematch, and we don't have a scorer," the man said in Spanish. And then he looked at Marcos. "Wait, you look like a footballer. Can you join us? It's the least you can do after canceling the wedding."

Nani blushed furiously. "Ay, Tío Román! He's not—"

"Then who are you?" the man asked, narrowing his eyes and balling his hands into fists.

"Nobody," she said at the same time Marcos replied, "I'm an old friend."

Her dad looked at both of them, forehead furrowed. "Which is it? Nobody or old friend?"

Marcos looked at Nani, hoping she would take the conversation from here.

"He's an old friend who also happens to be the venue owner." She sounded like she was confessing Marcos was a lover she'd kept secret since high school.

"Nice!" said the man she'd called Tío Román. Then he looked at Bisa, and leaning into Marcos and Nadia, he added, "Bisa's confused again, then?"

As if she'd heard they were talking about her, Bisa blew a kiss toward them, as she now circled the room with three of the women who'd arrived with Nadia's dad. Cousins, he imagined.

Bisa was having the time of her life.

"You don't have to go along, Marcos," Nadia said. "Seriously."

"I don't mind."

"Then come to our game," Tío Román said, clapping Marcos's shoulder. "Where are you from, by the way?"

"He's from here," Nani answered, a sharp tone in her voice like she wanted to cut this conversation before it got too far.

But Marcos didn't mind explaining. He liked Nani's family. He imagined his, in Uruguay, would be very similar to them, and he wished he hadn't lost contact with that branch of his family tree. What a pity he was stuck with people like Uncles Monty and George.

"My mom was from Colonia, Uruguay. My parents met there when they were very young and ended up settling here, where my dad's family's from," he said, looking at Nani from the corner of his eye.

He'd never shared much about his life and his family with her before.

"Your Spanish is excellent," Nani's dad, Ernesto, said. "You sound like an Argentine. I mean, once upon a time, Uruguay and Argentina were the same country. So—"

"Papi," Nani said, playfully slapping her dad's shoulder, but Marcos was laughing, and soon, she smiled, too.

Marcos had heard the jokes about the rivalry between Uruguay and Argentina all his life, and although he wasn't a soccer fanatic like the Palacio men seemed to be, his Charrúa blood called him during the World Cup and Copa America. Of course, he always cheered for his mother's country, which he secretly wished was his, too.

"I grew up speaking Spanish at home," he said. "Some days, my accent is horrible, because I don't really practice it a lot, but when I'm with other Spanish-speaking people, it comes back. Funny how that works."

"Yes, funny," Nadia said, but she was distracted by the group of her cousins and Bisa.

One of them, a tall, dark-skinned woman with a dazzling smile, kept making gestures and signals that Marcos was pretty sure had to be about him.

"And you drink mate?" Ernesto asked.

Marcos turned his attention to Nadia's father, whose eyes were narrowed as if he wanted to see through an illusion.

Marcos felt he was being examined, and for the first time in forever, he wanted to pass this test with full marks.

For her.

"Of course I do!" He bit his lip and looked at Nani, who was shaking her head. She knew his secret. He only liked the canned version, but it's not like he was going to confess this to her dad and uncles. What if they uninvited him to the game?

"Well, here's my number," Ernesto said, and Marcos exhaled like he'd been underwater for hours. "Come join us for the game next Tuesday night."

"Papá, stop it," Nadia interrupted. "Maybe he's busy. Aren't you, Marcos? Don't you have a wedding or something?"

"Let me see," Marcos said, taking his phone out of his pocket. He scrolled through his calendar, and miraculously, Tuesday was free. "My night is wide open."

She grabbed his phone as if she needed to see from up close.

"It's settled, then," her dad said, standing from the chair. "It's for the Latino league. I signed us up last year for this tournament. We can for sure use another player."

"What about Agustín and Pedro?" Nadia asked, obviously not thrilled about the prospect of Marcos spending time with her family.

"They won't arrive until Thursday. We have Ricardito's son, Thiago, and Noah. But the boys of this new generation only play FIFA on the PlayStation, if you know what I mean."

Tío Ricardo was chatting with the Coronel boy and Hernán. They were exchanging numbers to get together after Anthony's honeymoon.

The dance lesson seemed to be a success in more ways than one.

"Bring your friend to the game, Uruguayo!" Ricardo said to Marcos. "He says that he can be the keeper. He's short but athletic, and he's a good dancer."

Hernán was grinning from ear to ear, sweat beading along his hairline.

All smiles, the Coronels said goodbye to Kenzie, apparently satisfied with their dance lesson. Marcos was relieved that it had worked out. He'd have to call the Spanish dance instructor and ask why he hadn't even warned them he wouldn't be coming.

"Bueno, nene, chau chau," Bisa said to Marcos as she was heading out. "See you soon, right?" She stretched out her arms for a hug, and he made himself as small as possible to return the gesture.

It had been a long time since he'd had a loving grandma hug, the kind that means you're loved and accepted just as you are.

"I'll be there, Bisa. See you soon," he said.

Flanked by Nadia's dad and uncles, Bisa slowly walked to the car. She was still nursing her can of soda mate.

Marcos scratched his head. He really didn't have the time to play soccer with Nani's family. But honestly? He'd fallen a little in love with them.

Nani stood by his side, arms crossed, waiting to talk to him. Her cousins crowded around Hernán, who was showing them pictures of his girls, judging by the exclamations coming from the group.

"Thank you for being kind to her," she said.

"It's no problem, really," he said, distracted by the way the dying sun played on her face. He loved this time of day, golden hour, and his fingers itched for his good camera, so he could catch the way Nadia looked and keep it forever. His memory would have to do.

"You don't have to go to their soccer game."

"Your dad said it was part of your festivities. That the women are playing, too. I wouldn't miss that for the world," Marcos said, hoping he didn't sound like he was begging her to let him spend time with her family. He hadn't realized how lonely he was without his family until he'd been with hers.

She bit her lip, and this time, he couldn't help himself. He brushed her mouth with the knuckle of his index finger. "You're hurting yourself," he whispered at her wide-eyed expression. "Why do you keep doing that?"

She sighed again, her chest heaving as if she had a storm contained inside it.

"The caterer canceled on me," Nani said.

"What?"

"Yes," she said, her eyes flashing with anger. "I don't have a photographer, and now I don't have a caterer." She kept enumerating with her fingers. "I haven't found a dress, either. To make matters worse, if I don't send invitations to the treintañera, people will show up expecting to attend a wedding, and I really don't want to be giving any explanations the night of. That is, if I still go through with it."

"You still have two weeks for the party. I mean, it's late, but you can still send the invites. People will understand." Nadia seemed unconvinced, and Marcos added, "Once, my mom had only a week to plan a full wedding, from proposal to the real thing. She used to say, 'We're in the United States. Everything is easier here,' and she was right, you know?"

Nadia shrugged one shoulder, her jaw set. "Your mom knew the right people, Marcos. Everyone loved her. The printer I called said they're booked until the end of the year, and at this point, I might have to do with a virtual card."

"That's one printer, though, Nani," he said. "I have a list—"

"I called everyone from the list Kenzie gave me, and no one can take pictures, cater, or print invites for me."

He let her vent, but his mind was racing. A suspicion grew in Marcos's mind.

The photographer.

The caterer.

The dance teacher.

The printer.

Was someone keeping them away from Enchanted Orchard? Was someone sabotaging his business?

Would his uncles stoop so low?

Of course they would.

"Listen, I'm sorry for dragging you into a personal matter," Marcos said. "But . . . I think I know what's happening."

At that moment, Tío Román peeked into the ballroom and called, "Let's go, Nadia! Bisa fell asleep in the car!"

"I'm coming!" she said, and then she turned to Marcos. "I'll keep you updated. Don't worry. I don't have any good pictures for a highlights reel, either. Maybe it's a sign. In the worst-case scenario, you'll have an evening off on the night of the party. I'll let you know soon, though, in case you need to book it." She tried to smile, but the prospect of not having her party tinged the words with sadness.

But Marcos had other ideas. He wasn't going to let her fail.

"What if tomorrow we meet here for pictures? I'm an okay photographer."

"Tomorrow I'm going dress hunting," she said. "I won't be done until late."

Her cousins had followed Hernán to the pond. A few of them were posing in front of the swans. The light was glorious, and it cast Nadia in a golden hue. She continued talking about the dress, while he stared at her with abandon.

He wished he had a camera to preserve this moment for eternity. A vein pulsed in her throat as her chest rose and fell in harmony with her words. Her hair was coming undone from the ponytail she'd tied when she'd been dancing. He remembered the warmth of her skin under the flimsy fabric of her dress when she'd been in his arms, just minutes ago.

Wait. He had a camera.

Unable to stop himself, he said, "Don't move," as he took his phone from his pocket and snapped a picture of her. She didn't have time to look self-conscious or bashful.

He gazed at the screen for a second, satisfied with the shot. He'd caught Nadia mid-smile, as she brushed her hand through her hair, the sun highlighting all the right curves and angles of her face. She looked lit from the inside out.

"What do you think?" he asked, showing her his phone.

She bit her lower lip, as if she were bracing herself for something unpleasant, but when she saw the screen, her expression softened.

"How?" she asked, scoffing. "I never . . . I mean, I'm not photogenic at all, and you . . . ?"

"What do you mean, you're not photogenic? Are you just fishing for compliments, Palacio?"

The way she smiled at him . . .

"I think the one fishing for compliments on his photo-taking skills is you, Hawkins."

He should've looked away, but instead, he held her gaze. His heart was a runaway horse that wouldn't be contained with threats of the consequences that would follow if he were to ignore all the red flags around him.

"Let me AirDrop it to you," he said, fumbling with his phone. "I mean, look at it. I think it's perfect for an invite. I think you look . . . glorious. Should we ask your cousins?"

He clicked send, and there was another silence. A swan trumpeted in the distance.

"It's calling for her love," Nadia whispered, her gaze flitting to his lips.

"Nadia!" her dad called from outside, punctuating her name with honks.

"Ahí vengo!" she bellowed. Then she looked at him, as he tried not to laugh at the force of her voice and said, "Jeez! I'm sorry! When we're all together, I can't help matching their volume."

She turned to leave, but at the last second, she walked back to him. She rose to her tiptoes and kissed him on the cheek, cupping his other cheek with a small, cold hand.

He hadn't felt so overcome by an attack of butterflies in the stomach since . . . the first time they'd kissed.

She was gone before he could act on the impulse to place his hand on the small of her back and pull her close for a proper kiss.

"Someday," he promised himself as he watched her go.

Even if he had to wait another ten years, another lifetime, for a chance to make up for his mistakes of the past, he'd wait for the perfect moment to kiss her again.

Chapter 15

Nadia

"You're going to wear that picture out if you keep staring at it that way," Lola said on her way to the bathroom. She carried an assortment of toiletries and a pair of pajamas Isabella had lent her in her arms, so she couldn't return the high-five that Gianna sent her.

"Who can blame her?" Gianna said, sauntering downstairs. With an expert turn of her head wrapped in a towel, she dodged the small chandelier that swung like a pendulum above the spot where the kitchen table usually sat. They'd moved it aside to accommodate so many people in a house smaller than sixteen hundred square feet.

There were two showers at Nadia's childhood home. Although most of the older cousins had reservations at nearby hotels, no one seemed eager to waste a single moment when they were all on the same continent. In spite of the exhaustion of running all over the place, they took turns showering, cooking, and keeping Nadia company.

After the initial arrival early in the week, there had been a flood of visitors at the Palacios' home.

Tío Ricardo and his family (husband Francisco and twin girls a little younger than Olivia, Amara and Allegra) had finally arrived after being delayed in New York for over twenty-four hours. Although she'd been prepared, Nadia couldn't tell the girls apart, not even after spending days with them. They looked like teenage Snow Whites, with their creamy skin, dark hair, and big black eyes. They also spoke perfect English with a British accent. The whole family was obsessed with them. Later that week, cousin Gianna had arrived from Australia with her girlfriend, Marcella, a beautiful woman from Brazil who played professional soccer for a Sydney team. Nadia's parents' house was bursting at the seams, but no one wanted to call an early night. Especially after meeting Marcos, the mysterious wedding planner.

It didn't help that Bisa kept talking about Nadia's novio, pointing out little details that made Nadia feel like she was on fire.

"You should've seen them dancing. They were made for each other. And the way he looks at her!" Bisa bit her lip and shook her head. "That's a man in love if I ever saw one. Isn't he, Inés?" she asked Nadia, who'd been making signs to her mom that Bisa didn't know what she was talking about.

"Mamá," Abuela Catalina said. "This is Nadia, not Inés. And the man is just someone who works—"

"It's okay, Abuela," Nadia said, rushing toward Bisa to encircle her with her arms.

"But it's upsetting that she keeps confusing you with her dead sister, who, bless her soul, has been gone for more than fifty years," Abuela Catalina insisted, shaking her dark curls as she spoke.

Every time Nadia had been at Bisa's house in Argentina, she'd been fascinated with the photo of a girl from another century who had looked just like her. Tía Inés, Bisa's little sister, had died in a car accident. Looking at a face so much like hers had always been an eerie experience for Nadia. Her doppelgänger had been a girl who hadn't lived to her fifteenth birthday. A girl her Bisa adored, all these years later.

"It takes me out for a loop every time I look at her and remember the photos," Gianna said.

"Listen, Cata," Bisa said, lifting her chin at her daughter. "You know what's upsetting? How you talk to me, that is. I'm your mother. Don't forget. Maybe you're the one with memory issues." She started heading toward the front door.

"Where are you going, Mami?" Abuela Cata asked Bisa.

Nadia had rushed to the door to block Bisa's exit. But her great-grandma winked at her and then changed course and beelined for the couch instead. "I'm going to wait here for you, *Nadia*, so you don't forget to take me home with you. I can't stand this woman anymore."

Abuela Catalina cornered Nadia's mom at the hallway that divided the kitchen and the living room. For a second, Nadia and her mom exchanged a look of understanding, both sandwiched between grandma and great-grandma. Nadia had never experienced this before. It had always been Isabella who'd been side-to-side with her mom in this kind of situation. But Isabella and her family had gone back to their house hours ago. Noah had a game early in the morning.

In spite of the tension in the room, Nadia felt a moment of tenderness. Maybe, if she got lucky enough in this life, one day she and her mom would also be together at Nadia's granddaughter's wedding—that is, if she ever had a daughter to start. And if they bickered like Abuela and Bisa did, perhaps the other members of the family could play the role of peacemakers.

Still, the fighting was already tiring, and they still had days to go before the party.

Wanting to take charge, Nadia's mom had come over and said, "Nadia has a full day tomorrow."

"She can come dress hunting with us," Nadia said.

"What about work?" Virginia asked.

"I took the rest of the month off." Nadia was surprised at how easy the lie rolled off her tongue.

"On top of the week for the honeymoon? Were they okay with that?" her dad asked from the other corner of the kitchen.

"Yes, Pa," Nadia replied, rolling her eyes in an exaggerated motion. "They'll be okay."

Her mom must have suspected something fishy, because she didn't concede. "We have a room ready for you, Bisa. Don't hurt my feelings."

Bisa's face softened. "Bueno . . . I will stay for *you*, Virginia. Just tell your mother to mind her tone with me."

Crisis averted, Nadia sighed in relief. She didn't have a problem bringing Bisa home with her, but tomorrow would be a grueling day, and not only for her dress hunting. She had a lot of things to figure out. In a corner of her mind, she wondered if there was any excuse at all for her to swing by the venue, but she brushed the thought away.

"I promise you I'll bring you to my apartment so you can see where I live. Okay, Bisa?" Nadia said.

After all, they'd already scheduled a sleepover for all the "girls" to accompany Nadia on her last night as a single woman while Brandon slept at his parents' the days before the wedding. Now they could have a pre-party.

"Show me the picture again," Gianna said as she and Nadia headed back to the table. Abuelo Leo had just pulled a fresh onion pizza out of the oven.

Her cheeks blazing again, Nadia showed her the screen. She couldn't get over how Marcos had captured this look on her with just a phone camera.

"Are you going to use it for the invites?" Gianna asked.

"I'm not sure," Nadia whispered.

Right then, she got a torrent of texts from Madi and Stevie. Stevie:

R you effing me? This is gorg!

Madi:
Stop the world! He captured your inner goddess! Who is this man and when can we meet him?

"I guess your friends loved the picture," Gianna said, patting Nadia's hand.

Nadia laughed at the expression on her cousin's face. "The lighting was just right. That's all."

"That, and the fact that he saw you through eyes full of love. Don't you agree, Marce?"

Gianna's girlfriend, Marcella, had been all smiles since they'd arrived, but she had observed quietly from a corner of the kitchen, Tinkerbell on her lap, drinking soda mate. For all that the older matriarchs had hated on the drink, everyone seemed to love it. Nadia's dad had already made two runs to Costco for enough cans to keep the whole clan hydrated and caffeinated.

"The long-haired guy at the venue? He's definitely smitten," Marcella said in English with a strong Australian accent. "I don't blame Bisa for thinking he's your fiancé."

Nadia bit into her pizza and chewed, mostly to hide the smile of delight that kept creeping onto her face every time she realized that Marcos thought she was beautiful.

"I've missed you all so much," Gianna said as she crushed Nadia's fingers, lovingly. "I love talking drama with my family." Her eyes had a slightly crazed look of overexcitement, too much caffeine, and jet lag, as if flying across the world for a wedding that was no more, with strangers who only shared her blood and the roots of part of her family tree, were the most thrilling thing to ever happen to her.

Not for the first time, Nadia wished she and Gianna had grown up closer together.

Lola came out of the bathroom, grabbed a slice of pizza, and joined the conversation.

"I have a friend in Madrid who's a graphic designer. Let me send him the info and this picture, and he'll have an invitation ready for you to print, address, and send tomorrow."

"Are you sure I should use this picture, though?" Nadia asked.

"Yes!" The whole family, including the uncles, chorused from all over the house.

"I guess I have no choice, then," Nadia said, as her abuelo placed a slice of mozzarella in front of her.

The clock marked midnight when Lola got an email from her graphic designer friend.

"Que maja te ves, prima!" Lola exclaimed.

"Beleza!" said Marcella.

Bisa added, "Una muñeca!"

"Diosaaaa!" texted Stevie and Madi.

On an impulse, Nadia texted the file of her invite to Marcos. **What do you think?**

The three dots made her heart sputter.

We got ourselves a treintañera.

Nadia couldn't stop smiling. But she had a full day coming up.

If worst came to worst, they'd use disposable cameras to take pictures and have Abuelo bake pizzas. But she had a proper invite. Tomorrow, she'd get a dress.

Finally, Lola, Gianna, and Marcella packed their stuff in Nadia's car to head over to her apartment.

Luckily, Bisa had fallen asleep like a log before they headed out. If she insisted on coming with them, Nadia wouldn't have had the heart to go over the argument again.

Nadia's neighbor, the one with the Yorkie, was standing on the floor landing when Nadia and her cousins climbed upstairs. She nodded in approval at Nadia before she headed back inside.

"She told me the whole building had known Brandon was scum when I kicked him out," Nadia explained, embarrassment tingeing her words.

Gianna helped her unlock the door and said, "If I ever see him, I'll beat his ass, right, Marce?"

"Right," said her girlfriend, smacking her fist into the palm of her other hand.

"I'll ask one of my authors to make him a character in her book—and make sure he suffers a gruesome death," Lola said, making a clawing gesture with her hands.

It must have been her accent or the murderous look on her face. Or maybe the emotional roller coaster of the last few days was making a dent in them. Whatever the reason, they all broke into hysterical laughter.

When they'd recovered a little, Gianna said, "We can go find him now. Just say the word."

"It's okay," Nadia said, briefly entertaining and relishing the idea of her cousin and her beautiful girlfriend beating up her ex, and Lola taking notes for her author. But just for a second. "Like my friend Madi says, karma will catch up with him. You'll see."

Nadia had mentally and emotionally prepared herself for the agony of shopping for a dress. Isabella had crafted an itinerary, complete with addresses and contact information, to make the process a little easier for Nadia. Lola, Gianna, and Marcella went with her to the first shop. The same place where Nadia had bought her wedding dress, years and years ago. Back then, it had been a small boutique that featured vintage and modern couture. Now, it was a sprawling store that had absorbed the accessory shops around it. In addition to dresses, it now had a section for shoes, shapewear, and even a back room for a med spa that provided Botox as well as cool- and warm-sculpting.

Gianna studied a brochure as if the words were in Klingon. "Lola, you're the expert in words," she said. "Make it make sense."

Lola put on the reading glasses hanging from an old-fashioned chain around her neck. Her heart-shaped face and freckles contrasting with the thick, bottle-bottom glasses. She scanned the page and winced. "Tempting, but no thank you."

"What do you mean, it's tempting? You're a stick," Gianna said, smacking her cousin's arm playfully.

Lola pressed her lips and grabbed the sides of her waist. "A sedentary lifestyle and Mediterranean diet will give you these lovely handles, especially if you're over thirty."

They continued arguing about who needed a fat-sucking session the most, and concluded neither did.

"Más vale que sobre y no que falte, mamita," Gianna quoted one of the family's famous sayings.

Nadia agreed with the sentiment. It was better to have too much instead of going without. And even if the bickering of her family sometimes felt a little too much, she'd rather be surrounded with them than by herself while she went through her late-quarter-life crisis, as Stevie had called it.

Marcella, who'd been standing quietly by Gianna, gave Nadia a pained look.

"Are you okay?" Nadia asked.

Marcella lifted her eyebrows and huffed. "I've never seen so many white people in a place. It's kind of scary."

They had still not been attended to, but at ten in the morning, the place was already teeming with people. And now that Nadia noticed, yes, everyone was white, except for one of the store employees, who looked Asian, and them, of course. With her cream skin and greenish eyes she'd inherited from the Northern Italian side of the family, Lola could pass as white. That is, until she opened her mouth and started chattering in Peninsular Spanish, and when she spoke English, it was with a British accent because she'd learned it at school. But the rest of them stuck out like sunflowers in a rose garden. Especially Marcella, who was Black.

After years of making herself smaller and quieter to be as inconspicuous as possible, Nadia had stopped noticing how white her community was. Except when her people reminded her by asking where she was from.

It was true that with the influx of California and East Coast transfers, Utah had become a little more heterogenous, but in certain areas, she was usually the only Latina.

"I'm sorry," she said, patting Marcella's hand. "Hopefully, we'll be out of here soon."

By one in the afternoon, with blistered feet, hoarse voices, and frayed tempers, the women walked out of the store. "I'm never ever coming back here," Nadia vowed, slamming the door of her car.

Her cousins followed her, muttering insults at the last attendant who'd recommended Nadia get a dress from the mother-of-the-bride section at the mall.

"I can't believe she said that," Lola exclaimed, her cheeks flushed with anger. Or all the caffeine she'd had as they waited in vain.

"And how old is that girl that just walked in?" Marcella asked, still staring at the store with horror in her eyes. "She couldn't have been more than eighteen! Why is she getting married? What is the legal age here, Nadia? Where are we?"

Despite the fact that she hadn't found a single dress she liked, or one that fit her, Nadia laughed as she explained the strange wedding scene in a super-conservative society. "Marce, when you teach waiting until marriage for you-know-what, kids will get resourceful."

"But she was scheduling lip fillers and Botox! At eighteen!" Gianna said with outrage and a little envy. When she thought no one was watching, she'd tucked one of the brochures in her back jeans pocket.

Lola whispered, "Fascinating!"

Gianna, Marcella, and Lola broke into gossip about marriages that had started in adolescence and ended in either tragedy or bliss.

"There is this murder mystery podcast . . ." Lola was saying.

Nadia tuned them out as she tried to figure out what to do next. She had hoped to be in and out in a matter of one hour, two at most. Now she wondered if perhaps the mall was a good alternative after all.

Before Nadia entered the address of the next store to visit, she texted Stevie and Madi. Madi was meeting her and her cousins in the evening, but perhaps she had some ideas.

Although Stevie wasn't into the formal dress-buying scene, she was in El Paso, one of the quinceañera capitals of the country. Perhaps she had ideas of where to start even looking for a dress.

"Recalculating," the GPS said, as Nadia made the wrong turn out of the parking lot.

"Like your friend Madi says, let's manifest the best dress in the next store," Gianna said with fervor.

In reply, Marcella and Lola crossed themselves and chanted, "Amen."

By the time the cousins went back to Nadia's parents' house, they looked like they'd been to a war. It turned out that being in a time crunch, being picky, and not being a size 0 all made for a catastrophic combination.

Every dress Nadia liked had been too small for her.

"We only carry our most popular sizes, up to a 4, in stock," an old lady had explained to Lola when she had complained, via Gianna, who had translated. When Lola was agitated, she couldn't think in English.

"We can order it for you," the woman had said in a placating voice. "But if you need alterations, then it might not be ready in time. It is high wedding season."

"I see," Nadia had said, defeated.

In the end, she'd found a red cocktail dress at a quinceañera store in West Valley, where there was a sizable Hispanic population, and where they hadn't felt out of place at all.

"You need to love it, though," Marcella said.

Marcella, who so far had only worn high-end athleisure, was fiercely supportive in Nadia's parameters to find the most feminine, and yet not childish, dress.

"I just wanted to have something to show my mom, the abuelas, and the aunts tonight," Nadia said, grabbing the slender box from the trunk of her car. "But I'm not convinced."

"We'll keep looking until you find it, Nadia," Marcella said. She had dark circles under her eyes. The day had been exhausting. But at the same time, Nadia had enjoyed having her cousins with her.

Lola and Gianna exchanged a mortified look, but then Lola said, "Of course, we will keep looking, mujer."

"What do you want us to wear?" Gianna asked, as if she'd been wondering for ages and was scared of the answer.

Nadia sighed. "I have your bridesmaid dresses. You can wear those, or whatever you prefer."

The bridesmaid dresses were blush-pink, silk shift, with cap sleeves, to accommodate Brandon's sister's aversion to showing her shoulders. Nadia had just finished paying for them, but she wasn't going to subject the women she loved the most to them.

"Isabella said she can sell them like this," she said, snapping her fingers. "It's a lot of twelve, counting the ones for the younger girls. She's sure we will get our money back. That will offset some of the added costs, like new invites."

Marcella placed a hand on Nadia's shoulder. "Are you sure? I didn't have a quinceañera, but I know they, too, have a court, and a boy escort."

Gianna and Lola laughed raucously.

"Escort boy, ooh la la!" said Lola, which made Marcella roll her eyes.

"What do they call them then?" she asked.

"Chambelán," Nadia said. "Madi had three chambelanes for her quinces. The boys about had a *Hunger Games* kind of contest so she'd choose them, so she decided to pick all three. It was epic."

They headed toward the house. The sound of cumbia blared from the backyard, and the smoke of an asado made Nadia's stomach growl with hunger.

"Maybe if you ask nicely, that guy from the venue will be your chambelán," Gianna said, bumping Nadia with her butt.

Nadia bumped her back. "Don't even joke about it."

But she imagined Marcos in a tuxedo, dancing with her under the stars, while the swans trumpeted in their pond.

"Come on in, chicas," Tía Aimée said when they walked in the kitchen. "Wash your hands and head to the back patio. There are empanadas and asado and a whole lot of other things."

"Then you can try your dress on for us, mamita," Bisa said, carrying a glass of Malbec to Nadia, who emptied it with a gulp.

She'd need a lot of courage for a dress-fitting session with all the women of her family.

Nadia held her breath as her mom pulled the corset around her. She was trying on her old dress from senior prom. She hadn't attended, because she had the ACT the next morning, and with a broken heart, she'd kept the dress in the fancy bag that had come from the store in the mall she never shopped at.

The dress was a bright pink that would have gone perfect with her complexion, but so many years later, it didn't fit her anymore. Even if she gave up breathing, she'd have to take out a couple of ribs for the dress to zip up. It didn't help that she'd eaten at least five salteñas and two heaping plates of asado and ensalada rusa. But she had no regrets. Even if her mom was about to suffocate her.

"Stop, Mami," she said, huffing for air. Her armpits were prickling with sweat from the effort of trying to fit into the dress intended for a food-deprived seventeen-year-old. Even though she had a better relationship with food at almost thirty, and maybe because of it, her waist circumference was several inches larger. And if, for some miracle, her waist had remained the same, then her breasts ruined everything, because not even two bra sizes too small could contain them.

"She's going to faint, Tía Virginia," Gianna said, coming to her rescue. "Breathe, mamita. Breathe."

With Marcella's help, her mom undid the corset laces, and Nadia took such a gulp of air that she got lightheaded. "Oof!"

Her vision went black, and she could only see puffs of light like dust motes in a sunbeam. "It's not going to work," she said, despairing that the red dress hadn't received the approval of the older women of her family.

"It's too office-looking," Tía Romina had declared. Olivia and the twins, Allegra and Amara, had agreed with their aunt, and then everyone else had chimed in.

"It makes you look like a secretary," Bisa said, and that had sealed the deal.

The red dress was a no-go.

She stepped out of the silky fabric and sent the prom dress she'd kept in her closet a sad glance. "I think Olivia would love to wear it. What do you think?" she asked Isabella, who was sitting on the bed but hadn't stopped pecking at her phone with her index finger.

Isabella opened her eyes dramatically and said, "She'd love it for sure. Now it's Jason who might not go along with the idea. He refuses to acknowledge she's not a little girl anymore."

All the women in the room shook their heads. They'd all experienced overprotective fathers. All except for Gianna, whose dad had died when she was really young.

"It's a privilege, you know? Getting to grow up? Getting to see your daughter grow from little girl to woman?" Nadia said.

Marcella nodded.

"Let's give him time," Isabella said. "Maybe next year for her graduation, he'll come to terms with it."

"But what are we going to do with the dress situation?" Virginia asked, scratching her hair.

They'd spent years—and that wasn't an exaggeration—looking for Nadia's dream wedding dress. And when she'd finally found it, it had cost her a fortune to alter it to her size.

And all the effort had been for nothing.

She looked at her dream dress that hung, beseechingly, from the back door of her mom's room.

"Try it on," Bisa said. "I want to see what it looks like."

In the last several days with her extended family, Nadia had learned that she couldn't deny Bisa anything. She hadn't even been able to confess that Marcos wasn't, in fact, her fiancé, so correcting her about the dress and explaining to her why it was painful to even look at, much less wear it, was a lost cause already.

Madi had joined the group, along with Olivia and the twins, the aunts, Abuela, Bisa, Gianna, Lola (her fancy aloofness from the first day tossed aside), and Marcella, obviously uncomfortable in this ultra-femme meeting. All of them watched her, the same silent request in their eyes.

"Just for fun," Virginia said.

Nadia sent a look to her sister, who just shrugged and asked, "What can you lose?"

She considered for a second or two.

"Dale, nena," Bisa said, helping her take off her T-shirt.

Nadia recoiled. It really wasn't that she didn't want to try the dress on. She wanted to. More than anything, to take a last look. But she was terrified that it wouldn't fit.

"We all have the same body parts as you, nena," Bisa said.

"My equipment doesn't look like that in a T-shirt, but oh well," Lola said, rolling her eyes and sending her a little smile of encouragement.

Nadia smiled back, grateful for the support. Ah! She would miss her cousins when they went back to their lives.

She took a deep breath and took off her T-shirt, completely aware that so many pairs of eyes were roving over her body. But when she dared look into the faces of the women of her family, she didn't see judgment, or much less, condemnation. If anything, a few of them seemed kind of stunned by what they saw. Especially the younger girls and—Marcella?

Gianna seemed to notice, too, because she playfully slapped

her girlfriend's leg and tried to cover her eyes. "Hey, hey, hey," she said. "Don't go falling in love with my cousin now!"

Marcella replied by kissing Gianna fully on the lips.

Now the twins and Olivia couldn't unglue their eyes from the happy couple. Hilariously, neither could Virginia. It was as if a whole world of possibilities they'd never considered had opened up for them.

"Bueno, bueno," Isabella said, aware of her daughter's fascination by the PDA. Then she turned toward Nadia and exclaimed, "Help me out here, will you? You started it, after all!"

Nadia sauntered to the dress that was hanging by the mirror and stepped into the silky coolness of the expansive, and expensive, fabric. She turned around so her sister could help her button the back. To her relief and surprise, it fit. When she turned around, she first saw her reflection.

There she was. This was a dress she'd designed with her friends when she was still a teenager, after Brandon had kissed her for the first time. She'd added details and changed things as the style changed with the years, and for the last two years, she'd been making modest payments to the exclusive costurera in the exclusive shop, who'd made her dream come to life.

It had all been for nothing.

"You can get a lot of money when you resell it," Lola said appreciatively.

"Of course," Isabella said. "I'll add it to the listing at the BYU classifieds."

The women murmured about how much a dress like this would cost in London, Barcelona, Buenos Aires, Sydney, or Rio de Janeiro.

"You don't even have to say the circumstances behind it, you know?" Gianna said, her red lipstick sexily smudged around her mouth. Nadia felt a twinge of envy for the kind of love her cousin had in her life. But she quickly squashed that down. Gianna deserved that love, and Nadia wouldn't begrudge it.

Nadia swallowed the knot in her throat as she nodded.

The money wasn't the issue, really. What did they call it in her Econ 101 class? Sunken costs. That was it.

What hurt the most was that whoever bought this dress wouldn't know the illusions and dreams sewn into it with the sequins and pearls. How she'd changed her eating habits and life to fit into it, and in the end, the dress didn't fit her dreams anymore. Besides, if it had taken her years to get the perfect dress ready to celebrate her wedding, who knew how long it would take her to choose a dress to celebrate her commitment to herself? Going through it once was enough for a lifetime. How did people who got married multiple times manage this?

Slowly, she lost focus of her desolate, jilted bride image in the mirror and clearly saw the women standing behind her. She pictured all those who hadn't made it here yet, like Stevie, who was still in Texas and who'd been sending pictures of dresses all day. And those who loved her but had passed on, like her Grandmother Palacio, and the cousins who couldn't travel for her special day.

A wave of gratitude grew inside her and threatened to over-whelm her. Seeing all of them here for her, she blinked back her tears. She was so mother-effing lucky.

"I'm not ready to get rid of this dress," Nadia confessed.

She turned around to face her family. She wasn't the only one whose eyes were filled with tears, anyway. There wasn't a safer place to cry than with all these women.

"You can save it for when you meet your true love, you know?" Tía Aimée said with a matter-of-fact tone. "Your future husband won't need to know you've had it from another engagement."

The whole room exploded in disagreement. Even the younger girls had looks of horror on their faces.

"It's unlucky, Aimée!" Tía Romina said. "You can't reuse from a previous wedding."

"I know the superstitions and all that," Tía Aimée countered. "All I'm saying is that those things don't really matter. You can repurpose the dress and still have a happy life. Maybe not for this double quinces party. The wound is still too recent and fresh. But for . . . later, you know?"

She shrugged, like she was trying not to say too much.

Everyone knew she had a story she was squirming to tell, actually.

"Aimée, what are you trying to say?" Romina asked.

Mercedes, the seventeen-year-old cousin, looked at her mom like she hadn't seen her before.

Finally, Aimée took a deep breath and said, "Before I married Román, I was engaged to another boy . . . man."

"A boy or a man?" Gianna asked, her big eyes bright with curiosity.

Tía Aimée blushed, but she plopped on the bed, and hugging a pillow, said, "A man, but I think of him as a boy, because we were both so young! He was my next-door neighbor, and we dated all through our teenage years. Our moms were best friends and were delighted with our relationship. They started gathering my trousseau when I was fourteen!"

There was a murmur of horror, although Nadia felt heat creeping up her neck all the way to her face.

She avoided looking at her sister, in case she outed her and told the family that she'd been planning her wedding in a giant binder since she was about that age, too. What would the family say?

"But I met Román one day, and I couldn't go through it with Ramón—that was his name—you know?"

"It's practically the same name," Bisa said, voicing the obvious thought flashing through everyone's minds. "What a coincidence!"

"I broke up with Ramón because I knew the love of my life was Román. A couple of months after graduating high school, Román and I got married. I wore the same dress I'd had in my hope chest, and I kept everything else that was in there, too."

"The initials were the same. How convenient," Mercedes

said, and the teenage cousins surrounded her to lovebomb her. Her cheeks were bright red, as if she were embarrassed by her mom's story, or amazed at the force of her parents' love.

Tía Aimée and Tío Román didn't particularly look like a couple from the movies or romance novels, but if Nadia knew something, it was that appearances lie. Their love had survived the threat of the worst superstition.

"Was Tío weirded out that you had all the stuff you'd gathered to marry another person?" she asked.

All the women looked at Tía Aimée.

Defiant, she said, "And waste a perfectly good dress? With the economy we've had for decades? He didn't even say a peep! He had me, and he didn't care I'd been with . . . you know? Another man." She swallowed. This was the type of confession no one expected from a tía that had always seemed perfect. But honestly? This confession made her so much more human, that she was now truly perfect for Nadia.

"And Ramón?" Mercedes asked.

Tía Aimée sighed and smiled in a Mona Lisa kind of way. "He moved to Brazil." She looked at Marcella then, as if Gianna's girlfriend represented the land of samba and caipirinha. "And he started an imports business. He's a millionaire now. He married a girl who'd been one of Xuxa's Paquitas. I know he's very happy with her."

The laughter and hooting that ensued was deafening. Nadia had never seen a show by the Brazilian celebrity Xuxa in her whole life, but like a good Argentine, even one transplanted to the Northern Hemisphere right when puberty started, she knew who Maria da Graça Xuxa Meneghel was. A blond, beautiful Brazilian model, singer, and TV show host, she'd dated Pelé and Ayrton Senna, the Formula 1 pilot. Nadia's mom told her stories of when she was in high school and her biggest dream had been to one day be chosen as one of Xuxa's Paquitas, the assistants on her show. She dreamed of that, although she didn't sing or dance, and of course, wasn't blond, tall, or thin.

A Paquita had to look like a Barbie doll. That standard of beauty had wrecked the self-esteem of dark-skinned Latin American girls for generations.

"I was not expecting that plot twist," Abuela Catalina said, fanning herself.

When the sound of laughter died down a little, Olivia was the brave one to ask the million-dollar question. "And do you regret it, Tía? Have you been happy?"

The tension grew to the point that it hurt Nadia's ears.

Looking at her daughter Mercedes, Tía Aimée said, "I don't regret it for one bit. My life with Román has been magical. Hard, but beautiful, you know? And Ramón, my old friend, he's so much better off with that woman, but I'm so much better off with my Román, and it's not only because he's so much better looking than my first boyfriend."

Tía Aimée took her phone from her pocket, and she swiped through the screen, looking for something.

"If you don't believe me, see for yourselves," she said, and handed the phone to Nadia.

"Wow!" Nadia exclaimed, seeing the side-to-side collage photo that Tía Aimée kept in her camera roll, as if she had to look at it often to remind herself of how lucky she was. The man on the left was a balding, thin man with a face like a full moon. Maybe he wasn't that bad-looking in person, and this was a terrible shot, but compared to the glorious shot of Tío Román laughing, his head thrown back, swinging a blue-and-yellow soccer jersey with abandon, the old boyfriend looked decrepit. And Tío Román looked like white-bearded Ricky Martin from his photo shoot that had made Nadia question her taste in older men.

"I see," Nadia said, and she passed the phone around for others to see the photos.

"It's not only money or looks," Tía Aimée said. "But how you feel when you're with them, you know? Do you feel adored and revered? Desired? Or like a check mark waiting to happen,

236 • *Yamile Saied Méndez*

just because it's the easy and convenient choice? Do you love yourself when you're with him? When I chose Román instead of Ramón, I chose myself. I wanted to keep loving who I was. I wanted to discover who I could become. And let me tell you, the journey has been worth it."

There was a collective sigh of satisfaction, like when you reach the end of a romantic movie or book that makes you tingly and giddy.

Tía had chosen love, the real love of her life, herself, instead of convenience or expectation.

"See, mi amor?" Virginia said to Nadia as she enveloped her in a one-armed embrace. "You can still rebuild your life, even after Brandon broke up with you. You could—how do I say this?" Virginia looked around for help, but everyone's face was either blank or preemptively horrified for what Virginia was about to say. "Still have things to live for."

Nadia's vision went red. She'd kept this secret in her heart so long, she felt that if she didn't tell everyone what had really happened with Brandon, she'd throw up.

"Mami, I have things to live for already." Her voice was firm and resolute. "I've always had things to live for, even if sometimes I forgot."

Virginia's eyes filled with tears. "Oh, dear! I didn't mean—"

Nadia put a hand up, and she swallowed a sob that was threatening to come back up and ruin the whole thing. She tried to pretend she was in front of a judge and jury, but unlike other times in the courtroom, when she could try better next time, she wanted to get things right once and for all in front of some of the people she loved and respected the most.

Bisa looked at her, confused, and for the only time, Nadia faltered, but then she said, "*I* broke up with Brandon."

She didn't get the reaction she had expected. Either utter shock and surprise or support. But there was no reaction. And, as when it seemed Tía Aimée had a story to tell, this was a story her family was waiting for and expected.

"I have felt like a piece of crap for years next to Brandon. The thing is, he hasn't felt much better about himself with me by his side, either."

"Now, now," Gianna interrupted her. "Don't go looking at things from his perspective."

"Yes," Lola added, "we don't care about his side at all. You're the only one who matters now. Tell us."

So she told them. And with each word she unburied, she saw how she'd lived for years, trudging to a finish line of a wedding that had been just an illusion to mask everything that was wrong in her relationship with Brandon.

"I prepared the proposal, remember, Isabella?" she asked, looking at her sister. "I wanted it to be just as I'd always dreamed of."

Isabella and even Olivia nodded. Olivia had been little, but even she'd felt how forced things were the day Brandon had proposed in front of the family.

"And then, with the wedding, it's been the same. He wanted nothing to do with it, and it wasn't like he trusted me with the details. He just didn't want anything to do with it—or me," she said, sniffing, because although she was strong, saying the words was still like stripping her skin one inch at a time.

"It wasn't all like that," Isabella said, putting a hand up. "There was love, but not the kind you deserved. Good for you, Nadia. I'm proud of you."

Nadia held her breath. She had expected no different from her sister. But what about the rest of the family? Tía Romina had complained that they had to spend vacation time coming to the wedding, which they could've used to see the family back in Argentina. And Nadia felt guilty.

This might be the last time she saw Bisa, and it wasn't the wedding she'd dreamed of.

"Why did you do it now, knowing how hard it would be?" Lola asked in her posh British accent.

Nadia gave those translating the time to interpret the words into Spanish or Portuguese, the looks into emotions and conclusions.

"I wanted to celebrate myself," she said. "Make a commitment that I will love myself above all else, which isn't a permission slip to be selfish. I hope you will all still celebrate with me?"

To her surprise, Virginia started clapping. And then they all followed.

"Of course we'll stay and celebrate," Tía Aimée said when she hugged and kissed Nadia. "Tomorrow, we'll find a dress. You'll see."

For the first time, Nadia looked down and realized she'd been baring her heart to her family while only wearing a bra and panties, but she'd never felt more comfortable and protected around people in her life.

Chapter 16

Marcos

During the next several days, Marcos was immersed in preparations for the Coronel wedding party on Friday and a twentieth wedding anniversary on Saturday. A few months ago, if anyone had told him he'd be wedding planner and organizer and that he loved it, he would have laughed. But here he was, making sure every detail was perfect so people he hadn't previously known were happy, at least for one night. From the food to the photographer to the decorations, he double- and triple-checked so his clients didn't experience any nasty surprises, like Nadia had.

The day before, via text, she'd told him the florist had called her to confirm that the wedding had been canceled and the flowers donated to the local senior home.

Nadia had been frantic.

The florist had been adamant that a man had called with specific details, but since it was Nadia's name in the order, she wanted to make sure. Nadia had gone ahead and donated what would have been her bouquet and those of her bridesmaids.

Last year, she had picked sunflowers. She had told Marcos it would take her a while to forgive Brandon for ruining her favorite flower for her. But at least the yellow blossoms would brighten other people's lives. She'd made a new order for pink and cream roses, even if they cost more than her original selection.

Nadia's text read:

I think Brandon's trying to sabotage my party. It's very out of character, but I only wanted to let you know in case he tries to cancel there at the venue. Sorry to vent about this personal problem, but I thought you should know.

Marcos didn't think it was Brandon.

Nadia's ex was a coward.

Maybe his sister and mother were behind this flood of cancellations and misunderstandings? Maybe it was Kenzie? He hoped it wasn't his assistant. He didn't know what he would do if this suspicion turned out to be the truth.

Marcos answered:

You did well in letting me know. So far, the rest of the reservations are still a go. Your friend Madi confirmed with Cancún Querido. My friend Becca and her crew received the payment for the photos and the video. And Oscar said he's delivering the invites in your hand tonight. Let me know as soon as you get them if you like them.

He saw the three dots dancing on his screen. He held his breath in anticipation of what she would say. Tonight was the soccer game her family had invited him to. She hadn't mentioned anything about that.

She only sent a thumbs-up.

Marcos exhaled, disappointed.

But what had he expected? He'd only done what any other venue would do, connect clients with services and vendors and coordinate everything so their events would be as smooth as possible.

But then, his phone vibrated in his hand.

Nadia:

Thank you for everything, Marcos. By the way, Bisa says hi. She's excited to see you tonight.

The glow in his chest lasted him for hours.

That is, until Kenzie walked into his office with a thick envelope and dropped it on his desk as if it were burning her hands. The return address read, "Miller, Hunt, and Associates, Attorneys at Law" in ominous red letters.

"This was in the mailbox, Mark," she said. Her eyes were icy cold. "They're not going to relent until you give them an answer."

Marcos rose from his chair and grabbed the hefty envelope. "I can't decide anything until my sister's back from Phoenix," he replied.

That was not the answer Kenzie was hoping for, apparently. She squared her shoulders and lifted her chin. "I'll need time to find another job if you decide to get rid of—"

He placed a placating hand on her arm. She softened immediately, and he took a step back just in case. "Whatever decision my sister and I make, I promise we're taking into consideration the future of every person who has worked with my family all these years."

"Forgive me if I'm not thrilled at the sound of promises," she said, her voice dry and distant.

She turned to leave.

"Kenz," he said.

She stopped at the door of his office. "What is it?"

His heart hammered as he gathered the courage to ask if she was behind the attempts to sabotage Nadia's party.

"We've had a lot of problems with vendors dropping Nadia Palacio's reservations. The florist got a call from a man, canceling her order and sending the flowers to a senior home. Do you know anything about that?"

Kenzie's lips parted as she gasped in surprise. "Are you asking if *I* had anything to do with it? If so, just say it, Marcos."

She was either a good actress or innocent, but by her reaction, he gathered she hadn't done it, and now she was offended and hurt he'd asked.

"I only asked if you knew anything. Do you?"

She swallowed hard and shook her head. "I may not be thrilled with her party, but I'm not that kind of woman to bring down other women. You should know that."

Without another word, she left his office.

Marcos cursed himself, and without opening the envelope, he threw it in the garbage.

For hours, he debated whether he should go to the soccer game with Nadia's family. But just as he was about to head to the gym, Hernán texted him. He was coming along and bringing the girls. He included a picture with the three of them wearing Chile national jerseys. Lily had lost her two bottom teeth, and her smile was adorable.

They want to see their tío Marcos. Don't let them down.

Marcos laughed.

Manipulator.

Hernán:

Please, I need some time outside. Help me.

Marcos sent a thumbs-up and added:

See you at the pitch.

He grabbed a Uruguay jersey from a drawer in his desk and headed out. His excitement grew like dough left by a sunny window as he drove to the park. Once there, and still in the car, he put on his cleats that had languished in a closet for years. They were stiff for lack of wear, but they would work. He trotted over lush grass speckled with dried patches that exposed the hard-packed red dirt. A cloud of dirt haloed him as he approached Nadia's family.

"Uruguayo, you made it!" Nadia's tío Román greeted him.

He went around the group, shaking hands and kissing cheeks, but there was no sign of Bisa, or most importantly, Nadia, although three cousins who looked close to her age eyed him from a bench, as if they were x-raying his character. He gazed, hoping he wasn't being too obvious.

The cousin with red hair and a heart-shaped face must have understood his gesture, though, because she said, in Spanish with a European accent, "She couldn't make it."

It took Marcos's brain a few seconds to process her words.

"Lola means Nadia won't be coming," the tall cousin with the braids piled on top of her head said in English. This time, he understood the words all right, but the Australian accent threw him off. When this cousin turned toward the third one, an athletic Black woman, and kissed her on the corner of the mouth, his confusion was complete.

"What?" the redhead asked, "do you have a problem with them kissing?"

Marcos shook his head to clear his mind and find the perfect words to express his thoughts. "No. Not the fact that they were kissing. I mean, yes, I'm confused about that, but only because I thought you were all Nadia's cousins. We're in Utah, and still, I didn't realize you're *that* kind of family . . ."

The three of them exchanged a look and burst into laughter.

"Sorry," the redheaded one said, now in English with a strong British accent. "We didn't get introduced the other day. I'm Lola. How do you do? I'm Nadia's cousin on her dad's side, and this is Gianna, her cousin on her mom's side, and this is her girlfriend, Marcella. And your name?"

"I'm Marcos."

"The venue owner?" Gianna asked.

"And an old friend of Nadia's," he added, hoping they wouldn't see in his eyes a reflection of the memories that were flashing in his mind right now. Memories from ten years back that mixed with the ones formed after seeing Nadia again, and a few of the fantasies his brain curated when he dreamed of her—at night and awake.

Maybe they hadn't seen anything in his face, but they must have heard something in his voice, because they exchanged another look, and then, with conspiratorial smiles, walked up to him.

"Oh," Lola said, "I didn't know that about you and Nadia. You have a story? Tell us, how did you meet?"

He was sweating bullets. What mess had he gotten himself into?

"Tío Marcos!" Lucy, Lily, and Luna squealed in unison as they ran toward him, their arms wide open.

Marcos shot an apologetic smile toward Nadia's cousin, as if to say he'd tell her later after he'd said hi to his friend's daughters. She nodded once in approval, and for the next fifteen minutes, Nadia's three cousins watched as he played with the girls, threw them in the air like they demanded, and helped them tie their shoelaces. He couldn't be sure, but he thought he saw the three of them surreptitiously taking pictures or videos of him.

When he was about to resume the conversation, Nadia's dad called them to the game. The rival team, a hotchpotch of people of all ages from the same family in Brazilian jerseys, was already warming up on the field.

"Can you play as a nine?" Tío Ricardo asked.

Marcos hadn't played soccer in years, but he nodded, afraid of confessing he wouldn't live up to their expectations. He joined Nadia's cousins and nephew in the offensive. In the end, though, the one who ended up scoring time after time was Marcella. When he found out she played professionally in Australia, it all made sense, and a little bit of his self-esteem returned to him.

"You did well, Marcos. You have to come to the final," Nadia's dad told him, smacking Marcos's shoulder with appreciation.

"I don't know," he said. "I have to make sure everything's ready for Nadia's party next week."

He was excited to see how all the preparations would turn out, to see Nadia's face of happiness as she celebrated with this wonderful family, who obviously adored her. But he was also sad that his time with the Palacio clan was coming to its end.

Hernán must have been feeling the same, because he said to Nadia's dad, "If you'll still play after your brothers are gone, give me and Marcos a call. Right, Uruguayo?"

Marcos nodded along with his friend and tried not to look too eager at Nadia's dad.

But before Ernesto agreed to invite them, Gianna came up to Marcos and said, "Nadia just said she's so sad she couldn't make it, but she'll be here next time for sure. She was dealing with the cake."

Marcos's mind jumped to the worst-case scenario. "Are there any problems? Everything still okay?"

Gianna put a hand up and nodded. "Oh, no. Don't worry. It's all perfect with the cake, *and* the dress, but . . ." She bit her lower lip dramatically and looked at him with puppy eyes.

"What is it?"

"It's just that she doesn't have any professional shots of her in her dress for the highlights reel video my cousins and I are making of her."

Marcella and Lola were both typing furiously on their respective phones and sending Gianna amused glances. Gianna's phone vibrated in her hand and lit up with incoming messages, but she never once looked at it, continuing to stare at Marcos instead.

"The professional photographer you recommended can't be here until the day of the party, and then it would be too late to add these shots in the video. But wait—" Gianna stopped talking, her index finger up and a curious expression on her face, as if she'd just had the best idea. "Aren't you the one who took the shot for the invites?"

The corner of Marcos's mouth tugged up in a smile he couldn't conceal. "I am. And I'm so glad she liked it enough to put it in the invitation instead of sending them blank."

"Oh," Lola exclaimed. "She more than loved it! She's ecstatic with them, especially all the compliments she's getting! You can't imagine."

"Which is why I just thought of something amazing," Gianna said, "but that is . . . if you have time and the desire, I mean . . ."

Marcos had a glimpse of suspicion at what Gianna was hinting. His first inclination was saying no right away, before she got carried away. But when she added, "You have to see the dress her friend Stevie sent in a special delivery. It arrived this morning, and it fits her like it was made just for her. Wouldn't it be amazing if you took a few shots of her in her dress?"

He replied, "Yes," like a fool. He was stunned speechless by his rashness.

Gianna, who must not have expected such an easy resolution, blinked a couple of times and glanced at her cousin and her girlfriend, but she snapped out of her surprise faster than Marcos did.

"It's all settled then," she said. "Meet us the day of the final family soccer game at this address. The other day, Nadia said that this place was her dream location for bridals, but she had been too self-conscious to get them done in such a public space. Do you know where it is?"

She gave him a brochure for Thanksgiving Point, one of the most iconic landmarks in Utah County. There were gardens, a golf club, a yoga and dance studio, a Museum of Natural Curiosity, and a butterfly reserve. This late in September, it also featured a corn maze and a fall festival. Marcos had done countless shots for weddings and family pictures in this location, but not for several years now.

"The three of us are giving her this photo session and the

video as one of our presents. I've been looking at an old Instagram with your name and seen some amazing shots you've taken. Just let us know how much it is."

He couldn't say no, not to her cousins, not to Nadia's dreams, and not to the chance to see her unapologetically from behind a camera, trying to highlight all the beautiful things about her, which were countless.

"We'll see you next week then," Lola said, after high-fiving Gianna.

He wondered what kind of mischief her cousins had weaved and trapped him in. But the prospect of another excuse to see her again before the party kept him buoyed for days.

Marcos had made sure the plan was okay for Nadia. For all Gianna had insisted the photo shoot was a gift that the cousins were paying for, it was important that everything related to her party was exactly what Nadia wanted.

Marcos:

Is 7 okay for you? That way we can catch the best light.

Nadia:

It's good. The game is right after. Bisa might not be coming, so you don't need to stay if you don't want.

Marcos:

It's okay. I'll go to the game after.

She'd only sent back a thumbs-up emoji. It wasn't the message he'd been looking for that she, too, wanted to see him, but at least she hadn't uninvited him to come along with her family.

Now, he waited for her in the parking lot of Thanksgiving Point. He'd brought Kai. He'd been doing odd jobs at the venue like directing traffic, acting as valet, helping put things away. He was hardworking and eager to please. But as soon as Kai saw Nani coming down the sidewalk, all dressed up in her treintañera dress, Marcos regretted his decision to bring the boy.

"Holy mother of angels!" the boy exclaimed, without any

kind of filter. "Wow! I don't think I've ever seen a more beautiful woman in my life!"

Exasperated with the boy's lack of professionalism, Marcos turned around to tell him off, but when he caught sight of Nani, the words turned to sand on his tongue.

Holy mother of angels couldn't even begin to describe what Nani looked like.

The shocking neon-pink dress hugged her curves in a way that defied description. It wasn't only the plunging cleavage or that slit in the side of her already short skirt that challenged his wildest fantasies, but the way the light played on Nani's golden-tanned shoulders, her coily brown hair, and the apples of her cheeks as she smiled, attracting the attention of everyone standing in the way. The train of the dress draped over her arm. She wore a dainty tiara on top of her curls, and her piercing brown eyes had more power than a whip to which he'd happily submit for the rest of eternity.

Her three cousins followed her, along with several older women, all attractive and distinguished, most likely Nadia's aunts. They were all beaming, as if being by her side filled them all with pride. Marcos recognized her niece, Olivia, at the end of the swarm of stunning women. He was relieved that the object of Kai's fascination was her and not Nadia.

Bisa didn't seem to have come along, and he was a little disappointed. He wouldn't have the excuse of pretending to be the fiancé to hold her hand or just stare at her without guilt.

Next to him, Kai had become frozen, bewitched by the display of self-confidence and power. And how could he blame the boy, when at the mere sight of Nadia, he'd lost all control over his own body and thoughts?

If she'd asked him to whisk her away to another galaxy, he'd do it without questioning whether that was possible or not. It was a good thing that when she was in front of him, she only smiled and said a shy *hi* before she kissed him on the cheek.

If she'd asked him anything at all, he'd have been unable to speak.

"Hi, Marcos," one of the women said as she shook his hand. "I'm Isabella. Nadia's sister."

He couldn't help trying to gauge how much she knew about their situation.

"Hi, Isabella. Nadia has told me so much about you." Which had been true.

"Nice!" she said, but didn't say the same in return, and he was a little disappointed.

Nadia turned toward him and said, "Marcos, these are some of my cousins, my sister, my niece, and my two best friends, Stevie and Madi. They were going to be my maids, but now they're my royal court. Girls, this is Marcos. He's the venue owner and . . ." She looked at him, and his heart leapt in his chest as if he were an awkward teenager. "He's a friend," she added.

"Oh! We've already met el guapo Bisa was raving about!" Gianna said, and winked at him.

"Oh!" everyone said in unison.

Nadia's friends whispered to each other and sent her a curious look that she avoided.

What was the story there? He wanted to know. He was so engulfed in her charm that he had to shake his head to clear his thoughts.

Luckily, by the time he was done kissing every one of the women on the cheek, he'd gained a little more composure.

Isabella, who seemed to be in charge, informed him that after a couple of group pictures, the rest of her party were going to explore the gardens, while a couple of them helped with the pictures of Nadia.

He wished it was just the two of them, catching her every gesture during golden hour, so later, he could whisk her away just for him. But he had no right to begrudge sharing her with her family.

"Of course," he said. "You tell me what to do, and I'll follow through."

Nadia's friends, Stevie and Madi, exchanged a look that he didn't know how to read.

"This is beautiful," Nadia's mom said. "I love this place so much. The gardens become more and more stunning every year."

"I've never been to the gardens," Nadia said, gazing around through impossibly long lashes that cast shadows on her cheeks.

"Really?" He couldn't believe the airhead Brandon had never once brought her to see the tulips in the spring, or the dahlias and peonies riot in the summer, or her favorite, sunflowers in the fall. She was so gorgeous, she looked like the most beautiful flower. He'd always thought so, even when she'd been wearing those hideous polyester pants for work, and with this dress—which didn't so much show too much skin, but rather high-lighted all the right places—he felt that if he didn't kiss her, he was going to die.

"Let's get going," Isabella said, with a handclap like a teacher. And then, realizing the looks everyone sent her, she smiled sheepishly and said, "I don't want the good light to go to waste, of course. Sorry."

With a sigh, he turned toward Nadia. Her sister was now fussing with her hair, arranging it around her back like a fan. Nadia raised her eyebrows and smiled. "Thank you for helping me out with this. I . . . it's so indulgent, no?"

The rest of the group chatted like parrots as they paid the entrance fee. He had a pass, but it only covered him, the person being photographed, and a helper. Isabella headed to the front of the line, maybe to pay for everyone else.

"So what if it is indulgent?" he challenged her. "This is a big event, and photos are the best way to remember it."

"Is it?" she asked, doubt clouding her pretty eyes.

He shrugged and took her hand. "Let's go. Your sister's right. We're going to waste the best light." And then, turning to his assistant, who was chatting up Olivia, he called, "Hey, Kai! Let's go, buddy!"

Kai jumped like he'd been found with his paw in the cookie jar. "Coming, boss!"

Olivia watched the boy with the same expression that Kai directed at her. At least someone's feelings were being reciprocated.

Kai and Nadia followed Marcos into the gardens. Soon, the rest of the party joined them as he took shots of her in prepared spots or just candids. He was grateful for the filter of the camera between them and the excuse he had to stare at her to his heart's content, catching every expression on her beautiful face.

At first, when he asked her to pose a certain way, her movements were stiff and self-conscious. He made sure to press on the shutter to catch the transformation back to the confident, strong woman she was and every other gesture in between.

She smiled, hearing the laughter from her cousins and friends as they explored the gardens and took pictures on their phones. She gave a thumbs-up to someone, and when he turned, he saw Gianna leaving a duffel bag next to the rest of the cameras and equipment.

Kai had been the perfect assistant, hauling things all over the place and following Marcos and Nadia across the gardens. He'd been talking to Olivia and the other teenage girls, but suddenly, it was only Marcos and Nadia in a secluded area with an artificial waterfall in the back.

"Do you think we have plenty of good shots?" she asked, reapplying her lip-gloss while he changed the lens of his camera.

He looked at her over his shoulder, and he froze. The light was hitting her profile perfectly.

Oh, to be a sunbeam. To have the privilege of sliding down the slope of her flawless copper skin.

His hands rushed as he tried to prepare the camera for this one shot in a lifetime. It was even better than the one he'd gotten at the ranch.

She froze, and a look of suspicion crossed her face. "Why are you looking at me like that? Do I have a bug on me? Rocket, tell me right now."

Amazingly agile for wearing four-inch heels on the grass, she started scooting away from him. Dangerously close to an outcrop of boulders that loomed into a sharp drop below. Now it was his blood that froze.

"Don't move, Nani," he hissed, trying to balance himself, while he held Nadia's arm with one hand and his camera with the other. But if it came down to it, he'd drop the camera without hesitation. For him to let go of Nani, his arm would have to fall off. "Come here."

But Nani—stubborn, flighty Nani—didn't trust him. "Why did you tell me not to move if I don't have a spider in my hair?"

"Because you look fucking gorgeous, and I wanted to take a shot of you," he said through gritted teeth. "And now you're running away from an imaginary spider and are about to fall to your death."

Her face blanched. "Oh," she said, glancing at the air behind her. And below. She smiled tight-lipped and waved a little wave. "Yes, hi, boys. I hope you're enjoying the view."

Marcos about jumped out of his skin, trying to see whom she was talking to, but as he let her go, she wobbled. He quickly looked up at her and said, "Come here, Nani. We're going to fall."

Red-faced, she stepped toward him and fell into his arms. He could feel her heart racing through the flimsy fabric of her dress and his T-shirt.

He flipped the bird to the guys below, a bunch of bros, all carrying golf clubs and high-fiving each other. Pervs. He had the irrational thought to run downhill and punch them to pieces for daring to look up as Nadia was perched at the edge of the stone cropping.

But she was shaking in his arms now, gasping for air.

"Why did you run?" he asked. He pressed his lips against the top of her head and held her there for a second. How was he ever going to let her go?

Eventually, she pulled away from him and looked up into his eyes. A thunderstorm flashed in hers. "You scared me with that look and that voice, Rocket!" She accentuated each word with a pound to his chest.

"There's a smile," he said, pushing her chin up with his index finger.

No camera would ever catch the light playing across her face, so instead of trying to get both of them killed again, he just stared at her, vowing to remember this moment forever.

When he was sixteen, at the peak of his teen rebellion, he'd found his mom looking at him with a curious expression. She'd caught him at a rare moment; he was entertained with building an old Lego set of a *Star Wars* ship. Even at that age, he'd liked putting them together.

"What are you looking at, Ma?" he'd asked.

"You," she'd said, and he'd blushed, suddenly self-conscious. "I'm trying to take a picture with my eyes, so I'll remember this moment forever."

He had left all the pieces on the table and fled to his room. Several weeks later, when it was obvious that he wouldn't go back to finish that project either, the pieces were still there. It wouldn't be until the next holiday season that someone finally picked them up. But two things had stayed with him that day: that his mother had loved him and wanted to treasure every moment with him; and that, in spite of her love and the vote of confidence, he couldn't finish a single thing in his life without leaving a mess behind.

A rush of self-loathing swept over him. He wouldn't put additional stress on Nadia as she tried to figure out what to do with the rest of her life. He couldn't lean on her hard work. He had to find a purpose himself.

Nadia inhaled deeply, and he thought she was ready to say something about him scaring or holding her. But instead she said, "Your uncles want to take the property from you."

Marcos was so disoriented that he had to shake his head a little, as if to clear his ears. "What? My uncles?"

He pulled her along to a safe surface away from the cliff. Golden hour was long gone, but when he blinked, he still saw her profile lined by all the colors of the rainbow playing fantasies on her face.

He'd been right; it didn't matter that he hadn't been able to catch that shot. Her image was burned on his retinas.

But now, what was she saying about his uncles and the venue?

She was blushing again, her chest falling and rising, as if she were nervous.

Now it was his turn to become alarmed, as his mind rushed to the worst-case scenarios.

"I work . . . that is, I used to work at Miller, Hunt, and Associates."

She looked at him as if the name should mean anything. The name was familiar. A dreadful feeling fell on him as he remembered the envelope he'd thrown in the garbage. He shook his head. She worked for the firm that wanted to take the ranch away from him and his family?

She clicked her tongue. "The law firm that represents your uncles, Monty and George? They're your uncles, right?"

His heart lurched inside him. "Yes, how do you know?"

"Are you listening to me? I worked at the law firm that represents them. I know your case. They want to take your parents' venue and build either a new golf course or condos. Whatever will leave them the most money. They have a case. If they can't get you and your sister to sign, they'll get your dad to do it, however they can."

"They can't do that," he said, scoffing.

"You really believe that? Have you talked to your dad about

it? They call him constantly. Believe me, I've spoken with him before."

"My dad?"

"Your dad, before I knew who he really was."

Marcos hadn't talked to his dad in forever. His excuse was always that his father didn't know him anymore. But had he really tried to see what he wanted to do with the rest of his life? Had Marcos asked?

He hadn't. He'd assumed.

"If your dad signs, everything will be gone. It will be back to your uncles' hands, and your family won't receive a cent."

"How do you know all that?" he asked. His mouth had gone dry.

"I was assigned to this case. It was supposed to be my big break, Marcos. But I just couldn't go through with it."

He looked at her, blinking a few times.

She lowered her gaze and sighed.

"A year ago, I went to the venue for your dad to sign the papers. The reason I gave him when I met him was that I was interested in hosting my wedding there. But after talking to him, about what Enchanted Orchards meant for him, how it reminded him of your mom, I fell in love with the place and booked it for the wedding. I'm sorry for not warning you before, but if you want to hold on to your property, you should. There's a . . . special thing about that place. Maybe that's why I held on to the idea of doing my quinceañera there, even if it was a conflict of interest? Instead of finding a new venue, I quit my job. Maybe I should've just taken my losses. This party was a huge mistake."

Her eyes were full of tears, but she didn't flinch away from him. Before he could assure her that nothing was her fault, her phone rang. She fumbled in the layers of tulle until she seemed to find it.

Her eyes widened in alarm.

"Everything and everyone okay?" he asked.

"Yes," she said, "it's just that my cousins already left with Madi and Stevie for the soccer game. They assumed you'd be coming along. I'm sorry."

They were alone in the darkening gardens now, but he could tell she was blushing. The rushing sound in his ears didn't let him hear what she was saying. He was finally alone with her, and he was awkward like a lovestruck boy.

"Sorry for what?"

"They're heading to the field," she said. "They think I'm riding with you."

Marcos's phone vibrated, and when he looked at it, he saw the last message from Kai. He laughed.

"What?" she asked.

"My assistant ditched me, too. He said that when he couldn't find us, he offered Olivia and the girls a ride there. Since I'm driving you, he'll meet us at the fields."

Nadia's face blushed with embarrassment.

"Oh my gosh, I'm so sorry . . ." she said. "You don't have to drive me, though . . . I'll text my sister or someone. I'll get an Uber."

"It's okay," he said. "I'd love to drive you. Remember, I'm part of your dad's team now, too."

She pressed her lips and raised her eyebrows. "Sorry about that, too, but you don't have to come along or drive me, you know?"

But there was no way he'd go back on his word. He was still trying to process the fact that she'd quit her job instead of being complicit in the fall of his venue.

"No, I want to," he said. "I even brought my soccer boots from the good ol' college days. They still fit."

She tried to smile, but her eyes were still teary.

"Before we go, I need to change," she said. She grabbed the duffel bag Gianna had left for her a while ago.

"What? You're not going to run in those heels and that little dress?"

"Little dress?" she asked, her voice high-pitched. "It's yards of tulle!"

He wiggled his eyebrows. "In the train, because . . ."

Luckily, before he confessed how the dress didn't leave anything else to the imagination, he saw the sign for the bathroom. "You can change there."

"Guard the door for me, please. I don't want anyone to come in while in my underwear," she said, and he nodded, trying not to imagine her in underwear so tiny it hadn't even shown.

So many things whirled in his mind. What was she thinking right now that they were finally all alone?

He was so nervous that for the first time in years, he had the urge to smoke. He hadn't touched a cigarette since the summer between junior and senior year, when he'd had a coughing fit during his morning run. He'd started smoking to piss off his dad. He didn't remember why they had fought now. Did it even matter anymore? But it all had backfired when he couldn't breathe deep enough to run, so he'd quit cigarettes as easily as he'd become dependent on them.

Now, he was anxious like he'd been at sixteen, uncomfortable in his own skin, knowing he was letting everyone down. That he wasn't enough.

He exhaled, but without a nicotine hit, it just wasn't the same. He had the urge to run away. To escape from his feelings. But a voice that didn't speak in words told him there was no running away from her again.

"Ready?" she said, coming out of the bathroom. The fluorescent light didn't have the same effect of the sunset, but it still highlighted the shine in her hair and eyes. She looked as radiant in shorts and a T-shirt, which was painted like an Argentine flag, as she had in the dress she now held in her arm.

He pursed his lips, every cell in his body straining with the effort not to take her in his arms and love her in front of the whole world. "Is that how it's going to be now?"

He opened his duffel bag, pulled out a light blue jersey, and put it on top of his white T-shirt.

"Game on!" she said, brushing a hand over the Uruguayan Football Association logo on the top left of his chest. Instinctively, he flexed his pecs, and she laughed.

She didn't do this enough.

"It's el clásico of the Americas," he said.

"Let's go," she said, hooking her hand in the crook of his arm as they headed to his car, and then on to the soccer fields on the other side of the valley.

Chapter 17

Nadia

The soccer fields were teeming with life. It was the end of the summer, right before a weekend, when people flocked to meet their friends and rivals in a quest to feel a little of the rush they still remembered from their childhood years. Nadia didn't know how Marcos felt about the sport that defined their home countries, but she had a love/hate relationship with it.

Growing up, Nadia hadn't ever played soccer. She didn't even like it. This was all her dad's fault, though. When Argentina or his team from Rosario played, he'd watch it on their giant TV or listen to it on the radio. The otherwise mellow and peaceful Ernesto Palacio turned into a different, not very pleasant man when he watched fútbol.

When his team won, it was all hearts and rainbows at home. But when it lost . . . ay, when his team lost, he raved and swore and foamed at the mouth, throwing things around the house. Things got to a point that when the girls and their mom saw the TV on, they'd scurry away like mice, looking for a safe hiding spot. When they couldn't go anywhere to wait out his rages, they'd drive for hours, admiring the beautiful scenery in Utah, dreading what they'd find at home.

And when Argentina lost the World Cup final in Brazil in 2014, something broke inside Ernesto.

Nadia was telling Marcos about it as they walked from the car to the field. She had goosebumps from the memories and the coolness of the just-watered grass.

"We arrived home late that night, already knowing that Argentina had lost. To our surprise, everything looked okay. He hadn't destroyed the house like we'd feared. It was quiet. I saw him first, sitting out in the yard with el mate in his hand, looking at the fence. I thought he was dead, and when I ran to him and realized his eyes were open, he turned to me." She licked her lips as she continued the story. "And he smiled, tears falling down his cheeks, and he said, 'I'm sorry for being the way I am. I thought fútbol was the only way I was still connected to my family, but I realized it was what was pushing it apart from me. I'm sorry.'"

"Wow," Marcos said, a somber expression on his face. "That's . . . special."

"Yes," Nadia said, exhaling. "He follows the games now, and he'll swear every once in a while when Central loses, but it's nothing like it used to be. And after he started being more . . . civilized? Yes, civilized. After he started being more like a normal person, Isabella and I started liking fútbol, you know? Olivia now plays in high school. I wish I had. I was a cheerleader instead, and I liked it, but it wasn't the same."

He did a double take. "You were a cheerleader? I didn't know."

There were so many things he didn't know about her; why was he surprised? Still, his expression was endearing.

"And you?"

He was the one who exhaled now. He laughed sadly and said, "In my house, the fútbol fanatic was my mom. My middle name is Enzo." He looked at her as if she should get the reference, but she had no idea who Enzo might be.

"Enzo Francescoli, the Uruguayan fútbol national treasure."

"Like Luis Suárez or Cavani?" she replied. She knew those players because Olivia kept her updated.

"Francescoli was ten Luis Suárezes and ten Edinson Cavanis combined. He played in River Plate, so I'm sure your dad will know who he is. The thing is, she didn't expect me to become a soccer player, but everyone else around me did. My uncles, for example, filled my dad's head with stories of the great teams Uruguay had through the years. And in 2010, when they went to the semifinal, wow, I was obsessed. But my mom didn't insist on me playing. I wanted to, though. I wanted to be more Uruguayan than American, and I tried. I wasn't that good dribbling."

She laughed. "It's harder than it looks, right? Everyone sees Messi and thinks it just happens."

"Exactly," he said. "I couldn't dribble to save my life, but I was fast, so instead of torturing me, my mom signed me in track and field. And it changed my life."

In one of the fields they passed, there were kids playing a game, and on the sidelines, parents yelling like they were possessed.

Nadia and Marcos looked at each other and shook their heads.

"Our countries' relationship with soccer is so complicated, right? The culture is beautiful, but it can also be so toxic," Nadia said.

"And yet here we are."

Then she turned and looked at him. "You don't have to do this, you know? I mean, play with my family. My dad has calmed down watching games, but when he plays . . . he still gets intense."

"Don't worry," he reassured her. "He was fine last time. I survived, and they invited me back after all."

By then, the family, clad in blue and pink shirts, were waving at them. Her heart clenched. When she and Brandon had planned this night, they'd imagined their large families could make two teams, and they could have fun. Now it was only her family and a few friends, trying to fill in the blanks of her broken relationship. The men, her dad and uncles, seemed like they wanted to prove their manhood in the field, even if only to prove to Marcella, Gianna's girlfriend from Brazil, that they could still compete.

Nadia knew they really couldn't, and she worried about the aftermath.

Bisa saw them first and started waving Marcos over. "Come over here, guapo!" she said. "I'm cheering for you!"

Nadia laughed, because the other alternative was digging a hole in the earth and staying huddled in there until the end of the universe.

"Don't worry," Marcos said, placing an arm over her shoulders.

She looked at him through narrowed eyes. The field lights made a halo around his tanned face that made her stomach lurch with wanting to see him smile at her like this forever.

"Already in character, I see . . ."

He laughed, too, and drew her closer. "We need to make great-grandma happy. I mean, she's looking right at us."

"And if we don't get it right, we can try again next time. She won't remember," Nadia said, trying to laugh.

"Now, don't be sad. Let's have a fun time with the family."

The family received him as if he were the prodigal son. And for a second, Nadia let herself imagine that in an alternate reality, Marcos was really her fiancé, and they were playing this game before their actual wedding.

She would never have this with him again, and the Marcos-shaped hole in her heart would hurt, so she did all she could to memorize each of his expressions as he shared his soda mate with her uncles, and he chatted with her mom and her cousins.

While he was surrounded by the uncles, who all wanted to talk to him, Gianna took Nadia's arm and pulled her aside.

"What?"

Gianna had a mischievous expression on her face. "Nothing . . . I just want you to see something." She grabbed her phone from her pocket, scrolled through the screen, and showed her a picture.

It was a shock of reds, pinks, and oranges. The swirling technicolor sunset behind Marcos and her, as she snuggled close to his chest, in his arms, his head resting on hers, his eyes closed. If she'd come across this photo, she'd think it had been staged. But she remembered the rush of relief at being rescued by him before she fell to perhaps her death. Only because he'd scared her with that serious voice and expression, but that didn't show in the picture. Her insides melted as she remembered the warmth of his arms, and the scent of the sun and cologne on his skin. She imagined coming home to the promise of those arms every night for the rest of her life.

Why was she always thinking of what she couldn't have?

She hadn't missed Brandon at all this whole month. She imagined that once the family left, and the party was over, the reality would sink in.

She'd break up with her fiancé of more than a decade, and she'd quit the job she'd worked so hard to get.

Those two things didn't really hurt right now, and she imagined it was the shock.

But after her party was over, she wouldn't have an excuse to see Marcos anymore. For all she knew, he might sell the property. The venue would disappear.

Somehow, the thought of not seeing Marcos—even to pretend they were still friends—and not seeing the venue on her daily drive around town hurt way more. It was like her heart was being wrenched.

Once, after the third time she found out Brandon had cheated on her, she'd eaten a whole bucket of fried chicken and followed it with a full six-pack of beer, and the level of heartburn had traumatized her for life. Not even that pain could compare to what she felt now at seeing this photo and knowing she'd never have this with Marcos, ever again. The image had just been a blink her cousin had caught by accident or fate.

"What's wrong?" Gianna asked, brushing Nadia's hair. "The fake boyfriend obviously likes you . . . like, a lot. Why does that make you sad?"

Nadia wished her cousin didn't live in another hemisphere. She wished they'd known each other ten years ago, before she made a mess of her life.

"Because he and I already had an opportunity like this before, and life doesn't give you second chances. Besides, I promised myself I wouldn't depend on a guy to be happy ever again."

"So now you're going to let a guy make you unhappy forever? Isn't that why you broke up with Brandon? Because he made you feel like a turd? I see you with this . . . guy, Marcos. You light up like a torch when he's around. And he obviously feels the same way, too. Can't you see?"

Nadia turned, and she and Marcos crossed glances. For a second, her breath hitched when he smiled at her, as he helped Bisa change her shirt to match the blue one Marcos was wearing. Someone had crossed out BRANDON LEWIS with a Sharpie and written URUGUAYO. She smiled back at him. He deserved more than being a rebound guy.

"Nadia!" her dad called. "We need you in our team."

She kissed Gianna on the cheek and headed to join the pinks.

The game went as she had expected. Laughter, rolling around the grass, cheering, all served with a side of mate soda.

Although her dad and Marcella had made sure everyone knew the score (the women had won 9 to 0), the rest didn't even care about it. The result had been that they were all winners, all part of a big family, together again for the first time after years sprawled on different continents. She wanted to encapsulate this feeling forever.

But all things come to an end, and tomorrow was a big day

to prepare for her party. One by one, the families went back to their hotels or their homes.

Nadia kissed each person on the cheek, including her niece and nephew's friends, whose cheeks were already rosy, their eyes wide and bright.

"They've never seen grown men—or women, for that matter—have so much fun playing and not watching from the sidelines," Olivia told her. "Gracias, Titi Nadia. Everyone wants to come to your party. Thanks for inviting them."

Her smile was the reward that Nadia hadn't known she was chasing for.

"I'm glad they all had a good time. Even that boy, Kai," she said, wiggling her eyebrows.

Marcos was talking to Kai by the curb as the boy walked away from him. Nadia couldn't tell if it was because he was telling him off or giving him drop-off instructions. She hoped it was the latter, because although there would never be a perfect boy for her niece, at least Kai seemed totally infatuated with her.

Olivia blushed to the tips of her ears.

"Ready to go?" Kai asked her.

Nadia was surprised. She hadn't heard them approach.

Olivia, her eyes like diamonds and her smile like a rainbow, nodded.

"Drive safely," she said.

Isabella had already left in her van with Noah and his friends and the aunts and teenage cousins.

Madi had offered to give the older cousins a tour of the yoga studio and spa she had started working at. Stevie had, of course, said she'd come along, too.

They had all left one by one, and in the end, it was just Nadia and Rocket, watching her niece and his protégé go in a beat-up Honda Civic.

"Ah!" Marcos sighed, brushing his hair back from his eyes. "Young love!"

His forehead was glistening with sweat, and the scent of it, mixed with the leftover cologne from earlier, created a magical concoction that got to Nadia's head like the most intoxicating wine.

Nadia looked away from him so he wouldn't see all the emotions warring inside her.

"I hope they behave," she said, but it was mostly a reminder for herself to behave. To remember her promises to herself, her niece, her cousins, and her friends. She'd celebrate herself without the crutch of a man by her side.

"I doubt it. Someone's getting lucky tonight," he said. "He was asking me for tips."

"Not lucky!" She slapped his arm, and they were both laughing at the sound of her palm on his unflexed, naked biceps.

"Ouch! That hurt!" he complained as he rubbed his arm, but he was still laughing.

Nadia winced. She hadn't meant to do it so hard. Also, touching his skin like that had been a terribly unwise decision. Now she was all tingly, like an electrical current was running from her toes to the crown of her head.

If Madi were here listening to her thoughts, she'd say Nadia was having a kundalini awakening. Nadia knew better. This was plain, old-school horniness.

She hadn't been looked at, touched, spoken to, or admired by an attractive man since forever. The lack of physical affection was blatant, and it showed, especially when she was standing next to this man who radiated a gravitational force, pulling her toward him in spite of her determination and resolutions.

"They're babies! How dare you! If that boy doesn't behave with my niece, you'll pay." The mama bear inside her was coming out from the pent-up energy she felt.

His smile sobered a little. "Oh, I was joking. He'll behave. Don't worry."

That cleared her thoughts really quick. "What do you mean? You told him to?"

He looked around as if he wanted to make sure there was no

one to overhear his words. "Off the record, the one who doesn't want to behave is your niece. He asked me if he should go ahead and drop her off because he was scared of her kissing him, and he didn't know what to do."

She crossed her arms and tapped her foot on the sidewalk concrete. "I hope you told him to kiss her back, right? If he rejects her . . ."

His laughter broke free and loud as he threw his head back and clutched his midriff with both arms. She laughed, too. How could she not?

But their laughter was cut short by a hissing sound.

"A snake!" she yelled and jumped to hang from his neck.

"Where?" he yelled back, his voice squeaky with fear as he looked around their dancing feet.

But it wasn't a snake.

Jet streams of water crisscrossed in silver rays all over the fields, but before she could exclaim *Sprinklers!,* a burst of water doused her face and T-shirt.

Marcos fared the same fate.

"La puta madre!" he exclaimed, shocked.

She took his hand, and they ran toward the parking lot, Nadia screaming, "The dress!" each time a gush hit her.

He took the heavy duffel bag from her hand and placed himself in front of Nadia to protect her and the dress.

They reached the safety of the parking lot, gasping for air and laughing so much, she was afraid she'd pee herself.

"It was sprinklers, and you yelled snake? You know how afraid I am of them, and that's the first thing you say?" He was doubled over, his hands on his muscly thighs, as he tried to catch air.

"Didn't you hear that sound? How could I know it was the sprinklers?"

He looked up at her and said, "Hmmm. We're at the soccer fields at night, right after everyone leaves . . . yep. Snakes made more sense."

They laughed again, but the breeze started blowing from the canyon, and Nadia shivered, still hugging the dress. Marcos was cold, too, judging by the goosebumps covering his skin and his pointy nipples showing through the cutoff T-tank he wore.

Nadia could look at his perfectly sculpted body for hours. His legs were strong pillars that could have run faster than a bullet, but he'd chosen to run at her pace, even if he'd been deadly scared of snakes. His wet hair was plastered on his face, and when he pulled it up, the muscles in his arms popped in a way that shouldn't be allowed.

She'd never been attracted to muscles per se, but it must have been something primal in her DNA waking up, because all of a sudden, she wanted to see all of him, without clothes.

But after her big bash, he'd be gone from her life.

"Is the dress okay? I hope it didn't get ruined," he said.

But the dress was safe inside its stiff garment bag.

She shivered for cold and fear and was painfully aware that her nipples too were pointy and showing through the almost-not-there mesh fabric of the bra she was still wearing. She looked down and winced in embarrassment. The T-shirt was pink, but it was a faint pink that, under the floodlights of the park, made it look like she was really wearing nothing at all.

"Oh, my," was all Marcos said, and he pressed his lips as if he didn't want to laugh.

"Stop it," Nadia said, crossing her arms to hide her chest. But that meant she couldn't slap his arm playfully as she was burning to do. She just bumped him with the side of her hip. Although he was slender, he was taller and had several pounds on her. Still, she managed to move him, even if only a few inches.

"So that's how it's going to be," he said, and she saw a devilish glint in his eye that excited her. But she didn't scoot away. Instead, she turned to face him. His smile froze on his face, but a look of longing and wanting replaced it.

A million possibilities crossed her mind.

She knew he liked her. She wasn't so oblivious as to not notice how she still affected him, perhaps even more than she had when they were young. But he had told her he didn't want to be the rebound again, the one to come and pick up the parts of her heart when Brandon destroyed her.

She knew all this and still couldn't resist his magnetism and the cravings she had for his lips—and all of him. She stepped closer to him at the same time he stepped in her direction.

She shivered in anticipation. She'd been dreaming of this since he'd walked out of her life the first time.

Nothing could stop him from taking his uncles' offer and disappearing from her life once the venue wasn't an anchor for him anymore. And after her party was over, there would be no commitments linking one to the other besides the attraction they felt and the memories of how good it had been before life and responsibilities got in the way.

She felt his breath on her, and when she looked up, she saw all the same doubts crossing his face like storm clouds too dark to ignore.

But the night was balmy and clear, and the stars glittered with possibility, and she wanted him so damn much.

Before she made the crucial decision to stand on her tiptoes, he leaned in and kissed her.

At first, it was lips against lips, tentative, careful.

But then the hibernating instinct, and memory lying dormant in every cell in her body, took over. She stood on her tiptoes to reach as high as she could, as if the force of the kiss were making her float. But before she flew away by the sheer force of the whirlwind of her emotions, she wrapped her arms around his neck, as her lips parted to taste him and his want for her.

His hands moved over her back, and she felt his hesitation, but she pressed closer to him until he gave in to what she knew he wanted to do, and his hand cupped her butt.

She had often thought that after kissing him, her curiosity

and regret would be satisfied. That she could get closure and move on with her life. She had been wrong, as she was usually wrong on so many other things.

Because, after feeling the warmth of his arms again and tasting him on her tongue, she felt like a voracious fire had grown, and if she didn't explore every inch of his body and didn't have him inside her, she would die.

Someone wolf-whistled in the distance, and the two jumped from each other as if they'd been hit with a lightning bolt.

She felt steam rising from her wet shirt as it sizzled against her skin. He looked like a man who had been cut off from oxygen and couldn't stand to be apart from it.

"Come here," he said, and his voice was husky and promising.

She bit her swollen lip and shook her head, a sob of relief rising in her throat. All these years with Brandon, not feeling a single thing when he looked at her or touched her, she'd believed it was her fault. That she was broken. How else could she have explained not feeling a thing, as if she'd been dead?

But now her body woke up just at Marcos's eyes on her. She couldn't resist him, but if they didn't want to make a spectacle in public—or worse, be sent to jail for indecent exposure—they'd better find another place.

"Let's go to my apartment," she said.

It was the first time in her life that she could bring someone home and not worry about roommates or parents or anyone else judging her.

He nodded and leaned in to kiss her again, as if he couldn't help himself. She had the vague suspicion that once they huddled in his car, they'd have a hard enough time driving to her apartment.

She felt she was in a Bad Bunny song, and she was determined to live up to the lyrics playing in her mind.

Right then, his phone rang, the melody of Whitney's "I Will Always Love You" blaring over the sounds of the night. He ignored it at first, but when it rang again, he made a frustrated sound.

"It's my dad's nurse calling. I have to take it. I'm sorry," he said, grunting with the effort of breaking from her lips and arms.

"'I Will Always Love You'?" she asked.

He chuckled, and when he licked his lips, she would've jumped him and ravished him right there and then.

"It's my dad's favorite song," he explained as he dialed.

She felt the lack of his warmth as soon as he let her go, so she crossed her arms to keep the memory of his arms around her.

"Hello, Santiago. ¿Todo bien?" he asked, and he'd never been sexier, all worried and speaking in Spanish, his lips swollen from kissing her.

The voice at the other end of the call sounded calm, but the words must not have matched it, because a sudden fear jumped into Marcos's eyes and grew. He sighed and scratched his chin that had a couple of days' growth. He looked at her and pressed his lips, and she braced herself for bad news.

"Ya voy para allá. Okay? Don't let him sign anything until I get there."

Nadia's heart rate spiked. Sign what?

After a couple of words, Marcos hung up and, looking at her again, said, "It was about my dad."

"Is he okay?"

He sighed and swallowed hard, and then finally nodded. He stretched out his arms as an invitation for her to nestle into them again. She couldn't and wouldn't reject it. He hugged her tightly, and he kissed the top of her head.

"My uncles showed up at the house, and my dad asked to see me before he signed the papers. *Me.* Not my cousin Alexander. Santiago says he seems more lucid than he's ever seen him, as if he's just waking up from a dream."

She closed her eyes for a second. The words were hard, but she had to say them. "You have to go home and see him."

He nodded again, and then tipped her head up with his index finger. He gave her a long, languorous kiss that held so much promise and love, it almost made her drunk.

"I do, but it's early. I just thought that after I go home and talk to him, I'll come over to your apartment. Would you like that?" He swallowed, his Adam's apple bobbing up and down. "You can say no. You should say no. But I love you, Nani," he said, closing his eyes and exhaling in spasms, as if saying the words unlocked something inside him that finally let him free but still caused him pain. "I love you, I love you, I love you, and if I don't tell you and show you for the rest of my life, I know I'll regret it forever. But if you don't feel the same way, just tell me. I'll go. I won't pressure you in any way. I want you to savor this freedom you've fought for so hard."

The way he looked at her.

She felt so powerful, that he looked at her that way and respected her enough to even ask.

As for the only answer, she looked into his eyes, and whispered into his lips so he'd taste her promise forever, "Go to your dad, and then come back to me forever, Rocket. You can tell me you love me for the rest of our lives." And she kissed him.

Chapter 18

Marcos

Marcos drove back home in a high. He was still reeling after Nadia's last kiss, which held such a promise not only for tonight, but all the nights to come.

He didn't know what the future held for them, but all he cared about right now was that he'd be by her side. This time, he wouldn't run.

Life had given him a second chance, and he wasn't going to waste it.

But when he arrived home, the prospect of seeing his father and facing the moment of truth he'd been running from for so long left him momentarily paralyzed. Still, he promised himself he wouldn't run from this, and he steeled himself for the emotional roller coaster he was about to board—now with no safety belts or nets to catch him if he fell.

He'd have to know how to unfurl the wings he'd been keeping hidden all his life without harming those closest to him.

When he opened the door, the scent of his mom's tomato sauce that Santiago must have prepared for his dad took Marcos to the past. How many days and evenings had his family sat by the round table to talk about their days, eating pasta, drinking mate, playing a round or two of truco? His mom always said spaghetti and meat sauce was the easiest, most "rendidora" meal to make for a large family, with plenty for friends or even a strange face that might show up.

Now the table was empty except for his dad, sitting in front of a photo album, which he looked at quietly with a smile on his face.

At the sound of the door creaking open, Santiago called from inside the house, "Is that you, Marcos?"

Stuart Hawkins looked up, alarmed at the intruder in front of him.

Marcos's mouth went dry. He held his dad's blue gaze.

"Yes, it's me."

His heart started beating so fast, he was afraid it might leave bruises on his chest. What if his father still didn't recognize him? What if he was too late, all because he'd stayed a few more minutes with Nadia?

But a flash of recognition passed his dad's face. He smiled, and it was like seeing the old father, the strong pillar and protector Marcos had missed so much.

"Good to see you, Rocket," his dad said, and he sipped from the mate in front of him.

A warmth spread all over Marcos's chest, melting the ice that had grown around his heart like barnacles on a sunken ship. "Hola, Pa."

His father signaled at the chair in front of him with his chin and said, "I've been waiting for you, son. I've missed you."

Marcos sat down, as a million emotions battled inside him. He wanted to say that he'd been right here, waiting for this moment, that it was his dad who had been gone. But that wasn't the truth. At all.

His body had been home, going through the motions, but in his mind and heart, he kept escaping, not even to a place or a person, but to nothingness. No wonder he'd felt so empty all this time. It wasn't until he'd started being here in the now, instead of the past or the present, that he felt at peace again.

"I've missed you, too," he said. "The uncles were here?" He pointed at a stack of papers on the table with his chin.

"Yep." His dad scratched his blond hair gone platinum with age and sighed. "I know it's been hard. I should've sold the land to my brothers a long time ago, but . . . I'm a weak man. Hosting weddings and big parties for families made your mom happy, you know? I think it's because all her life, she lived so far from her family, that she liked to think each celebration she organized was for her family."

Marcos didn't know what to say, and his dad continued. "My brothers have been pestering us for ages to sell. When your mother died, they came like vultures trying to pick the best part of my life . . . but I didn't care about the money. And Sarita, your sister, was helping me, and she was happy. Being at Enchanted Orchards is like being with your mom, continuing her legacy. But I don't want that legacy to be a burden."

Marcos nodded, his heart easing about the decision he hadn't known he'd make until he had heard his father's voice.

His dad continued, "Now that I'm out of commission, and with Sarita's family growing, maybe it's a sign that we should give in before they find another loop in the law and take everything from us without leaving us a penny. We can't assign it to someone not from our family if we don't want George and Monty to take it from us. Today I was alert when they showed up. But if we sell voluntarily, at least we'll get some money to help your sister and you."

Marcos swallowed. What he said next would determine the path of his life for years and years to come. He hadn't taken this decision lightly.

"There's another option," he said after clearing his throat.

"Which is?" His father passed him the mate.

Marcos took a sip. The sweet greenish taste of mate flooded

his senses. This couldn't compare to the soda mate in a can. It was an abomination to compare them. Instead of feeling artificially caffeinated and unmoored, the mate grounded him and gave him the strength to say the next words. "I'll take over the venue. I'll keep Mami's legacy going."

His father shook his head and placed a warm hand on Marcos's. "Your mother wouldn't want you to do things out of family duty or, worse, guilt."

Marcos swallowed the knot in his throat. "It's not out of guilt, Pa."

"Vamos, hijo. No me mientas, por favor," Stuart said in his flawless Spanish, the language that for Marcos meant love and family. The language in which he could never lie. "I know you think the accident was your fault, but—"

"Pa—"

"Marcos." His voice was firm and unwavering. "It wasn't your fault. It happened. I hate it more than anyone would know. I lost my best friend, the love of my life." His father looked at him, tears teetering on the edge of his light lashes. "But the real tragedy would be to lose you too, son. I know it's not easy to live with me in my condition, and I'm so fortunate to have you and Sarita taking care of me at home. Your mom will be happy, even if the venue is no more. The memories last forever."

Marcos nodded; the tears in his eyes didn't hold on to his lashes and fell on his cheeks. This was the moment he'd been waiting for. This was the redemption he'd lied to himself about, saying he would never get.

He cleared his throat and said, "I know her legacy would continue without the venue. I know we can get a lot of money from the land, but if it's okay with you, I want to stay."

His dad's eyes lit up with a hope that hadn't been there before, as if the possibility of Marcos staying were too big of a fantasy to even consider.

"I'm good at this job, too, Pa. Give me a chance," he begged.

Santiago was watching them from the sofa, quiet. His face

showed no judgment, but when Marcos caught his eye, he nodded once, as if saying *good job.*

His father sighed and said, "If that is what you want . . ."

"It is," Marcos promised.

"It's not easy to deal with the brides and their mothers all the time," Stuart said. "Your mother sometimes had to lock herself in the bathroom for a long bath to get rid of the bad vibes."

Marcos just looked at his dad.

"But she also cried with happiness when she'd get an update on those couples, a baby picture, a simple thank-you note, the reservation to host an anniversary. It never got old."

"We're doing quinceañeras now," Marcos confessed, and sipped from the mate before the yerba got cold.

His father nodded. "I've heard about that. Your mom would have loved it."

After a few minutes in which it wasn't necessary to fill the quiet with words, his dad said, "I might forget your name, or why you're here, but I'll never forget I love you, even if I'm saying nonsense words. Even if I appear angry at you. I love you, son, and I'm proud of the man you have become. Thank you."

They embraced, and for the first time since he was a little boy, Marcos and his dad cried in each other's arms, healing tears, cleansing tears. Tears of forgiveness and love that two men who loved each other allowed themselves to finally shed.

Armed with a clean conscience and the love he'd seen in his dad's eyes as he tucked him in bed, roles reversed, Marcos found Nadia's number and typed:

Still okay if I come over?

He read it over and over. His doubts growing, he deleted and typed the same sentence, changing a word here or there, adding a smiling emoji, leaving out the question mark. No matter what he changed, the text read too much like a booty call, and this wasn't what he wanted with her. But he didn't know how else to phrase it. He couldn't just show up.

Finally, he clicked send before he was really ready, but once the message was gone, he quickly added:

No pressure.

He reread the messages, and when the three dots appeared, his ears started humming so loudly he thought he was going to pass out from nerves.

What was a grown-ass man getting all flustered like a teenager for?

He almost called her and told her to never mind.

Her party was in two days. He could wait for after. He *should* wait for after.

Then came her reply:

Waiting for you.

And her address.

He texted back:

On my way.

And darted to get a flash fast shower. He only put on a deodorant instead of dousing himself with cologne. He wasn't that kind of clueless guy, after all. Before heading out, he peeked into his dad's room. His dad was already sound asleep.

"Bye, Santi," he said. "I'll be back soon."

"Don't lie, Marcos!" Santiago said.

"I'm not lying!" But he couldn't keep his face straight. He felt he was beaming, light coming out from his every pore.

"Mira," Santiago said, taking his reading glasses off and putting the book he was reading down on his lap. "I haven't seen you smiling like this in the whole time I've known you. Judging by the shower and the effort in your clothes, I assume you're seeing a . . . friend? Gal, guy . . . ?" He made a motion for Marcos to continue, to confess.

Marcos narrowed his eyes and said, "It happens to be a gal friend. An old girlfriend, actually." He pictured Nadia and how she'd looked earlier at the gardens, the sun playing on her skin, her face luminous and badass, and he couldn't help smiling.

"Is she the one?" Santiago asked.

Marcos considered seriously and then nodded. "We had a very intense relationship when we were still kids, you know? This is a second chance at a life with her." The words pressed on the tip of his tongue for him to finally recognize what he'd known all his adult life. "Yes, she's the one."

Finally saying it aloud, he felt like the steel binds that had crushed his heart had finally melted.

"I have to tell you the story someday," he promised.

"Just tell me this, is she a one of a kind?" Santiago asked.

Marcos wiggled his eyebrows. "One of a kind? She's unforgettable."

Santiago laughed and waved Marcos away with a hand. "Go ahead then, cowboy. Don't let your lady wait."

Without hesitation, Marcos said bye, grabbed a bottle of wine from the basement, and headed to Nadia's apartment, his and Nadia's song blaring on the English radio.

He stopped by her favorite fast-food place and got two peach shakes with fries and fry sauce. He could almost taste her lips infused with the sweet coolness of the ice cream, and something in his stomach flip-flopped. They could have the wine after . . .

After whatever.

For the first time in as long as he could remember, Marcos wasn't running from his happiness, but towards it. The blue tail of a shooting star streaked past in the indigo sky.

He felt his mom approved.

What a sign, if there ever was one.

Marcos parked by the curb so his car wouldn't get towed. He wanted to minimize any and all threats to the happiest weekend of his life.

He checked and double-checked the address, and when he saw her Subaru parked under a carport, he knew he was in the right place. He looked up toward her apartment and took a big breath perfumed with the roses blooming on the hedges. He hoped the perfume came with a dose of courage and clear-mindedness. He didn't want to fuck anything up.

Everything had to be perfect.

He balanced the shake carrier and brown paper bag with the fries and the wine bottle. He took each step deliberately. This walk upstairs to her apartment would mark a before-and-after.

He knew it was perhaps best not to set his expectations super high, but he indulged in the anticipation. He knew from experience with Nadia that his fantasies would pale compared to reality.

"Good evening," a tall, statuesque woman said. Her head was wrapped in a white turban, and when he looked again, he realized she was wearing a white silk robe. She had a little dog tucked under her arm.

"Good evening," he said, impressed that she took her dog out while still wearing a full face of makeup. He lowered his head in a sign of respect and moved out of her way.

Marcos heard music playing from Nadia's apartment, some romantic country. He didn't expect her to like that kind of music, but maybe her musical taste had changed with the years.

The neighbor was watching him still, and he gave her a tight smile. "Good night," he said, and without a word, she got the message and walked away, down the stairs, her flip-flops slapping the ground with each step.

Marcos wondered if he should've texted Nadia with a heads-up that he was coming up. But doing so seemed ridiculous, like a round of "¿Lobo está?," the wolf game he and his sister had played with their mom when they were little.

No. It was better he'd come up. He knocked on the door and waited.

The sound of footsteps coming in his direction made his heart rate ratchet up. Stupidly, his mouth watered, anticipating his lips on hers, his hands on her silky skin, wrapping his fingers around her should—

"May I help you?" asked the voice of the person who answered the door.

Marcos was so surprised, he stepped back as if he'd seen a ghost.

No. Worse.

A devil.

"You?" he and Brandon said in unison, the same loathing and disdain in their voices.

After all these years, Brandon would still be considered handsome, but there was none of the dignity men their age usually acquired with the experience of a life well lived.

Time hadn't been kind to him. An air of decay surrounded him. His brown hair was thinning, and his blue eyes had a coldness, a cruelty that leaked into his voice. Red splotches on his cheeks contrasted with his pale skin. He looked like he spent a lot of time at the gym, judging by his arms, but Marcos wasn't afraid of taking him on. In fact, he craved it. A yearning to punch the smug expression off his face ate at him like hunger.

A cold drop from the milkshakes fell on the top of Marcos's shoe, and looking down broke the tension of the moment.

"What are you doing here?" they both asked.

Marcos exhaled, disgusted. He didn't want anything in common with this guy who'd broken Nadia's heart into smithereens, to the point where she had doubted not only that she could love again but, worse, that she would ever be worthy of love.

"I don't have to give you any explanations, Lewis," Marcos said, stepping forward. He tried to see if Nadia was inside the apartment. Or was she? Why had she told him to come over, that she was waiting for him, if Brandon Lewis, her ex-fiancé, was here?

But Brandon blocked his way.

"Where do you think you're going?" Brandon asked.

"I came to see Nadia. It's got nothing to do with you," Marcos said, trying to sound calm, but his heart hammered against his ribs.

Brandon closed the door behind him and pursed his lips. "You've got no business coming to see my fiancée at this time of night. I don't like it."

"Your fiancée?" Marcos's heart pulsated all over his body as he spat the words. "I don't give a fuck what you like or you don't. That train left the station a long time ago. I came to see her. She's waiting for me."

Brandon made a gesture with his hands, palms up, as a smirk crossed his face. "Tough luck, buddy. You're too late. I came to claim what's mine. Things are back to normal now."

"What do you mean?"

"That there's a wedding in two days' time. I don't even care if she keeps her pink decorations. The reception's for the bride and her mom anyway, right? I just want *her*. That's all I care about."

Marcos's thoughts rushed like rats trapped in a maze. This had to be a test of some kind. To see if he'd run again, if he really meant it when he'd said she was special, the one. The love that fate had brought back to his path for a reason.

"Why don't you call her so she can tell me in my face?"

Brandon shook his head and said, "She's in the shower right now. You know what I mean?"

"You son of a b—" He took a step toward Brandon, ready to smash his face, when a voice behind them asked, "What's going on here?"

It was the neighbor lady, with her Yorkie under her arm.

"Good night, Ms. Betty," Brandon said, as if he'd just seen his savior.

She eyed him suspiciously, her eyes moving back and forth over Marcos and Brandon as if trying to assess the situation.

"I thought she'd kicked you out," she said. "I heard her say, and I quote, 'If you show your face around here one more time, I'll call the cops and haul your ass in jail.'" She paused and added, "Didn't she say that this is her apartment, and you coming here would be considered trespassing?"

Brandon's face looked like a pomegranate. "Yes, she did, Betty. But she's the love of my life, and I crawled back to her feet to ask for forgiveness, which she gave. The wedding is on." He looked at Marcos with a sanctimonious smile. "Thanks for keeping her entertained, but I'll take her back from here."

By now, other neighbors had popped their heads out of their balconies on floor landings to see what was happening.

Some greeted Brandon, and he waved back at them with an apologetic expression on his face, but also a hint of smugness, because he was on his turf.

Marcos left the milkshakes on the little bench by the door, along with the fries and the wine. When he'd stepped forward, Brandon had blanched, as if expecting a punch. The coward.

If this clown was telling the truth, why had Nadia invited him over? Was he so late that she'd changed her mind in the time it took him to drive from his house to her apartment? Was her heart that fickle? Was the wedding all she wanted, and all the plans for her treintañera only a foil for her true desires?

Science says that when threatened, humans flee, fight, or freeze.

All his life, when he'd faced a threat, Marcos had run. But now, although his heart was demanding him to fight for Nadia's love, Marcos decided to pause before he made a mess of his future—and Nadia's.

He had to talk to her, but not with Brandon around.

Marcos exhaled, took a last look at the apartment, and headed downstairs.

"Bye, nice to see you," Brandon said, his cockiness back.

Marcos couldn't help it. Fury and frustration took him. He turned back, climbed the stairs three at a time, and grabbed the back of Brandon's shirt and pulled him back.

"Don't hit me," Brandon pleaded. "She deserves good photos from our wedding, right? Don't ruin this for her."

Marcos wanted nothing more than to pummel this idiot until he was so unrecognizable, the sticker of an emoji on the photos would be better than his face. But he thought of Nadia.

Was *this* what she wanted? Marcos had been sure they had a connection. That the bond that tied them all those years ago was stronger than ever. He hadn't misread the clues, had he? That almost-kiss at the storage, and then those kisses at the park, her request for him to come over? Those hadn't been his imagination, had they? All the longing he read in every gaze, brush of her fingers against his, the sighs and tension, all those signs had to be reflections of what he felt for her. They had to.

What would have happened if he hadn't gone home to talk to his father? He would've been here when Brandon showed up, and she wouldn't have answered the door, or if she did, he wanted to think she'd have been strong enough to shut the door back in Brandon's face.

Was she really in the shower now? He hadn't taken that long at home. Had that small window of time wrecked his future forever?

But although it hurt to think that he had lost Nadia and everything else she represented—her family, her culture, the friendship—he didn't regret speaking with his father.

"If you hurt her, I will kill you," he hissed in Brandon's face. "I don't care what happens to me, but I promise, I'll kill you."

Marcos shoved Brandon back against the door.

And fuming, he went back to his car.

Chapter 19

Nadia

Nadia woke up with a headache from crying herself to sleep. The tears were a mixture of rage and fear and relief.

She could hardly open her eyes, and when she felt with her fingertips how swollen they were, she exclaimed, "Ay Dios mío!"

She wished she could sleep for a hundred years.

Seeing Brandon at her door had made her feel like she'd stepped into an alternate reality.

To say he wasn't the man she'd been waiting for, had prepared for, was the understatement of the year. Although it really wasn't that funny, she laughed, still drunk with the adrenaline of having done the impossible, for a second time in less than a month: She'd kicked Brandon's ass out the door.

Literally.

Last night, she had arrived home in a frenzy, worried that Bisa would be here or the rest of the cousins, ready to ambush her in a prank.

But to her delight, the apartment was delightfully empty. There was a meal from Cancún Querido warming in the oven and a bottle of her favorite rosé cooling in an ice bucket. Madi and Stevie had been here, and it showed. Nadia would have bet a thousand dollars that it had been Madi's idea to light the candles in the bathroom and draw a bath and put flower petals in it. It looked sexy and comforting as hell, and Nadia's heart sped up just thinking about spending the night here with Marcos.

She'd showered and put on the special nightie she'd reserved for the honeymoon that she wouldn't go to. But it didn't matter. She wasn't getting married this weekend, but her life had never seemed more exciting, even though she didn't even have a job anymore. Like Madi often said, the universe had a way to put things into place, if only one knew how to step out of the way.

Anxious as she checked that the bathwater wasn't getting too cold, Nadia had jumped when Marcos had texted her. The phone slipped from her recently moisturized hands and fell straight into the bathtub.

"No!" she screamed, as if she were losing her soul. In a way, she was. How would she survive without her phone? On the eve of her party? She didn't even remember her friends' numbers by heart. Or worse, Marcos's. She only knew her mom's landline, and it's not like she was going to call her while wearing a transparent outfit as she waited for her future lover to show up.

She fished the phone out of the tub, hoping there was a ten-second rule or something that would rescue her.

The only grace she received was a brief glance of his message: *On my way*, before the screen went gray and then black.

She felt her curls straightening up in frustration. Why did this have to happen now? But then, she had the thought in Stevie's voice that said, *Everything happens for a reason, Nadia.*

Nadia exhaled her frustration. Marcos was coming. True, she couldn't reply or even tap the message and give it a heart, but maybe he'd take her silence as her consent, and he'd hurry over.

But then there was a knock on the door.

There he is, she said to herself.

She checked her image in the mirror. She didn't need to put

on any blush or highlighter; she was all lit up with the promise
of spending the night with him—and all that implied. She'd arrive to her second quinceañera not a virgin, but quite the opposite, completely energized after a night of hot sex with the man
of her dreams.

There was another knock as she tried to figure out the stereo.
It was the only thing Brandon had actually bought for their
apartment, and in the rush of kicking him out, she hadn't even
considered giving it back. He'd lived rent-free, leeching off her
love, for years. Let this be part of the payment for that.

"Lucinda," she commanded the smart speaker, "Play romantic bossa nova."

Soft, seductive music filled the apartment. She took a deep
breath of the scent of the roses scattered all over the place.

Her heart skipped a beat when she saw the faint shadow of
a tall man at the door, his head down, as if praying before he
stepped over the threshold.

When they were younger, she and Marcos had such different
goals and interests, their love hadn't been enough to keep them
together. Now that they were more experienced and mature, life
was giving them a second chance.

"I'm coming," she said, her voice full of promise.

Aware that in the semidarkness of the room, she would appear naked, she threw her curls back and threw open the door.

"Finally," she exclaimed, smiling so wide she thought her
face muscles would sprain.

But at the sight of the man at the door, the smile first got frozen, and then it fell to her feet as she, pointlessly, tried to cover
herself from Brandon's eyes.

"What are you doing here?" she practically shrieked.

"Shhh," Brandon said, walking in, el caradura, as if this were
his house. "I knew you'd be happy to see me, despite what Lisa
and Mom said, but I wasn't expecting this kind of welcome. I've
missed you, too, hon." He opened his arms as if she were going
to fall into them. As if she were going to let him touch her.

Instead, she opened the coat closet next to the door, grabbed a giant cardigan she hadn't worn since May, and threw it on.

"Nads, what are you doing that for? All our years together, I fantasized about something like this, and the one time it happens, you go and ruin it?"

The nerve! She wanted to claw out his bright blue eyes. She wanted to slap that smug smile off his face. She wanted to rip out his voice box, so she would never have to hear that whiny tone ever again. How had she ever thought she loved this man?

Why had she lied to herself for so long?

She was so angry, she felt like a volcano made woman. But her anger wasn't really directed at this poor excuse of a man. No. She was angry at herself. For the lies, the gaslighting, the undermining, the self-sabotage, the lack of love and confidence, the lack of loyalty. She deserved better. From herself. If she wasn't getting all this from herself, what right did she have to demand this from anyone else?

"What? Aren't you happy to see me? You're speechless, but your face—"

"Shut up!" she said. Not yelling. Not screaming and giving him the chance to say she was hysterical. She threw back the cardigan from her shoulders, and pointing at him, said, "What are you doing here? You don't want to get married, at least not to me. You don't love me. You don't even love yourself, Brandon. Why are you here?"

The mask of self-confidence he wore fell off like an autumn leaf. She was the one not wearing clothes, but he was the one who was vulnerable, with no shield or mask to hide behind.

He scratched his head. "I wanted to come see you so many times. But my mom told me to take a break, to give you some space to think things through. She said that eventually, you'd realize how ridiculous it was to throw yourself this party, that you'd let me come back. We could go back to the original plan. I still want to get married. We still can, hon."

The electricity crackled between her and Brandon, and not in a good way.

"You think you can blame your mother for going MIA instead of fighting for our love, instead of even explaining like a man? You think I would even consider taking you back?"

He hadn't considered the alternative that she wouldn't want him again; that much was obvious by his expression of shock. Brandon didn't know how to be rejected. But she couldn't feel sorry for him anymore. He was a grown-ass man. He had to figure things out on his own.

She exhaled, exhausted. "Go away, Brandon. Let's cut our losses. Thirteen years together. Five years engaged. We tried. It didn't work out. Leave now."

He seemed confused. "So you weren't waiting for me with this getup? Who are you with now? And why—"

"I don't have to explain anything to you."

"You're crazy," he said, throwing his hands up in the air. "I should've known when I heard you were doing a birthday party. So indulgent and immature!"

She couldn't hold her anger in check anymore. "Immature that I'm choosing to spend *my* money in a celebration of my life? Okay, I'll take it! But look who's talking about being immature, the guy who jacks off with videos of his old affairs. Get out of here! You disgust me."

There wasn't a thing she liked about him. There wasn't a thing she liked about herself when she was next to him.

Trying to channel the energy from the matriarchs of her family, she said, "I'm going to go to my room. You have five minutes to leave before I call the police."

Of course, she had no idea what phone she'd use to call the police, but he didn't need to know that.

"You know you don't mean that, babe," he said. There was a smirk on his face as he stretched out his hand to her. It made her blood boil.

She took a big breath. He must have thought she was going to give in, but instead, she exclaimed, "Don't touch me, you motherfucker de mierda, or I'll tear your hand off!"

More than the threat, it must have been the swearing that shocked him. He actually scuttled back like a cockroach.

Victorious, she stormed to her room and slammed the door behind her, shaking from the adrenaline.

She looked at herself in the mirror. She loved what she saw. Her hair fanned over her shoulders like unruly snakes. Her cheeks flushed, like she had an inner fire. She'd stood up for herself. She hadn't cried for him. She hadn't even considered taking him back. She hadn't even leaned on her new relationship with Marcos for that.

She was wholly on her own.

She heard the door open and close a few times, and then silence.

After a while, she looked out the window. Brandon was just now driving away in his white BMW.

She didn't even wish him good luck.

The bathwater was getting cold. The candles burning low.

Nadia went back to the kitchen to make sure Brandon was really gone. But on the counter sat an envelope, a peach milkshake from Nadia's favorite place, and a bag of fries.

A note in Brandon's handwriting read, *Enjoy your feast, chubbers. I doordashed it for you. I hope you choke.*

Tentatively, she opened the manila envelope. The wedding certificate was there, just waiting to be signed by the wedding officiator, Nadia, and Brandon.

"Hijo de puta," she said.

She considered throwing it all in the garbage, but she wouldn't let him ruin peach milkshakes and fries for her, too. So she tore the certificate in little pieces like confetti, sat on the stool, and savored each fry like it was ambrosia from the gods and the milkshake was nectar.

When she was finished, she checked the clock.

It was way past midnight, but . . . Marcos had never shown up.

She had no way to call him, and she worried he'd had a car crash or something. She considered getting her laptop, to resurrect some of her old social media accounts she never checked anymore, to send him a message. But she wasn't going to beg him to come over, either.

If she was to be alone, then so be it.

She was with the love of her life. Herself.

For all her positive self-talk, waking up alone in the morning hurt. But she remembered her treintañera was hours away. There were so many things to do. Wasn't that how she always dealt with heartbreak? With work?

But if it had to be work, at least it would be for her.

She jumped from bed.

She showered, put on a little bit of makeup to hide the bags under her eyes, and then drove to her parents' house.

No one commented on her cutting voice. Her moodiness before a big event was legendary in the family, and they all let her be.

When, in a not-so-subtle tone accompanied by a wink, Madi asked why Nadia hadn't been answering her phone, she replied curtly, "My phone fell in the tub and died."

Madi and Stevie exchanged a worried look. They knew something had gone really wrong, but Nadia couldn't tell them the truth. She was too heartbroken. She felt raw, like she had fallen from a high-speed bike and her soul was all road-burnt and broken.

"Well, since she couldn't get in touch with you, Sarah Hernández from Enchanted Orchard called me to let me know she's back from Phoenix. She said she'll be our contact for today and tomorrow," Stevie said in her saleswoman's voice.

At the mention of Enchanted Orchard, Nadia's heart sputtered and started racing.

"Sarah Hernández? Who is that?"

Madi passed Nadia a cup of coffee and said, "The other venue owner? Isn't she, like, Marcos's sister?"

"Where's Marcos?" Nadia asked, feeling the blood draining from her face.

"What's going on?" Isabella asked, walking into the living room, where they had been whispering in a charged tone.

Nadia took a sip from her coffee.

Isabella looked at Stevie and Madi for an answer.

"Nothing . . . it's just that Sarah said she'll be our contact for the party. Marcos is gone," Madi said, wringing her hands.

"Really?" said Isabella. "Didn't you spend the night with him? What did you do?"

Nadia shook her head, trying to dispel the sudden urge to throttle her sister. First of all, how did she think they'd spend the night together? And second, why did Isabella assume Nadia had done something wrong? "Nope. We didn't sleep together." She considered leaving things unexplained, carrying her sorrow alone, like she always did.

But if her sister or her friends did this, she'd feel hurt, not trusted. What were friends for if not to support you when a man breaks your heart?

Nadia sighed and confessed. "In true Rocket fashion, when things got good, he made a run for it and left."

"What?" Stevie exclaimed, smacking her hand on her hip, her eyes flashing.

"And Brandon showed up to convince me to go ahead with the wedding. He even brought the wedding certificate that he got in the mail. Can you believe it?"

"Canallas! Both of them!" Bisa exclaimed, coming out from behind the curtain, all confusion and cloudiness gone from her face. "But we're not going to let them win. We're going to celebrate that you didn't only survive the battle and the war, you're thriving. The best is yet to come. Life in crescendo!"

"The best is here, right now," Madi said softly, holding Nadia's hand.

Nadia looked around at her family, all together to celebrate her, and she couldn't agree more. She wasn't striving to be the best anymore. From now on, she'd be Nadia Noemí Palacio, unapologetically herself.

The day before her treintañera, she treated her family to a spa day at the place where Madi worked. The men got haircuts and manicures, and brow and nose waxes. The women got massages and mani/pedis. Nadia got a facial and her lashes filled, while her mother and aunts laughed until they cried in the sauna.

Once they were back home, the family insisted on cooking all her favorite foods: gnocchi, empanadas, sandwiches de miga, and clericó, Tía Romina's famous fruit salad with vermouth.

Nadia pretended not to see Olivia and the twins sneaking into the kitchen to sample the fruity concoction.

Olivia came up to her and kissed her on the cheek. "You're the best, Tía. I love you," she said in perfect Spanish.

"We all want to be you when we grow up," Amara said, and Allegra nodded next to her twin.

Gianna clicked her tongue from the other side of the kitchen.

"Jealous that she's the favorite cousin?" Marcella asked Gianna, and planted a kiss on her lips.

The girls all giggled at the PDA, blushing, and Gianna replied, "Jealous? Are you kidding me? I'm proud. That's what I am." She came over to Nadia and hugged her tightly. "We got you, prima. We got you."

And it was true. They wouldn't leave her alone long enough to wallow in self-pity. Every time Sarah from the venue called with a question, one of her friends or cousins would take care of it. They showered her with a love so genuine, Nadia almost didn't have time or room to think about Marcos. Almost.

Stevie said everything happened for a reason, and maybe the reason that she and Rocket had crossed paths was to see how much she'd grown. Life wanted to see if Nadia had learned to love herself first.

Still, she missed him. Missed what could have been. She wouldn't lie to herself. But she didn't need him to celebrate. Love wasn't lacking in her life.

And when she woke up surrounded by her family on the day of her celebration, she wasn't faking the joy bubbling inside her. She noted how everyone in her family gave her a blessing in their own way.

"I have something for you, mamita," her mom said, after Nadia had come out of the shower. They were alone for the first time in weeks, maybe even months. This was a moment when Nadia imagined her mom would try to give her "the talk" before her wedding, and she blushed in commiseration with herself in an alternate life, one in which she was getting married today. But now, she was curious to know what her mom would say.

But at first, her mom didn't say anything. She only walked into her closet and came out with a little pink jewelry box nestled in her hands.

"Open it," she said.

Nadia's hands shook as she opened the box and saw a thin gold chain with the number *30* and a letter *N* intertwined. Little diamonds glittered on the edges of the charm.

"What's this?" Nadia asked, her gaze fixed on her mom's face.

Virginia's eyes were filled with tears. She shrugged and swallowed, but then she said, "Isabella got one for her quinces, and I even made one for Olivia, remember?"

Boy, did she ever. Nadia had coveted a charm like this since she was eleven years old. She had tried to pretend not to care when Olivia had received hers, although she hadn't had a party, but she had been jealous.

"Mami, it's beautiful, thank you!" she whispered, full of emotion.

Her mom took the chain from the box, walked behind Nadia, and clasped it around her neck. Her fingers lingered on Nadia's skin tenderly. And when Nadia turned around, she hugged her mom and broke into tears.

"Shhh," Virginia said, lovingly. "Shhh, mi niña. No tan niña anymore, though," she whispered, as if she were talking to herself. Then she added in a firm voice, "You're such an incredible woman, my Nadia." She held Nadia's face, and looking into her eyes, said, "I'm so proud of you, and I can't wait to show you off to the whole world, to celebrate you like we should have way before now."

Nadia nodded, sniffing her tears.

"Now let's go get you ready for your treintañera."

Nadia had debated if she would wear the same pink tulle dress from the photos, the one Stevie had sent her from El Paso. It would forever remind her of Marcos. But the other option, a black shift dress that fit her like a glove, didn't feel right. While she decided, Gianna fixed her hair, plumping up her curls that framed her face. Lola did her makeup. She was an expert in the smoky-eye technique.

Her mom, Abuela Catalina, and Bisa, the three generations before her, gave Nadia a blessing in the shape of a kiss on the forehead.

"It's time to head out!" Olivia exclaimed, peeking into the room where the preparations were taking place. When she saw Nadia in her robe, her smile fell. "Put on your dress, Tía! The limo Tío Román ordered is here!" And she clapped a hand on her mouth as the rest of the women groaned that she had ruined the surprise.

"Sorry," Olivia said sheepishly, ducking. "I didn't know it was a surprise."

"I'll still be surprised. Don't worry," Nadia said. "Now help me put on my dress."

"Which one?" Isabella asked, the pink dress in one hand and the black one in the other.

"The pink one, duh," Nadia said, and Madi and Stevie high-fived each other as the other women cheered.

They dressed her tenderly, and when she sat down, Virginia helped her clasp her dainty crystal shoes.

"You look like Cinderella," Amara said, her face rapturous.

"A kick-ass Cinderella, that's who," Allegra, the shy, quiet twin added, and everyone laughed and clapped.

Nadia savored every moment. She wasn't becoming a woman just because she was having a party. She'd been a woman for a long time now, but she'd hidden her real self under the guise of living up to other people's expectations, instead of honoring who she really was.

"Let's go," Ernesto bellowed from downstairs, and all the women left the room, throwing her kisses so they wouldn't ruin her makeup.

Nadia sat on the pouf in front of the mirror for a second. The first time on her own. She threw a kiss at her reflection and headed out.

When she walked downstairs, she was beaming, and not because the fabric of her long train tickled her legs. She loved to see the expressions in her family's eyes.

Her dad kissed her cheek and said, "You look gorgeous, mi amor."

She smiled at him. He'd put on a tuxedo, even though he hated looking like a penguin, as he used to complain. Then he took her hand and placed it in the hook of his elbow, and together, they walked to the limo, flanked by her family and a few neighbors, who'd come out to see what the party was all about.

Nadia and her parents rode in the limo, behind the caravan of her family's cars.

She would switch to the horse-drawn carriage that her family had decorated in pinks and golds for her. Although she was sure people in the street couldn't see her, she waved like she was a princess. The limo drove around town a couple of times to give her family time to reach the venue. Summer was saying goodbye with a show. The tips of some trees were already tinged with orange and yellow, and the sky was a deep indigo. From behind Mount Timpanogos rose a full moon—a harvest moon.

Time to reap all that she'd sown.

The limo turned toward Mountainville and into the gravel road that led to her party. The parking lot next to the big barn was filled to capacity. When the limo stopped at the entrance of the venue, Kai opened the door.

"Welcome, Miss Palacio," he said respectfully.

Nadia took the hand he offered and winked at him as she got out of the limo after her parents. Kai blushed to the tips of his ears.

Nadia looked around, and her heart swelled at the sight of the sign on the marquee. It read: NADIA, TWICE A QUINCEAÑERA. LOVED AND CHERISHED FOREVER.

"Gracias, Mamá y Papá," she said, hugging them.

"Welcome," said Sarah Hawkins Hernández.

She looked so much like Marcos, it kind of hurt Nadia to see her, so she couldn't speak.

Sarah continued, "You look stunning."

"Thank you," Nadia replied, her heart dying to ask about Marcos.

"Thank you also for setting up a trend."

"A trend?" Virginia asked.

"Word of your party has spread like wildfire." Sarah laughed. "We've had so many calls for treintañeras, and even for triple and quadrupled quinces."

"There's even one for a ninetieth birthday that this woman from Salt Lake is throwing for herself. She's not even a Latina," Kenzie said.

She looked lovely in her all-pink pants set.

"You brought new life to our business, and we can never

thank you enough," Sarah said, and her eyes sparkled with tears. "My brother was so grateful for this chance, you know. I know he loved planning this event with you."

Nadia swallowed the knot in her throat. "He did a wonderful job," she said, and although she had promised she wouldn't ask about him, she couldn't help it. "Is he here today?"

Sarah lowered her gaze and shrugged. When she looked up at Nadia, there was sadness in her eyes.

"Is everything okay?" Nadia asked.

Kenzie said, "He's with his father tonight. The nighttime nurse canceled at the last minute. But Marcos left precise instructions to make sure you have the party you've always dreamed of."

The party Nadia had dreamed of lately featured Marcos by her side. But she wasn't going to undermine what it meant to walk into this party on her own.

"Thank you," was all she said.

The music for her entrance broke the sound of the mountain night. This was their cue. Hadn't they practiced it enough?

"Ready?" her dad asked.

Nadia smiled, pushing away any thought of Marcos. The people who mattered were here. Her family and friends were with her. "Ready," she said.

Her dad offered his arm to her mom. Together, they walked ahead of her. Her mom didn't check once over her shoulder to see if Nadia was following them. Whether or not she did, they would love her.

That was all she ever needed in life.

With that knowledge, she looked at Sarah and Kenzie and said, "Thank you."

They nodded in respect.

Nadia took a deep breath, squared her shoulders, and walked forward, sure-footed in spite of how thin her stilettos were.

Her shocking pink dress showed so much skin, even though she wasn't going to be on any magazine covers for being the most fit or slender. But she loved how the dress made her feel. Wasn't that the most important thing?

When she reached her parents, who were waiting with flutes of champagne in hand, the room exploded into applause.

She saw friends from middle and high school and all the way to law school. Girls from the EL program where she volunteered. Girls from the cheerleading squad. Clients, her parents' friends, a few teachers, and neighbors were all here. Marcos's friend, Becca, took picture after picture, and a boy followed Nadia with another camera.

Her cheeks were already hurting from smiling so much, seeing so many loved faces, but her heart caught in her throat when she looked up and saw herself on giant banners, hung all over the room, from the photo session with Marcos.

As when she'd seen the photo of her invitation, she was amazed at how her image looked so fulfilled, so accomplished.

Was that how Marcos looked at her?

If so, why hadn't he come over the night before? The thorn of disappointment stabbed at her heart, but Nadia didn't have time to wonder.

After the entrance toast with her parents, she grabbed the microphone and spoke to those who loved her. She hadn't prepared a speech or anything. She just spoke from her heart, mixing both English and Spanish, because they were both her languages.

"Thank you all for being here, even though it wasn't the celebration you had signed up for. I love to see your faces. I love to be part of you, mi familia. Mis amigas y amigos, thank you for helping me become the woman I am today."

The applause was deafening.

The caterers started serving the food from Cancún Querido, and the band started playing softly, instrumental versions of all of Nadia's favorite songs that spanned a multitude of languages, decades, and styles. She ate; she chatted with people she hadn't seen in years; she smiled for pictures; she savored the champagne on her tongue after Madi, Stevie, Lola, and Gianna took turns for the speeches. She got teary-eyed when her parents and Isabella spoke, and before she broke into tears, the DJ announced the father-daughter dance.

She glided on the floor in her father's arms.

"I'm glad I didn't have to give you away to a man, but to the whole world," he said in her ear.

She laughed. "Papi, you made it sound really weird."

Her dad, who hadn't meant it like that at all, laughed, too.

And then Tío Román stepped in for a turn to dance with her, and she went from arm to arm, dance companion to dance companion. Her uncles, her cousins. Her friends from high school, college, and law school. Her nephew and brother-in-law.

And in the end, a voice: "May I have this dance?"

She looked up and saw Marcos, in a dark suit that made the angles of his face more cut and chiseled. She would have fallen into his arms, but she only nodded.

"Bailar Pegados" was playing. Her head fit right in the crook of his head and shoulder. She could stay there until the end of the world.

"You came back," she said. "I thought you had run."

He didn't reply right away. Then he sighed and said, "I came over last night, but Brandon was there. He said the wedding was still on, and I just couldn't take it. I tried calling you, but you wouldn't answer, and I thought it was just what I deserved. To have this second chance from life and then lose it in a blink. But if it was what you decided, then, who was I to stop you? I just admire you and love you so much, I was glad you let me be part of this." He looked around. "Thank you."

She swallowed as thoughts whirled in her mind.

"How did you know it wasn't a wedding after all? Why did you come tonight?"

"I had promised I'd dance with you tonight. I wasn't going to break this promise." He glanced over his shoulder and smiled. "And . . . actually, Kenzie told me that if I didn't haul ass and make it before the dance, she was going to quit, and honestly, we can't afford for her to quit. Not now that I'm going to be in charge of all the operations."

Marcos twirled her, and Nadia caught a peek of Kenzie, watching them from the entrance, a smile of approval on her face. Nadia smiled back at her.

"You're not leaving then?"

He shook his head. "This is home. I'm good at this party-planning thing. I'm staying put."

He hadn't run away. He'd come back for her.

And then, when she was about to kiss him, someone tapped Marcos's shoulder. A friend from college said, "May I have a turn?"

There was still a line of people who wanted to dance with her, and Marcos smiled, yielded her hand with a respectful nod, and stepped away. But before she looked away, she saw him wink at her, and there was so much promise in his eyes.

He made good on that promise a couple of hours later, when the cotillion was at its peak, and everyone was having too much fun to notice what she did or where she went. Marcos had been looking at her the whole night, so he caught the meaning of the glance she sent him as she walked out into the garden.

The night had a chill that cooled her sweat from dancing so much—and the nerves of finally being alone with him. She followed the path to an orchard lined with rosebushes that made it seem like a room in another world. The music was faint and distant, and fairy lights blinked overhead. She didn't have to wait long to hear the sound of running footsteps.

His smile when he saw her made a warmth bloom in her belly. He stopped a few feet away from her, but she had waited too long to waste time in words. She breached the distance in a stride, and he caught her in an embrace. His heart beat against her cheek. She looked up at him and cupped the nape of his neck in her hand and brought his face down toward hers. She tasted the mint from his mouth and the coconut ChapStick from his lips. His tongue met hers, and he let out a sigh of relief, of coming home.

Her party raved in the barn as Marcos and Nadia kissed with abandon behind the rosebushes. A little girl's voice pierced the sounds of nightbirds and kisses. "Hey, Mr. Swan!" she called. "You dropped this!"

They peeked through the branches and saw Hernán's little daughter chasing the swans, holding a black feather in one hand, a white one in the other. The swans hobbled side to side as they ran away from the little girl. Before they touched the water of the pond, they took flight and glided on the glittery sky.

"I didn't know they could do that!" Nadia whispered through bruised lips for all the kissing.

"Do what?" he asked, looking at her with adoration, like she was even more magnificent than the birds.

"Fly!" Nadia said, extending her arms and flapping them like a goddess.

Epilogue

Nine months later

"Ready?" Olivia asked.

Marcos checked his pockets. He had his and Nadia's passports in one, and a box with a diamond ring in the other.

"Ready," he said.

They were surrounded by people celebrating Olivia's graduation with honors from high school. The summer glittered with promise ahead of them. A little part of Marcos regretted that he wouldn't be here when his sister's new baby was born next week, but another couldn't wait to be touring South America with Nadia, like they had both always dreamed of.

"Does she know about the party at Bisa's house?" Olivia asked, eating the slice of cake from Isabella's new pastry shop in downtown Salt Lake.

Marcos shook his head. "She has no idea. And then we're flying out to Australia for Gianna and Marcella's wedding. Lola will meet us there, and then we're off for Europe."

"What a life," Olivia said with longing. "When I grow up, I want to be like Tía Nadia."

Nadia stepped from behind Olivia and hugged her, planting a kiss on top of her head. "A lawyer?"

A month after her treintañera, Nadia and Shanice had started plans to open an office together. The inauguration of Palacio, Johnson, and Company was a success. Nadia loved solving hard cases everyone else gave up for lost. And she had the best staff around her. Soon, the money followed.

"Yes, I want to be that, but also something else," Olivia replied, her eyes beaming. "A kick-ass dreamer."

Nadia and Marcos laughed. She still smiled in satisfaction when she remembered the headline announcing Laramie Hunt had been accused of harassment by his last assistant, whom Nadia was representing.

Right then, Kai arrived, bringing a plate of cookies. Olivia ran to his side without looking at them once.

"Ah, young love," Nadia said, stretching her arms to the sky. Her yellow sundress showed off her new sleeve tattoo of the Fool tarot card, and a magnificent cleavage that made Marcos want to pick her up and take her back to their apartment.

"My eyes are up here," she said, jokingly.

He leaned in and kissed her. He could never get over the thrill of being able to kiss her anytime, in front of everyone, with nothing to hide.

She'd chosen him because she wanted to, because she loved him, flaws and all. Not because of the potential she saw in him, or the things she wanted to fix, or to complete him. Life had given them this second chance, and he could never live long enough to say how grateful he was.

"Your bags ready?" he asked.

She laughed. "They've been in the car for a week. You know me."

They held hands as they watched the kids play in the sprinklers with her parents. His sister cradled her belly as Nick talked with Hernán and Jason, Isabella's husband.

Life wasn't perfect. Who knew what challenges the future would bring? But for now, he was with Nadia, and that was all that mattered.

Acknowledgments

The years 2020 and 2021 were two of the hardest of my life. Like always, stories, the ones I wrote and the ones I love to lose myself in as a reader, saved me. During the summer of 2020, Nani and Rocket arrived in my mind and heart fully formed and I took dictation from them as I typed as fast as could. I hope I make them proud.

Although I'm the one who created these characters and their families, this book wouldn't have been possible without the encouragement and support of Linda Camacho, my dear agent to whom this novel is dedicated. Thank you, Linda, for that email. Your "what if?" set my dreams on fire. Look at what we made! I'm so proud of us! Thank you also to the Gallt & Zacker Literary family.

Thanks to Norma Perez-Hernandez, my brilliant editor, for manifesting her wish to the universe that brought us together! Also, my eternal gratitude to the Kensington Books family for taking me in and helping me tell my stories: Carly Sommerstein,

Jane Nutter, Lauren Jernigan, and Kris Noble. Thanks also to copy editor Scott Heim.

Thank you to my Plot Twister Sisters: Megan Jensen, Jennifer Maughan, Kalie Chamberlain, Ellen Misner King, for the friendship and a special care package while I recovered from the plague! Thank you for making room in your group for me!

Thank you, Kalie Chamberlain and Melanie Jacobson, for your wonderful feedback and suggestions.

Also, I wouldn't have ever finished the first chapter without the encouragement of my dear Veeda Bybee, my friend and accountability partner. Thank you, Amparo Ortiz, for your friendship and camaraderie! Te adoro!

Thank you, Zoraida Córdova for being my fairy godmother although I'm way older than you!

Thank you, Rachel Seegmiller and Sofy Price! Nothing would be done without your help and the love you have for my family.

Gracias totales a mi familia, especialmente Julián, Magalí, Joaquín, Areli, and Valentino for cheering me on always. And most of all, gracias, Jeffrey, for being the love of my life. I love who I am when I'm with you and I want to be with you forever and ever! Te quiero!

Thank you, Giselle, Denisse, Lucy, Mariana, Annie, Tania, and Mariana for your friendship.

Thank you to all the Romancelandia community for paving the way and for opening your arms to me! I'm humbled to be part of you.

And finally, thank you, readers. What an honor that you choose to share time with my books. Thank you!

TWICE A QUINCEAÑERA

Yamile Saied Méndez

ABOUT THIS GUIDE

The suggested questions are included to enhance your group's
reading of Yamile Saied Méndez's *Twice a Quinceañera*!

Discussion Questions

1. Usually when we speak of coming of age, we think of teenage characters who are figuring out what to do with their lives. We meet Nadia as her life plans take an unexpected turn and instead of her wedding, she's now planning a double quinces. From weddings to quinceañeras, bat mitzvahs, graduations, and sweet sixteens, what are some rites of passage and/or coming-of-age events discussed in the novel, and what effect do they have on the protagonists and those around them?

2. Some people debate that quinceañeras or debuts are outdated customs, vestiges of a patriarchal heritage—events that commodify girls and women. But others argue a celebration of girlhood and womanhood is inherently an act of resistance against patriarchy. How do you consider Nadia's double quinces?

3. Food and drink are things that connect families to their roots. How do the characters' relations to food show their emotional journey?

4. The order in which we are born sometimes determines the roles we play in our families and society. How is being the younger child different for Nadia and Marcos as far as what their families expect of them?

5. Having a support system is vital for everyone, especially women. From her best friends Stevie and Madi, to Nadia's sister and her mom, and her cousins, aunts, grandmother and even great-grandma, how are Nadia's relationships with other women crucial to her character development?

6. Marcos runs away from family, friends, and love to escape the expectations that weigh on his shoulders. What does a support system mean for him?

7. How do their relationships with their mothers influence Marcos's and Nadia's views of marriage, family, and celebrations?

8. How are Marcos's and Nadia's views on second chances, love, and commitment similar or different?

9. Brandon is the villain of Nadia's story, but how would he tell his version of the events?

10. What do you envision for the characters a year after the epilogue?

Visit us online at
KensingtonBooks.com
to read more from your favorite authors,
see books by series, view reading
group guides, and more!

BOOK **CLUB**
BETWEEN THE CHAPTERS

Visit us online for sneak peeks, exclusive
giveaways, special discounts, author content,
and engaging discussions with your fellow readers.

Betweenthechapters.net

Sign up for our newsletters and be the first
to get exciting news and announcements about
your favorite authors!
Kensingtonbooks.com/newsletter